ASSASSIN'S STRIKE

BOOKS BY WARD LARSEN

*Published by Forge Books

ASSASSIN'S STRIKE

WARD LARSEN

A TOM DOHERTY ASSOCIATES BOOK
New York

ASSASSIN'S STRIKE

Copyright © 2020 by Ward Larsen

All rights reserved.

A Forge Book
Published by Tom Doherty Associates
120 Broadway
New York, NY 10271

www.tor-forge.com

Forge® is a registered trademark of Macmillan Publishing Group, LLC.

The Library of Congress Cataloguing-in-Publication Data is available upon request.

ISBN 978-0-7653-9156-8 (hardcover)
ISBN 978-0-7653-9157-5 (ebook)

Our books may be purchased in bulk for promotional, educational, or business use. Please contact your local bookseller or the Macmillan Corporate and Premium Sales Department at 1-800-221-7945, extension 5442, or by email at MacmillanSpecialMarkets@macmillan.com.

Printed in the United States of America

0 9 8 7 6 5 4 3 2

Once again, to Rose.

The best weapon against an enemy is another enemy.

Friedrich Nietzsche

ONE

Few people presume to whisper into the ears of presidents. Fewer still are duty bound to do precisely that.

Ludmilla Kravchuk sat with practiced calm in a straight-back Louis Quinze chair. She wore a heavy skirt that, even when seated, fell demurely below her dimpled knees. Her shapeless blouse was cast in neutral beige, not by chance blending seamlessly into the curtained backdrop. Her earrings were modest, small cultured pearls in a gold claw setting. Her only other accessory of note was an ordinary wristwatch, this shifted above the cuff on her right wrist. It was conceivable she might be asked the time, but to be seen checking it of her own accord would be a grievous faux pas.

Ever so discreetly, Ludmilla reached down and slipped a finger into the heel of her right shoe. Sensible flats, battleship gray, the shoes had been furnished specifically for this occasion, chosen so as to not clash with anything worn by the two main actors of today's show. Unfortunately, the shoes proved to be a size too small. No doubt, she would be rewarded with a blister by the end of the day.

Ludmilla would be situated at President Petrov's right shoulder, her chair perfectly placed in the staged meeting area. The two larger and more comfortable sitting chairs were situated at a perfectly diplomatic slant, the armrests canted toward one another at a thirty-degree angle. Anything less might appear aloof. Anything more confrontational. This would be President Petrov's first summit with the newly elected Iranian president, Ahmed Rahmani, and it was not to be mishandled. Or as the adage went in diplomatic circles, *If everyone does their job, a completely forgettable event.*

As if to keep the world off-balance, the meeting was taking place in Damascus. The Syrian regime was desperate to put the

war behind it, and playing neutral host to its two greatest bene-
factors—or coconspirators, some might say—was a baby step back
onto the world stage. In a notable snub, however, the Syrian president would not take part. He had been left behind near a tray of
scones at the breakfast table while the two principals pursued the
world's real business.

They were presently standing at the head of the meeting room,
the presidents of Russia and Iran, posing and smiling for a band
of official photographers—three Russian, one Iranian—who were
capturing a series of wooden smiles and handshakes to be beamed
over news wires later that day. Under a backdrop of whirring and
clicking, the two men approached the upholstered chairs with a
decorum that would have sufficed in any house of worship. Once
comfortably seated, there were more handshakes and strobes until,
all at once, the presidential smiles blanked like a pair of lights being
switched off. The photographers took their cue and were ushered
from the room. Next to go were two small contingents of support
staff, followed at the end by the respective security details, two
clusters of serious men, one Slavic, the other Persian, who eyed one
another with that mix of suspicion and bravado invariably reared
into the type. When the great double doors finally closed, a disconcerting silence fell across the room.

Ludmilla took a deep breath. The meeting today would be
among the most unusual between heads of state, a pure one-on-
one: no whispering advisors or busy stenographers. Had the two
men shared a language, even in the most rudimentary sense, Ludmilla was certain that she and her Iranian counterpart would not
be in attendance. As it was, the specter of misunderstanding demanded their inclusion.

Her eyes connected briefly with those of the attractive young
Persian woman seated to the left of the Iranian president. Ludmilla
thought she looked nervous. There had been no words between
them since arriving in the room, although they'd met earlier at the
hotel, as interpreters often did, to establish a few ground rules. Her
name was Sofia Aryan, and she had admitted tautly to Ludmilla
that she was nervous about the meeting: this was but her second
occasion interpreting for the new Iranian president.

Ludmilla harbored no such insecurities. She had studied Mideast
languages at the prestigious Lomonosov Moscow State University,

and later honed her linguistic skills at the special language academy of the Ministry of Foreign Affairs. Mastering both Farsi and Arabic, she had thereafter served in various embassies across the Middle East: Iran, Jordan, Oman, and most recently two postings to Syria. It was this, her experience in both Tehran and Damascus, that had put her at the president's side for this summit. She would be his linguistic filter, expected to catch every verbal nuance and colloquialism, to neither editorialize nor embellish, and to present herself with paramount dignity. More subtly, but no less important: she had to do it all as a chameleon, blending into the surroundings.

In the three weeks since learning of the assignment, Ludmilla had committed herself fully. She'd memorized the name and location of every military base in Iran, and could cite employment statistics from the most recent government economic report. She knew the Iranian president's extended family tree, his relationship with the ayatollahs, his penchant for European football, and that he enjoyed fishing for trout. Ludmilla would of course never steer a conversation toward any of these subjects, but if they arose naturally she would be comfortable with the vernacular in every case.

She waited patiently for one of the two men to break the ice. Russia's ties to the Iranian regime went back to the revolution, and the war in Syria had brought the nations closer yet—an alliance of convenience by any measure. Now the two heads of state were meeting in the heart of the killing grounds.

Not surprisingly, it was Petrov who began.

"I am glad we could meet," he said in Russian.

Ludmilla listened closely to Aryan's translation—not so much for content, which was basic enough, but to get a feel for her pacing and volume. At this level, interpreters were expected to operate with carefully governed modulation, the volume subtly loud enough for their counterpart to double-check, and the interval not stepping on the other principal's reply. Aryan seemed on task, if a bit measured.

"As am I," Rahmani responded.

"I hope we can someday meet in the new villa you are building. The pictures I have seen are inspiring."

The Iranian smiled, but a trace of discomfort shone through. Construction of the villa—the word *palace* carried uncomfortable connotations, regardless of how apt—was supposed to be a closely held secret, a necessary accommodation in a country whose economy had been suffering for years. The president of Russia, who began his career as a KGB officer, had made his first point: on matters of intelligence, Rahmani would be at a disadvantage.

With alpha status established, Petrov meandered to a bit of small talk about families and acquaintances. It was the usual banter of two leaders getting to know one another. Then, after some off-color humor about the American president, Petrov induced a sudden shift.

"My people have swept this room thoroughly," he said, waving a hand through the air. "We can speak freely."

The Iranian gave the slightest of nods.

"It is best to not be obtuse," Petrov continued. "You know what I have come to discuss."

Ludmilla felt Rahmani's eyes hold her for a moment, before he said, "Of course. The new capability you have offered us."

Petrov said, "I am convinced the transfer of this technology will help stabilize the region."

"Yes, a bit of stability is always welcome in our corner of the world."

"Indeed. Iran is surrounded by Sunnis, and Israeli strike aircraft are never more than a few hours away. Then, of course, you have the Americans blundering about as ever."

"I am happy you recognize our dilemma," said Rahmani.

Petrov might have smiled.

Ludmilla was keeping up well.

Petrov said, "The logistics on our end are in place. The delivery will take place in the coming days. As you can understand, we must be extremely careful about such transactions."

"And this is why you've selected such a remote location?"

"It is. Tell your people that the timing will be rather fluid. Expect a window of a few days for the transfer to take place. I can also tell you that the man making the delivery is not provably Russian. He comes more from your part of the world than mine."

"But clearly you trust him."

"As much as I trust anyone," said Petrov with a stone face.

Ludmilla's ears reached for Aryan's translation, making sure she did not editorialize these words.

"I am glad we have earned your confidence," Rahmani replied. "We accept what you are offering with a due sense of responsibility.

We of course have our own program in this area, but Russia has always been on the leading edge."

Ludmilla stuck to her task as the conversation deepened, yet soon it veered onto ground that had not been in her briefing guide. Ground she never would have imagined in her preparations. It was the kind of thing, she supposed, that heads of state might discuss with trusted military advisors. Yet such an open dialogue with a foreign leader seemed acutely misplaced. She tried to maintain focus, and saw Aryan struggling as well.

This was long the conundrum faced by interpreters—try as they might to detach themselves during work, they were in the end humans. Individuals with sentiments and opinions and souls. And as Ludmilla knew all too well, what was heard could never be unheard.

She did her best to stay on task, concentrating on verbiage and tone and detail. Trying not to be distracted by the bigger picture. After ten minutes, the essence of the meeting was inescapably clear. Five after that, Petrov abruptly declared the meeting complete. The president of Russia stood, headed for the door.

Rahmani followed.

Ludmilla remained frozen in her seat. Only her eyes tracked the two presidents as they neared the door. It was Iran's leader who turned and glanced at her. His gaze then shifted to Sofia Aryan. He gently took Petrov's elbow and whispered into his ear—the first direct, unfiltered words between the two. She wondered what language they shared. Broken English? Whatever it was, Rahmani's words seemed to register with Petrov. He, too, looked at Ludmilla and Aryan, as if recognizing their presence for the first time. He gave a slight nod, and the two men disappeared into the hallway.

The room fell uncomfortably still. Ludmilla heard the gentle rush of air from a vent, a door closing down the hall. The welcome return of the ordinary.

Her thoughts still spinning, she stood slowly, deliberately. She absently smoothed her perfectly pressed skirt. Aryan rose, and they exchanged an uncomfortable look. Still cordial, but newly laced with suspicion. A wariness born of the words of others. Words they had both been forced to hear and speak.

"That was . . . unusual," Aryan said, her flawless Russian faltering.

Ludmilla didn't respond.

"What do you think they said as they were leaving . . . when they looked back at us?"

"I'm not sure what you mean," Ludmilla said unconvincingly.

Aryan gave her a plaintive look. "What they were discussing—"

"*What* they were discussing is no business of ours!" Ludmilla interjected. "We are paid for our language skills, not our opinions."

"Of course, you are right. It is just that . . . certain things are difficult to forget."

"Perhaps, but forget we must. That is our duty." Ludmilla hoped the conviction in her words belied what she felt. She had interpreted for many important meetings. Never had she come away with her thoughts in such disarray. She was confident her translations had been accurate, but she also knew she'd hesitated distinctly on realizing what the two men were proposing. Aryan's unease was understandable. Even so, Ludmilla would not fuel it further.

"The Four Seasons is a very nice place," Aryan ventured. "How long will you be staying?"

In a tone that held no regret, Ludmilla said, "Regrettably, I am scheduled to leave tomorrow."

"Too bad. Perhaps we could have met for coffee."

Ludmilla recoiled. Such contact would be blatantly unprofessional. Still, she found herself thinking about it. By pure chance the two of them, a Russian and an Iranian who would likely never meet again, had been bonded by circumstances. Tied by a secret neither could share with anyone else on earth.

"No," Ludmilla said decisively, "that would not be possible."

Aryan nodded to say she understood. She seemed suddenly smaller, her pretty face gone pale. She looked like a woman being pushed to sea alone in a lifeboat. It occurred to Ludmilla that she would have to report this conversation. A part of her—the old Soviet part of her youth—imagined that the exchange they'd just overheard was only some convoluted test. An assessment of her loyalty. Could Petrov really have sunk to that kind of thing?

Aryan walked toward her, still at sea, and offered a hesitant handshake.

Ludmilla gave her that much.

With a tortured smile, and in a shuffle of crisp polyester, Sofia Aryan turned toward the door and disappeared.

TWO

Situated centrally in Damascus, on the northern bank of the Barada River, the Four Seasons was as close to a luxury hotel as remained in Syria. As with the rest of the country, a decade of war had taken its toll. The pool was closed, the hot water intermittent, and half the items on the room service menu were no longer on offer. A letter squared on the writing desk, immaculately scripted in the general manager's hand, offered his personal apologies for these running inconveniences, and asked guests for their "forbearance in light of our nation's ongoing troubles."

It was all of little concern to Ludmilla Kravchuk. As she stared distractedly down from her twelfth-floor window to the empty pool and vacant deck, there was no room in her mind for regrets about not having the opportunity to sunbathe. She turned into her spacious suite, her thoughts no less a maelstrom now than when she'd returned from the palace two hours ago.

The meeting remained stuck in her head, segments of disjointed conversation looping time and again. She'd had misgivings after meetings in the past, but they had mostly centered on her performance. Had she used the right words? Captured accurately the principals' tones? Today was different. In that unique affliction suffered by interpreters, every word arrived in her head with an echo—in this case, once in Farsi and again in Russian. She searched for faults in her translation. Prayed for them even. Try as she might, there were none. Her work had been unerring. The problem was the subject matter.

Ludmilla's meandering ended near the nightstand. She stood stock-still in front of the full-length dressing mirror. She thought she looked suddenly older, her face weary. The subtle lines in her forehead had gone to grooves, and her shoulders drooped as if she were hauling heavy bags. She had been working for the foreign ministry for twenty-two years, long enough to draw a modest pension. And what more did she need given her situation?

Ludmilla had married young and impulsively, and for a time it had worked. Then Grishka had lost his job at the tractor factory, and soon after she began a series of foreign postings. He had left her ten years ago for a woman half his age. Two years after that he'd been found dead in a ditch on a sub-zero January morning, an empty vodka bottle by his side. They'd never had children, which was probably just as well. Aside from a sister in Murmansk she hadn't spoken to in years, Ludmilla had no immediate family.

Perhaps it's time, she thought. *A small cottage near the Black Sea.*

She turned away from the mirror, not liking its company. She strove to regain her interpreter's composure. Subject matter aside, Ludmilla had sensed something unusual today in the current of Petrov's words. His constructions had seemed crafted with inordinate care, almost as if rehearsed. Conversely, she'd sensed caution, even mild surprise in Rahmani's responses—an impression she would include in her after-action report. *If I could only collect myself long enough to write one.*

A knock on the door rattled her back to the present.

Ludmilla edged toward the peephole and peered through. What felt like a shot of stray voltage coursed through her spine. The face in the fish-eyed lens was painfully familiar. Close-cropped black beard, heavy brow, fearsome eyes of coal. Cinderblock head on crossbeam shoulders. It was Oleg Vasiliev, the head of Petrov's security detail.

She hesitated, wondering if she might call out that she was in the shower. Of course she knew better. Ludmilla was a product of the new Russia, and a near-confidant of its czar. She strongly suspected they'd wired her room. It was a discomforting thought, but one she'd grown accustomed to—one of the prices paid for the privileges she enjoyed. As a more practical matter, Ludmilla recalled what she'd been told in her arrival briefing. The Russian delegation had taken over the hotel's two highest floors in their entirety. She was on the penultimate level, directly beneath the presidential suite, and as head of security, Vasiliev had in his possession a key that would open any room on either floor. An accommodation made by the Four Seasons, she supposed, for the security chiefs of visiting heads of state.

After a bracing inhalation, she pulled open the door.

Vasiliev barged inside. "Your shoes," he demanded.

"I beg your pardon?"

"My man brought you a pair of shoes last night—you wore them at today's meeting. They must be returned."

Ludmilla blinked. It was not uncommon for interpreters to be issued wardrobes, particularly for head-of-state summits. Indeed, her closet at home displayed an entire rack of grain-sack-cut skirts and neutral blouses, issued like so many uniforms to a diplomatic corporal. As far as she could remember, this was the first time she'd ever been asked to return anything.

She set out toward the closet, feeling Vasiliev's eyes on her. It was more a watchdog's gaze than anything leering. This Ludmilla knew all too well. She had not been chosen as the president's interpreter based solely on her language skills. Solid as they were, a dozen men and women in the foreign ministry were every bit as proficient. What set her apart were her physical attributes—or, more bluntly, her lack thereof. Her peasant's jowls and thick build had been with her since childhood. So too, her stern facial set and officious manner. Yet what had proved a social handicap as a young woman she'd turned to an advantage amid her small community of interpreters. At the apex of Russia's male-dominated pyramid of power, she had claimed a niche with her plain, undistracting appearance. Payback of sorts, she told herself, for a lifetime of doors not being opened and catcalls missed.

She went to the closet and saw the shoes in back.

As an interpreter, Ludmilla was something of a professional listener, an expert in the nuanced details of spoken phrases. That being the case, she recalled precisely what Vasiliev had just said: *a pair of shoes*.

Singular.

His minion had yesterday delivered the dress she'd worn to the meeting, along with *two* identical pairs of shoes—two, she'd been told, because they had been unsure of her size. It seemed rather wasteful, but Ludmilla thought little of it at the time. This morning she'd slipped on the larger pair. They were tight—her mother's side of the family was cursed with big feet—yet by the end of the day the shoes had broken in nicely. She also thought them rather stylish, at least more so than the chock-heeled black wedges that dominated her closet back home.

In a decision any Russian would understand—and one that would soon change her life forever—Ludmilla retrieved the smaller pair she'd never worn and handed them to Vasiliev.

He took them in his hairy hand and was out the door.

THREE

The second knock on Ludmilla's door came twenty minutes later. She assumed Vasiliev had come back for the second pair of shoes, and prepared to feign forgetfulness. One look through the viewing port, however, converted mere disappointment to alarm. An agitated Sofia Aryan stood rocking on her heels, her gaze alternating between the door and the hallway.

Ludmilla put on a stern face and opened the door. "You should not have come here!" she admonished.

Much like Vasiliev, Aryan shouldered in without invitation. "They are following me!" she said breathlessly.

"This is highly . . ." Ludmilla's protest faded. "*Who* is following you?"

"Two men—I'm sure they are VAJA," she said, referring to Iranian intelligence. "I was returning from lunch and they tried to seize me on the sidewalk outside the hotel. As they dragged me toward a car I began screaming, and fortunately a group of soldiers were passing on the sidewalk. They tussled with the men long enough for me to get free. I was able to get away in the confusion, but I can't return to my room—it is the first place they'll look. I didn't know where to go. Then I remembered that you were staying at the Four Seasons as well."

"How did you know my room number?"

"During our coordination meeting this morning . . . you used your key to access the business center. I saw the room number on the sleeve."

Ludmilla stared at the woman with newfound respect. She was clever, or at the very least observant. She was also clearly terrified.

Her hair was mussed, and one cuff of her dark blue overcoat had suffered a jagged tear.

Aryan took Ludmilla's hand and looked at her pleadingly. "You are the only one who could understand. We are in the same position . . . you *heard* the same things I did today. You know what is being planned by—"

"No! None of that concerns us! It is a grave breach of protocol for us to discuss anything we've heard!"

The gentle lines in Aryan's pretty face deepened, and her lively dark eyes lost some of their luster. "You know what it is like in Iran. I can't go back now. If they find me, they will—"

"Out!" Ludmilla demanded. "Out of my room now!" She herded Aryan through the still-open door and into the hall. The woman looked on the verge of panic.

"Don't you understand?" Aryan argued. "If they have come for me, they will come for you as well! If not VAJA, then Petrov's SVR! You and I heard far too much to be allowed to—"

Ludmilla slammed the door shut and threw the bolt.

She expelled a great breath and put her shoulders on the door as if to prevent another assault by Aryan. She waited, expecting her pleading voice or frantic pounding. What she heard was something else.

A man somewhere down the hall was shouting in Farsi: *"Stop! We mean you no harm!"*

That was followed by multiple footfalls. The first set were light and quick, scampering like a deer. These were followed by what sounded like a stampede of bison. More shouting, the words unintelligible. Ludmilla heard a door slam somewhere down the hall.

Then an uneasy silence.

She tried to remain calm.

She crossed the room tentatively, retrieved a bottle of mineral water from the bedside stand. Cracking the cap, she took a deliberate sip, trying to right her disjointed thoughts. She recalled the panicked look on Aryan's face. Then the conversation the two of them had heard and translated this morning. *And now?* Now Iranian thugs were chasing the poor woman down the hall. It was some minutes later—how many she could not say—that the last underpinnings of her steadfast world were removed. It would prove to be the moment she remembered above all others. The one that forced its way to her nightmares.

A scream.

It began with disconcerting suddenness, full-throated and desperate. More curiously, the cry changed swiftly in pitch and volume, like the screech of a passing subway car. She didn't know precisely where it was sourced, but it ended with dreadful abruptness. Soon after, Ludmilla was drawn to the window by a chorus of shouts. Ever so slowly, reluctantly, she crossed the room.

She looked down at the pool deck. No longer vacant, three uniformed hotel employees stood in a perfect triangle, and between them a body lay splayed facedown on the stone patio. A body in a dark blue coat. The arms were outstretched, almost as if pleading. A puddle of red was growing quickly beneath, oozing toward the empty pool.

Ludmilla's knees buckled, and she leaned involuntarily into the wall next to the window. She gasped for breath, as if the room had suddenly gone to a vacuum. Thoughts that had been brewing only moments ago, fleeting and ill-defined, seemed to fuse with a crushing weight. More shouting broke the spell, this time from above. The words were muddled, yet the tone was easily distinguishable. An alarm being raised. Commands given in Russian.

It was coming from Petrov's suite.

She stood frozen, stilled by indecision. A lifetime of conformity collided with far more basic instincts. The likes of fear and self-preservation. Slowly, glacially, Ludmilla's methodical nature reasserted itself. She knew what she had to do . . . at least in the next sixty seconds.

She retrieved her purse from the nightstand, double-checking that her passport and wallet were inside. She suspected her phone could be tracked, so she set that aside. She considered packing a bag, but a door slamming somewhere above ended the thought. She yanked her light jacket from a hanger in the closet. On another day she might have remembered sunglasses, or perhaps a scarf with which to cover her hair. Then again, on another day she might not have been so bold. Only later would Ludmilla realize that the most crucial decision she made in those seconds was quite accidental. From the closet she picked out the shoes she'd worn that morning.

Moments later she was out the door and rushing through the hall. The elevator seemed quickest, and she breathed a sigh of relief when the door opened to present an empty car. In the lobby she made a beeline for the front entrance where the doorman ably waved up a taxi. She gave the driver an address that she knew to be across town—not because it was her destination, but because she didn't have one. She needed time to think. As the car pulled away, Ludmilla glanced over her shoulder. She saw two men bustle out the hotel's revolving front door. They skidded to a stop on the curb and began conferring with the doorman. He pointed to her receding cab like a witness pointing out a murderer in a courtroom.

Ludmilla shrank instinctively in her seat. She opened her purse and pulled out a fistful of Syrian pounds—she'd intended to go shopping, but had run out of time. In an impulse that was completely at odds with her frugal nature, she threw a wad of cash into the front seat. "I wish to change my destination!" she said in perfect Arabic, adding the name of a hotel less than a mile away. "Please hurry! I am late for my daughter's wedding!"

The driver glanced at her in the mirror, then looked at the lump of cash on his seat. The car accelerated.

Ludmilla ventured a final look back as the cab turned onto a side street. She didn't recognize the two men as being from Vasiliev's detail, but their Slavic features and the way their eyes tracked her cab left no doubt.

There were Russian.

And they had come for her.

FOUR

News of Ludmilla Kravchuk's disappearance spread through the top floor of the Four Seasons like fire through a wood-rotted saloon. Her harried departure, witnessed by the SVR team who'd been sent to collect her, had all the hallmarks of a defection. That scenario seemed even more likely when it was learned that the woman now splattered on the hotel's Italian travertine pool deck was in fact Kravchuk's Iranian counterpart.

Petrov, who had been enjoying a late lunch on the expansive balcony, made a series of snap decisions. To begin, he ordered his regrets to be given for a state dinner with the Syrians scheduled for that evening, explaining that he faced "pressing business on the home front." In seeming contradiction, he declared that he and his entourage would stay in Damascus for another day, perhaps two. The presidential finger then landed squarely on his security chief.

Vasiliev trailed Petrov into his private suite like a wayward student being led into the principal's office. As soon as the door closed, Petrov began in a low voice: "Do we know why this woman has run?"

"Who can say?" Vasiliev said weakly.

Petrov, of course, already knew the answer: the woman feared for her life. After this morning's meeting, President Rahmani had pulled him aside, in full view of both interpreters, and suggested that the women had heard more than they should have. Petrov, whose English was only passable, recalled falling back on one of his standard catchphrases: "I will take care of the problem on my side." He had arranged for Kravchuk to be sequestered and debriefed once they returned to Moscow, and to be reminded that for a woman in her profession, discretion was inviolate. In Petrov's Russia, no more was necessary.

Not so, apparently, in Rahmani's Iran. The Iranian president had taken care of his half of the problem by unleashing his VAJA thugs whose inelegant solution was to throw the interpreter off the roof. In all likelihood, Kravchuk had seen it happen and fled for her life. A perfectly understandable reaction.

But what risks does it introduce? Petrov wondered.

He circled the room like a caged animal. He recalled seeing a cursory background check on Kravchuk. She had a solid reputation at the foreign ministry, nearly twenty years in service. Her linguistic skills were solid, although professionally she was seen as something of a plodder—not necessarily a bad thing. She had interpreted for Petrov twice before without issue. There had been but one red flag, and that a distant one—her husband had died eight years ago, not long after an awkward separation.

Had that affected her allegiance? Made her unstable? It seemed unlikely, but not impossible. At the very least, it was something Petrov should have considered. The woman had few remaining ties to Russia.

He paused at the window and regarded the Damascus skyline. Compared to the glass and steel of Moscow, the mosques and sandstone architecture before him seemed from a different world. Petrov cursed inwardly. Given what was at stake, he *should* have looked at Kravchuk more closely. Would he have made such a mistake twenty years ago? Had he gotten lazy, become too reliant on those around him? He had risen through the ranks of the KGB as a detail man, finding every threat, identifying weaknesses to be exploited. Over time, as the scale of his empire expanded, he'd been forced to delegate more and more. That was an inescapable consequence of having reached the pinnacle. Yet today seemed different. For an operation of this magnitude, of such importance, he should have been more careful. The woman had heard too much.

And now she'd disappeared.

Petrov turned back to the silent Vasiliev, his reptilian eyes fixed. His voice was calm when he said, "Your job is to keep me safe, and you have done so admirably. Today, however, I need something more. I cannot stress enough the importance of finding this woman."

"I have men searching for her," Vasiliev said, his tone reflecting more confidence than he likely felt. "But please understand, we brought only eighteen men to Damascus. Nearly all of them are needed to maintain security here. We will have to rely on the Syrians to find this woman. They have unlimited manpower, and we are on their ground."

"See to it then."

Vasiliev said that he would. "She cannot evade us for long. She is not trained." He then paused before adding, "I should tell you, sir . . . there is one other problem."

Petrov's gaze never wavered.

"It has to do with the shoes. It seems she was given *two* pairs."

"What are you saying?"

"Mikhailov wanted a good fit . . . to ensure that she wore them. I had no knowledge of this until only moments ago. When I went to her room to retrieve them, she returned only a single pair— according to our technician, they are not the ones she wore to the meeting. We have checked her room, but the other pair are gone."

A barely perceptible twitch came to the presidential brow. "Are you telling me that she—"

"We are trying to find out. I sent a man to check the hotel's video footage from the lobby."

After a motivational pause, the president said, "Do you have any doubts as to your current mission?"

"None sir!"

"Then get on with it!"

Vasiliev did precisely that.

FIVE

Vasiliev wasted no time in sending a message to his Syrian security liaison, a midlevel man in the Ministry of the Interior. That the request was coming directly from Russia's president caused considerable hand-wringing in the ministry's upper ranks. After an unusual amount of departmental churning, orders were sent down to the Damascus Police, criminal investigations division. A certain inspector was to report without delay to the Four Seasons Hotel and give every assistance in the matter of a missing Russian interpreter.

His name was Omar Hadad.

Hadad was a long-tenured captain and senior inspector in the division. He was a slightly built man with thinning hair and a methodical nature. Wire-rimmed spectacles sat upon a thin nose, and behind them were a set of inquisitive brown eyes. He was, by most accounts, including those of his colonel and his wife, a serviceable man. Hadad had been on the force for twelve years, a detective for eight. In the course of his career he had earned a solid reputation, although the consensus was that he'd reached the top rung of his personal ladder.

Hadad was given instructions to begin at the hotel, and when he arrived he took the elevator to the twelfth floor. He found the Russian he was to meet in the room where Ludmilla Kravchuk had been staying. He extended a hand and introduced himself in passable Russian. A number of the detectives in his section had a rudimentary grasp of the language, a consequence of the two nations' long and arduous history.

The man, whose name was Vasiliev, shook his hand wearily and launched straight into business. "It is imperative we find this woman. She is a traitor to Russia."

Hadad nodded sympathetically. "My orders were very explicit. I can assure you every national resource is at my command."

Vasiliev gave a quick rundown of what he knew so far—or at least, what he was willing to share. His level of angst, Hadad thought, likely reflected that of the Russian president himself. He sensed more at stake than a simple defection.

The first order of business, the two agreed, was to establish a constellation of checkpoints: every highway leaving the city had to be covered. "That," said Hadad, "should at least confine the field of play. Do you have a photo of our quarry?"

"There is a digital image on my computer upstairs. I can send it to you."

Inspector Hadad scrawled down an email address on hotel stationery. Vasiliev headed for the door, promising to be right back.

Alone, Hadad began wandering the room. As he did so he took up a series of phone calls, bounding between various regional police divisions. He emphasized the importance of finding Kravchuk, and while everyone agreed to help, Hadad recognized the all-too-familiar hallmarks of dysfunction: many of the regional commanders suggested the woman had likely fled to a quarter more lawless than their own. Just as Hadad's last call ended, he saw an email notification and opened it. He studied a decent image of Ludmilla Kravchuk, and wondered how much damage could really be wrought by such a nondescript suspect.

The inspector had ended near the window, and he was looking down toward the pool when a second email arrived. It was from his sergeant, who'd begun interviewing the staff.

Vasiliev returned moments later, and Hadad said, "The Iranian interpreter, Sofia Aryan. Are you aware she was thrown off the roof?"

"Thrown?" Vasiliev repeated.

"Apparently there was a witness, the hotel gardener. He heard a scream and looked up, saw a set of hands helping her over the edge."

"Did he see who it was?"

"No."

Vasiliev's face crinkled beneath his beard. "I am a soldier, not a detective. But . . . do you think Kravchuk might have murdered this woman?"

"The way she fled so suddenly . . . it has to be considered. For the time being, it helps drive our search. We can call her a suspect in a murder investigation."

"I suppose it might help. But make no mistake: President Petrov does not want this search to be taken public. Kravchuk's disappearance is to remain an internal Russian matter."

"I understand," said Hadad.

And truly he did. Given what he knew so far, Hadad would bet his pension that Ludmilla Kravchuk, by all accounts a mild-mannered interpreter and matron of Russia, had probably never thrown trash on a sidewalk, let alone a healthy young woman from a thirteen-story building. He smiled reassuringly at Vasiliev. "Tell your president to rest assured. She cannot have gone far."

Although Hadad would not realize it for days, he was in fact quite right.

SIX

The woman they were looking for was, at that moment, wandering the streets of the nearby Arnous district in a daze. The city around her seemed a blur. Noxious clouds of diesel belched from buses and crowds choked the sidewalks. Street vendors sold meat from grills, the scent of cooking flesh drifting past in waves. Because Western clothing was more or less the norm in Damascus, Ludmilla drew little attention from passersby.

But it was not the casual faces on the sidewalk that worried her.

Not for the first time, she wondered if she'd made a terrible mistake. Bolting from the hotel had been rash and impulsive—completely at odds with her typically thoughtful conduct. She tried to imagine some way to surrender herself, a rational reason for her unconscionable blunder. Every time she did, the disturbing images came back, flickering like so many snapshots in a terrible scrapbook. The two presidents at the door whispering to one another. The glance back at their interpreters. A desperate Sofia Aryan coming to her room, pleading for help. And soon after—Aryan's scream as she fell from the roof of the building.

The associations couldn't be clearer. Couldn't be more damning.

No, Ludmilla thought, there was no turning back. Petrov's men had seen her running away. She had served in the foreign ministry long enough, even as a lowly interpreter, to know how such defections were handled. Only last year she'd seen an army major try to defect from the embassy in Cairo. He was captured within hours by the SVR, put hurriedly on a specially arranged flight back to Moscow. The rest could only be imagined. A car ride to an FSB interrogation facility—nothing so explicit as Lubyanka, but one of the smaller off-the-books prisons that were today preferred by the agency.

And then?

Ludmilla didn't want to think about it.

Like it or not, she was committed. Running for her life.

She was completely lost in this bleak train of thought, and stepping across a dirty curb, when out of nowhere a hand clamped over her arm. Ludmilla jerked upright, and in the next instant a bus rushed past, horn blaring. Recoiling in a swirl of dust, she half turned to see an old man, his bony hand on her bicep. He stared at her with the compassion one might confer upon a stray dog.

"Thank you," she said in Arabic.

The old man gave her a quizzical look, then went on his way. The light turned red and the traffic came to a stop. Ludmilla fell in with the crowd crossing the intersection. Her heart was racing, her nerves shot. She felt near a breaking point.

This dilemma was unlike any she'd ever faced. Hers was a world of meeting minutes and transcripts. Of staid conferences and numbing briefing papers. But now? Now her life had been distilled to something far more elemental—she had to get out of Syria alive.

Since ditching the cab an hour ago, she was sure she'd made a hundred mistakes. Ludmilla forced herself to think logically. She needed help, and there seemed but one obvious source: the Americans.

The logistics of that, however, were not so simple.

It had been decades since the Americans kept a diplomatic presence in Syria. There was no longer any embassy or consulate, the relationship between the countries having long ago sunk beneath the threshold of such pretenses. Ludmilla knew, however, that there was one possibility. As was customary in such diplomatic estrangements, the United States had arranged for a third party—in this case the Czech Republic—to serve as its diplomatic surrogate. Getting word to the Americans, therefore, meant going through the Czechs.

Ludmilla began stepping more quickly as her plan took shape. She soon realized that before she attempted contact, more pressing needs had to be addressed. To begin, she needed a place to stay.

No, she corrected, *I need a place to hide.*

A bus approached a stop just ahead, and she hurried to board it. Settling into an empty seat near the back, her paranoia began to ease. Like public transportation the world over, everyone on the bus was wearing their thousand-yard stare. Ever so slowly, the shock was wearing off.

Ludmilla realized she was not completely helpless. She had been posted to Syria twice, most recently three years ago. She spoke the language fluently, knew the local customs. In her time at the embassy, she'd received countless briefings on how to stay out of trouble. She knew which neighborhoods to avoid and where the militias prevailed. Her best resource of all: Ludmilla had once had her share of friends.

But which would still be here?

Who was safe to approach?

The first few names that came to mind were staff from the Russian embassy. She'd had a handful of close acquaintances, and some might conceivably still be posted in Damascus. Ludmilla had also gotten to know a handful of Syrians, locals who were tied to the embassy by various means: messengers, caterers, cleaning crews. Her hope then faltered when she realized that all such contacts had to be avoided. The staff at the embassy would soon be apprised of her disappearance, ordered to report any contact.

She had to find help elsewhere.

The solution came in the middle of a busy commercial block when through her window she saw the marquis of a high-end hair salon. As it turned out, Ludmilla knew of another such place, although decidedly more egalitarian. During her time at the embassy, the salon's owner had become the closest thing she'd had to a friend in Syria.

And a friend was very much what she needed.

Her feet were aching twenty minutes later when Chez Salma came into view. Ludmilla paused at the front window and peered inside. The business day was nearing its end, and she saw the proprietor unwrapping strips of foil from a customer's hair. The other two stylist's chairs were empty.

Ludmilla walked in, and Salma saw her immediately. The two exchanged a warm embrace before, predictably, the hairdresser pulled back. She regarded Ludmilla's much neglected pageboy with a jaundiced eye and a *tsk tsk* noise. Her brown hair was due for a tint, the gray beginning to win.

"I know," admitted Ludmilla. "I need the works."

"I can put you on the schedule tomorrow."

"That would be wonderful. How is business?"

Salma frowned. "Terrible. Too many husbands tell their wives that food is more important than style."

"How shortsighted."

This brought the slightest of grins. "Everyone has cut back during the war. Everyone except those living in Qasr ash-Shaab," she said, referring to the presidential palace. She looked up and down at Ludmilla's dress and shoes. "Are you back at the embassy?"

Ludmilla faltered. It was a question she should have predicted. "Yes . . . but only for a short time. They are performing some renovations in the temporary living quarters at the station, so I need a place to stay for a few nights."

She held her breath, hoping things were as she remembered. Salma lived on the second floor with her husband, who drove a bus in the city. On either side of their residence were small rooms they rented out. Ludmilla remembered Salma complaining about the high turnover rate.

When Salma didn't reply, Ludmilla prompted, "Perhaps you should ask your husband."

The hairdresser's expression went cold. "Adil died," she said flatly.

"Oh God, no," Ludmilla said. "I am so sorry."

"It's been two years," Salma said, as if that made a difference.

"And Naji?" Ludmilla asked, referring to Salma's son who'd been an infant when she'd last seen him.

"He was two when his father died. In the beginning it was easy, but now Naji asks about him every day. I tell him what I can, the stories I remember. But there was so little time when we were all together. That's what war does to families—it steals their chances to make memories."

Ludmilla looked around the salon. As an infant Naji had often been in a playpen in the corner. "Where is he now?"

"Upstairs. My mother watches him most days. One day each week we go south to Mezzeh. Naji has become close with an uncle there."

"Achmed, the one you once told me about?"

Salma nodded. A hard silence descended until she forced a smile and said, "As it turns out, you are in luck. One of my renters moved out last week. But I haven't had time to clean the place."

"I'm sure it would be fine. I could tidy it up myself."

And just like that the deal was struck. Ludmilla settled on a price for five nights, thinking that would give the Americans plenty of time. She used half the cash in her wallet to pay in advance. Salma gave her a key, then went back to the coloring in progress.

"There is one more thing," Ludmilla said.

Salma looked at her inquisitively, wet foil in her hand.

"My phone has stopped working." She pointed to an old computer and a hard-wired phone at the front desk. "Might I look up one phone number and make a call?"

Salma waved a hand to say that she could.

SEVEN

The call to the Czech embassy went smoothly, or so Ludmilla thought—clandestine communications were not her forte.

She had tried to think everything through beforehand. It was crucial that she give enough information to draw interest, some of which had to be backstopped as verifiable. Once that was settled, she took the direct route. She called the embassy's switchboard, asked if the line was being recorded. The operator assured her it was, and for the next thirty seconds Ludmilla stated her case. She ended by giving a time and place for a rendezvous, then abruptly disconnected.

Salma was putting the final touches on her last customer of the day, and with an hour to kill until her rendezvous, Ludmilla headed upstairs to see her new flat. She was nearly to the second-floor landing when she wrenched the heel of one shoe on a crooked board in the staircase. She caught the handrail, righted herself, and reached the landing. Room 3 was at the end of the short hall. Ludmilla unlocked the door, stepped inside, and sank the deadbolt behind her. For the first time since this morning she felt safe.

Her first look at the room reinforced what Salma had said— it *did* need to be cleaned. There was trash on the floor, the bed was unmade, and dead bugs lay strewn about the tiny kitchen. *No matter,* she thought. *I'll have plenty of time.* It was a small room, even by Russian standards, everything wedged into a continuous space. There was a bed in one corner with a mattress like a taco shell. Someone had thrown a sheet over the listing couch. Ludmilla made the mistake of lifting it and saw upholstery that was grossly stained. She sighed and thought wistfully of her tidy flat on Tverskaya Street.

A place she would never see again.

She let out a long sigh and settled on the couch. The springs groaned in protest. After her rendezvous later, there would be nothing to do but wait. Hours, days, weeks. Whatever it took for someone to rescue her. She reached down, removed her shoes, and began to massage her blistered right foot. As she did, she remembered catching her heel on the stair. She picked up the right shoe, held it by the toe.

And that was when Ludmilla got her final shock of the day.

Thirty minutes later, across town from Chez Salma, Tomas Kovacs walked out of the Czech embassy into a gathering evening. He took up a purposeful stride along the ruined sidewalks of Al Jalaa Street. Having been posted to Syria on three occasions since joining the foreign service, Kovacs had a good measure of the city's suffering. Once-thriving coffee shops and bakeries had gone under, never to return, and municipal funding for the likes of roads and sewers was all but a memory. Still, people adapted. Planks spanned washed-out gutters, and traffic cones appeared to mark the worst potholes. Damascus today was like an aging ship—a serviceable craft that carried on wearily, disinterested in whatever storms lay ahead.

Kovacs was dressed for the office: a stiff button-down shirt over tan chinos, dress shoes that had not yet been broken in. He'd had no time to change into something more suited to counter-surveillance. His usual jeans, Barcelona jersey, and trusted Nikes were in his apartment closet. Lamentably, cold contacts were like shooting stars: they never came with advance warning.

Kovacs was an ordinary man in appearance. He carried ten more pounds than he should have, had a modestly receding hairline, and was generally soft spoken. Less prosaic was the fact that for two years running he had been the U.S. State Department's default proxy in Syria. Or in the lexicon of his D.C. liaison, who'd played American football in college: their Hail Mary receiver.

In practice, of course, most of those who tried to contact the Americans via the Czechs tended to be cranks, lunatics, or amateur terrorists. This was no less a problem for the Syrians, who knew full well of the arrangement, and who put considerable effort into intercepting the embassy's incoming calls and emails. Still, everyone played along, spy versus spy, on the odd chance of the system working—some desperate contact providing critical intelligence.

Today's caller had, if nothing else, sounded desperate.

The recording from the embassy's communications center was of an anxious woman who claimed to have vital information regarding Iran and Russia. The few details offered were intriguing, and it hadn't been lost on the embassy staff that the woman made her claim in reasonably proficient Czech. An astute staffer in the communications center recalled that the Russian president was indeed in Damascus that day for a summit with his Iranian counterpart. There had also been rumblings about a dust-up at the Four Seasons, where both delegations were staying. It was far less a long shot than most tips, and enough of a coincidence that the duty officer committed to a response.

He dispatched Tomas Kovacs.

EIGHT

Kovacs approached Sibky Park with a casualness that was not entirely manufactured. It was a lovely evening in Damascus, the low sun bathing in a gentle breeze. With the war winding down, people were getting out, pent-up wanderlust after so many years of bunkering up. Even the birds and squirrels seemed more active, instilled with a new freedom.

For Kovacs, however, this posed a problem.

He entered the park with diminishing ease. The crowds were thick, coursing over sidewalks and roaming the lawns. A band was setting up to play on a makeshift stage in the distance, a few dozen people already staking out the front row with blankets and coolers. To undertake a meeting in such a public place, in Kovacs' view—and in broad daylight no less—was a dreadful bit of tradecraft. There were too many people to have any hope of spotting a tail. He put the odds at fifty-fifty that he was already being followed. To say the park was centrally located in the city was a gross understatement. To the east he saw Syria's Parliament building. To the west was embassy row, at least a dozen diplomatic stations—some friendly, others less so—in plain sight. Kovacs imagined there was not a more heavily monitored ten acres in all Syria.

To the positive, he was not in any personal danger. The Syrians followed him regularly, at least to the limits of their manpower, which had been strained during the war. The Mukhabarat knew perfectly well who Kovacs was and what he did for the Americans. This made him something of a known evil, and imbued him with a kind of immunity—the Syrians had never once bothered to pick him up during meetings gone bad. The same could not be said for those on the other end. He'd watched helplessly on a half dozen occasions as government defectors and hopeful asylum seekers had been swept up and thrown into cars—or in one case, the trunk of a ZIL limousine. The Muk had its charms.

He walked directly to the meeting point, a surveillance detection route being pointless. His instructions were to proceed to the center circle and stand by a specific topiary. Kovacs reached the spot and stood with his hands in his pockets as if admiring the sculpted gardens. He felt about as unobtrusive as a tour guide with a pink umbrella.

He saw the woman coming from a hundred paces. Her dress had an almost rectangular fit. Indoor complexion and purposeful gait. Take away the cheap sunglasses, and he was looking at his accountant's receptionist back in Prague.

She came straight at him, and without any salutation whatsoever said in heavily accented English, "Should we take a walk?"

Kovacs weighed a smarmy reply that running might draw more attention. He said, "Why not."

They set out on the nearest path, wandering beneath the sparse shade trees. Kovacs considered her selection of language. She'd spoken Czech when she'd talked to the embassy operator, but it had been rough and rather rehearsed—he'd listened to the recording three times.

"Why are we speaking English?" he asked.

"I thought it better for us to not use Arabic in such a public place and my Czech is not the best. I am more comfortable with English and I assumed you would be proficient."

Kovacs considered her logic, allowed that it was solid. "You are Russian?" he ventured, fairly confident of her accent.

"Yes. I am an interpreter."

"With the visiting delegation?"

A pair of young men approached in the opposite direction. She waited for them to pass before saying, "Yes. I was Petrov's interpreter for his summit this morning with President Rahmani."

Kovacs came to a stop. The woman did the same. Nothing in her face caused him to doubt what she had just said. "You are Petrov's interpreter?"

"For this trip, yes. And on a few other occasions."

"And the information you claim to have . . . it relates to today's meeting?"

The street was a short distance ahead, and the woman turned and began walking back the way they'd come. Kovacs rolled his eyes and fell in beside her.

"Let me start at the beginning," she said. "My name is Lud-milla Kravchuk . . ."

For the next five minutes Kravchuk talked quickly. She explained what had happened to Sofia Aryan, and covered her escape from the Four Seasons. Then, in a very general way, she told Kovacs what she'd heard at the meeting.

"An attack with a chemical weapon?" he repeated.

"Yes."

"Do you know what the target will be?"

"What I know is for the Americans."

"All right. And is there anything else you want me to pass along?"

"I want them to get me out."

"Out of Syria?" he asked, just to be clear.

"Yes."

In truth, Kovacs was relieved. He had been half expecting the woman to ask for refuge in the embassy—ever since Julian Assange had commandeered Ecuador's London mission, it had become the de rigueur request.

He said, "I can't speak for them, of course, but I will pass along what you've told me. If it is enough, they may wish to get involved."

She looked at him incredulously. "How could it *not* be enough?"

He steered her toward a new path with fewer passersby. "You must understand . . . what you are asking carries great risk. The Americans get many vague promises of 'things overheard.'"

"There was nothing vague about what I heard—and I can prove it." She told him what she'd found in her shoe. "I don't know *why* this was done, but I can tell you the device ended up in my posses-sion quite by accident." She explained the confusion over two pairs of shoes.

As had been the trend for the last fifteen minutes, Kovacs' inter-est ratcheted up another notch. "How can you be sure it is what you think it is?"

"I admit, I am not a technician. But I know our president better than most. It is precisely the kind of thing he *would* do."

Kovacs considered it.

In that pause the woman's agitation seemed to grow. Her eyes flicked across the park. Kovacs doubted she was sensing a specific threat, but rather a more generalized fear. He knew the signs all too well.

Kravchuk stopped and gripped him by the elbow. "Whether I have the proof or not, the Americans must be informed."

He nodded and pulled away slightly. "Very well. I will pass along what you've told me. From there, you understand, it is out of my hands. Where will you be staying?"

To his utter surprise, Kravchuk gave not only an address, but told him how to reach it and explained why she'd chosen the place.

"Do you think that is . . . safe?" he asked.

"The woman who owns the salon is a friend."

He thought, *She won't be after the Mukhabarat batters down her door.* What he said was, "All right. I suggest you go back now, and don't venture outside."

Kravchuk hesitated, then turned and hurried away. In that moment she looked more like a grandmother late for choir practice than what she was—a presidential interpreter walking the tightrope of treason.

Kovacs watched her until she disappeared. To his mild astonishment, no squad of regime thugs materialized from the trees. No cars bounded to the curb to cut her off. Kravchuk simply blended into the crowds and disappeared. Not lost on Kovacs was that she was heading directly toward the address she'd given him.

Against all odds, she'd somehow succeeded. She'd called the embassy on an open line, arranged a clandestine meeting, and gotten away with it—right under the Muk's nose.

"God have mercy on the amateur," he mumbled. Turning back toward the Czech embassy in the waning evening light, he wondered what might come of it all.

NINE

Two days later

As counter-surveillance routines went, it was the most epic David Slaton had ever run. But then, he'd never had such motivation to stay clean.

He kept a steady pace on the sidewalk, doing his best to blend in. In the heart of Montevideo, it was less a chore than might be imagined. He was slightly over six feet tall, and his sandy hair and regular features were vaguely Scandinavian. Fortunately, nearly ninety percent of native Uruguayans traced their lineage to Europe. Slaton had a number of more distinguishing physical characteristics, but these—the various scars that marked his body—were not in view.

He did not carry a bag or a coat, or for that matter anything to suggest he was a traveler. It had taken him two days to reach Montevideo, one of the world's oft-overlooked great cities. Three airplanes, one train, two buses, three taxis. And today, at the end of it all, countless miles of walking. For all the world's procedural funnels—the increasingly complex web of passport control stations and immigration queues and municipal camera networks—the simple act of walking through an urban maze remained the most effective countermeasure against being followed.

The best chance to disappear.

In truth, being tailed here would not be of particular concern. More pressing was to not leave a single crumb, no trace of a digital footprint that could be tracked to the origin of his journey. For the first time ever, Slaton was more worried about concealing where he'd been than giving away where he was going.

He paused at the final crosswalk, a buzz-saw intersection in the heart of the old city. Behind him was Parque Rodó, and beyond that the temperate shoulder of Rio de la Plata, the wide estuary that bounded the city's southern shore. In the course of two previous forays to the city, Slaton had never visited this park. On general appearances it was the sort of common found in virtually every capital, with all the usual adornments. There were walking paths and gardens for those prone to contemplation, amusement rides for those seeking thrills. Calorie-laden confection stands seemed planted on every corner, and the playgrounds were thick with darting children and hovering parents.

If there was a uniqueness to Parque Rodó, Slaton decided, it would be the countless specimens of artwork scattered across the broad lawns. Statues dominated, although not the portrayals he would have expected. There was the odd Spanish explorer and a few Uruguayan legends, but the majority of the subjects held a more scholarly outlook. Einstein was depicted in stony contemplation, and Confucius stood reflectively before a thick glade. More lightheartedly, an entire ensemble of stone clothing stood as if worn by invisible bodies. Slaton found it all bemusing, but rendered no judgment. He himself was something of an artisan when it came to stone, yet sculpture was not his domain. His expertise leaned toward the more practical: the creation of retaining walls and patios and foundations. By any measure, masonry had become his second career.

Unfortunately, repercussions from his first career intervened all too regularly.

The light at the intersection changed, and Slaton crossed amid a thick crowd reveling in the welcome October spring. On the far side he referenced his watch before turning right on the sidewalk. He glanced back and saw nothing suspicious.

The address he'd been given was near, across the street to his right. This was his preferred method of approach: studying an objective from across a street gave a wide perspective, and the traffic served as a defensive barrier if anything went wrong.

It turned out to be a three-story residential building, a nondescript façade of brick, mortar, and glass. From the walkways of the park he'd performed a more distant survey and found the place unremarkable. He saw nothing to change his opinion up close. It was a building like a thousand others in Montevideo. Like a million across the world. He'd been given no unit or apartment number, and that omission was telling. Slaton had arrived in the right place at precisely the right time. The rest, he was sure, would soon become evident.

He knew perfectly well who he was here to meet. Indeed, there were but two people on earth he trusted enough to draw him away from his family. One was Anton Bloch, the former chief of Mossad. Bloch had recruited him into that service, an act of malice Slaton had forgiven only after Bloch, some years later, had risked his own life to save Slaton's wife.

Today, however, it was the other person Slaton had come to see.

She appeared right on cue.

He spotted her behind the wheel of a dove-gray Nissan a hundred feet ahead. The car edged out of light traffic and drew smoothly to the curb. There was no tap on the horn, no flicking of headlights. The two hands high on the steering wheel made not the slightest of gestures. The driver simply waited. Knowing he would see her.

Slaton never broke stride. He climbed in the Nissan's curbside passenger door, and for the sake of anyone watching even manufactured a smile. He wasn't surprised when the driver, a Nordic-stock blonde, leaned in to exchange an amiable peck on the cheek. They could have been husband and wife, brother and sister, or simply close friends. All the bases covered with one simple gesture.

Anna Sorensen pulled cautiously back out into traffic.

"Hello, Anna," he said.

"Hi, David. Thanks for coming."

"I'm not completely sure I had a choice . . . but you're welcome."

She shot him a guarded look. Anna Sorensen headed up the CIA's National Clandestine Service, Special Activities Center. In effect, she ran the agency's black operations across the world, and kept a direct line to the director of the CIA. That Sorensen had herself come to meet him at the bottom of South America, certainly undercover, was testament to the secrecy of their affiliation.

"I told you before," she said. "You always have a choice."

Instead of arguing the point, Slaton studied the car's interior. An envelope tucked between the seats told him they were riding in a rental. The gas tank was full, the back seat empty. His right hand dropped to the side of his seat. No electric buttons, but a manual recline lever—good to know if he needed to duck in a hurry. He adjusted the seat for a better view of the right rear quarter in the side mirror.

Sorensen was watching. "You never let up, do you?"

"Given my circumstances, would you?" His gaze snagged on an unfamiliar device on the dash. The unobtrusiveness of its design was certainly intentional. Made of smooth gray plastic, it was the size and shape of a Styrofoam coffee cup, albeit inverted. It appeared to be mounted on the dash with an adhesive pad. "That's no air freshener," he said.

"It's a jammer," she explained. "The rental car companies all track their fleets these days."

"So, it blocks the GPS signal?"

"Among other things. I've been told it covers a wide range of frequencies. I think the DST guy used the term 'barrage jammer.' It supposedly scrambles the most common devices used for tracking." DST was the agency's Directorate of Science and Technology.

"You don't sound convinced," he said. "I think my paranoia is rubbing off on you."

"Maybe so. I see it as a layered precaution. I was very careful in how I got here."

"Not as careful as I was," he assured her.

Slaton's relationship with the CIA was something new. Less than a year ago he'd single-handedly pulled the agency out of an epic bind, thwarting a nuclear attack by North Korea. In the course of it, his wife and son had been kidnapped. Everything turned out as well as it could have, and when the dust settled he'd had a very long talk with Christine. They agreed that, for the safety of their son, Davy, only one option remained. It was time to make a pact with Langley. Or more precisely, with Sorensen.

A longtime Mossad operative, Slaton had tried to leave the black world behind for a normal life with his family. He'd parted ways with Israel years earlier and gone off-grid, becoming, effectively, a man without a country. His disappearance was aided by the fact that he'd been reported on at least two occasions to have met his demise. Despite it all, his attempts at isolation were a failure. Try as he might, Slaton repeatedly found himself drawn back into the folds of both Mossad and the CIA.

After the previous year's close call, however, he realized his only hope was to strike a bargain, and of the two devils he chose the Americans. The CIA had placed Slaton and his family into their "asset protection" program. New identities, new lives, security as needed. It put his family on a tightrope, the only net being anonymity. Or at least, that and a damned well-stocked gun safe. So far, the scheme had worked, yet that sanctuary came at a cost: Slaton allowed that the CIA might occasionally call upon his services for certain missions.

The kind of services few could imagine.

David Slaton was, by all accounts, the most accomplished assassin ever created by the state of Israel—given that nation's rich clandestine history, something akin to being the fastest car ever built by Ferrari. When combined with his ethereal background of recent years, it made him something unique: a top-flight assassin who, in an increasingly connected world, was as close as one could be to a ghost.

The question of what missions Slaton might be tapped for remained unclear. The CIA's Special Activities Center, or SAC, kept a full stable of competent special operators, some internally trained, others drawn from elite military units. The problem with those assets, for all their expertise, was that they could invariably be linked to the United States. Slaton, by either fault or virtue, offered a new and unique option: a first-tier operator who was virtually untraceable.

The arrangement with Sorensen had been sealed over café Americanos in the Cape Verde islands. Christine had been in attendance, and she'd agreed reluctantly in principle. After the debacle in North Korea, she reasoned, something in their lives had to change. Or as she'd put it so succinctly, "The safety of our son is everything."

While Sorensen had gone back to Langley to make the arrangements, Slaton and his family sailed to Brazil. They sold the boat and receded into their new life. All had been going well until two days ago.

That was when Slaton received the first call from his new employer, arriving via an ultra-secure comm device—he kept the handset in the basement of his Idaho farmhouse inside a special gun safe that not only gave physical security, but also acted as a Faraday Cage to keep electronic intrusion at bay. Twice each day he removed the phone and checked for messages. On the day in question, after preparing lunch for his son—peanut butter sandwich, no jelly, with a sliced banana—Slaton checked a screen that for seven months had remained blank. And there, finally, he saw a message. There were no allusions as to why he was being summoned, no hint of what he would be asked to do. Only an address along Calle Patria in Montevideo, along with a time and date that gave a reasonable allowance for travel.

That afternoon he'd discussed the summons with Christine, and they agreed to terms. Slaton would make the meeting with Sorensen to find out what was being asked of him. Yet he would accept the mission only if certain requirements were met. That much settled, Slaton had responded.

Will comply, require backup.

Two hours later, a contingent of six serious individuals, five men and one woman, had arrived at the front gate of their ranch. Slaton gave them a thorough briefing, and they'd asked enough questions—the right questions—to convince him they were competent.

Security in place, Slaton had set out toward Spokane. Thirty-six hours later, he was standing on the given street at the prescribed time.

"How are Christine and Davy?" Sorensen asked. She knew them both, having personally overseen their security during a previous mission.

"They're good," Slaton said. "Davy started preschool."

"Preschool? They grow up fast."

"I know, right? And thanks for the team you sent. They were a solid bunch."

"I'm glad you approve."

"What about you?" he asked. "Still seeing your flyboy?"

"Jammer? Yeah, he's good. If we both weren't so busy, something might come of it."

"Don't wait too long. This business we're in . . . it can swallow your life whole."

"You of all people would know."

"Where are we going?" he asked.

"Somewhere quiet. We need to talk, and I've got a few things to show you."

"Okay." Slaton settled back in his seat and relaxed. Having come this far, he decided he could give Sorensen the courtesy of patience.

TEN

Traffic was modest by big city standards. Slaton liked the choice of Uruguay for their meeting. It was among the most stable countries in South America, a placid harbor amid the continent's ocean of scandal and corruption. Even better, a place where few clandestine services were active. An under-the-radar venue.

As they progressed eastward Sorensen opted for small talk, or at least what passed for it in intelligence circles. She inquired about the security measures Slaton had installed around his ranch, which somehow led to the vulnerability of Israel's settlements in the West Bank.

With practiced discretion, Slaton studied Sorensen as she drove. He thought she looked different from the last time he'd seen her, although he couldn't say precisely how. She wore a stylish scarf around her neck and a pair of large-framed sunglasses. Her straight blond hair had gone askew, a few locks tumbling forward over her face. He was certain it was all deliberate. Indeed, he imagined that the CIA, given its expertise in facial recognition technology, had somewhere on its staff a hair stylist who specialized in maximizing pixelated confusion. Sorensen's guise was just understated enough to be effective. She might have been the wife of a sales rep tagging along on a business trip, or a schoolteacher on sabbatical. Anything but the director of the darkest division of the world's most mighty clandestine service.

The city fell behind them, giving way to broad coastal plains. The day seemed unusually bright. Clear air and a high sun. A sign declared they were entering a region called Maldonado. Open expanses stretched to the horizon, tawny hills flecked by farmhouses and barns, the occasional village nestled in the creases between hills. Weary dirt side roads disappeared into dusty pastures, and small herds of goats and sheep wandered through it all. Slaton saw teenage boys riding muscular horses, all of them rough-hewn and weathered, moving slow on a fast-warming day.

Sorensen finally turned off the main road onto a bolt-straight dirt path. "Here we are," she said.

Rows of trees stood in what looked like military formation, reaching high into the gentle hills. Slaton knew what kind of trees they were—the type was common throughout Israel's Upper Galilee.

"This is your quiet place?" he asked. "An olive farm?"

"Trust me, it's very secure. Wholly owned and operated."

He stared at her for a moment. "The CIA is procuring olive farms in Uruguay to use as safe houses?"

She met his gaze with a dazzling smile. Sorensen was an undeniably attractive woman. Slaton guessed her to be in the neighborhood of forty, although in the short time he'd known her, just over a year, he thought she seemed more mature. It wasn't crow's feet or gray hair, but something more insidious. A faint strain in her voice, a burden in her eyes. Slaton had seen more advanced stages of the affliction in his sage mentor at Mossad, the now septuagenarian Anton Bloch. Also like Bloch, Sorensen conveyed no small measure of conviction in her words and tone. A requisite trait, he supposed, for successful spymasters.

"I wasn't talking about the company," she corrected. "The farm is owned by my family. My grandfather bought it nearly sixty years ago. Two hundred and fifty acres of mature Manzanilla olives on a perfectly terraced hillside."

"Does he live here?"

"No. He and my grandmother went back and forth to Sweden seasonally for many years—harvest every March or April, depending on the conditions. But they're getting on now, so they stay in Malmö full time. They hired a local couple to run the farm. Pressing and bottling are handled by a local distributor."

"Not a bad arrangement. I worked on an olive farm in Israel for a year, when I was a teenager. We harvested by hand. I recall that if you don't process the olives within a few hours, the oil begins to degrade."

"True—one of the reasons we use mechanical harvesters now."

The rows of trees seemed endless as they progressed up the long drive, and Sorensen had to veer around the occasional pothole.

He asked, "Are you sure this place can't be traced to the head of the Special Activities Center?"

"I wouldn't have brought you here if I thought it could. My name was never associated with the property. I haven't been here in twenty years. My sister and I came twice when we were in college to work the harvest."

"That's an unusual spring break. And you never mentioned this on your company security declarations?"

"No. I actually hadn't thought about the place in years. I couldn't go to Idaho, and I knew you wouldn't want to come to D.C. This seemed ideal. There's a small main house. The caretaker, Gabriella, lives there with her husband most of the year. I sent a message, told them I was coming with a guest. She said they would take the chance to visit family up north."

"She probably thinks you're having a tryst."

"Probably—which is good cover. We'll have the place to ourselves, very discreet."

On balance, Slaton approved. Meeting at an off-the-books family-owned farm was decidedly intimate. But then, his relationship with Sorensen held an intimacy few could comprehend: that of assassin and controller.

The cottage was small, a weathered raft of whitewashed earth floating atop a minor hill. There were wooden shutters on every window, each a different size and seemingly attached at a different angle. The barrel tile roof might once have been orange.

Sorensen led the way to a front door that wasn't locked. Indeed, Slaton saw no security of any kind other than a corroded iron hasp and handle that was probably decorative fifty years ago. Inside the place was solid and warm. Crossbeam ceilings carried the length of the main room, and a thick wooden counter at the far end defined a kitchen. Next to that a butcher block table was surrounded by four slat-back wooden chairs. Plain curtains above the kitchen sink fluttered, giving away that the window behind them was open.

Strike two for security, Slaton thought.

Sorensen crossed the room and put her satchel on the table. She pulled out a laptop computer, and as it booted up she pushed back one of the chairs and took a seat. Slaton followed her lead, sliding a second chair beside her.

"Before I give you the briefing," she said, "we need to establish some ground rules."

"Rules?"

"When we arranged to protect your family, David, I promised there would be no quid pro quo. I don't have any authority to order you out on a mission. I can only convince you that what we're proposing is justified."

"That's a good start. In my experience, operators who don't believe in what they're doing are rarely effective."

"Are you referring to your years with Mossad?"

"Things went pretty well for a time . . . until I realized my whole recruitment had been based on a lie."

"Point taken. I understand that your first allegiance is to your family now . . . as it should be. But to my section you offer certain unique qualifications."

"Chief of which is expendability?"

She held his stare.

"Okay, sorry," he said. "Let's just say I'm your ultimate cutout. If things go sideways, there won't be blowback on the CIA."

"Essentially, yes."

He studied her for a beat. "You mentioned authority a moment ago. At the risk of sounding like a lawyer, where is that sourced?"

She hesitated.

"Look . . . we both know there isn't much chain of command above you."

"All right, it's a fair question. At my request, Director Coltrane approached the president to request authority for special missions. I won't get into the details, but the end result was a highly classified national security directive signed by the president. It gives me authority to conduct operations using assets outside normal agency channels. It's only to be used in extremely delicate situations—instances in which using in-house personnel might be viewed as either illegal or unsafe."

"That sounds broad. Does Coltrane have oversight?"

"The directive doesn't require it, but I promised him I would keep him informed. Not specifics—just a general outline of what's being planned. For what it's worth, none of this is set in stone. What we're talking about today would be the first operation down the chute."

"Is any of this legal?"

"We tried to keep the JAGs out of it. In the president's mind, it's necessary."

"Don't you think Coltrane will guess I'm involved? He *has* seen me work."

"Probably. The point is to have the highest possible degree of separation."

"One man's 'degree of separation' is another's lack of accountability," he countered.

"True . . . but that falls into the realm of politics."

"Look, I've seen murky setups like this before. What I'm hearing puts you firmly on the hook for any screwups."

"Not as much as you. If a mission goes bad, David, I'll help you as best I can. I have virtually all agency assets at my disposal. But there are limitations. If you end up in prison in some godforsaken backwater, don't expect State Department lawyers or a Delta Force extraction team."

He sat impassively.

"Can you still work for us knowing that?" she asked.

Slaton blew a humorless laugh. "I've been working under those rules most of my life. It gives a pretty strong incentive to not screw up. But I do have one request."

This time Sorensen was out front. "Whatever happens, you have my word that Christine and Davy will be cared for."

"For however long it might be," he added, his implication clear.

"Yes."

"All right," he said, "so let's get down to it. Who do you want me to kill?"

"It may surprise you, but that's not the mission. I actually want you to save someone . . ."

ELEVEN

"We want you to exfiltrate a woman from a precarious situation," Sorensen said. "Her name is Ludmilla Kravchuk. She's an interpreter with the Russian foreign ministry, a Mideast language specialist. We've had her name on file for a few years—she occasionally works high-level meetings."

"Have you ever tried to contact her?"

"No. She was never an agent, never targeted for recruitment."

"Then what's driving your involvement?"

"Two days ago, Kravchuk made a cold call to the Czech embassy in Damascus—the Czechs serve as our surrogate point of contact in Syria. She asked for an immediate meeting."

"In Damascus?"

"Broad daylight."

"That's bold."

"As it turned out, I think desperate is more like it. The Czechs did well. They sent a man to meet her, and the rendezvous went down with no apparent hitches. He said Kravchuk seemed nervous. She claimed to have information that could be very valuable to us, sourced from a meeting that morning between the presidents of Russia and Iran."

"Did you verify that?"

"As far as we could. We knew the Syrians were hosting a summit between Petrov and Rahmani. It was put together on short notice—according to the press releases, some kind of trade initiative. Our analysts didn't have any trouble placing Kravchuk at the meeting. She can be seen in the background of the grip-and-grin photos that were put out by Russian news services."

Sorensen called up the first image on her laptop. Slaton saw a generic photo op: two presidents smiling through a handshake, their interpreters blending in discreetly in the background. There was no question which of the two women might be named Ludmilla Kravchuk: she was a babushka in the making, sitting stiffly with her hands folded in her lap.

"So, she's legit," Slaton said.

"As far as we can tell. After the photographers finished, the room was cleared. By all accounts it was a one-on-one meeting—only the presidents and their interpreters."

"And this valuable information she's offering? It's her account of the meeting?"

"Apparently. Kravchuk gave one hint as to its substance. She said it involves a pending attack—one that will employ chemical weapons."

Slaton stiffened ever so slightly. "That's a serious allegation."

"It is. And Kravchuk says she has proof."

"Proof?"

Sorensen explained what the interpreter claimed to have in her possession.

"If that's for real, it could be pretty damning."

"I thought the same thing," Sorensen agreed. "And that's when I decided to call you."

The shoe sat on the table in front of Ludmilla. She regarded it as one might a sculpture in a museum—reflecting on the deeper meaning. She'd been studying it, on and off, for the best part of two days now. In the world's continuum of gray pumps, she'd hardly thought them special. Not until she'd caught the heel of one on the uneven staircase.

After reaching her room that day she'd taken a closer look. The first thing she noticed was an exposed blue wire. Curiosity piqued, she'd tracked the wire by feel, through the leather siding, and realized it ended at the decorative brass button on top—a circular bauble the size of a ten-ruble coin. On closer inspection, she noticed that the button was in fact surfaced with fine metal mesh. It didn't take an engineer to realize what this was: a microphone.

She'd used a knife from the kitchen to pry the heel apart, exposing a nest of wiring, a tiny circuit board, and something she recognized instantly—a compact memory card, very much like the one in her SLR camera at home.

At that point, Ludmilla's technical expertise was exhausted. The greater revelation, however, was inescapable: someone had fabricated an audio recording device into her shoe. A shoe that had been given to her by Petrov's staff. Because she'd spent a career in foreign service—and perhaps more so because she was Russian—the discovery of a hidden microphone came as no great surprise. It explained why Vasiliev had come to reclaim the shoes directly after the meeting. Also, why an extra pair had been provided: they didn't want to take the chance that she might reject them due to a poor fit. Then came the classic bureaucratic blunder. Nobody told Vasiliev she'd been given *two* sets of shoes, and Ludmilla had kept the pair she'd worn to the meeting. That mistake had worked in her favor. And the discovery of a recording device only further cemented her conviction: she'd done the right thing by running.

If only poor Sofia Aryan had been so lucky.

She tapped the loose heel contemplatively. Ludmilla wasn't sure how to find out what was on the memory card—assuming the device had even worked. Gadgets had never been her strong suit, yet she knew they had a way of malfunctioning. Still, the chances were good that she now possessed a perfect transcript of the meeting—and undeniable confirmation that an attack was in the works.

More than ever, she realized she needed help.

She got up and went to the sink, filled a kettle with water. The kettle was rusted and the handle broken, probably the reason the previous tenant had left it behind. She lit a burner on the stove and set the water to boil. The instant coffee was long gone, the dregs of a bag of grounds spent on her first morning here. She remembered seeing a few old tea bags in the back of a drawer during her foraging. She was searching for them when a door banged shut down the hall. Three days ago, she wouldn't have given a second thought to such a noise. Soft footsteps receded down the stairs. The young waitress who rented the other room.

Again Ludmilla sat at the table. She wondered if the man from the Czech embassy had been able to contact the Americans. Was a scheme being hatched to get her out of Damascus, and if so how long would it take? Or had her plea gone wrong? Perhaps the man from the Czech embassy had thought her a crackpot—Ludmilla knew from her time in foreign service that a high percentage of informants were solidly in that category. And if her story had been forwarded, would the Americans deem it credible?

If only I could have given them a sample of the recording, she thought. *That would have brought them running.*

She looked around the room uncertainly, wondering how long she could hole up here. Since her outing to meet the Czech, Ludmilla had barely set foot outside her pied-à-terre, and even then, she'd ventured no farther than the salon—on the first morning she'd let Salma work her stylist's magic. It was a Spartan existence. She was still wearing the clothes she'd arrived in, the only difference being a set of athletic shoes borrowed from Salma. She'd found a bit of leftover food in the cupboards, and had so far gone through one can of salmon, half a box of pasta noodles, and a small container of couscous. Unfortunately, all that was left was a partial bag of very stale cereal and a can of mushroom soup. The moldering piece of cheese in the sputtering mini-refrigerator she'd vowed not to touch. Grocery shopping was out of the question, but if things got desperate she might have something delivered—she could use the phone in the salon after hours. Then again, after literally throwing money at the taxi driver, followed by paying Salma for the room and "the works," she was desperately low on cash.

On the bright side: the diet she'd long been putting off was well under way.

More vexing than the lack of food was being in the dark about what was happening in the outside world. The room had no television, and she'd intentionally left her phone at the Four Seasons. It left her with no access to news. She'd tried the computer downstairs, sneaking down late last night, but it had been shut down and she didn't know the password. Asking for that was a bridge too far—Salma had so far been understanding, but Ludmilla didn't want to press her luck.

She wondered if her disappearance had created a diplomatic row. She decided it was unlikely. Petrov would try to keep the matter quiet, especially given what had been discussed during the summit—a meeting whose infamy could be proved by the recording in her possession. In the end, Ludmilla decided there was nothing to do but wait. A few days at least.

The kettle began to whistle and she took it off the burner. There was no teapot, and she was about to drop the two scavenged tea bags into the kettle when she paused. She took a chipped mug from the counter, filled it with hot water, and used a single bag.

She took the mug to the table, set it down to steep next to the ruined shoe. In that moment Ludmilla felt incredibly alone. Her job, her husband, her homeland . . . she had lost them all. Her world had shrunk to a few hundred square feet of living space in a war-torn foreign land. Venture outside that, and people would be searching for her.

Right on cue, paranoia made its visit. Having worked with Petrov before, Ludmilla had a more unvarnished view of the president than most Russians. She had seen how he treated oligarchs who double-crossed him. Seen what came of agents who fled to the West. The question of how he would deal with a midlevel foreign ministry employee who'd absconded with an extremely incriminating recording: that required no interpretation.

The president of Russia, and all those who served him, would want it back.

Want it very badly indeed.

TWELVE

"You need to understand what you're getting into," Sorensen said. "Ludmilla Kravchuk isn't a trained intelligence officer. She knows nothing about tradecraft, and probably little about communications security."

"Sometimes that can be an advantage," Slaton replied.

"And sometimes it can get you killed."

"How exactly did she contact the Czech embassy?"

"She called their central switchboard."

"Did she at least use a burner?"

"The Czechs captured the number, but that was all. Their ability to pathway connections in Syria is pretty limited."

"And yours?"

"It took the NSA about thirty seconds to nail it down. Turns out, it wasn't even a mobile number. She placed the call from a landline at a hair salon in the Al Salhiyeh district."

"Okay, that's not so bad. She walked in off the street for a haircut, then asked to use the phone while she waited her turn."

"No, David, that's what *you* would do. She's a complete amateur."

"Meaning?"

"She came right out and told our Czech contact she was staying in a room above the salon. Apparently, she was a regular there during her time at the Russian embassy."

Slaton went silent.

"You see the problem," Sorensen prodded. "This woman has put herself behind the eight ball, and she has no idea how to get out. I've counted at least a dozen faults in what she's done so far. Most obvious is that the Syrians know full well that the Czechs serve as our proxy in Damascus. The Mukhabarat tries hard to monitor every call. We give the Czechs technology to counter it, but it's a running game. We put in frequency-hopping software, Russia helps the Syrians hack into it. As things stand, I give it a fifty-fifty chance that the Muk has already collected Kravchuk. If so, they'll be interrogating her at Sednaya."

Slaton knew she was referring to the notorious military prison north of Damascus, a place where so many thousands of extrajudicial killings had occurred during the war that the regime had been forced to add a crematorium.

"I don't think so," he countered. "If the Syrians find her, they'll hand her over to Petrov's SVR thugs."

"Maybe so."

"Either way," Slaton extrapolated, "if Kravchuk has been found, they'll be keeping watch on the salon to see if anyone shows up to meet her."

"True."

He weighed it all. "But there's another side to your odds. Our interpreter could be above that salon right now, sitting in a closet full of hair gel and bleach while she's waiting to be rescued."

"No way to tell."

"Have you been watching the place?"

"We're doing what we can. NRO satellites sweep over Damascus pretty regularly." She was referring to the National Reconnaissance Office, lord and master of the country's orbital assets. "We've identified the building, and I was able to get priority for a few overheads. I'll show you those later, but as far as we can tell, everything looks normal at Chez Salma from two hundred miles up. The bad news is, we don't have much in the way of eyes on the ground in Damascus. Our human networks were lousy before the war, and the regime has cracked down since then in the name of survival."

"Sounds like I'd really be on my own."

"That's only going in. On the way out, you'll have a civilian on your back."

Slaton was losing count of the traps in the mission.

"If I could reach her, what's the best egress?"

"I'd leave that up to you. Basically, you would have to make it to a border. Israel is nearby and they would help if we asked—especially given that you're involved. Jordan is a possibility, and Lebanon's not out of the question. You could make for the coastline, but you'd have to find a way to reach international waters. That's risky given the new Russian naval base in Tartus."

Slaton took a moment to consider it. Sorensen was leaving the planning up to him, which appealed in a way. Most spymasters were micromanagers. He was being given a clear objective and an open field in which to run. "So, you want me to go in, snatch a woman out of central Damascus, then make a run for the nearest border."

"Something like that. If you can't find Kravchuk and things go south, I can offer you one bailout option. Mind you, it's a last-ditch maneuver, and only applies to you. We've developed a new extraction system for solo operators trapped behind hard borders." Sorensen navigated to another image on her computer.

Slaton did a double take. What looked like a standard Reaper drone had been modified with an improbable addition.

"Is this a joke?" he asked.

"No, it's very real. One of my snake-eaters came up with it— former Raider Battalion."

"A Marine. Why am I not surprised."

Sorensen offered a few more details, then hedged with, "It's never been used live in the field, but we've tested it with some success."

"*Some* success?"

"Look, if you don't like it, no problem. The system has been deployed downrange, so I wanted you to be aware of every option."

"Okay, consider me briefed. But as far as I'm concerned . . . you can send that one back to the ACME Corporation."

She turned the screen away and met his gaze. "All right . . . that's the basics. If you tell me you're in, we can go deeper. What do you think?"

Slaton got up and walked to the kitchen window. He pulled the curtain aside and looked out across a rolling hillside of olive trees basking in the southern spring. "Could you preposition some equipment by tomorrow?"

"Anything we have in theater."

"Active support?"

"Limited once you cross into Syria. We can track you if you want, and you'll have comm available. The entire mission is under my control. You can't expect any material support or reinforcements, but I'll honor any request that's within my power. Reconnaissance, comm intercepts, an extraction team to meet you at the border. It will all be standing by. The only caveat is that nothing can tie us to the mission."

"What about that drone you just showed me?"

"We fly Reapers and Predators all over the Middle East, including Syria. It would be more suspicious to not have aircraft overhead. For attribution of an extraction op—it's a dead end."

"Just like me," he said.

"Just like you."

Slaton was silent for a time. The deep shadow of a thick cloud swept over the hill. He turned back to Sorensen, and said, "All right then . . . let's do it."

THIRTEEN

"Nothing," said a frustrated Inspector Hadad late the next morning. "The woman has vanished, I tell you."

Vasiliev looked at him disbelievingly. "How can that be? She disappeared *three days ago*!"

Hadad inhaled deeply, trying to hold steady.

They were separated by his desk at district headquarters—once a refuge, but no more. The Russian had been stalking him incessantly, or so it seemed. Twice he'd encountered Vasiliev at the Four Seasons, four times here. The man had even been waiting when Hadad stepped out of his car last night on the curb in front of his house. That had crossed a line, and Hadad had sent the feckless Russian packing.

It wasn't that he didn't have sympathy. Hadad had been dressed down himself by his colonel for not getting results. Poor Vasiliev, he was sure, was being hounded by no less than the president of Russia.

"There are no new leads," he reiterated, his hands wringing the arms of his chair. "Our checkpoints are searching every vehicle leaving the city. I am convinced she's still in Damascus. It can only be a matter of time."

"What have you done since we last spoke?" Vasiliev asked.

"We interviewed the cab driver a second time—the one who picked her up at the Four Seasons. His story remains consistent. Kravchuk originally gave him an address across town, then changed her mind barely a kilometer away. From that point her trail went cold."

"Were there no CCTV cameras where she was last seen?"

Hadad shook his head. "You must understand, for years our

government has spent every penny on bullets and bombs. We've been fighting the rebels, ISIS, the Kurds. A state-of-the-art surveillance network in our fair city would make my job far easier. Unfortunately, it has never gotten past the planning stages."

Vasiliev diverted to a map of Damascus on the wall. It was stuck with pins of various colors to represent possible sightings. None had proved useful.

"We are going to check the hotel again for leads," Hadad continued. "I would still like to know what you were looking for." His evidence team had arrived the first night to find Kravchuk's room already turned over. The suite looked like a storm had blown through, every drawer pulled and emptied, the mattress sliced open. The closet doors had been ripped from their hinges.

"I told you," Vasiliev insisted, "it wasn't us."

Hadad frowned. He'd seen hotel CCTV footage that suggested otherwise—proof enough that the Four Seasons had already sent the Russians a bill for the damage. He decided not to waste time arguing the point.

"Your president is still in Damascus?" he inquired.

"Yes. He was hoping to stay until this matter was resolved. Unfortunately, affairs of state can no longer be put on hold. Petrov will leave today. His plane is being prepared as we speak."

This Hadad already knew—it was his business to know such things. He said with undisguised relief, "Then I wish you a happy journey home."

"I'm afraid you won't be rid of me so easily," Vasiliev countered. "President Petrov has ordered me to remain behind. When the interpreter is found, I am to personally oversee her return to Moscow."

A cautious Vasiliev entered the presidential suite twenty minutes later. He found Petrov on the balcony flicking through his daily briefing reports.

"The preparations for your departure are complete," he announced.

Petrov lowered the papers and looked at him expectantly.

"I have just seen Inspector Hadad," Vasiliev said. "He reports nothing new in his department's search for Kravchuk. He does, however, believe she is still in the city." Vasiliev thought he'd phrased it well, as much blame as possible deflected toward the Syrians.

The president looked at him as he might a stone that had been removed from a shoe. "I have one more meeting to conduct before we leave the hotel." He explained how and where it would take place.

"The parking garage?" Vasiliev remarked.

"Is that a problem?"

"No, sir, it can certainly be done. The cars are in place. But I will have to adjust the perimeter."

"Do what you must."

"Who will you be meeting?" Vasiliev asked.

"A man you have seen once before, I think . . . this summer. He came to my room during our visit to Tashkent."

Vasiliev remembered, if hazily.

Petrov continued, "Bring him to my car when everything is in place. You will find him waiting outside the hotel, near the south service entrance. He is wearing a tan jacket."

"I will have to search him for weapons."

"You should. But make it quick, and be sure to avoid the hotel's cameras. This is a meeting I do not want documented."

Security was intense as Petrov was marshaled down to the Four Seasons parking garage. The primary limousine, a big armored Mercedes, was wedged in a tight corner between concrete walls. No one other than Petrov's personal detail had a view of the proceedings. This had come straight from the president, further emphasizing the nature of the meeting.

As Petrov slipped into the back seat, Vasiliev dismissed the two men in front. Without comment, the driver and team leader got out and positioned themselves a discreet distance away, their attention focused outward. Vasiliev thought back to Tashkent, recalling similarly shadowed arrangements. He'd been working for Petrov long enough to know the hierarchy of the man's wishes. If there was any constant, it was his insistence on privacy in certain situations.

With Petrov secure, Vasiliev set out through the garage. He knew perfectly well the layout of the hotel, and had a good idea where the cameras were located. As he made his way toward the service entrance he encountered no one but his own men. No watchful Syrians with earpieces or uniformed local police. Best of all, no wandering hotel guests with smartphones. *Everyone with a mobile phone these days is an aspiring videographer.*

He had no trouble finding the man he was looking for. He stood with his hands in his pockets near a stairwell door. Calm but expectant. He *did* look familiar, Vasiliev thought, although he wouldn't have made the connection to Tashkent had Petrov not mentioned it. The main difference now was a more-or-less trimmed beard above a black push-broom mustache. The more Vasiliev looked, the more he remembered. He saw nothing to alter his original impression that the man was not a physical threat—something good security chiefs could recognize on a glance. Average in height and build, with dark olive skin, the stranger had distinctly Middle Eastern features.

When Vasiliev came near, the man lifted his hands from his pockets and held them out for inspection. A thorough pat-down turned up nothing, and without a word spoken between them, Vasiliev nodded for his charge to follow. As they made their way through the garage, he noticed that the man walked with a faintly uneven gait.

The right rear door of the Mercedes was open when they arrived. An undeniable invitation. Vasiliev watched like a hawk as the man slid inside with the president of Russia. He saw perhaps a slight nod between the two, but no handshake followed. The door closed with the finality of a tomb.

FOURTEEN

"We were supposed to meet yesterday," said the man next to Petrov in heavily accented Russian. "My schedule is very tight."

The president of Russia nearly smiled. He knew his guest was not uneducated—indeed, he knew a great deal about him. Their last meeting had been conducted in English, which was fast becoming the lingua franca of the world. So why had he learned a bit of Russian? Was it for this moment? Because he believed it would help pave his path to destiny? There seemed no other reason. The cloistered meeting in Tashkent had been an extended affair, the genesis of a plan now six months in the making. *But for him,* Petrov thought, *it has been a lifetime.*

"There has been a complication," Petrov said flatly, switching to English.

"Your wayward interpreter?"

Petrov allowed no trace of surprise. News of Kravchuk's defection had been tamped down, but the man had contacts. More damningly, the Syrian government had more leaks than a Ukrainian fishing boat.

"Yes, she has disappeared."

"How critical is it?"

"She was present during my entire conversation with the Iranian president."

"The one you so carefully arranged?"

This time Petrov shot the man a hard look. "The problem will be contained." He made no mention of the recording that might be in her possession. That would remain his problem. Or at least Vasiliev's.

"It could complicate things," the man said. "But more for you than for me."

"I'm not so sure. It is possible that connections could be made to your work in the coming days. The transfer of the material, your travels."

A thoughtful nod, then, "My precautions are sound. Nothing will be found except what I want to be found."

"Let's hope. In any event, I advise you to tread carefully."

"Was there not another interpreter present—on the Iranian side?"

"There was, but she seems to have met an untimely end."

The visitor raised an eyebrow.

"The Iranians took matters into their own hands. Unfortunately, they were clumsy. We believe it's what spooked our own woman."

"For our purposes, it speaks well with regard to Rahmani. He has no idea where he is taking his country."

"Perhaps." Petrov looked blankly out the window. "Give me an update on your preparations."

"I have been in Sudan all week. Nearly everything is in place for the demonstration."

"Including the Iranian team?"

"They checked into the hotel in Khartoum yesterday. I told them to book through the weekend."

"How many did they send?"

"Three. One specialist, one for security, and a confidant of Rahmani's in command."

"What have they been doing?" Petrov asked.

"Waiting patiently, I'm told."

Petrov's gaze narrowed inquisitively.

"I have an arrangement with a certain member of the hotel staff. She is keeping an eye on them, and also acquiring a few things from their room."

The president of Russia smiled, having a good idea what he was referring to. It was rare he encountered someone whose ruthlessness rivaled his own.

The man next to him said, "I told them to rent a car. Yesterday I began sending instructions—a rendezvous far outside the city. It will put them out of the room and raise their visibility. They'll be seen. My plan is to abort the first few delivery attempts. I'll tell them I am exercising extreme caution."

"They might think you are running scared."

"I hope so—it will heighten their conviction. The timing of the events in Sudan must be convincing. On the third or fourth day, after the demonstration takes place, I will permit the transfer."

"One canister?"

"We can't send them back empty-handed. It will be a dead drop . . . so to speak."

"And this demonstration—you don't know exactly when it will take place?"

"That remains one of the few variables."

Petrov looked at his guest sternly.

"I couldn't exactly ask for volunteers, could I? The way things are designed . . . it's rather like fishing. I have no doubt the bait will be taken."

"And you put everything in place yourself?"

"Technically, it wasn't difficult," the man said. "The fewer who are involved, the less chance of failure."

"Will the results be convincing?"

"It will take a day, perhaps two to be discovered. In the end the Western intelligence agencies will have no doubt as to who is responsible."

"And nothing to forewarn of our true target?"

"The dispersal hardware would be the only clue—it has a unique design. There are only eight units like it in the world. But without understanding its true function, no one could guess our employment method."

"What of your Saudi contact?"

"He remains in position . . . under the radar, you might say."

Once again, Petrov's measure of the man shifted. He could jest against the backdrop of a chemical weapon attack. With nothing more to ask, he said, "Very well. We should not meet again."

"Oh, we will," said the visitor.

Petrov didn't reply, his gaze going to its stony best.

"And next time, we will not have to be so secretive."

Petrov watched him get out of the car and walk away. The hitch in his gait was almost imperceptible, no doubt something he'd been masking since he was a child. A minor imperfection that had transformed his life—and, as it turned out, also saved it.

He saw Vasiliev waiting a discreet distance away. Petrov spun a finger in the air, and Vasiliev repeated the gesture. The driver and his partner returned, and soon the garage was reverberating under the snarling engines of eight armored vehicles. The convoy began crawling toward the exit.

Petrov remained deep in thought, so much so that he never noticed a dutiful wave from Vasiliev. He stared blankly at the passing concrete walls. A great many people came to him with schemes. The oligarchs were the worst, but at least they were predictable, wanting nothing more than to enrich themselves at the expense of either the state or a rival. A few foreigners came begging, mostly for weapons to be leveraged in the overthrow of political enemies.

But this man was different. Very different.

Petrov played his favorite internal game, distilling him to a single word. The one that came to mind was *patient*. Given his lineage, that seemed preordained. Yet it came without the usual serenity. More of a doggedness, he thought. A terrier with a rat in its jaws. It wasn't really surprising. He had researched the man's background exhaustively, and knew beyond a doubt that he possessed the one thing that could not be bought or learned: a blood lineage.

The convoy burst into sun-blanched streets, plowing north toward the airport. Petrov took solace that Russia's part in the scheme was now complete. He had only to sit back and watch. Wait to reap the rewards. The matter of Ludmilla Kravchuk remained, but surely that was manageable. More critical was that the delivery of the precursors was imminent, the target confirmed.

It occurred to him that only a handful of people in the world knew the lame's true identity. Over the course of the next week that would change. They would come to know a man who had been born in Iraq, but who'd spent the bulk of his life in Jordan. The name on his documents was Ahmed Sultan al-Majid, and for forty-two years that had sufficed.

Yet others had recently bestowed the lame with another name. He would become the new Rashidun. In Islamic legend, the Rashidun were the caliphs of the rightly guided, four ancient rulers who steered the faith after the death of the Prophet Muhammad. It had always mystified Petrov how Muslim leaders looked back thousands of years for guidance. He himself kept to an operating model that was far more assured. He selected carefully a crew of loyal oligarchs from a populace who'd grown up hungry under the old Soviet system, men who would trade their very souls for a pipeline contract or a bauxite mine. The two business models could not have been more different in their inspirations, yet he supposed the same result was had: control of the masses.

And that was where the lame was headed. With Petrov's help, a Fifth Rashidun would soon rise.

And he was going to start a war.

FIFTEEN

Hours later, as the president of Russia sped northward in his private jet, Slaton was high above Italy on a scheduled commercial flight. According to the monitor before him, his destination, Amman, Jordan, was four hours ahead. He'd just finished a surprisingly tasty seafood pasta dish, and had even allowed a glass of Chardonnay as an accompaniment—the last drink he would have for the foreseeable future. With the food service complete, the flight attendants dimmed the cabin lights to promote a period of restfulness among their charges—and with any luck, also for themselves.

Slaton was traveling business class—Sorensen's idea, not his—and he motored his lie-flat seat back until he was staring at the ceiling. He clasped his hands behind his head and closed his eyes. He'd been riding airplanes for the better part of a day, using the reprieve to fine-tune his plan: how to snatch a fugitive Russian interpreter from the heart of Damascus. His strategy for getting in was simple. For getting out he saw nothing but contingencies.

His mind saturated, he decided to let his thoughts drift elsewhere. Perhaps it was the wine, or too many variables in mission planning. Whatever the case, Slaton found his thoughts drifting away from the mission to the question of why he'd accepted it in the first place.

The most obvious answer was that he felt, in spite of Sorensen's insistence otherwise, an obligation to the CIA. He was confident that Davy and Christine were safe in the wilds of northern Idaho, protected by their new identities and, for the time being, a crack security detail. For that he was grateful. He'd been tempted to call home, if only to hear their voices. Any traveling salesman would have done so, any conference-bound doctor. In the end, Slaton knew better. When he was away, operating, surveillance could never be completely discounted.

An old saying came to mind: *The measure of anything's worth is to imagine yourself without it.* When it came to his family, that simply wasn't possible. Without them he would be lost.

Yet his arrangement with the CIA was only part of the equation. The second factor was one he never would have considered himself—something Christine had brought up recently in an off-the-cuff way. She'd suggested that as much as he detested his former work, there was some part of him that needed it. Perhaps even craved it. Slaton had never considered himself any kind of adrenaline junkie—he was an operator who accepted measured risk in order to achieve a desired outcome. But even at that moment, relaxing in a plush recliner six miles in the sky, he could not deny the heightened state of his senses. He was no longer checking fence lines in the Rockies. He was hurtling headlong into Syria.

The airplane rocked momentarily in a pocket of turbulence. It seemed to shake the idea from his head, and a third possibility arose. The recovery of Ludmilla Kravchuk, at least as presented by Sorensen, was as near a noble mission as he'd ever been assigned. He was being asked to save someone who claimed to have information that might forestall a terrorist attack.

The dim lighting, along with too many time zones, began to have its effect. Travel weary, and with organized thought faltering, the third case kept running through his head. Going forward, he decided to make it part of his calculus: using his skills for the betterment of the world. A high bar for an assassin.

As the turbulence faded away, Slaton drifted into the deepest sleep he'd had in seventy-two hours.

SIXTEEN

An illegal entry into Syria was Slaton's first objective. By the time the cityscape of Amman began filling the oval window, his initial plan was set.

From a purely geographic standpoint, there had been no shortage of options. Syria had fourteen hundred miles of land border. Of that, only the fifty-mile frontier shared with Israel was monitored with any sense of urgency, a watch kept partly by Hezbollah guerillas. For that reason, he'd decided that entering Syria by way of his homeland was off the table.

Everywhere else Slaton saw opportunity. Over the course of the long-running war, Syria's borders with Turkey, Iraq, Jordan, and Lebanon had become the most porous in the world. Literally millions of refugees had fled outward during the conflict. Running in the other direction were tens of thousands of fighters yearning to join ISIS, Al-Nusra, and the volatile stew of militias that made the war what it was—a horror with no end. If that wasn't enough, smugglers had for years hauled in arms and spirited out human cargo. Now, with the war winding down, all those exoduses had slowed, and some even reversed. The upshot of it all was over a thousand miles of desert boundary that existed as little more than lines on a map.

Slaton had briefly considered an approach by sea, crossing the eastern Mediterranean from Cyprus. He'd hired a smuggler there some years ago to successfully insert himself into Lebanon. Unfortunately, that relationship had ended when the Nicosian tried to double-cross him—leading to considerable pain for the fisherman. Slaton supposed he might find another boat, run by another duplicitous sea captain, but a greater problem loomed: the Syrian coastline was simply too narrow and well monitored. Worse yet, such an approach would leave hundreds of miles remaining to reach Damascus. The same could be said for entering from Turkey or Iraq—those borders were simply too far from his objective. Lebanon was closer, but traveling there was a risk in itself.

For all these reasons, Slaton decided Jordan was his best option. Using the identity Sorensen had given him, he was sure he could enter the country with minimal chance of being noticed. And while Jordan's western border with Syria, separating Amman and Damascus, the largest population centers, was closely guarded, the shared border farther east was little more than sparsely populated desert. There would be occasional patrols, the odd bands of smugglers and refugees, but with over a hundred miles to work with, Slaton was confident he could find a gap.

These calculations had all been made yesterday, after leaving the farmhouse in Uruguay. He'd given Sorensen a list of exactly what he would need upon his arrival in Amman. There hadn't been a great deal of time, but she'd promised everything would be in place.

Now, looking down at the city with all its sharp angles and tawny shadows, Slaton felt the uncomfortable twinge that came before every mission: the realization that all the easy choices were behind you.

The Boeing 787 landed at Amman's Queen Alia International Airport backdropped by a deepening sunset. Slaton quickly cleared immigration under the guise of a Canadian businessman, the CIA's identity package holding up faultlessly. Keeping in character, he took a taxi into town and, with the sun throwing its final burnt embers on high stratus clouds to the west, was dropped under the main portico of the Intercontinental Hotel.

Slaton settled with the cab using cash—a credit card had been included with his travel legend, but he preferred not to use it. When the taxi pulled away Slaton ignored a welcome from the hotel's doorman, instead setting out along the street with a small carry-on in hand. He followed the simple directions Sorensen had given him, and two blocks later, in a public parking lot, he found the vehicle precisely where it was supposed to be. Third row, fourth spot.

It turned out to be a modest work van, not new, not old. The color could best be characterized as off-white, and faded lettering on the side advertised something called Hasina Construction Services. Beneath the name was a phone number that, were anyone to go to the trouble of calling, would lead to a vaguely worded recording.

Slaton scanned a full circle as he approached the van. No one seemed to be watching. He set his carry-on down near the driver's-side door, knelt down, and unzipped the bag's main compartment. While one hand foraged inside, the other curled beneath the inner lip of the rocker panel—bumpers and wheel wells were far too obvious. It took two swipes back and forth to find the small box secured with tape to the underside. In the old days it would have been a magnetic box, but plastic trim had taken over.

The engine cranked right to life and held a smooth idle. The gas tank was of course full. Before setting out, Slaton turned on the dome light in the van's cargo compartment. He maneuvered between the seats and performed a quick inventory. All the main components he'd requested were there.

Sorensen had done well.

From this point forward, the op was his to run. He'd been given a sat-phone for critical communications, but no one at Langley knew his plan. In truth, he himself knew nothing beyond the first steps. The next two days—his best-case estimate—would adhere to no blueprint. It would instead unfold as a series of decision points. Options taken, others discarded.

Which was exactly how Slaton wanted it.

He left the parking lot without referencing a map. He'd memorized the route out of town during his long journey from South America—at least, enough to put him on the correct outbound road. He steered onto King Hussein Street, then merged onto Queen Noor Boulevard—the kind of royal procession so embraced in the Mideast.

Night took hold as he cleared the city, the van's headlights cutting into featureless desert. Slaton drove at a reasonable speed and saw few other cars. In the rearview mirror, the gently rising terrain gradually cut off the lights of Amman. No city, no oncoming headlights, no people. He was as alone as he could be.

Only after forty miles did Slaton consider his next move. He began searching the endless void of desert to his left.

SEVENTEEN

For Sorensen, compliance with the oversight requirements of the special authority through which Slaton had been deployed felt like a kind of predictive confessional. In a cloistered setting, she would engage in a one-on-one meeting with the high priest of her agency and, in effect, plea for forgiveness for impending sins.

Weary from two days of travel, she was ushered straight into the CIA director's suite. Thomas Coltrane was waiting.

"Good afternoon, Anna."

"Good afternoon, sir."

Standing behind his desk, the director was framed by a great window that looked out across a glade. The maple and hickory trees were nearing the peak of their seasonal color, and the blustery wind brought shimmers of red and orange. Coltrane's perfectly groomed hair and eternal tan looked out of place against the backdrop of an onrushing winter. The director was not a political appointee, but a born-and-bred CIA man who'd hit the pinnacle. He'd also had no small hand in Sorensen's rapid rise at the agency.

"You look tired," he said.

"It's been a busy few days. Thanks for making room in your schedule to see me."

"Is this about what I think it's about?"

Sorensen paused. "It is—I've activated Corsair."

The director nodded. "This has been a long time in the making."

Slaton's code name had been chosen by Sorensen, drawn from the seafaring Mediterranean bandits who'd thrived trafficking for both sides when the Ottoman Turks battled the Christians for supremacy of Europe. It seemed a natural moniker for an operative who was not only lethal, but who shunned affiliations.

"You're not having seconds thoughts, are you?" she asked.

"Of course not. You?"

"Constantly."

Coltrane smiled. "Then I've trained you well. I might make a director out of you yet."

Sorensen didn't dignify that with a response. "So . . . how much do you want to know?"

"Honestly? I want to be fully briefed in until it's over. At that point, I'll wish I never knew anything, especially if things don't go to plan."

"For what it's worth, there is no plan. At least, none that I know about."

"You are not instilling me with confidence, Anna."

The legal ice they were traversing could not have been more thin. But then, that had long been the problem: the country had lost far too many opportunities to strike terrorist organizations because agency or DOD attorneys bogged down response times on perishable intelligence. *Verbal quicksand,* as one Delta Force commander had put it.

The newly elected president, Elayne Cleveland, wanted a fresh approach. She had called Coltrane to the Oval Office soon after taking charge, and over gin and tonics he'd floated the idea of using outside assets for delicate agency operations. The ever-astute Cleveland sidestepped, neither approving nor disapproving of the notion, but saying that she had "all confidence in the agency to keep America safe." The final product of that meeting was given the most insipid name possible: National Security Presidential Memoranda 14.

It was, Coltrane knew, as close to a green light as he would ever get. The directive gave the CIA authorization to conduct "offensive operations in time-sensitive circumstances" without the president's express approval. Within certain parameters, the decision of who, what, and where to strike was delegated to the head of the Special Activities Center—at that moment, Anna Sorensen. Sorensen, in turn, was obliged to provide operational updates to the director of the CIA. Attorneys at both the White House and CIA had rebelled against the concept, but to no avail. The president was determined to cut the red tape.

And SAC was happy to oblige.

From there Sorensen had taken over. She'd waited patiently for a mission that would test her new authority, not to mention her new operative. The rescue of Ludmilla Kravchuk seemed an ideal opportunity. The chance of collateral damage was low, and Sorensen had been reasonably sure Slaton would accept. If he succeeded in getting Kravchuk out of Syria, the concept would be proved. And if not?

She didn't want to think about that—for Slaton's sake.

Coltrane said, "I know it's not part of your mandate to divulge Corsair's identity, even to me . . . but I suspect we're talking about our Israeli friend?"

Sorensen wasn't surprised he'd nailed it—the director had seen Slaton work on at least two occasions.

"We are," she said.

"Is he already in play?"

"He's en route. I selected him for this op because I judged his skills to be both necessary and appropriate."

Coltrane took on a pained expression that might or might not have been genuine. "Necessary and appropriate skills? I'm not sure I like the sound of that. We both know what he is. I've personally seen the man sink ships and destroy jet fighters."

"I have no reason to believe this mission will be so . . . kinetically inclined. Slaton has a wide range of abilities. He also has extensive experience operating in the region in question."

"Which is?"

"He's going to enter Syria. We need to locate and extract a Russian defector who claims to have intelligence regarding a terrorist attack."

Coltrane's words became measured. "What kind of attack?"

"We don't have many details yet, but apparently it involves chemical weapons."

"Does this relate to the interpreter?"

"I see you've read your morning briefing," Sorensen said, referring to the "current intel" synopsis given each morning to all top agency officials.

"I do so without fail."

Sorensen explained how Kravchuk had made contact through the Czech embassy.

"And this slipped past the Syrians?" Coltrane asked.

"Apparently so. They're searching intensively for this woman, and it's a safe bet the Russians are too. If we're going to get her out of the country, it'll have to be done quickly."

Sorensen went through a rough timetable and covered the possible pitfalls. She explained that if Corsair could spirit the woman to a neutral border, the CIA would take over from there.

"It seems like a reasonable plan," said Coltrane. "Do we know where this woman is at the moment?"

"We think so. On last contact she was holed up in a hair salon in one of the central districts."

"Let's hope Corsair lives up to his reputation."

"He will," Sorensen found herself saying.

"Are you monitoring his progress?"

"No. He has the ability to contact me, and we'll get situation updates. But we won't be watching his every move. That keeps the risk of comm intercepts low, and also aligns with our desire to avoid attribution."

Coltrane said, "All right. Once we have the woman in hand, I want to hear what she has to say. Hopefully it will be worth the risks we're taking."

"I hope so too," Sorensen said. "But let's not forget—it's Corsair who's taking the real risks."

EIGHTEEN

When viewed from the driver's seat of a utility van at night, all the world's deserts look the same. The landscape is gentle, the sky overhead unbroken by canopied trees. That impression would change, Slaton knew, the moment he stepped outside. The texture of the earth would take hold, carried on soft unfiltered air. He would breathe in the scents of parched brush and night-flowering succulents. Even hints of autumn could be discerned by those familiar with the region. And Slaton was indeed familiar. He'd spent many of his formative years not far from here, two borders to the west within sight of Mount Meron. He could never have imagined, in those peaceable days, how the lessons of his youth would be applied.

Selecting a launching point for his raid across the border was easier than expected. He had seen but one official vehicle since leaving Amman: ten miles outside town, a lightly armored truck parked beside the road. There had been no sign of the attendant soldiers. They might have been on patrol, resting nearby, or addressing a call of nature. Perhaps the vehicle had broken down weeks earlier and been abandoned. Slaton didn't care—no threat had appeared, and ever since, the desert on his left had been free and clear.

The headlights cut the night a hundred yards ahead. Because the van wasn't built for terrain, Slaton began scouting for a prepared road. He'd seen a handful in the last few miles, unevenly formed and marginally maintained, that were unquestionably meant for military use. The few villages and farms he'd seen had all been to his right, and none were less than ten miles from the border—wary settlers keeping their distance from the crazy neighbor.

Slaton pulled to a stop at the next westbound offshoot. He studied it carefully in the wash of the van's headlights. The road curved gently into flat terrain and disappeared a hundred yards ahead. From the main road it looked passable. He drove cautiously for the first half mile—it was vital to not hang up the van in a washout within sight of the main road. He navigated by a mapping application built into the phone Sorensen had given him. On all appearances it was a brand-name satellite phone, yet a special application, only accessible by a scan of Slaton's retina, activated an entirely separate operating system with a menu of special functions.

The navigation mode ran military-grade GPS accuracy, and the terrain database would have made any platoon leader smile. Slaton used that accuracy to drive within a half mile of the border. There he veered onto a section of level ground surrounded by stands of brush and a few stunted trees. Not perfect concealment, but the best he could expect given the topography.

He turned off the engine, stepped outside, and stood for a moment. The only sounds were the ticking of the van's cooling engine and the buzz of an unseen insect. The night seemed unusually still, and as expected, he sensed the desert's resinous fragrances.

He scanned 360 degrees, searching for unnatural shadows, any trace of movement. There was nothing. Slaton went to the van's rear cargo door and pulled both sides open. Before him, strapped tight to the floor, was his core request—a Hayes M1060 dirt bike, designed specifically for Special Operations work.

He guessed Sorensen had pilfered the motorcycle from the unconventional motor pool of some forward-deployed SEAL unit. The tires were foam-filled run-flats, and the model he'd chosen had an automatic clutch. The exhaust system was suppressed for sound and surrounded by baffles to minimize heat signature. The engine was modified to run on a wide variety of fuels. Diesel, Jet A, biodiesel, along with all common military-grade fuels. The bike would get reasonably good gas mileage, minimizing the need for spontaneous assaults on gas stations. An integrated GPS nav system would back up his phone—the last thing he wanted was to get lost in hostile territory on a dark night.

He'd given considerable thought to what type of bike to request. Japanese bikes were commonplace in Syria, yet the Hayes was obviously a military item. If he were to run into anyone en route, civilian or otherwise, he would not have the option of posing as a wayward European adventure traveler who'd taken a wrong turn into a war zone. The idea of riding a standard bike straight into central Damascus had crossed his mind, yet while it might have worked in some cities, Slaton didn't like it here. Few riders in Syria wore helmets, and his sandy hair and loosely Nordic features would stand out glaringly. In the end, he couldn't escape the Hayes' one great advantage—its stealth would be invaluable for getting him near the city.

Once he arrived on the outskirts of Damascus, Slaton knew he would have to improvise to reach the center of town—where Ludmilla Kravchuk was holed up. That, he knew, would be the most dangerous part of the mission. He spoke a number of languages fluently, but Arabic was not among them. For that reason, blending in would be critical. He retrieved the bag he'd traveled with, removed a set of clothes, and began to change: tan cargo pants, two cotton shirts, the outer long sleeve, and a sturdy pair of boots. There was also a thin jacket, dark blue, with a hood. All of it was gently used, and could have been purchased at any retailer in Damascus.

Slaton loosened the ratcheting tie-downs on the Hayes. Someone had had the foresight to include an eight-foot-long plank in the cargo compartment. He slid the board outside, leaned it on the bumper, and walked the bike down the makeshift ramp. Returning to the van, he inventoried the rest of his gear.

In a heavy-duty rucksack he found the weapons he'd requested: one MP5, one Sig Sauer P229 with a right-hand thigh holster. The MP5 was a Spec Ops variant with a collapsible stock. The barrel was threaded for a sound suppressor, also included, and the ammunition was subsonic—a calculated sacrifice of range for stealth. Three spare magazines for each weapon were provided, and enough ammo to fill them all. Slaton hadn't come to start World War III. Any firefight he couldn't resolve with two weapons, and more than 150 rounds, was one he needed to avoid.

The guns looked flawless, but all the same he inspected them under the cargo compartment dome light. He seated a full magazine in each weapon and chambered a round. Slaton looked out over the silent desert. He saw not a single light anywhere on the horizon. The main road was far behind him, and he'd encountered virtually no traffic during the last half hour of his journey. At ten thirty at night, he guessed there wasn't another human within ten miles.

It was all the isolation he needed.

He looked around the van's interior, and his eyes settled on a box of paint cans, brushes, and rags—no doubt remnants of the vehicle's past life. He took a paint can that, judging by its weight, was roughly half full. Slaton walked thirty paces to a clear area and set the can on the ground.

He went back to the van and picked up the Sig. Its weight and grip were familiar in his hand. In the years since he'd left Mossad, there was a period when his training had turned spotty—when he'd lived off-grid with his family on a sailboat. Slaton's most recent outing with the CIA had been a wakeup call. Resolving to do something about it, he'd set up a tactical range on a remote corner of his Idaho ranch. The Sig and MP, by no coincidence, were favorites in his private arsenal.

He extended the Sig in a comfortable grip and addressed the paint can. He aligned the forward sight in the rear notch, relaxed his breathing, and sent a single round. A trickle of blue paint bubbled from a hole dead center. He next issued a quick two-shot pairing, followed by three more singles. The gun was true. Six hits in a reasonable two-inch grouping.

He switched to the MP and did the same, finding a very slight variance to the three-o'clock position. Because he didn't have the required sight adjustment tool, and because the correction was minimal, he left it as a mental note. The paint can was by then mottled in blue, an oozing cobalt puddle spreading in the dim light.

Slaton secured the guns, filled the spare magazines, then topped off the ones he'd just used. From the van he removed the rest: a German-manufactured night optical device with an integrated ranging feature, three water bottles, a half dozen energy bars, a combat knife, and a tactical flashlight. All of it went into the rucksack, which wasn't cut from military-style camo fabric, but rather heavy-duty black nylon. Better to blend in as a civilian if it came to that. There was also a stack of Syrian pound notes in various denominations. After a rough count, he divided it between two thigh pockets.

It occurred to Slaton that, aside from the bike, none of what he was carrying, should it fall into Syrian hands, could tie him to the CIA. Even the Hayes was used by Special Forces units of other nations. He briefly wondered if the local CIA officer who'd put his package together had been given details about the mission. Probably not, Slaton decided. An untraceable vehicle, tactical dirt bike, guns, ammunition, and energy bars. It was the kind of mission support intelligence staff in this part of the world likely arranged on a daily basis.

He collapsed the stock of the MP5, and it fit perfectly inside the ruck with the rest. The Sig went into the thigh holster, secured by a Velcro strap. He retrieved the paint can and dropped his brass into the jagged new opening. Holding the can by its wire handle, he spun like an Olympian throwing the discus and launched it far into the desert. He closed the van, locked the doors, and dropped the key in a back pocket. He doubted the van would be noticed for some time. All the same, anyone who saw it—a border patrol unit, Bedouins, a wandering refugee—would likely investigate. Aside from its odd location, the painter's truck with Jordanian commercial plates was completely unremarkable.

He noted his present position on the dirt bike's GPS. Slaton committed the coordinates to memory. He doubted he would leave Syria the same way he was going in—even so, the van was an option to keep, quite literally, in his back pocket.

The bike's seat extended far enough to support a second rider, but just barely. Behind that was a small rack crisscrossed with bungees. He secured the rucksack on the rack, making sure the MP5 was easily accessible. Slaton donned the thigh holster, adjusting it for a natural right-hand reach.

He mounted the bike and turned the key. The engine fired to life. Idle came at an unusually low pitch, suggesting the power resonating beneath. Like a racehorse primed in the gate.

He looked ahead into the pitch-black night. The border in this area was unmarked, but Slaton knew it was less than a mile distant. He had made it this far with Sorensen's help. Travel, equipment, weapons. That kind of support was now at an end. It was time to assume the identity Sorensen was after. That of a ghost. A man with no country or allegiance. Only a mission of vital importance.

Slaton gave the throttle a turn, put the bike in gear, and shot into the desert leading a rooster-tail of gravel.

NINETEEN

The As Suwayda Governorate of Syria was vast and sparsely populated. The few villages Slaton encountered were easily avoided. More problematic, and the reason there were so few inhabitants, was the daunting terrain.

The night optics proved essential as he negotiated the topography. Using the gray-scale image, he ran a twisting path through what looked like sunbaked moonscape. The valleys were little more than rain-carved ditches, while the high ground was pocked with circular craters. The entire region rested atop an ancient volcanic plateau, mile after mile of cinder cones and vents baked into a Mad Max panorama.

Slaton's progress slowed considerably near the heart of the plateau. He slalomed the bike amid rock outcroppings, the earth's molten offerings hardened by a million cycles of cooling and heating. He sought out trails that kept the right general course, and on the best of them he managed a decent speed, but invariably the paths would fade to nothing and he found himself steering through what looked like a giant volcanic quarry. He put down one foot or the other to pivot sharp corners, and realized he should have asked for riding boots.

Progress became slow and tortuous, but this was not unanticipated—after studying the satellite images Sorensen had provided, he was convinced this was the best route for avoiding detection. The gap he was threading was narrow. To the south were more populated areas, inhabited mostly by Druze who'd established towns and farms in the fertile valley. Conversely, to the north was the As Safa lava field, eighty-four square miles of lifeless rock and hardened volcanic vents. The terrain there was all but impassable, so much so that it had become a defensive fallback in conflicts for a thousand years—most recently, the Islamic State had retreated to As Safa to make its unsuccessful last stand in the south against Assad.

As he rode, Slaton's attention alternated between the terrain immediately ahead and the distant horizon. He'd so far seen few signs of life, but that wasn't going to hold. According to the bike's nav display, five miles ahead lay his first man-made obstacle—a primary paved road connecting the village of Shahba to the Duma district. If he saw no traffic, his plan was to take that road west, followed by a right turn and a dash toward Damascus. At this time of night, there was a good chance he wouldn't see another soul.

How close to the city he could get remained an open question. Inevitably, a transition would be necessary, some alternate means by which to reach a particular hair salon in central Damascus. At the farmhouse Sorensen had presented him with the CIA's latest assessments. Slaton had taken particular note of Syrian army checkpoints and patrols. The roads leading to Damascus were a brick wall—every one was being monitored. Yet the off-road approaches from the direction of As Suwayda showed little government presence. The desert bordering Jordan was sparsely populated, making it a low priority for a regime still stamping out endless pockets of resistance in the north.

Not all of this was in Slaton's favor. The laissez-faire treatment of the southern governorates fostered a measure of lawlessness. It was the usual cast of suspects. Druze militias were ever watchful around their villages. Bedouin tribes had been walking these sands longer than anyone, and bands of smugglers ran between them. Hezbollah also roamed, although they were a more transitory lot. Even remnants of the Islamic State made the occasional appearance— like a bulge in a water balloon moving to the area of least resistance. Slaton simply had to keep his head up—only by avoiding all of them did he have a chance of reaching Ludmilla Kravchuk.

He checked the nav display. The road lay three miles ahead. He brought the bike to a stop and used his NODs to search a full 360 degrees. He saw nothing worrisome.

He put the bike in gear and set out along another dusty trail.

Slaton spotted the road ten minutes later. On first look he saw no vehicles, but wanting to be sure, he guided the Hayes toward a minor hill and paused at its base. He studied the rocky rise through his optic. No more than fifty feet high, it was little more than a weathered outcropping of dirt over black basalt. He parked the bike, deciding the hill would give him a good view of the surrounding area.

He scrambled up the rise on hands and feet, tiny streams of dirt and stone avalanching down behind him. Slaton paused just short of the crest and settled on his knees for better purchase. He popped his head over the peak and again brought up the optics.

He first looked west, where the road ran a relatively straight line to the horizon. He knew from his planning that this particular road bypassed Damascus to the south, but connected to Highway 110 which led into town. There were no vehicles as far as he could see in that direction, which, given his elevation and the magnification of the optics, he reckoned to be at least five miles.

His plan seemed solid. A ten-minute ride west would put him at the junction, leaving no more than fifteen miles to the outer reaches of the city. Somewhere along that stretch he would go into cover and search for a better way into Damascus. *So far so good,* he thought.

Slaton was beginning to feel more confident. He was making progress. The moment he looked in the other direction, that promise was lost in the ether of a soon-to-be-shattered night.

TWENTY

As was typically the case, it was motion that caught his sniper's eye. Irregular movement in an otherwise tranquil panorama. And a great deal of motion at that.

Slaton was looking at a convoy.

The string of vehicles was two miles away, heading in his direction. He'd seen a great many military formations in his time, everything from elite armored units to gaggles that looked like circus trains. Tonight he was looking at something in the middle of the spectrum. In both the front and back of the lineup were paired technicals—pickup trucks with large-caliber guns mounted in their beds. Between these were three larger vehicles. Slaton recognized them as Ural-4320 transports—the Russian equivalent of a standard army deuce and a half. In the surreal amplified image he could make out the heat signature of engines and frames, while the canopied load bays of the Urals appeared relatively cool. In the wake of it all a miasma of dust shimmered in the cool night air. At a glance, Slaton knew perfectly well *what* he was looking at.

The matter of *who*, however, was far more relevant.

The most telling feature of the formation was that it was traveling lights out. This was why Slaton hadn't spotted it sooner when he'd been riding without the optics, even though the trucks were barely two miles away. It was a damning set of circumstances: moving in the middle of the night, heavy escort, lights out. Whoever this was, they didn't want to be seen. And whatever the trucks were carrying, it was important.

Oddly, Slaton realized these deductions did little to settle who he was looking at. In the badlands of As Suwayda such a formation could be assembled by any of a half dozen players. He studied each vehicle, beginning at the front. It took only one to give him an answer: snapping on a pole secured to the back bumper of the lead technical was a flag. Slaton could easily make out the image in his magnified view, and while the green and white colors were washed out, it was a standard any Israeli knew all too well: the unmistakable shape of a raised hand clutching a Kalashnikov.

This was a unit of Hezbollah. The self-proclaimed Party of God.

It was a sight to instill caution, and Slaton was struck by the possibility that the hot engine of the Hayes could be seen from the road. The drivers in the formation, at least those in front, were probably also using night optics.

He scrambled down from the promontory and pulled the bike tight against the hillside. Just to be sure, he bent down and checked the opposite line of sight. He couldn't see either the road or the convoy. Satisfied, he scrambled back uphill to his perch.

He moved a pair of football-sized rocks in front of him to provide better concealment—anyone looking in his direction would naturally scan the high ground carefully. The convoy was roughly a mile away, traveling at perhaps thirty miles an hour. A judicious speed. In approximately two minutes it would reach the closest point, passing a hundred yards from where he lay.

Slaton studied a man in the bed of the third technical. He had the heaviest gun in the wagon train pointed skyward. Slaton recognized it as a ZSU-23, a classic Russian-manufactured anti-aircraft gun. The soldier was scanning the heavens through the targeting reticle like an astronomer looking for nebulas. With this last bit of information, the rest fell into place.

He was looking at a Hezbollah arms shipment.

For years the group had been stockpiling guns, mortars, rockets, and missiles along the length of the Israeli border. The shipments mostly came from Iran, either flown into Syrian airbases, overland via Iraq, or brought in through the sea port of Tartus. From those transit points, Hezbollah loaded the munitions and ran operations like the one he was watching. Three truckloads of armaments to be dispersed along the border with Israel—most likely in Syria, but Lebanon was a possibility. The governments of both countries, who manifestly hated the Jews on their own volition, turned a blind eye to the entire affair.

Not so visionless were the Israelis. They had long ago identified the developing threat, and the Israeli Air Force regularly launched airstrikes across its northern border. Some shipments were targeted during transport, others immolated in place once they arrived at their destinations. Hezbollah, of course, did its best to conceal and defend the shipments. The caches being delivered were kept intentionally small, limiting the potential damage from an airstrike by Israel's jets. For Hezbollah, it was a reasonably effective strategy, a war of attrition they accepted as the cost of doing business. Over time, enough shipments got through, dispersed into storage armories and underground tunnel networks, to justify the losses. And when the next war came—as it always did—Hezbollah would have the firepower in place to respond against its Zionist foe.

Had Slaton still been in the employ of Mossad, and if he had a direct means of communication, he could have called in an airstrike then and there. Or at the very least, reported the position of a vulnerable target. Tonight, however, he had a different mission. He needed to find a way into central Damascus. He was sure this conga line would go nowhere near the city—it was destined for a tunnel complex or a warehouse far to the south.

These disparate facts began blending in Slaton's head. Details and assumptions. The requirements of his own mission. When it finally reached critical mass, an opportunity crystallized. One that might very soon be lost.

He scrambled back downhill, details falling into place as dirt and stones dislodged under his steps. At the bottom he unzipped his backpack and extracted the MP5.

TWENTY-ONE

Sixty seconds later Slaton was ready. Lying in wait like the sniper he was.

He shifted his sight between the leading vehicles of the convoy, settling on each one at a time. He did so as an exercise, tracking the front quarter panel of each and reckoning a lead correction for his shot.

He'd already measured the range using his optic—to the nearest point on the road, 110 yards. A simple shot under most circumstances, but one that tonight came with complications. To begin, his targets were moving at roughly thirty miles an hour. His subsonic ammunition had a substantially lower muzzle velocity than a standard round. That meant more lead and a greater bullet drop, even at short range. In his favor, his intended target was quite large. Also, thanks to the suppressor, not to mention the mechanical clamor of a seven-vehicle caravan, he could afford multiple shots.

Best of all: he had three chances to make his plan work.

With only moments before the convoy reached the nearest point on the road, Slaton checked his sat-phone. He was extremely careful to shield the screen's glow. He'd turned it on moments earlier—the first time he'd done so since crossing the border. He checked and saw a solid connection to a satellite somewhere overhead. He typed out an urgent request to Sorensen. He had no idea if she could provide what he needed. If not, he would simply have to find another way.

He pocketed the phone and shifted his attention to the scope of the MP5. In the magnified image the leading transport looked like a cruise ship. Slaton settled the reticle on the front quarter of the truck's cab, slightly behind the bumper. He applied what felt like a reasonable lead.

Ever so slightly, he began to pressure the trigger. Waiting for the familiar break.

Sorensen was at home, getting into her nightclothes after a long hot shower, when the message from Slaton arrived. Because she carried the CIA's most secure communication device, and because messages from Corsair were routed immediately for her eyes only, it arrived without having been filtered through Langley's operations center.

She read through one long paragraph of text. Then she read it again.

"You gotta be shittin' me, David!" she muttered to herself.

Sorensen closed her eyes, but only for a moment. Sixty seconds later she was talking to the CIA's Defense Department liaison at SOCOM headquarters. Thirty after that, she was talking to the commander on shift. An Air Force one-star named Smithers was in charge of the country's special operations that night.

"You want *what?*" he asked incredulously.

"A little close air support in southern Syria. I have an operative on the ground who urgently needs assistance."

"Syria." A pause. "All right . . . I'm looking at it now." A longer pause. "No, I don't show any ordnance in the sky near those coordinates."

"What *do* you have?"

"Closest thing is a pair of F-22 Raptors. They're about a hundred miles out—just came off a tanker in western Iraq. But they're loaded for air-to-air, internal missiles only. We keep a combat air patrol running most days just in case. To tell you the truth Miss . . . ah . . ."

"Sorensen."

"Right, Sorensen . . . even if these jets were packing bombs, I'd pretty much have to wake up the president to drop inside Syria."

"I never said I wanted bombs."

"Well then, what the hell—"

"General, what my guy needs is very simple! And you won't have to wake up the president to do it . . ."

As had been the case for three hours, Corporal Mahmood Arian's attention was padlocked on the bumper of the Toyota Hilux twenty paces in front of him. Arian was not wearing night vision gear—the only sets they possessed were reserved for two men in the lead Hilux. The rest of the drivers had only a dim moon and starlight to work with.

To that end, wanting to keep his night vision at its peak, he had dimmed every light on the instrument panel in front of him. For the most part it worked. The tailgate ahead was a steady, albeit muted reference on the narrow two-lane road.

"You are too close again," fussed Captain Quraishi from the passenger seat next to him.

Arian let up on the gas. The captain had been berating him for the last fifty miles, although he suspected it had less to do with his driving than a simple case of nerves—they were now squarely in the killing grounds, the southern desert where Israel preferred to make its airstrikes.

After backing off a bit, Arian was accelerating back to speed when a loud bang sent him rigid in his seat. The steering wheel pulled to one side and the truck became difficult to control.

"What is it?" Quraishi bellowed.

"I . . . I don't know, sir. Something is wrong with the truck." He brought the Ural to an awkward stop, its hood canted to the left in the middle of the road. Arian saw his captain looking up at the sky, then heard commotion on the radio.

"What is wrong?" said a voice Arian recognized—Jamal, the driver behind them.

Arian picked up the dash-mounted microphone. "I don't know. Something happened to my truck."

Everyone sat still, waiting for the worst. When nothing happened, the captain ordered, "Well don't just sit there, Corporal! Get out and see what is wrong!"

Arian turned off the engine. He stepped down on the wide running board, then to the ground. He saw the problem right away. The truck's left front tire was flattened under its rim, and a section of the sidewall had shredded. Arian felt the tension wash away as if cleansed by the night breeze.

He said, "We have a flat tire, sir."

The captain climbed down and stood next to him. "Did you not inspect them before we left?"

"I did," said Arian.

The captain looked again at the sky. He frowned, and said, "Well . . . don't just stand there. Fix it!"

TWENTY-TWO

Slaton checked his watch.

Fifteen minutes.

He took another look through his optic. The lead Ural had come to rest crookedly in the road. Two soldiers were torqueing the final lug nuts off the pancaked front wheel. No one seemed to suspect that the tire had been shot out. He knew because no guards had been posted, and the perimeter wasn't being watched. What little caution he saw from the platoon was directed up at the sky. A wariness he'd been banking on. And one he hoped to soon exploit.

Since the convoy had ground to a halt, things were playing out nicely. Half the men had dismounted and were milling about their respective trucks. Most were smoking cigarettes and bantering casually. A pop music playlist was running on somebody's phone. It was the kind of delay soldiers dealt with on a daily basis—particularly those who served in scattershot armies like Hezbollah.

From his hide Slaton kept his eyes fixed on the stricken truck—its driver had disappeared behind the cab minutes earlier. He again checked the time. Sorensen had acknowledged his request seventeen minutes earlier.

He fired off another message: Were you able to get fighter support?

The reply seemed to take forever, but in fact came after only twenty seconds: Just arrived at staging point. Awaiting three-minute warning.

No sooner did that message arrive than Slaton saw his cue: the driver and another man dropped the big spare tire from its stowage rack behind the cab. Slaton thought it better to err on the early side, even if it meant more work for himself.

He sent what he hoped was the last message of the thread: Three minutes! Go!

Seventeen miles east, and twenty-two thousand feet up, a flight of two F-22 Raptors, call sign Bones 22 from the 95th Fighter Squadron, were wheeling in a makeshift holding pattern. The unit had been deployed for two months, and the hundreds of missions flown so far had been largely uneventful: a lot of air refueling and holding patterns, a lot of radar work and gathering electronic intelligence. But when it came to turning and burning engagements, things had been slow.

Which was why, when the unusual order came via datalink, both pilots' attention ratcheted up. The flight lead addressed his wingman on a secure radio. "Okay, we're turning inbound. Go loose trail."

The wingman, Bones 23, acknowledged and performed a hard S-turn to separate. Once established a mile behind his flight lead, the wingman said, "Tell me again what our objective is."

"You saw the orders as well as I did. It's not anything we ever trained to do, but it seems simple enough."

"Boss, we *are* in Syrian airspace."

"That's why we have stealth, Fledge. Flares armed, radars air-to-ground mode. We paint this convoy and light 'em up."

The flight lead pointed his jet toward the given coordinates and initiated a gentle descent. He studied his primary tactical display. The radar painted their targets like a spotlight on a prison break. "Sure enough, there they are. Okay, Bones 23. Push it up!"

Slaton looked at his watch, then scanned the pitch-black sky. Thirty seconds to go. He saw and heard nothing.

His eyes were locked on the disabled truck. The new tire was in place, and a soldier—surely the lowest ranking—was torqueing the lug nuts with the wheel still jacked up off the ground. Elsewhere he saw cautious glances and clipped exchanges. The music had been turned off, and cigarette butts had long been flicked into the desert. The unit had been here, sitting still, for longer than was healthy—the mood was that of a flock of ducks who'd been on a pond too long during hunting season. Even the vehicles, dispersed along the road shoulder and parked at odd angles, exuded an aura of wariness.

Ten seconds. Slaton hoped the Air Force kept a good time hack.

To his surprise, he saw the assault before he heard it. A momentary glint in the pale moonlight before an arrow-like shape shot past in impossible silence. At impossible speed. It was like a bolt of lightning without the thunder. Slaton understood why because he'd been forewarned—and because that was the point of the entire exercise. Streaking at no more than two hundred feet above the ground, the jet was traveling so fast it was outrunning its own sound.

The jet was gone in a flash and the sonic boom hit, shattering the cool night. That was followed almost immediately by the shriek of engine noise. The crack from the second jet came seconds later. The sonic booms were still reverberating amid the hills when the night came alive with light: self-defense flares and afterburners, a veritable fireworks show in the sky. The result was exactly what Slaton wanted.

In a word, chaos. The ground that he owned.

The convoy erupted to life like a kicked termite hill. Soldiers began running, and the guns on two of the technicals opened up, lacing the night with tracers. A handful of the more belligerent troops pointed their AKs upward and began spraying lead into the sky. The return fire was ungoverned, frantic, like a stunned drunk swinging at air after being punched in the nose. The odds of hitting two jets that couldn't be seen, and that were traveling faster than the speed of sound, was effectively nil. Yet as random as it all was, it *was* a response, which was why Slaton was surprised when the jets made a second pass.

If it hadn't been nighttime, he imagined, it would have looked like an airshow, sleek jets sweeping low over the dunes before climbing straight up. On the second pass Slaton never even saw the Raptors, and he suspected they'd offset by maybe a mile—a reasonable precaution, he supposed, to stay clear of the small arms fire. Even so, the second iteration of sonic booms was as convincing as the first.

There was nothing for Slaton to do but sit back and watch. If he hadn't been working solo, deep inside enemy territory, he might have smiled. The Hezbollah men, clearly convinced they were under air attack, responded with all the orderliness of an exploding bomb. Twenty-odd men, who'd moments ago been milling about nervously, ran and jumped into their vehicles—and not necessarily the ones they'd rode in on.

A better trained bunch would have reacted differently. Climbing into a vehicle during an air attack, with the intent of driving away, was like hiding behind a paper target on a gun range. The best defensive move would have been to throw themselves in the ditch along the shoulder of the road. Yet once the first vehicle began moving, the frenetic die was cast. None of what Slaton saw surprised him.

And it suited his needs perfectly.

Within a minute six vehicles—the four technicals and the two Urals that were still in service—were thundering westward down the road. Two of the technicals were weaving drunkenly, as if side-to-side movement would negate the tracking of a precision-guided bomb. The drivers of the Urals, which were too heavy for evasive maneuvers, simply went for speed. Altogether, it bore no resemblance to any kind of defensive formation. More like a stampede.

From the Hezbollah commander's point of view, there was one minor victory. As far as Slaton could see, not a single man had been left behind. The stricken Ural delivery truck remained in the middle of the road, its left front wheel jacked in the air like a hospital patient in traction. The new tire had been put in place, and on the ground next to it Slaton saw a discarded crowbar. The flat tire was on the ground nearby.

He couldn't have drawn it up any better.

He waited.

The roar of engines soon faded, both on the ground and in the air. The desert reverted to its customary silence.

TWENTY-THREE

Slaton gave the silence another five minutes. The pinballing convoy was completely out of sight, having disappeared down the road. They would return at some point, most likely a small detail dispatched to see if anything was left of the stranded Ural. Slaton doubted that would happen before daybreak, when the sky could be watched more closely. Once everyone's heart rates got back to normal.

He scanned all around the abandoned truck, particularly in the brush along the road's shoulders. He was reasonably sure every man was accounted for, but during the chaos it was possible some right-minded junior officer might have opted for the desert.

Seeing no signs of life, Slaton decided the coast was clear.

He sidestepped quickly to the bottom of the hill. The Hayes, he decided, could be left where it was, concealed in a dense thicket. He did, however, take the time to note its GPS position before switching the nav unit off. With his optics he carefully memorized features of the hill and surrounding terrain. Slaton didn't plan to return for the bike, but one never wasted a backup plan. If it came to that, he wanted to be able to locate the bike in a hurry, preferably without electronic help.

He shouldered up the backpack, then made his way to the road with the MP5 leading. By the time he reached the truck Slaton was convinced he was alone.

The first thing he checked was the truck's cab. The key was still in the ignition. Slaton tensed momentarily on hearing distant voices, but then realized it was only the truck's radio—it was still on, tuned to a tactical frequency. His Arabic was poor, but he caught a few words. Something about continuing ten more kilometers. In spite of his fractured translations, the radio could prove a priceless source of intel—if the unit reversed to collect the truck they'd left behind, he was sure he would get warning.

He stepped out of the cab and checked the left front tire. The spare had been mounted, two lug nuts remaining on the ground. He picked up the crowbar, used the wrench end to install them, then tightened those already in place. The jack was a peculiar design, and he didn't immediately see how to lower it.

No matter.

Slaton backed off a step, took a solid stance, and put one boot on the driver's-side running board. He pushed and the cab wobbled away slightly. He let it come back, then did it again, beginning a cyclic rocking motion. On the fifth shove the jack gave way. The truck's front end dropped twelve inches to the ground, bouncing twice on its huge tires before going still.

Slaton torqued each lug nut one last time, then with the crowbar still in hand, he moved to the back of the truck. The large cargo bay was topped by a steel frame and desert-tan canopy. Slaton climbed onto the rear bumper, then a second step put him inside the bay with the payload. In the dim light he stood looking at twenty-odd crates, each the size of a kitchen stove. From his pocket he removed his tactical flashlight and switched it on. The writing on the crates was in Cyrillic—no surprise there—and he couldn't decipher the words. He did, however, note that all the crates had a similar model number.

He was sure he was looking at a cache of Russian-manufactured weapons, most likely supplied by Iran. The only question: what kind?

With due caution, he eased the crowbar into a gap beneath the first wooden lid. He worked his way around and had it free in less than a minute. Slaton pulled the lid clear, trained his flashlight inside, and could not suppress a smile. He was looking at a Shmel-M rocket launcher, a 90mm Russian weapon designed to be carried and employed by a single soldier. He uncorked another crate and saw a slightly different version, the smaller Z-model—an incendiary weapon that was technically classified as a flamethrower. After digging deep into both crates, and doing a bit of math, he estimated the truck was carrying nearly 250 man-portable rockets.

He pulled out the topmost M-model and grounded the stock to his shoulder, trying it on for size as a more genteel man might a dinner jacket. Satisfied, he set the rocket aside, worked the lid into place, and hammered down a few nails using the crowbar. He did the same to the other open crate.

Slaton noticed a stack of folded blankets in one corner, and he took one from the top. It was stained with black grease, which was just as well. He wrapped up the rocket launcher, returned to the truck's cab, and placed it on the passenger seat. He took a long look at the detritus in the road all around—a byproduct of the unit's hasty departure—and decided it might be worth a look. Slaton walked through a sea of cigarette butts, spent water bottles, and at least one cheap mobile phone. On the shoulder of the road he found a camouflage jacket. It looked like it had been run over, foot-wide tread marks stamped across the back. He picked up the jacket and took a closer look. It displayed no unit insignia, but that was hardly a surprise. Hezbollah was an irregular force by any measure. He'd noted earlier through his optic that every man had been dressed differently. Most wore fatigues and camo of some kind, but they'd all seemingly shopped at different stores, been fitted by different tailors. There was nothing "uniform" about it. He tried the jacket on for size. It was a snug fit, but not bad. Best of all, it came with an integral rain hood zipped into the collar.

He was about to turn back to the truck when something in the distance caught his eye. He walked a hundred feet up the road, and there, smack on the centerline, was the Hezbollah flag he'd seen flying from the lead technical. It had obviously fallen off in the scramble. Slaton picked it up and, without bothering to brush away the dust, carried it back to the Ural. After some searching near the rear bumper, he wedged the pole into the canopy frame just above the tailgate.

Slaton mounted the cab and fired up the engine. The big diesel rumbled obediently to life. He put the Ural in gear and accelerated in the same direction as the fleeing convoy. The radio was silent, and he guessed the unit commander had either ordered a switch to a different tactical frequency, or more likely shut down UHF communications altogether. It wasn't a bad call—radio usage could give away a unit's position. Either way, Slaton doubted he would see anyone for the next ten miles. Which was all he needed. From that point, a right turn onto the adjoining highway would place him on a collision course with Damascus.

The big Ural rumbled southward in a riot of noise and flapping canvas, its suspension groaning under the weight of more than two tons of rockets. In the truck's wake, the flag of Hezbollah snapped smartly in the soft night air.

TWENTY-FOUR

The three Iranians left Khartoum's Corinthia Hotel well before dawn, all looking weary as they passed beneath the great modernist portico. Their rented Land Rover was in the parking lot, and as they slid inside three sets of eyes squinted against a dome light that seemed inordinately bright.

The call had come thirty minutes ago, waking them out of a sound sleep—directions for a second rendezvous.

"I hope we have better luck than yesterday," grumbled the leader from the front passenger seat. "Seven hours in this damned car, and nothing to show for it."

"Considering what we are taking possession of," said the driver, who was in charge of security, "I am glad the Russians are being careful."

The third man, who was the technician, said nothing. He'd always been the least social of the bunch, and his reticence this morning was magnified by a raging hangover. After yesterday's frustration, they'd all gone to the hotel bar, and "one drink" had led to far too many. Alcohol was generally prohibited in Sudan, just as it was in Iran. Yet in the capital city certain allowances were made for foreigners. And what their controllers back in Tehran didn't know wouldn't hurt them.

The driver turned on the GPS receiver, turned off the radio, and set out into the still-black morning. The other two settled back for what promised to be another long day of driving.

As the Land Rover turned west onto the main road, it was watched carefully from the window of room 442. The housekeeper, whose name was Yusra, waited until the SUV was completely out of sight. Once it was, she went to the hall and used her passkey to enter 444—directly next door.

Yusra closed the door behind her, let her eyes drift across the room. She couldn't contain a heavy sigh. The place was a mess. The Iranians had been complete slobs since arriving. Each man had his own room, but they all looked the same: food trays and trash and towels strewn everywhere. Today she saw an empty gin bottle next to this one's bed, and the place smelled like someone had vomited. Every day it was something new, and so far not even a dollar left for gratuity. Truth be told, Yusra felt a bit of satisfaction in what she was about to do.

She ignored the mess for the time being—she would come around later with her cart, after the morning shift started—and headed straight to the bathroom. From her apron pocket Yusra removed the kit she'd been given. She followed her instructions to the letter. First she removed a pair of nitrile gloves and snapped one on each hand before extracting the set of tweezers. The kit contained three sturdy Ziploc bags, already labeled 1, 2, and 3. Room 444 correlated to number 1, and she set that bag on the sink counter. Having already performed one collection yesterday, she knew it was important not to mix the samples.

Yusra was not an educated woman, yet she'd seen enough Hollywood movies to understand, at least in a general sense, what she was being asked to do. She began at the tub drain. Two days ago there had been nothing but a hole, but the man who'd hired her had provided three special metal screens, one for each room, that fit perfectly over the drains. She checked the screen and saw two hairs, one long and straight, the other short and curly. She put them into the bag using the tweezers. She collected another hair from the floor near the toilet, and two from the sink counter.

From her apron pocket she removed a disposable razor and a toothbrush. Both were freebies provided by the hotel, and still in their cellophane packaging. What the Iranian guests couldn't know was that the sundries, while complimentary, were generally provided only upon request, a bit of emergency aid for travelers whose luggage had been lost. As a housekeeper, of course, Yusra had access to an unlimited supply, and she'd been instructed to provide a fresh item to each man every day.

Yesterday's razor and toothbrush, both of which appeared to have been used, went into the bag labeled 1. She placed the new razor and toothbrush on the counter.

Going over the rest of the room, she collected one more hair from the bed. Yusra was ready to move on to the next room when she was again struck by the sour scent of alcohol-infused bile. She looked around and finally saw the source. Someone—most likely the room's occupant—had thrown up in the ice bucket. This gave pause. The man who'd hired her had been generous, and she recalled that he'd promised a bonus for any blood or fecal samples. She wondered if drunken vomit was in the same category. It was a fleeting thought, but then the housekeeper in her took hold. She emptied the putrid bucket into the toilet, flushed, then filled it with water at the tub. She would deal with the rest later.

Yusra went to the window and checked the parking lot. She saw no sign of the Land Rover. Yesterday they'd been gone nearly eight hours. All she needed was another twenty minutes. She slipped into the hall and gasped when she almost ran into someone.

She was relieved—only just—to see that it was Emil, the vile old Eritrean who kept the toilets flushing. He leered at her unabashedly.

Yusra gave him her haughtiest look before turning down the hall. She quickly disappeared into the next room.

TWENTY-FIVE

Morning was barely a promise when the glow of Damascus first came into view. By the time Slaton had the Ural rumbling into the city's outskirts, only a few of the most stubborn stars remained in the brightening sky overhead. The rising sun was low at his back, which was always an advantage—like a fighter pilot sneaking up on an unsuspecting adversary. At that early hour there were few vehicles on the road, and those he did see were strictly civilian. His run of good fortune ended at the edge of the first official township.

Slaton spotted a checkpoint ahead near a gentle bend in the road.

He slowed to a judicious speed, donned a pair of cheap sunglasses he'd found on the truck's glare shield. He pulled the hood of his jacket completely over his head—his hair and skin were too light to blend in locally, and his limited Arabic would be a dead giveaway if he were challenged. Slaton was running a calculated risk: in his experience, a military truck flying the Hezbollah flag would not be stopped by the police. He'd seen it before in the course of Mossad missions. But had something changed in recent years? Was there a new dynamic between the two forces after so many years of war? He was betting heavily against it.

All the same, the MP5 was ready on the seat next to him, secured with the muzzle down. He'd removed the thigh holster, but the Sig was in the right thigh pocket of his cargo pants. And the Shmel-M rocket? That was pure overkill.

He quickly discerned two police vehicles. A pair of men stood beside the road, machine pistols hanging loosely across their chests. A third uniformed officer was leaning casually on the fender of one of the cars. Slaton was, if there could be such a thing, something of an expert on the subject of roadblocks. He knew that good ones could be all but impenetrable. He knew that most were something else.

What he saw from a distance was a catalogue of shortcomings. The cars were not *in* the road, but parked parallel on either side. There were no secondary barriers or backup units nearby. On appearances the men might have been waiting for a bus, their posture slouched and relaxed. What little attention he saw was focused in the other direction, on traffic coming *from* the city. This was telling. Combined with the lack of barriers, it implied a temporary checkpoint. Slaton wondered if it had anything to do with Ludmilla Kravchuk. Sorensen had told him the Syrians were searching for her, and this might well be part of the strategy. He hoped that was the case. It would mean they hadn't found her yet. It would also make getting *into* the city easier.

Getting out would be another story.

Slaton downshifted to a lower gear, and the pitch of the big diesel rose. As expected, it got the policemen's attention. All three turned and stared at the approaching truck, flying the Hezbollah flag.

Slaton's eyes were fixed on the road beyond. In the distance he saw two cars nearing. He slowed further, needing time to evaluate the geometry. One of the cars was a taxi, the other a dated sedan.

He was half a mile from the checkpoint, the two approaching cars somewhat less in the other direction. One of the policemen noticed the cars, and he directed everyone's attention toward them. The two men with weapons stepped into the middle of the road. The officer pushed away from the fender. He glanced back once at the Ural, but the focus was clearly in the other direction.

More proof of where the scrutiny lay.

Slaton governed his speed carefully. With a hundred yards to go, the taxi reached the checkpoint and came to a stop. The two policemen in the road began circling the vehicle, searching in earnest. The second car came to a halt behind the first, waiting its turn. The taxi driver got out and opened his trunk. This was no random shakedown—they were searching for something specific.

Someone specific. The importance of Ludmilla Kravchuk, and what she might know, was being reinforced before his eyes.

A hundred feet away, Slaton had the truck down to jogging speed. The officer glanced at him once, but nothing more. Thankfully, he never raised a hand for Slaton to stop. The gap in the road was wide enough for the Ural to pass. Slaton sped up slightly. Two truck-lengths away, he revved the engine and played the clutch to maximize the noise and commotion. The policemen couldn't talk to one another if they wanted to. A cloud of black smoke spewed from the exhaust.

The Ural arrived in a flurry of dust and diesel fumes. Passing only yards from the nearest policeman, Slaton raised his fist out the window, angled precisely to help conceal his face. He shouted one of the few Arabic phrases he could deliver convincingly.

"Allahu Akbar!"

He imagined that these policemen, like most Syrians, would agree that God was great. And like most Syrians, they would have little patience for the zealots of the self-proclaimed Party of God.

The officer waved him onward, turning his head away from a belching cloud of smoke. For his part, Slaton breathed much more freely. As the checkpoint receded in the tall driver's-side mirror, he shifted his attention ahead. Rising in front of him, like a great earthen jungle, was the war-torn city of Damascus.

TWENTY-SIX

At the same moment Slaton was violating one of his checkpoints, Inspector Hadad heard, "She has lived in Syria before!"

Hadad looked up from his desk.

Vasiliev, the ill-mannered Russian, was barging into his office. He wore a fearsome expression, although given his coal-black beard and stormy features, Hadad doubted he could have appeared otherwise. His arrival was not unexpected—the odd investigative couple had agreed to an early meeting.

"What are you talking about?" Hadad asked.

Vasiliev searched for a place to drop a folder—Hadad's desk was a shipwreck of files. "I only recently learned of her history," he said. "Kravchuk was posted to our embassy here three years ago."

"She *lived* in Damascus?" Hadad asked incredulously.

Vasiliev nodded.

The search was still not going well. For four days the city had been locked down, and the police and Mukhabarat had been rousting entire neighborhoods. They so far had nothing to show for their efforts. Hadad opened the file and began to read. He said nothing for almost a minute, then slapped the folder closed. "I have been searching every car leaving Damascus since Monday . . . and *now* you tell me she might have friends here?"

"I went through the file myself, but see no one who is likely to be harboring her. Yet there is an address, the apartment building where she used to live. Start there, question her neighbors. You might find something useful. Maybe ideas about who would give her refuge."

Hadad had taken on a crimson shade. With forced calm, he said, "Go back to your embassy and find out what else I haven't been told! Perhaps she has a Syrian lover as well!"

The Russian glowered, then turned on a heel and left.

Hadad stared blankly at the file.

I need to find this damned woman!

He picked up his phone and began making calls.

Overdue as the lead was, Hadad was happy to have *something* to chase.

He immediately mustered a squad and set out to the building where Kravchuk had lived, three years earlier, during her posting to the Russian embassy. They started by rousting the building's owner, who easily produced records showing that the interpreter had indeed rented a small flat on the third floor. The room was presently let to a Lebanese businessman. Hadad doubted a search of the place would turn up anything useful. More relevant, in his mind, were the units on either side. Both were occupied by long-term tenants who, according to the owner, had been friendly with Kravchuk during her time there.

After some deliberation, Hadad decided the right tone should be set through brute force. Two tactical squads were organized and, simultaneously, the doors of both flats kicked in. The residents—an elderly couple in one, a twice-divorced schoolteacher in the other—were taken completely by surprise. This, of course, was part of the method. An invasion by armed police was always an attention-getter, particularly in a place like Syria where the notion of due process was aspirational at best.

News of the raid—there was no other word—tsunamied quickly through the rest of the building. There was no sign of Ludmilla Kravchuk—Hadad had never expected to be so lucky, but hope sprang eternal. As reality took its grim hold, the on-site interviews began. As it turned out, six of the building's current residents remembered the quiet Russian interpreter. None confessed to seeing her in the years since she'd left.

Most of those interviewed spoke freely, the rest fearfully. Those who showed the slightest reluctance were given an ultimatum: declare everything they knew immediately, or be escorted to the basement of the district station for more spirited questioning. Any remaining reservations were fast resolved. Within two hours the interrogators had all they would ever get, and it was not without use. They learned which restaurants Kravchuk had frequented, which dry cleaner she used, and where she'd gotten repairs to her beaten old Volkswagen. They also extracted the name of a local librarian who was the only close friend anyone could remember.

The librarian, unfortunately, turned out to be a dead end, the woman having perished last year from a staph infection gone systemic—the kind of thing that rarely happened outside war zones, but that took its toll in times of government-imposed austerity. The last morsel of information came from the schoolteacher. She said Kravchuk had kept regular hair appointments at a nearby salon. To Hadad's frustration, the woman couldn't remember the name of the place, and a quick check of his phone showed more than twenty within a two-mile radius.

He put the salon on his list of things to track down—directly beneath nine restaurants, one dry cleaner, and an auto repair shop, all of whose names he already knew.

The city rose promptly at daybreak.

Ludmilla Kravchuk did not. She lay on the collapsed mattress, studying the water-stained ceiling above in dim light. She had stirred awake on a dream of better days. Parts of it were familiar, recurring. The house on the Black Sea where she and her husband had spent their honeymoon. The two of them walking paths on the nearby cliffs through an evergreen forest, no other people in sight.

They had never gone back after that halcyon week. Never so much as talked about doing so. In the years since Grishka's death, as she lay awake at night, trying and trying to sleep, Ludmilla often found herself going back. Forever walking through the low hills, breathing in the briny air. There had been something inordinately Russian about the place. Something enduring.

Now, however, everything had changed. She knew she would never go back. She had lost the only dream she'd ever had. Yet it might not be a bad thing. Perhaps the house on the Black Sea would be replaced by something new. Something better.

She thought about Salma. She too had lost her husband, but at least she had Naji. Ludmilla wondered if she might meet someone to share the coming years with. Perhaps there was a chance—if she could only escape Damascus.

She stared at the room's only window. Outside, the new morning was muted under a nickel-gray sky.

Ludmilla waited.

For what or who, she didn't know.

Slaton carefully guided the big truck into the center of town. He was not overly restrained, and certainly not reckless. To anyone watching, he handled the Ural precisely as any junior enlisted man in Hezbollah would: with a duty-bound furtherance of the will of God.

The city was busy, heavy traffic in spots and bustling sidewalks. The war was easing, fuel becoming available. Spare parts for cars were getting through, and sons were being granted leave from the hot spots in the north. Not life as it had been, but traces of normalcy returning.

Ludmilla Kravchuk was supposedly holed up in the Al Salhiyeh district. Slaton had committed the address to memory, and he'd spent hours studying overheads of the surrounding area. He'd seen right away that the building could never be reached covertly. That being the case, he'd settled on the other extreme—overtness. He would make his approach by hiding in plain sight.

He bypassed the Citadel of Damascus, the one-time residence of Saladin, leader of the first battles against the Crusaders, and crossed the Barada River on the shoulder of the Old City. For the first time since calling in a simulated airstrike hours earlier, he turned on his CIA-issued phone. At this point, he reckoned the risk from being tracked was less than that of making a wrong turn—to put this rig into a dead-end street, especially given the load he was carrying, could prove a fatal mistake.

He'd had a handful of interactions since arriving in town, none of which were surprising. Most of those on the sidewalk paid him little attention—military vehicles were a ubiquitous presence throughout the country. Hezbollah, however, was not a fixture in the capital. Those who did look his way had varied reactions. Hezbollah was an indigenous faction in Syria, but one that was widely viewed as being bought and paid for by Iran. Slaton saw a few supportive raised fists, but far more indecent gestures. He returned them all in kind—again, exactly as a low-ranking militia driver would.

Ten minutes after crossing the river he was rumbling through Al Salhiyeh. Soon after that, Slaton got his first look at the building in question. What he saw, unfortunately, caused him to drive straight past.

TWENTY-SEVEN

The police car was parked directly across the street from Chez Salma, hard against the curb in front of a European-themed restaurant. Slaton's initial reaction was guarded, and he passed without slowing. Then in his mirror he saw two policemen emerge from the restaurant.

This brought relief, if not outright encouragement. A patrol car would never have been dispatched here if the authorities suspected the interpreter was hiding nearby. Moreover, if Kravchuk had already been found and detained, the Mukhabarat would be watching the place like hawks. No uniform would be allowed anywhere near.

Slaton rounded the block at a crawl. By the time he again reached Kravchuk's address, the patrol car had departed, a blue-and-white speck in the distant traffic. He parked across the street, one shopfront removed from the restaurant—which turned out to be a secondhand furniture store.

He set the parking brake and studied Chez Salma. Lights were burning in the salon's first-floor window, and the front door was blocked open with a brick. Kravchuk had told her Czech contact she was staying on the floor above. Slaton saw two second-floor windows facing the street. Neither was open, but even in daylight the room on the right was full of diffuse white light. He had no idea if that was the correct flat, or even how many rooms were in the place. He'd never been given a room number, and had no way to contact Kravchuk. Sorensen had searched for a floorplan for the building, explaining that the NSA had hacked into many of Syria's municipal databases. Unfortunately, she'd come up empty on this address.

Slaton considered the salon's invitingly open front door. Try as he might, he could imagine no pretense of walking inside that wouldn't lead to a conversation in Arabic. He needed another way to get inside the building. Was there a fire escape in back? He couldn't see much of the roof, but the neighboring building to the north might give access.

He simply had to find a way. And he had to find it before he got out of the truck. Once his boots hit the sidewalk, the risk level ramped up exponentially. Anyone might stop him to strike up a conversation. A zealous teenager wanting to join Hezbollah. A widow with a question about the militia's food handouts. Slaton would ignore any such approaches, but that might not solve the problem.

He stared at the two high windows. They glared back invitingly. So close, yet so far.

The good news was that things seemed quiet. He'd caught no glints from windows across the street. Saw no suspicious vehicles along the curbs. Slaton glanced down at the seat next to him. A blanket covered both his MP5 and the rocket launcher he'd plundered from the arsenal in back.

He pocketed the truck's key. When the time came, he would leave the cab unlocked. War-torn Damascus might be rife with petty crime, but even the most adventurous thief would steer clear of a truck full of weapons flying the Hezbollah flag.

He looked down the street in both directions, saw nothing inspirational. Then he checked the first side street, and his gaze settled on a large work truck. He actually couldn't see the vehicle directly, only the front bumper and grille. Yet an image of the rest was clear, reflected in the broad window of a corner grocer. And there, glimmering like a mirage in the midday heat, Slaton saw the answer to his dilemma.

Mustafa Barak secured the arm of his truck in its cradle, then powered down the hydraulics. He climbed down from the bucket to street level and found the black-jacketed young man waiting.

"It works!" his customer remarked.

"Of course it works," Mustafa responded. He edged between his truck and the building, a narrow gap where there was no sidewalk.

The black jacket followed him into the shadows. No one on the nearby street could possibly see them. Mustafa held out his hand, and the young man filled it with a wad of U.S. dollars—Syrian pounds were always second choice.

Mustafa had worked for the Ministry of Electricity for twenty-five years, long enough to know that no lineman could make a decent living without a bit of work on the side. He paid his dispatcher a kickback to keep his schedule relatively light. In most months, Mustafa made twice his regular wage from what he called his "concierge work." Power lines had long been strung over Damascus like a dropped bowl of spaghetti. Those who knew what they were doing tapped into the main lines themselves. Those who didn't fell into three camps. A few connected to power the official way and received a ruinous electric bill every month. Others engaged linemen like Mustafa. It was the third group who were the least fortunate— they suffered electrocution.

"My brother-in-law called," said the black jacket. "He also would like you to install a line."

"Where does he live?" Mustafa asked.

The young man edged out of the shadows and pointed to a window two buildings down.

"Okay, but the price will be double."

"Why?"

"Because I'm sure you didn't tell him what you paid."

The young man looked at him, then couldn't contain a smile.

"Can he have the money within the hour?" Mustafa asked.

"Sure."

"Then I'll take care of it after lunch."

The young man walked off, and just then Mustafa's partner, a new kid named Ahmed, bounded down from the cab of the truck. He'd been on his phone for the last ten minutes. Mustafa peeled off Ahmed's share: one-quarter of the take. Seniority had its privileges, and the dispatcher had to be paid.

"Easy money," said the kid, beaming like a dog getting a treat.

"As ever." Mustafa handed over the cash. He looked up the street once, then said, "We are ahead of schedule. Let's take a long lunch today."

Ahmed's smile widened further—as Mustafa knew it would. The kid had been seeing a girl who lived only a few blocks away, in the center of their usual territory. Her parents both worked during the day, and whenever Ahmed was allotted an extended lunch break, he invariably succumbed to appetites that had nothing to do with food.

"When should I be back?" he asked.

Mustafa considered the new job. He could easily manage it alone, and still have time for a kebab. "Two hours," he said.

"Two hours?" Ahmed looked like he might explode. Mustafa hoped the poor girl was as fervent as her boyfriend. Ahmed tossed his hard hat and yellow vest into the cab, and Mustafa watched him set off down the street.

He retrieved a pair of traffic cones, then edged back between the truck and the building. Looking up the street through the narrow gap, he noticed a tall man wearing a hooded camo jacket walking toward him.

Mustafa sighed. *Some days, some neighborhoods. I could get rich if I had the time.* As he threw the cones onto the truck, he debated whether he wanted any more work that day. By the time Ahmed got back, he decided, they would have to tackle their real schedule.

He turned toward the approaching man, and was halfway through the motion when he had the distinct impression that a sledgehammer had struck his crotch. Mustafa doubled over, retching in pain. His vision went to a blur. When focus began to return, the first thing he saw was his hard hat spinning on the pavement like a child's top.

Then everything went black.

TWENTY-EIGHT

Ludmilla sat looking at the empty teacup on the table in front of her. The lump of a twice-used tea bag sat cold and wet in its center. She was wondering whether she might be able to pilfer something from the coffee machine downstairs when a thump from behind startled her.

She turned toward the window and was stunned to see a man waving at her from outside. He appeared to be hovering in midair, like a superhero in an action movie. Only he was wearing a yellow vest and a hard hat. Then she noticed a plastic panel in front of his thighs. Ludmilla stood, saw more of the picture, and finally realized what she was looking at—a worker in the bucket of a cherry picker.

He was manipulating a controller with one hand, and the platform wobbled slightly before grounding against the window. The man was looking straight at her. Her thoughts went into overdrive. If she were in her apartment in Moscow, Ludmilla would have no doubt that he was a window washer or repairman. Or in the worst case, given how he was staring at her, perhaps a voyeur. In her present circumstances, however, she knew better. Was this a raid by the police? Had they managed to track her here? Ludmilla instinctively stepped back. She weighed dashing for the door. The window was closed and locked, but that was hardly a comfort.

Before she could settle on a response, the man began deliberately mouthing something. Like any good interpreter, she had a knack for reading lips. She made out the individual letters *L, U, D, M* . . .

He was mouthing her name.

She took one cautious step toward the window.

He mimed opening it. Ludmilla noticed that his movement inside the plastic bucket seemed constrained, as if something else was inside. She took another step toward the window. The man put his face very close to the glass. He said something aloud, muffled words that penetrated faintly through the thick pane.

"The Americans sent me! I'm here to help you!"

The telling break in Inspector Hadad's search came from a source, he later realized, that he should have leveraged sooner: Vasiliev the irksome Russian.

Hadad had called Petrov's man twice that morning to fill him in on what they'd learned from the raid on Kravchuk's old building. He was in his office, having just refilled his coffee mug, when a call came in the other direction.

"I have been interviewing embassy personnel," Vasiliev said. "Three remain from the days when Kravchuk was assigned there. One of them, a receptionist who is a local contract employee, claimed to be quite friendly with her. I mentioned what you told me earlier, and she said she might know the hair salon—apparently Kravchuk asked for a recommendation, and the receptionist gave her one. Over time she gained the impression that Kravchuk and the owner had become friends."

"What is the name of the salon?"

"Chez Salma. This receptionist still goes there, and she mentioned something else—apparently the owner lets out two rooms above her shop."

Hadad cursed inwardly—he'd let his dislike of Vasiliev cloud his vision. "Very well. I will investigate immediately."

"I was thinking of going myself—" Vasiliev began.

"Absolutely not!" Hadad barked. If Kravchuk *was* at the salon, the last thing he wanted was a band of Russian intelligence thugs barging in. The phone remained silent, and Hadad began to have second thoughts. He knew the matter of the wayward interpreter was playing out far above either of their pay grades. For the sake of his career, he said, "I will call back as soon as we have her. But stay out of the way and let us handle it!"

Hadad rang off and made a call to the operations center. He was informed that two patrol units were nearby and could reach the address within minutes. "Order it! Tell them to seal off the building!"

He tore his coat from a hook and headed for the door.

Slaton grounded the bucket hard to the building, just below the frame of the window. Ludmilla Kravchuk pulled the window open like a damsel uncaging a lion in a circus show. She took a tentative step back, which was just as well—the first thing Slaton did was dump a body over the sill.

"*What . . . ?*" Kravchuk stood wide-eyed, staring at the lifeless form on the floor. He was wearing the uniform of a municipal worker.

Slaton straddled the bucket and stepped into the room. He regarded Kravchuk and decided she looked very much like the pictures from Sorensen's file. Solidly built, mid-forties, undeniably Slavic features. The only differences now were the natural results of stress. Deepened lines in her face, dark patches under her eyes, a hesitant posture.

"It's going to be okay," he said. "My name is David. I've been sent to get you out of here."

"My message got through?" she asked, still seeming uncertain.

"Yes, the one you sent through the Czechs."

She eyed him warily. "But you are not American."

"How do you know that?" he asked, not bothering to argue otherwise.

"I'm an interpreter. Languages are my specialty, and your accent is Continental." She looked expectantly out the window, and asked, "Are you alone?"

"For now, yes."

He took in the room at a glance. It was the kind of shoebox lodging that might have had a dozen tenants in the last year. What little furniture he saw was mismatched, piecemeal acquisitions left behind by previous renters or salvaged from an alley. The paint on the walls was flaking in spots, tiny reveals of drab green beneath a ten-year-old spruce-up of beige. The scent of the salon was unmistakable—a chemical stew of hair dye, gel, and floral-scented shampoo.

Slaton dragged the unconscious man into a corner. Back at the window he glanced outside, then collected the rest of what was in the lift's bucket—wrapped in an olive blanket like a sleeping toddler, one MP5 and one grenade launcher. He took a more careful look up and down the street. The man he'd taken out had a partner, and there was no telling how soon he would return. Some interval, he guessed, between retrieving a takeout lunch and addressing a call of nature. Slaton knew the two were freelancing, which was endemic throughout the region—municipal employees augmenting their inflation-racked paychecks by squeezing in private jobs. The man he'd overpowered was obviously the senior of the two. That being the case, the fact that the truck had moved slightly up the road, and was now apparently engaged in a new job would hardly be unusual.

The man's disappearance, however, would be.

"Is he dead?" Kravchuk asked. Her English was effortless, only a mild accent.

"No," he said truthfully, not speculating on his victim's long-term prognosis. "Are you alone here?"

"Yes."

"Is the front door locked?"

"Of course."

"Is there any other way into the room?"

"No, except . . . the one you took."

She was frozen, still staring at the man in the corner. He hadn't stirred, but he seemed to be breathing. A goose egg on his skull had stopped bleeding. Slaton gave the interpreter his most reassuring smile. "Look, it's going to be okay," he said a second time.

She finally met his eyes and seemed to ratchet down a notch.

"He's unconscious, but I don't know for how long. I need to make sure he's restrained."

Slaton went to the kitchen and began rummaging through drawers. He came back with an electrical extension cord, a roll of packing tape, and a dishrag.

He rolled the man onto his stomach, wrenched his hands behind his back, and bound them with the electrical cord—a harsh irony, given his profession. The dishrag he taped over the man's mouth as a gag, making sure he could still breathe through his nose. Slaton hurried to the only closet in sight, opened the door, and was happy to find it empty. He dragged the man over and shoved him inside, propping him in the corner in a sitting position—the best option to keep his airway open. His victim began to stir, emitting a low groan.

Slaton closed the door. *Out of sight, out of mind.*

He returned to the window, sided up to the frame, and peered outside. A police car had appeared directly below on the street. An officer was standing at the driver's door talking on a mobile phone. *Not good.*

"We need to move," he said, stripping off and discarding the yellow vest and hard hat he'd appropriated from the truck. He had already ditched his camo jacket, which wouldn't have worked with the rest.

"Move?" she asked. "How?"

"I don't know."

Kravchuk seemed disappointed. She was probably expecting the imminent arrival of a black helicopter on the roof. Slaton only wished it were so easy. He also wished he could debrief Kravchuk right now, go over at least the basics of her story. There simply wasn't time. Yet he did need to cover one thing.

"You said you had a recording of a meeting between the presidents."

"Yes." Ludmilla led him to the tiny kitchen table. There Slaton saw a disassembled shoe. Its heel was detached but remained connected to the rest by a wire. He picked it up carefully. A circuit board and tiny memory card had been artfully crafted into the one-inch block heel.

"I was given these shoes," she said. "They told me to wear them to the meeting. I had no idea they contained a recording device—not until I arrived here."

"Are you sure it worked? Have you checked what's on the card?"

"No. I wanted to, but I'm not very good at that kind of thing."

Slaton picked up the shoe. He ripped the heel free, separating the circuitry and SD card—the rest, he was sure, was nothing more than a microphone which was of little intelligence value. He stuffed the heel into the hip pocket of his cargo pants.

Ludmilla looked at him suspiciously.

"It makes more sense for me to keep it," he said. "If we get separated, you have a first-hand account of the meeting. I'll have the recording. It doubles our chance of getting the information out."

He knew his math was dubious, and the question of why they

might get separated he left unaddressed. All the same, the logic seemed to quell her reservations.

More commotion outside, tires scrubbing over asphalt.

"Why did you choose this place?" he asked sharply.

"What do you mean?"

She sensed his urgency but seemed confused. It struck Slaton that the challenges in his situation were mounting—and very quickly. The police could arrive en masse at any moment. Kravchuk wasn't in a good frame of mind. He noticed she was wearing a pair of running shoes, which seemed oddly appropriate, even if they didn't match the sedate dress she was wearing. She suddenly seemed to gain confidence.

"The owner of the salon is an old friend," she said. "I recalled that she rented out rooms above her shop . . . it was the safest place I could think of."

He considered it. "How did you get to be friends with a stylist in Damascus?"

"I was a regular customer when I was posted here at the embassy."

"Is she making you pay for the room?" he asked, wanting to establish the depth of their friendship.

"She took some money, yes. But that doesn't mean we aren't—"

"Does she have a car?"

"I don't know. She used to, but that was years ago."

Slaton did his best to recall the satellite images of the building. He remembered an alley behind the salon, a few cars parked among the trash bins and debris. Unfortunately, the aspect of Sorensen's overheads had been limited. He hadn't been able to confirm points of entry into the building.

"Does the salon have a back door?"

"Yes. I checked myself after Salma closed on the first night. It's through the storage room at the base of the stairs."

Slaton was encouraged—not only for the fact that there *was* a back door, but because Kravchuk was showing a few instincts after all.

He pulled a thick wad of Syrian pounds from his pocket, cut it, and put half in her hand. "Here's what I need you to do . . ."

TWENTY-NINE

Ludmilla rushed downstairs and found Salma in the middle of a balayage. Her assistant, Malika, was sweeping up beneath another stylist's chair. Naji was sitting quietly on a tiny wooden stool in the corner—he was looking at a Dr. Seuss book, holding it upside down.

Ludmilla approached her friend with an urgency she didn't have to manufacture. "Salma, I need a favor. It's very important."

The highlighting brush paused.

"One of my old friends from the embassy has fallen ill. She lives across town, and I may need to take her to the hospital. If you still have your car, I'd very much like to borrow it."

Before Salma could answer, Ludmilla discreetly held out the cash Slaton had given her. Salma looked at the cash, then outside. A police car was visible through the wide shopfront window. She looked back at Ludmilla skeptically.

Ludmilla tried to think of something credible to say. Nothing came to mind.

Salma left her customer, nodding for Ludmilla to follow. At the back of the shop, near the stairs, Salma said, "A friend called me this morning, the owner of a salon a few streets away. She said the police had come by. They asked her if she'd ever had a woman customer from the Russian embassy."

Ludmilla remained silent.

"Of course, she told them no. But she remembered that I had once mentioned a regular who was Russian."

Ludmilla asked cautiously, "Did you tell her I was here?"

Salma looked at Naji who was now running a plastic car up the wall. Watching him with a vacant gaze, she said in a whisper, "I never told you *how* his father died."

"No . . . you didn't."

"The army conscripted Adil two years ago. They said if he could drive a bus for the city, he could drive one for the army just as well. He was forty-three years old, a peaceable man. He tried to get out of it, but of course they didn't listen. The Alawites gave him a uniform, and two days later he was transporting soldiers from one battle to the next. He did what they asked for six months. Then one Saturday morning, outside Aleppo, Adil drove straight over a bomb that had been buried in the road. He was the only one on the bus."

Ludmilla could think of nothing to say.

Salma ignored the cash. "I still have the car." She went to a nearby counter and pulled a key from a drawer. "Where will you go?"

Ludmilla hesitated, then said, "I'm not sure. There is a man upstairs, an American. He has come to help me get out of the country."

Salma straightened. *"An American?* In your room? But how did he—"

"Please, there's no time to explain!" Ludmilla looked plaintively at the front window. The police car sat like an omen.

Salma's gaze fell to Naji. After a prolonged silence, she said, "I will give you my car. But I want something in return . . ."

Slaton realized his run of luck had ended when the third police car arrived.

The first hadn't moved—it was parked not far behind the Ural. Two more had appeared up the street to the right, and now four uniformed officers were huddled in an impromptu conference. One was talking on his mobile.

Slaton turned away from the window and glanced hopefully at the door behind him. Kravchuk was supposed to retrieve him once she'd gotten the keys to the car—assuming there *was* a car. How long had she been gone? Five minutes? Six? He wanted to keep an eye on the situation outside, but time was becoming critical.

He looked again to the street. The Ural was directly across from the window, no more than a hundred feet away. The nearest police car was twenty feet behind it, the other two fifty yards farther back. He leaned tentatively out the window, just far enough to survey the street in both directions. He spotted more trouble on the right, two big sedans lacing through traffic.

He looked again at the door, willing it to open.

The little group of policemen remained in their huddle, like a group of referees trying to agree on a call. All of a sudden, one seemed to notice the cherry picker with its bucket grounded to the window above the salon.

Time was up.

Slaton reached down and selected his weapon. He'd brought both the MP5 and the rocket launcher, hoping to use neither but keeping his options open. Now his hand was being forced. He prepped the rocket launcher, and was arcing it toward the window when he heard hard steps on the stairs.

Too heavy and quick to be Kravchuk's?

He immediately switched to the MP5 and trained it across the room. The door burst open. Ludmilla appeared, completely out of breath. As if not realizing she was looking down the barrel of a gun, she said, "We can go now!"

Had she come ten seconds sooner, they might have done just that.

"There is the building, just ahead!" said Inspector Hadad's driver.

Hadad was in the back seat of the leading sedan, another unmarked unit behind them. He cursed when he saw the scene. Three patrol cars were parked along the street in front of the salon. He'd wanted to contain the building quickly, but now he realized he should have told the uniforms to stay out of sight.

"Stop!" Hadad shouted.

The driver complied.

Hadad got out and stood in the street for a moment to take in the scene. He saw the salon's front door, its streetside window. One of the black-and-whites was parked directly across the street. He also saw the mouth of an alley behind. He cursed under his breath and got back in the car.

"There is an alley in back!" he said. "We must contain every escape!"

He used the radio to send the trailing car ahead to cover the back. It quickly shot past toward the top of the alley.

Altogether, there were seven men in the two unmarked sedans. All were so focused on the front entrance and the alley that no one gave a second thought to the truck from the Ministry of Electricity parked next to the building, its lift extended to an open second-floor window.

Also ignored: the military troop carrier, flying a Hezbollah flag, that was parked diagonally across the street.

THIRTY

"Salma's car is in the alley!" Ludmilla said. "But we must hurry—the police are outside!"

Slaton didn't bother to explain that he was intimately aware of the tactical picture. There was an impulse to stand down and egress. The ride they needed was waiting. A clean escape in hand.

One last look outside changed his mind.

The sedans were very close, and multiple silhouettes inside confirmed they were delivering trouble: men presumably more formidably armed, and better trained, than the street cops outside.

As if to prove the point, both sedans skidded to a hard stop. The back door of one opened and a man stepped out to survey the situation. Slaton edged away from the window, but kept watching. The man was thin and agile, his eyes alert behind wire-framed glasses. He wasted little time with his evaluation, soon disappearing back into the car. Moments later, certainly after coordinating by radio, the trailing car leapfrogged ahead. It slowed enough to climb a curb and bypass traffic, the dark shape of the driver mirroring every jolt. The other sedan didn't move.

Slaton knew immediately what was happening—one car was advancing to block the alley, while the other remained in front. A textbook move for secret police the world over. The second car swerved amid traffic, the engine revving. In a matter of seconds, it would pass the Ural. A few beats later, the car would blockade the alley—all before he and Ludmilla could even get downstairs.

Their best avenue of escape was about to be shut down.

"Go down and start the car!" he shouted. "I'll be right behind you!"

Thankfully, Kravchuk disappeared without a word.

Slaton lifted the rocket launcher a second time. As he scanned outside he saw the policemen on the sidewalk, but no bystanders in the immediate area. This made his calculus even easier.

He rotated the grip into place and flipped up the optical sight. He'd chosen the M-model for its larger thermobaric warhead—twelve pounds of high-explosives that packed the same punch as a 155mm artillery shell.

The inaptness of the weapon didn't escape him. Slaton was a highly trained sniper, virtually peerless when it came to precision shooting. This was anything but. The system in his hands had an effective range of six hundred yards, but was essentially a point and shoot weapon. No wires or lasers. No guidance of any kind. Only ballistics and Kentucky windage. He looked at the scene through the window and decided it hardly mattered. With his target no more than forty yards away, the recommended *minimum* range was of greater concern—the distance at which an unprotected shooter risked fragging himself.

Slaton had only one shot. He settled the sight on his target, slightly above the passing sedan's hood, and depressed the trigger.

The results were instantaneous.

The solid-propellant engine ignited, creating an overpressure that blew the front and back discs clear of the launcher tube. As the rocket flew outbound, a plume of back-blast shrouded the room behind him.

In the time it took to blink, the rocket flew straight and true. It struck its target dead center.

The devastation that occurred in the next seconds was indistinguishable to the human eye. The projectile penetrated the Ural's canvas canopy uneventfully, but fused on contact with the first true resistance—the lid of one of the crates holding twelve incendiary Z-versions of the weapon. The initial explosion was predictable, a product of years of engineering: an immediate overpressure in the local area, followed by a perfectly shaped cone of speeding shrapnel.

What occurred next only a supercomputer could have modeled.

Within milliseconds, a half dozen warheads in the first crate exploded, adding to the growing fireball. At the same time, the propellant in three rocket motors ignited, launching those weapons into neighboring crates from a range of less than a yard. The reactions multiplied from there, and in less time than it took to draw a human breath, nearly a hundred rockets in the back of the Ural were in various stages of detonation creating a fireball that topped the adjacent buildings.

If the initial blast was spectacular, the aftermath was sporadic. The rockets that hadn't exploded right away began cooking off in the ensuing inferno. Secondary explosions were, as a rule, highly unpredictable. Slaton had seen ammo caches light off countless times in his career, and some were more spectacular than others. Less intense fires produced a slow burn, giving the potential of setting off rifle rounds hours after the initial blast. What Slaton saw now was closer to Chinese New Year.

The initial blast had upended the moving sedan, putting it on its side. This was probably fortunate for the car's occupants, since it allowed the chassis to absorb the subsequent storm of fire and shrapnel. Slaton saw two policemen down in the street. Another had thrown himself behind a now-smoldering patrol car. On the fringes people were running away, and every building in sight had been peppered by shrapnel. The Ural itself, ground zero, was barely recognizable, a flaming mass of metal with the occasional rocket whizzing outward. The world's biggest Roman candle sputtering to an end.

The street quickly vanished in boiling curtains of smoke, either gray or black depending on the source. Slaton would use that to its fullest advantage. He dropped the launcher tube, picked up the MP5, and ran for the door.

He had created a window of escape but it wouldn't last long. He took the stairs two at a time, turned left at the bottom. The back door was ajar and he flew outside. Slaton quickly spotted what had to be his ride, a dated tan Hyundai beside a dented dumpster. A trickle of gray smoke at the exhaust told him it was running, and Kravchuk had the car pointed toward the alley's exit. He ran flat out to the passenger door, flung it open, and settled into the seat with the MP5 in hand. The interpreter was indeed at the wheel. Only then did Slaton notice the car's other occupants. A thirtyish woman sat in back. She looked at him expectantly. At her side was a boy of no more than four. Her arm encircled him protectively.

"What the hell?" he said, his eyes going back and forth between Kravchuk and the two in back.

A great explosion reverberated, and shards of flaming debris spun through the street ahead.

Kravchuk said, "There is no time! I will explain later!"

Slaton didn't argue. "Okay . . . go, go!"

The engine revved and the Hyundai jumped toward the street. Kravchuk navigated around the hulk of a burning car that Slaton barely recognized—since he'd left the window, the second of the two sedans, the one that had been trying to blockade the alley, had taken a direct hit from a stray rocket. It was now on its roof, a smoldering mess. Up the street he saw a visual Hiroshima, cars scattered like bowling pins, smoke swirling and blooming. The Ural's body was ablaze, its cab unrecognizable. Part of the high frame was still intact, bent and twisted, and shreds of canopy lay over its smoldering skeleton.

"Turn here!" the woman in back commanded.

Kravchuk veered onto a secondary street, the Hyundai's tiny engine racing. Moments later, the chaos behind them was lost to sight.

Hadad was flat on the floor behind the shattered front seat, smoke swirling all around him. Through the ringing in his ears he heard shouting outside, the occasional muffled explosion. Still dangerous, but only a fraction of the hell that had been unleashing moments earlier.

He lifted his head tentatively. The first thing he saw was the fearful eyes of his driver—he and his partner were lying flat on the front bench seat, as much of their bodies as possible curled into the floor wells. Hadad looked out through the front windshield—or more precisely, the jagged cavity where it had been moments earlier.

Four cars lay flaming in the street. Two were overturned. The big military truck at ground zero looked as if it had melted. The body was charred and molten, the tires belching black smoke. The back canopy had been shredded, the remains fluttering over the wilted frame like a combover from the apocalypse. Hadad had no idea what just happened, but one inescapable thought rose to the forefront.

Ludmilla Kravchuk, the Russian interpreter he'd been chasing, was not alone. She had found some help.

THIRTY-ONE

Sultan arrived in Khartoum at nine o'clock that same morning via an air route that had taken less than three hours. He mused that his next crossing—the divide between Africa and the Arabian Peninsula—would prove far more daunting.

Since meeting with Petrov he'd been traveling non-stop. He'd been forced to spend last night in Dubai, having missed a connecting flight, yet he'd gotten a good night's sleep because of it. It was the last he would have for many days. He bypassed the rental car counter and headed straight to the main parking lot. The aged Fiat sedan, purchased one month ago, was right where he'd left it. He got in and immediately rolled down the windows, the heat inside being oppressive. Having spent most of his childhood in Jordan, nearly a thousand miles north, he was accustomed to having some manner of seasons. Here, on the threshold of the Sahara, there was only summer. He supposed it was just as well: Sultan would take any constant in a mission so fraught with variables. Just to be sure, he'd watched the forecast closely. For the next few days there would be no frontal weather, which even here could bring rain and wind.

Ideal conditions for his mission.

Traffic was light, and he made his first stop less than three miles from the airport. The Corinthia Hotel was centered in the business district, overlooking the confluence of the Blue and White Niles, and the cable-suspended Tuti Bridge. The hotel was among the most modern in the country, a hundred-million-dollar luxury project in a nation desperate to attract business and investment. Sultan thought it a hopeless undertaking, and to his eye the twelve-story façade seemed cast in the image of an obese robot—in all likelihood, not the architect's intent.

He parked behind the hotel, in a niche where a three-sided wall concealed a row of dumpsters. He got out, paused to survey the area, and saw nothing out of the ordinary. A pair of women with shopping bags were traversing the sidewalk of a distant overpass. Two blocks away, a short queue of taxis lay parked along a curb, the drivers leaning on fenders, huffing cigarettes, talking animatedly. He closed the gap to the hotel's service entrance, and as he did so the line of sight to all of them was cut off by a high block wall. On his first visit he'd verified there were no cameras nearby. This service bay, he was sure, was as discreet a meeting place as could be had within the bounds of hotel property.

He pulled out a burner phone and sent a three-word text message.

The maid arrived four minutes later. She stopped in front of him and smiled, probably because that was her nature. She was small and thinly framed, although there was nothing frail about her. He guessed her to be not much more than twenty years old, a clear-eyed and lively thing, imbued with the vitality of youth. Without so much as a greeting, she handed over a nylon grocery bag.

Such was the nature of their relationship.

He looked inside and saw the labeled plastic Ziplocs he'd given her, six in all. Through the clear plastic he inspected the contents of each, one by one. He saw multiple samples of hair. The razors and toothbrushes, of course, were a given.

"Numbers one and three provided the most," she said in Arabic. Her voice was surprisingly strong, her diction precise, albeit colored in her lilting Sudanese accent. Sultan was accustomed to more northern dialects, but communication was not an issue.

"No blood or feces?" he asked.

She showed no sign of distaste—nor had she when he'd first mentioned it. He'd surmised then, as now, that any housekeeper in a Sudanese hotel, even a young one, would hardly be put off stride by a few bodily fluids. As if to prove the point, she said, "I saw no evidence of those. One did vomit, but I wasn't sure if you would want that."

Sultan considered it. An interesting prospect, and one he hadn't considered. Bile would certainly be identifiable, but it might prove a contradiction for his specific purposes. "No, you did well."

She held out a hand for the balance of her payment. "If you ever need my help again, you have my number." She said it with the confident air of a car mechanic who'd just repaired a leaking radiator.

He set the shopping bag on the ground and reached into his pocket. "Actually, there is one more thing you can do for me."

Sultan's next movements came smoothly—he'd practiced them repeatedly in the mirror of his hotel room. He drew a sheaf of cash from his pocket, beneath which was concealed a hypodermic needle filled with an amber liquid. He held out cash at arm's length, in the way one might feed a bird in a park. When the girl reached out for the money, he flicked off the needle's plastic cover with a thumb, took one step toward her, and plunged the needle into the soft flesh of her outstretched forearm.

She pulled back, the look on her face more one of surprise than fear.

Sultan had no idea what was in the syringe. The Russian who'd supplied it had promised only two things: the agent would work quickly and, by any analysis, the victim would appear to have succumbed to heart failure.

The girl opened her mouth as if to say something, but no perfectly clipped words came forth. She listed to one side like a tree catching a gust of wind, then stumbled toward the great cinderblock wall. There her entire body went rigid, and she toppled toward him like a plank of lumber. He tried to catch her as she fell, not wanting any contusions to muddy the manner of her passing.

By the time she reached the ground, her breathing had shallowed out precipitously, tiny gasps beyond her control. Sultan waited, his eyes sweeping the surrounding area. They were still concealed by the high wall. A few ragged gasps came at the end before all life left her. Her almond-shaped eyes remained open, fixed in eternal astonishment.

He looked around, and decided to pull her body closer to the dumpster. He'd already decided that he wouldn't elaborate the scene with a trash can or spent vacuum cleaner bags—it would likely do more harm than good. After a final survey, he decided there was nothing more to be done. He pocketed the cash she'd never touched, then recovered the plastic cover to the hypodermic and capped the needle. He retrieved the bag and began walking calmly toward his car. If there was any remorse it was fleeting, overtaken by the satisfaction of a smooth operation. After so many years, so much preparation, his plan was finally under way.

Sultan looked over his shoulder only once. He had never killed anyone before, and was glad to have the first behind him. That, he'd been told, was the crucible. The moment a man realized what he was capable of.

Now he knew.

A good thing, given the magnitude of what was to come.

Sultan drove the Fiat across town, to the far western edge of what could still be called Khartoum. He turned into a latent industrial area that had, on appearances, fallen on hard times. He'd leased a storage garage from an enterprise at the back of the property, a half acre of corrugated lock-ups where in good times oil exploration and drilling companies warehoused pipes and trucks and machinery. And where, in less prosperous stretches, sheds were rented out unquestioningly to itinerant foreigners who needed storage space for no apparent reason.

He drew the Fiat to a stop next to a standard single-door unit. The compound looked deserted, as it had every time he'd come. Leaving the engine running, he removed a heavy padlock and rolled up the accordion metal door. There was enough space inside for both his vehicles, and he pulled the Fiat inside next to a beaten Toyota pickup truck. The truck had obvious aesthetic shortcomings, but was mechanically sound. Where Sultan was going, he couldn't afford a dead battery or a failed water pump.

After killing the Fiat's engine, he got out and set straight to work. He began with the Toyota, taking a careful look at what was in back. On his last visit he'd painstakingly inventoried the equipment in the bed. He double-checked now to make sure nothing was missing. Sudan was a thieves' paradise, and he'd had doubts as to whether the shed would be secure. As a telltale of sorts, he'd left a new iPhone in its original box on top of his heap of equipment, reasoning that no thief could resist such a valuable, easily marketable piece of electronic bling.

The box was still there. The phone was inside.

Sultan was glad nothing seemed to be missing. Much like the truck's mechanical condition, there were no hardware stores in the territory ahead to deal with shortcomings. Inventory complete, he pulled a tarp over the bed, covering it completely, and secured it with multiple tie-downs. The bag the housekeeper had given him went on the floor in the truck's cab. The key to the Fiat he decided to keep.

He cranked the Toyota to life and backed outside. Rolling down the shed's door, he resecured the heavy padlock. Sultan checked the time. Still on schedule. He'd paid for the shed through the end of next month, a transaction executed entirely by way of emails and wire transfers. Landlords rarely bothered with face-to-face meetings these days—particularly when euros were delivered in advance.

He put the truck in gear, its transmission shifting smoothly, and set out west toward the bleakness that was Darfur.

THIRTY-TWO

Ludmilla was driving, and to Slaton's eye doing a respectable job, keeping good positions in the flow of traffic. Better yet, she knew her way around the city. At that moment they had no destination in mind—only a departure from the chaos behind.

They'd seen little of the police since leaving Al Salhiyeh, but a passing patrol car two minutes ago, siren blaring through an intersection, had put everyone on edge. Ludmilla glanced down at the MP5 canted against Slaton's right knee. "Shouldn't we hide that?" she asked.

"Better to have it available—just in case."

Her eyes went back to the road. Slaton turned toward the back seat, and the woman there met his eyes. The young boy did not, preferring the view out the window to the stranger in the front seat. He clutched a toy truck in his lap; one of its wheels was missing.

"I think it's time for introductions," Slaton suggested. "Can I assume your name is Salma?"

She nodded, and said in heavily accented English, "This is my son, Naji. He speaks no English."

On hearing his name, the boy looked forward. Slaton smiled at the child, adding a friendly wink.

The boy turned back to the window.

"He does not like soldiers," Salma said.

"Right now, neither do I," Slaton said. He'd ditched his camo jacket, but he *had* brought a weapon into the car. That, apparently, was enough to make the label fit. He knew it was a common affliction in war-torn areas. Children didn't know one uniform from another. They simply learned to be frightened of all combatants, save for those who were close family relations.

"We only wanted to borrow your car," he said. "It would be safer for you and your son if you got out at the next corner."

"No, we come with you," Salma argued.

"Come *with* us?" he repeated, exchanging a glance with Ludmilla. "Where do you imagine we're going?"

"America, of course."

Slaton held fast. He settled on a logical reply. "I'm not even American," he said. "I'm Israeli."

Salma looked confused at first. Then worry set in.

Ludmilla mirrored her expressions, and said, "But you told me—"

"Look, I know," he said, cutting her off. "It's complicated. I work for the Americans. And yes, I'm here to get you out of Syria." He shifted his attention to the mother and child. "There's no way I can get you and your son to the United States. Right now, I'm going to have a hard time getting the two of *us* to the border."

Salma spoke to Ludmilla in a stream of rapid-fire Arabic.

"She wants to know what you would have her do," the interpreter said.

Slaton stared at Salma. She was an attractive woman, dark-eyed with raven-black hair. There was a resoluteness about her that seemed familiar, an aura of conviction that would not be easily sidestepped. Only then did Slaton make the connection. She reminded him of the mother of another preschooler—the one he'd married.

Salma spoke again to Ludmilla, who translated. "She says that for seven years she has struggled to keep her business going. For the last two it has been particularly hard because her husband was killed in the war. Now, thanks to us, her salon is surrounded by the police and Mukhabarat. They will discover she has been harboring me."

"Salma could say she was only helping a friend. She couldn't have known the police were looking for you."

Ludmilla said, "Actually, the owner of another salon recently called her. She told Salma the police had come looking for me at her own place. Anyway, none of that would matter to the Muk. Salma is gone, along with her car and her son. They will learn I was staying there, in the very room from which you just launched an attack. There is no way they can go back."

As much as he didn't like it, Slaton knew she was right. Salma had burned her bridge—or more precisely, he and Ludmilla had burned it. This mother and son were now fugitives every bit as much as they were. He heaved a sigh and looked outside. In the distance he saw an ambulance running in the opposite direction down a parallel street. Of course he knew where it was going.

Slaton hadn't come to start a war. Yet that was exactly what he'd done. Now they had to get out of town, and it wouldn't be easy. The checkpoints he'd seen on his way in would be reinforced, every car leaving Damascus searched thoroughly. Every policeman and soldier not already on duty would be called in to comb streets and conduct raids. Getting Ludmilla to safety had suddenly become exponentially more difficult. And now he had Syria's two newest refugees in tow.

Yet it wasn't all gloom. His deficiency when it came to speaking Arabic was no longer an issue. He now had a perfectly fluent interpreter, even if she could never pass for a local on appearance, and two native speakers, one of whom was intimately familiar with the city. It was a start.

"Okay," he said. "Tell Salma I can't make any promises about citizenship, but I'll do my best to get her and Naji out of Syria. The first order of business is to ditch this car."

"Go to Mezzeh," Salma said.

Slaton eyed her skeptically, and she expanded, "My uncle, Achmed, lives there. He will help us."

"How?"

"He has a garage. We can hide this car, and he will get us another."

Slaton had no better ideas, but caution ruled. "Do you trust him?"

"I—"

Ludmilla interrupted with, "Achmed lost two sons to the war."

The women exchanged a pained glance.

Slaton looked at them in turn, then blew out an extended sigh. "All right. Uncle Achmed's it is."

From his office window, Petrov regarded a day whose bleakness matched his mood. The sky was gray and sulking, and a sharp wind kept heads down and brushed waves across the river. October was rarely kind to Moscow. *But then,* Petrov mused, *who was these days?*

This morning's briefing had been unusually dire. Unusual not because the national condition hadn't long been one of suffering, but because one of his minions had dared to speak the truth. General Markarov, who was fast nearing retirement, had taken it upon himself to speak candidly.

It was getting more difficult to control the masses, he'd said. Every time the government issued good news, organizers on the internet would shoot it full of holes. A burgeoning protest yesterday had been shut down by police, only to have cretins using WhatsApp move it three blocks away. The technology division disabled WhatsApp, only to see the crowd switch to a different application. It was like chasing ten thousand butterflies in a swirling breeze. The information blunderbuss Petrov had built for his trolls, so effectively when it came to meddling in the West's affairs, was now being turned against him. A digital anarchy that no one controlled. After Markarov had left, Petrov was left shaking his head somberly, not unlike Khrushchev in his final days.

The red phone on his desk chirped its signature tone. The handset was his most secure, and rarely used. On this day Petrov could imagine only two reasons why it would ring: impending nuclear annihilation, or the arrival of an important call he'd been waiting for.

He picked up, and said, "Tell me you have found her."

A hesitation. An audible swallow. Vasiliev said, "We found the hair salon where she was hiding, but the Syrians bungled the arrest. Kravchuk escaped before we could reach her."

"I heard an absurd rumor that half a city block was destroyed."

Silence in return.

"Have we underestimated our interpreter? Perhaps she is not an amateur after all."

"It's not that," said Vasiliev. "There is significant evidence that she's gotten help."

"Help?"

"To begin, the salon owner is missing, along with her young son. There is also a report of a stranger." Vasiliev told him about the lift bucket found against the window, the semiconscious municipal worker who'd been in the closet. "Whoever this man is, he managed to steal a Ural from Hezbollah, then used it to enter the city. The truck was carrying a full load of rockets which exploded just as Inspector Hadad and his team arrived."

"Not by chance."

"No."

"Did Hadad survive?"

"Yes, he's fine. He is already going over the apartment where Kravchuk was staying, and there is one bit of news." Vasiliev hesitated. "He asked me about a pair of shoes he found on a table. I told him nothing, of course, but asked him to send me a picture. The one with the recording device has been disassembled, and the heel containing the memory card is gone."

Petrov held steady. This was bad news, but a scenario he'd been contemplating since Kravchuk's disappearance. If nothing else, it confirmed what he was up against.

"This man who is helping her," he prodded, "who do you think he is?"

"Two witnesses saw him, but according to Hadad their descriptions weren't of much use. Whoever he is, he clearly has operational experience."

Petrov felt a sudden worm of anxiety. The last time he'd had such a feeling was last year, at his palace on the Black Sea, when an assassin had nearly gunned him down. *Surely not,* he thought.

He forced himself back to the matter at hand. "Does Hadad have any idea where they might have gone?" His tone was that of a teacher addressing his most simple-minded student.

"No, but he is confident they remain in the city. The police and army have locked down every outbound road."

"What if they don't use a road?"

"Well . . . the airports are also being watched."

Petrov hesitated for effect. "This problem is expanding—there are now four people who must be found. Can you and Hadad manage it?" he asked. "Or should I send in someone else?"

It was nothing short of an ultimatum.

"We will find them," Vasiliev said none too convincingly.

"Then do so . . . and *quickly!*"

Petrov rang off.

The president turned away from his desk. The cheerless visage of Red Square was still there. Framed by the sky and river, a veritable masterpiece of dullness. He could only assume Kravchuk, or whoever had rescued her, was carrying the recording. The device in her shoe had been a precaution, a potential bit of leverage for certain contingencies. It had never occurred to Petrov that it might fall into the wrong hands. He found himself trying to recall the exact words he'd spoken four mornings ago. Did it matter if someone disclosed them? Or even put the recording in its entirety on the internet? No, he decided. Voiceprints could be fooled, conversations digitally manipulated. And anyway, denial was his specialty.

His words had been damning, to be sure, but the damage was not insurmountable. And if Vasiliev could recover the recording? Then that problem would be solved.

Either way, the greater plan could no longer be stopped.

THIRTY-THREE

They called him Happy but he no longer was. His given name was Jamal al-Badri, yet the playful name bestowed upon him as a child, a consequence of his sunny nature, had pursued him relentlessly into adulthood. For forty-something years—he'd never bothered to count birthdays—the nickname had mostly fit. He'd married, had six children, and by local standards led a prosperous life. Ultimately, however, the hardships of Darfur had taken their toll.

The high sun was giving its worst. With aching feet, Jamal plodded across parched terrain, his loose sandals kicking up clouds of dust with each step. The rainy season had once again come and gone without living up to its name, less than an inch falling through the high summer months—a fraction of the meager standard for Western Sudan. There had been storms of a kind, great tsunamis of dirt that blotted out the sky and rolled across the land, but they brought no moisture. The wind would howl, whipping the sand to sting faces and rearrange the landscape, yet in the end the haboobs did little more than spit on the cracked earth. The imam in Kuma faulted the idolatrous Christians for offending God. The government blamed the rebels, the rebels the government, although how either side could have any effect on the skies Jamal didn't know. A Western doctor at a clinic Jamal had visited—he'd needed a rotted tooth pulled—told him it was all due to something called global warming. Jamal didn't really care who or what was responsible. He only wanted grass for his herd and a well from which to drink. A year of that, perhaps two, and his old name might fit once again.

He paused to wipe sweat from his forehead, his leather-skinned hand sweeping up through close-cropped black hair. He jabbed out with a stick to prod his lead animal onward. The bull was the best of his herd, although the brute had come up mildly lame a few months back. He could still travel, still sire, but he was no longer any good behind a plow. One more source of income lost, meager as it was—the farmers, too, had largely given up, many of them abandoning the land for the treacherous passage to Europe.

He turned and saw his youngest son behind the herd. Musa was sixteen, but looked four years younger. He was small and frail, although Jamal had come to view it as a blessing—a reversal of thinking compared to his older boys. Adan and Manute had grown tall and strong, and for that reason they'd been taken away, one requisitioned by the Janjaweed, the other by the rebel alliance.

Jamal had not seen either of them in years, and the hope in his heart had fallen to little more than a flicker. He feared it was only a matter of time before someone came for Musa. A new militia, a new alliance. Spindly as he was, the boy was growing, and soon his rising stature would intersect with the militias' declining standards. He'd heard they were taking young boys these days, eight and nine years old. Even girls who showed a willingness to fight. His three daughters, at least, were safe. They'd gone south of Nyala to live with a cousin, the only option after his wife had succumbed to the fever last year.

While he strived for optimism, Jamal was at base a realist. He'd reached the point in life when one spent more time reminiscing about days behind than dreaming of those ahead. The only livelihood he'd ever known, that of the *baqqara*, or cattle-keepers, was fast coming to an end. For a thousand years his ancestors had wandered these lands without respect to borders, their herds grazing pastoral hillsides. Today only eight beasts remained in his herd, from what had once been a wealth of over a hundred. The survivors were little more than skin and bones, and he'd been blessed with but one calf this year—bartered away for food last month.

Jamal looked ahead, toward the east. His vision had been getting worse in recent years, an opaqueness settling in, but in the bright sun he could easily make out the scalloped hills in the distance. The landscape in Darfur seemed the one remaining constant, tawny undulations beaten by the sun and reorganized by the wind. He wasn't precisely sure of their location—somewhere north of Mount Teljo, which was still visible on the horizon—yet he was sure they'd mounted the southern plateau, skirting the edge of the great Sahara. What lay farther east was a mystery, but Jamal decided it had to be better than what was behind him. Western Darfur was again becoming treacherous, the rebels launching a new campaign. The land there, the only home he'd ever known, seemed closer to dying each day.

Fortunately, the militias couldn't be everywhere. The frontlines of the conflict ebbed and flowed, and according to the latest rumors the east was calm. Jamal thought it might be true, although few of the *baqqara* had ventured there. He prayed the land was better than what he saw now. Here even the toughest shrubs, the black thorn and sage, were withering to straw, and the earth beneath his feet was cracked from dryness. It occurred to Jamal that his herd was raising a considerable cloud of dust. This was yet another complication of living in the new Darfur: any movement could be seen for twenty miles, making it impossible to hide from the various factions. There was little to be done about it, other than avoiding known encampments by the greatest possible distance.

"There!" came a shout from behind.

Jamal stopped and turned. He saw Musa pointing toward a basin in the distance, slightly to the left. Jamal squinted and saw what had drawn his son's attention. A lalob tree was the most prominent landmark, suggesting a source of water. Beyond that he saw a small cluster of buildings.

Musa came and stood next to him. "It is exactly where they said it would be."

"Do you see anyone?"

Musa studied the place with his sharper eyes. "No, it looks abandoned—just as promised. Perhaps the well still gives water."

Jamal nodded cautiously.

They'd journeyed here, to this forgotten valley, based on whisperings that had been sweeping through the souk in recent days. A visiting merchant had spread the word that conditions in the east were vastly better. He said the rebels had moved away, and that the valleys at the distant heel of the great plateau were thick with green grass. Jamal had talked to the man briefly, and found him convincing. He wasn't a local, and spoke Arabic from the north, but his glowing recommendation seemed sincere. Jamal would not normally be swayed by such gossip, but between the fighting and the drought, conditions at home had reached the point of desperation.

He'd discussed the idea with a few of the other *baqqara,* and slept on it that night. By the next morning he was convinced: it would be a three-day journey, but someone had to take the initiative. As far as he knew, he and Musa were the first.

He looked to the horizon, and thought the far-off hills might perhaps be just a bit greener. The small compound had also been mentioned: a forgotten waystation where a man could water his herd and take shelter for the night.

He turned to his son, and said, "All right, then. Let's have a look."

It took thirty minutes to reach the tiny outpost—things in the desert were invariably farther away than they appeared. Jamal beat his herd along a dry wadi for the last half mile, and in the low channel he lost sight of the small cluster of buildings. Even so, he could navigate easily by referencing the distant hills. He eventually saw the lalob tree, and soon after that the compound came into view.

There was still no sign of life. No goats tethered to stakes or blankets strung up for shade. Best of all, Jamal saw no vehicles. The buildings were in a state of near ruin. The largest had two misshapen walls, and the smallest, little more than a shed, was topped by a skeletal roof of rotted branches, probably taken from the tree decades earlier.

Of the three, the center building was the only one that might be habitable. There were four walls and a roof, but the door was missing and he saw only one open-air window. The construction was archetypical, earthen walls blending seamlessly into the land from which they'd been drawn. An animal pen in front suffered a buckled segment of fence, and where it abutted the building Jamal saw a watering trough. Not surprisingly, all three buildings showed telltale pockmarks of varying calibers—on appearances, a series of minor engagements, with perhaps the odd wedding celebration thrown in. Virtually every rural building in Sudan was so adorned.

Fifty steps short of the compound, Jamal brought his herd to a stop. He exchanged a look with his son, then nodded to send him ahead. Quiet as things seemed, it was best to check the building out. Musa moved ahead surely. Frail or not, the boy was gaining confidence. Growing into a man.

Jamal watched him pass beneath the shade of the big tree. Musa paused near the collapsed pen, and called out, "The trough is full."

A herder at heart, Jamal smiled. They could water the cattle.

Musa approached the doorway of the midsized building cautiously. Jamal held his breath. Some months ago, they'd come across a similar shack that appeared abandoned, only to find two nervous and heavily armed teenagers inside guarding a cache of rebel weapons.

He watched Musa lean toward the entrance and peer inside. When he turned back he was grinning. "There is no one inside . . . only some equipment." Musa disappeared into the shadowed interior.

A relieved Jamal began prodding the herd forward. The bull was the first to arrive at the trough. He dipped his head, and soon two cows were at his shoulders. Jamal noticed a tall wooden pole next to the house. At the top he saw what looked like a few long threads of yarn. The yellow strands danced festively in the light breeze. He took in the surrounding brushland and wondered if any other *baqqara* had used this place. He supposed they had, although more likely in the summer months.

A momentary glint caught his eye at the base of a low ridgeline. He studied the spot for a time, but discerned nothing of interest. *Only my old eyes playing tricks on me again.* Jamal moved into the shade of the tree. He'd just put a hand to its ancient trunk when Musa called from inside.

"Father—"

He looked at the earthen shack, but didn't see his son. He did however hear a peculiar sound—a sharp crack, followed by a faint hissing sound. It reminded him of air being vented from the valve of a bicycle tire. The sound soon faded, then there was nothing for a time.

"Musa?" he called.

No reply.

Jamal felt the first pang of discomfort. His eyes went back to the spot below the ridge. "Musa! Are you all right?"

Still nothing.

What happened next took Jamal completely by surprise. The cow nearest the window lurched back as if startled. She issued a terrible bleating sound as her front legs wobbled, then buckled completely. She fell facedown into the dirt before tumbling on her side. All four legs began to spasm violently.

Jamal ran toward the pen, but before he could reach it the bull did much the same, falling into the dirt with its great legs twitching wildly. Jamal skidded to a stop in the dirt. He was suddenly very afraid—and not for his herd.

He looked guardedly at the open doorway. "Musa! Where are you?"

Again, no reply.

He moved warily toward the doorway. Before he'd gone two steps, Musa appeared. His son staggered into the threshold. He put one shoulder heavily to the earthen wall, then collapsed.

Jamal ran and kneeled beside his son. There was vomit on the front of his robe, spittle coming from his mouth. It looked as if every muscle in his body had gone rigid, and he was sweating profusely. Then Jamal noticed his eyes. They seemed vacant, staring blankly skyward, the pupils no more than pinpoints.

"Musa, can you hear me?" he said desperately.

There was no reaction, no recognition at all. Musa's breathing was choppy and shallow, gasping for air but somehow not finding it. Jamal cradled his son's head in his hands, felt the rigid muscles in his neck. Behind him the bull gave a horrid wail. Jamal couldn't take his eyes off his son. He wondered what affliction could befall both men and cattle, what could seize them so quickly. He peered into the shadowed recesses of the room and saw walking sticks, spent water bottles, a few empty crates. Then at the back, something shiny . . . two heavy metallic bottles.

Musa's gaze became fixed, stilled in a terrible forever stare. "No!" Jamal cried out, cradling his son's head. *"Musa!"* Tears began streaming down his cheeks. Then, through his grief, Jamal felt a terrible aura of foreboding.

Sweat began dripping down his face, and there was an awful constriction in his chest. The hands holding his dead son's face went rigid, and his arms seemed to seize. He fell helplessly onto his side, his vision blurring. He felt the warmth of urine spreading across one leg. *But his chest* . . . that was the worst. A pain like nothing he'd ever experienced. Jamal felt like he was being crushed, some unseen weight expelling every bit of air from his lungs.

He lay on the ground, trying to focus. Trying to breathe.

Then he saw it . . . coming at him like a nightmare.

It approached from the direction of the tree, and was vaguely in the shape of a man—arms and legs, a body of sorts, but all of it bloated inside what looked like a great yellow balloon. Where the face should have been was a wide glass plate, and behind that, perhaps, the visage of a man. *Or am I only seeing things?*

Jamal retched once, then again, a spastic expulsion that made breathing more difficult than ever. When his eyes opened again the apparition was closer, only a few steps away. The creature came to a stop and stood over him. Watching and waiting. Jamal reached out a hand, pleading for help. The figure didn't move, and for the first time Jamal heard what sounded like flowing air, an in-and-out stream that was almost mechanical. It seemed to mock his own seized lungs.

The world began to go dim.

His last vision was of the figure kneeling down next to him. Jamal felt two slight stings—first one leg, then the other. Against so much agony it hardly registered. He shuddered and drew one final breath. Then his body racked violently and the world went black.

THIRTY-FOUR

The midday sun seemed to beat down through a magnifying glass as they made their way across Damascus. The car was serviceable, but had seen better days, and the air conditioner showed no signs of life. To Slaton it was less an issue of comfort than security—it forced them to keep the windows open.

There were sirens in the distance, but distance was the operative word—that meant safety, preoccupation. He was intensely attuned to their surroundings: every nearby car noted, every intersection approached with caution. He'd already confirmed that everyone's phones were off. They'd so far seen no roadblocks; Slaton guessed those would eventually appear inside the city, but not before the perimeter was sealed. Given the scale of battle he'd begun, it wouldn't take long.

Kravchuk was still driving, Slaton riding semi-automatic. They made halting progress, moving for a time before shifting into cover, ducking into parking areas and alleys. They avoided main arteries wherever possible. With the traffic at a crescendo, and moving with utmost caution, it took nearly two hours to reach their destination.

"How much farther?" he asked.

"We are almost there," replied Salma.

He half turned and saw her eyes reaching up the street. Naji remained silent at her side, his three-wheeled toy truck clutched to his chest. They were winding through a dated residential neighborhood, somewhere on the distant south side of town. Ordinary people going about ordinary lives. The homes were in various conditions. Some were old but well maintained, a few token trees. Others looked like junkyard offices surrounded by building material and scrapped cars. The only common theme seemed to be walls between every property—creating a warren of routes for possible escape. *Or assault,* Slaton corrected.

"There!" Salma exclaimed.

Slaton followed her gaze and saw a beaten residence fronted by a struggling acacia tree. The house looked fragmented, a charmless collection of mismatched rooms that seemed to have been added one at a time—what happened when an owner had no chance of a mortgage and simply added a room or a shed when times were good. The roof seemed vaguely crooked, and if there had ever been paint on the block walls it had faded to obscurity. Salma had assured him there was a garage, and while Slaton saw no sign of it from the street, a pair of rutted tracks to the right hinted at something in back. Every window in the house was covered with either blinds, sheets, or both, and paint peeled from the rotted fascia like sunburned skin.

Up and down the street Slaton saw a scattering of similar residences. The front yard next door resembled a municipal dump, and a house across the street was dominated by geriatric citrus trees and a tattered windsock. A stray dog ambled indifferently up the middle of the road.

Slaton saw no immediate threats. All the same, the MP5 was ready at his knee, two spare mags in his thigh pocket—an undeniable comfort when operating under thrice-removed confidences. He had decided to trust Ludmilla. She, in turn, was relying on her hairdresser. Now Salma had put everyone's lives in the hands of a relative neither of them had met. It was a lot of transferred faith, but in that moment Slaton could think of no better option—which spoke volumes about how quickly the situation had degraded.

He gestured to the driveway that led around the home's right side. "Is the garage around back?"

"Yes," Salma replied. "Achmed keeps his work van inside, but he'll understand. Should I call and ask him to move it out now?"

"No, all phones stay off. I want you to go to the door and make sure he's home. If he is, ask him if he's okay with us crashing in."

"He will welcome us," she said confidently.

Ludmilla pulled the car to a stop directly in front of the house. There was a time, not so long ago, when Slaton would have demanded that Salma leave her son in the back seat. From an operator's perspective it would be the solid move, providing a degree of insurance. From a father's point of view, unfortunately, it was an unfathomable ask.

Salma addressed her son, and Slaton caught one word: Achmed.

Slaton saw the boy smile for the first time. A great smile, deep and genuine. They got out of the car and walked to the front door hand in hand.

Slaton's eyes shifted between three front windows. He saw no blinds being fingered back, no sign of lights being turned on or off. When the mother and son reached the front steps, he turned to Ludmilla and said, "She seems convinced her uncle is going to take us in."

"He will."

His eyes narrowed. "Because he had two sons killed in the war?"

"Actually . . . that was not truthful."

He held her eyes with a level gaze.

"Achmed never married," she admitted. "He has never had children."

Slaton remained silent.

"In the moment, there wasn't time for argument."

His eyes went back to the house, and he said in distant voice, "So, you manipulated me."

"Yes. But I am telling you the truth now."

"What about Salma? Was her husband really killed in the war?"

"Yes, although I myself only learned of it today. But I truly believe Achmed will help us."

"Why?"

"He was always Salma's favorite. He's very close to her and Naji, even more so since her husband died. And there is something else you should know about Achmed—the reason, I am sure, she thought of him in the first place."

Slaton felt as though he was waiting for a bad punch line.

"As it turns out, he is a businessman who makes his living . . . outside normal channels."

"How far outside?"

She cocked her head and pursed her lips, a classically Slavic gesture. "Achmed is an importer of goods, but he has no official license."

"You mean—"

"He is a smuggler."

The front door opened. Salma and Naji went inside.

They both sat watching the door, which remained ajar, for a full five minutes. It seemed like hours. Slaton saw no movement anywhere. Not inside the house. Not on the driveway to the right.

He sensed Ludmilla shifting in her seat. The assuredness she'd displayed earlier was ebbing. With his eyes fixed outside, he said, "If we have to move, drive straight ahead. Hit it hard and take the first left."

"Do you think something is wrong?"

He thought, *We're fugitives in Syria being hunted down by a bloody regime, not to mention Russian intelligence. Everything is wrong.* He said, "No, we're good. But having a plan costs us nothing."

"Shouldn't they have come out by now?"

"Yes."

"Perhaps we should go inside."

"No."

More shifting. Her fingers grasped rhythmically on the steering wheel. "Was it a mistake to come here?" she asked.

"Given what I was *told*, it seemed the best option at the time."

"But now?"

He shot her a sideways glance. "It's all right. Leave the worrying to me."

"I can't."

"Why?"

"Because I'm Russian," she said.

Finally, Salma appeared with Naji at her side. His hand gripped her pocket as if connected by Velcro. A man appeared behind them. He was grizzled, perhaps fifty. Thick build, cheeks covered with a salt-and-pepper stubble.

Salma pointed toward the Hyundai. The man who had to be Achmed nodded. He pointed a bony finger at the car, then flicked it toward the side of the house.

"Okay," Slaton said. "Let's pull around back. But there is one more thing . . ." He briefly put his hand over the shift lever for emphasis. "If you ever lie to me again, you're on your own."

THIRTY-FIVE

Sultan remained stock-still in the shade of the great lalob tree. He cut a bizarre figure in his square-edged, head-to-toe yellow suit. His lack of movement was quite intentional. The falling afternoon sun was relentless, and the suit had become unbearably hot. He was glad he'd had the forethought to drink a bottle of water before donning it.

He checked the cheap digital watch he'd taped to the inside of his faceplate. Eight minutes had elapsed since the initial exposure. By the criteria he'd been given, there were two minutes to go.

He used the time to collate the observations he'd made so far. The younger of his two subjects had lasted less than a minute. The older almost three. But then, it was hard to say precisely when each had come in contact with the agent. He wasn't sure how to assess the fate of the cows—for all his planning, that had never been a consideration. Curiously, one member of the herd was still standing—by some feral instinct it had scurried fifty meters away. *Smart cow,* he thought. He checked the tails of yarn he'd put high on the wooden pole. They were pointing, more or less, in the direction the cow had gone. He watched the beast carefully. It took another minute. The creature staggered sideways once, almost righted itself, then fell to the ground and began convulsing.

When the ten-minute point was reached—the planned exposure interval—Sultan lumbered back to the entrance of the hut. His first thought on arriving was that he was happy to be breathing fresh air in an over-pressurized suit—both victims were surrounded by a host of bodily fluids, expelled by the resulting spasms, and the smell had to be appalling.

He stood over the body of the older man, and with clinical

detachment regarded the two syringes sticking out of his leg. Had they made any difference? he wondered. The man had drawn one breath near the end, a long gasp before succumbing. The agent had prevailed, of course, yet there might have been some slight mitigation from the atropine injection. *Noted.*

He turned a full circle, taking in the panorama around the building. He saw death in every quarter. Sultan squared his shoulders and eased into the shack with the utmost of caution. Despite having practiced, he found moving in the suit exceedingly awkward. It was like walking inside a giant balloon. Visibility through the faceplate was poor and the glass fogged constantly with moisture. He undertook each step cautiously, and was once more thankful for his preparations: on his first visit here, he'd carefully cleared the floor of any tripping hazards. Fall now and tear the suit, and he would be frantically jabbing needles into his own thigh.

He referenced the watch and saw that he'd been in the suit for twenty-one minutes. He needed to pick up the pace. His air supply was limited, and there was still a great deal to be done. Sweating profusely, he cursed the herders for not showing up closer to nightfall. Unfortunately, certain parts of the equation had always been out of his control. In truth, he was surprised anyone had gotten here so quickly—he'd always reckoned that tomorrow was more likely. He put it down to the despondency of the local situation.

Three days ago, an associate, a Sudanese he'd paid handsomely, had made a trip on Sultan's behalf to Kuma, a village twenty miles to the west. At a gathering place for local herders, he'd spread word of this outpost to a half dozen of the *baqqara*, painting it as a waypoint to ever-greener pastures. Sultan had no doubt the story would circulate, and that, given the severity of the drought, *someone* would be drawn east. The only questions were how long it would take and how many would come. The journey from Kuma, he'd reckoned, would take at least two days, so he'd been mildly surprised when, soon after pulling the Toyota into the nearby valley, he'd seen a small herd materialize. They headed straight for the compound, and by the time Sultan had finished unloading he knew his scheme had worked. Now he had to finish the job.

He reached the back of the room and paused near the table holding the equipment. The most prominent components were two canisters. One resembled a miniature scuba tank, while the other was thinner, like a small fire extinguisher. Both remained in place on the table, connected by a minor network of silver tubes and regulators. On top of it all was the dispersal nozzle, which looked like a small inverted showerhead. He had activated the system from fifty yards away using a transmitter modified from a garage door opener. He'd considered using a motion-activated initiator, but had ruled the idea out, not wanting some curious jackal to set things off prematurely.

On appearances, the system seemed to have performed well. If anything, the efficacy of the binary mix was more lethal than anticipated. A check of the pressure gauge confirmed that the larger canister had fully depressurized. The smaller cylinder didn't have a gauge, so leaving the flexible hose attached, he lifted it from its stand and gave the container a shake. He felt a slight sloshing inside. Eighty percent usage, he guessed, of the aerosolizing mixture.

It occurred to him that he might have brought a scale to get a more precise measurement. Sultan discarded the idea just as quickly. He already had enough to keep track of. *Simplify wherever possible.* By this same mantra, he'd already decided against trying to take pictures. Manipulating a camera in the heavy gloves would be all but impossible, and mounting a GoPro inside his helmet seemed problematic given the expected fogging. It hardly mattered. Others would take pictures soon enough.

Back outside, he walked past the big tree and down a gentle embankment to a familiar stand of brush. The two large duffels were right where he'd left them. He hauled them into the building, straining in the cumbersome suit. After catching his breath, he went straight to work.

From the first duffel he extracted a biohazard suit identical to the one he was wearing. He'd already removed it from its plastic shipping bag to insert what the maid had provided. He dragged the suit across the dirt floor, and for good measure wiped its rubbery exterior across the tabletop where the canisters were set up. He crushed the suit into a ball, returned it to the duffel, and extracted second. This he gave the same treatment. From the other duffel he removed two pairs of boots—twins to the oversized set he was wearing. He swept them back and forth across the shack's dirt floor. Last to be contaminated were a dozen foot-long strips of ChemTape. With one last look at the scene, Sultan was satisfied. Everything went back into the duffels, and gripping one in each hand, he set out for the staging area.

The heat was interminable; he'd now been wearing the suit for over thirty minutes. His bad foot ached by the time he reached his destination, a prominent rock outcropping a quarter mile downwind from his truck. He opened the duffels and extracted the contaminated suits, boots, and ChemTape, positioning all of it haphazardly around the rocky enclave. The rest of the scene was already in place, strewn randomly nearby. One pair of scissors, two partial rolls of the special tape, a few rags, and a collection of empty food wrappers and water bottles. Near the largest rock were two pump spray containers of decontamination solution, both half empty. He'd spent ten minutes earlier misting the surrounding dirt like a groundskeeper killing weeds. After one last look, he decided to scuff the ground a bit more.

He set out again in the direction of his truck, one last stop to be made. By the time he reached the true decontamination area the gauge on his breathing tank showed five minutes of air remaining. He could tell the suit was sagging in spots, the overpressure effect nowhere near what it had been earlier. Exhausted from his exertions, he was glad to have had the forethought to preposition everything.

With air running critically low, he went through the protocols he had so diligently practiced. The first task was probably overkill, but he'd already committed to going through with it. Sitting down on a rock, he picked up an auto-injector, removed the safety cover, and sank the needle straight through his suit and into the meaty part of his left thigh. He watched the syringe to make sure it fully expelled before pulling the needle clear. He'd already taken a regimen of pyridostigmine. When he removed the suit, he would be theoretically protected if he made any mistakes or if the wind suddenly shifted.

Theoretically. Not a comforting modifier for a man who had seen what he'd just seen.

He used a pump sprayer to bathe himself in five gallons of decontamination solution. By the end his suit was dripping with the amber fluid. That done, he retrieved a doubled garbage can liner and, leaning on the rock for support, placed his feet inside the opening. He peeled the tape from the seams of his hood, then the wrist seal on each glove. He rolled down the suit from top to bottom, undulating like a molting snake to free himself from the protective garment. He'd practiced the maneuver countless times: leaning on a hotel room bed, on a dinner chair in a Damascus safe house. All for this one moment.

The desert breeze, hot and arid as it was, gave instant relief. Soon the yellow suit was puddled in the trash bag at his feet. Still wearing the outer gloves, he pried his feet from the oversized boots, beginning with his aching right foot, and stepped clear of the plastic bag. The outer gloves were next to go. Then, still wearing the inner glove liners, he unstrapped the air tank and dropped it onto the pile of gear. When he at last took off the glove liners, his hands were wet and clammy beneath.

Only after sealing the bag, with the entire ensemble inside, did Sultan allow himself a momentary pause. The warm air felt like freedom itself. It struck him that the desert here was different from the one he'd been born into. More heat, perhaps, less moisture. Sudan was a more populated country, yet somehow it seemed more desolate. Greater expanses and fewer small villages. Bands of nomads roaming the great desert. Sultan's eyes swept the valley 360 degrees. He saw nothing but brown desert and blue sky.

His thoughts turned to the two victims. He wondered if they were father and son, and decided it was likely. *At least they were together in the end.* A pair of vultures wheeling in the distance caught his eye. Would they be the first to arrive? If so, there would be two more carcasses to add to the show.

He abandoned his musings. The most challenging task was behind him now. He broke a leafy branch from a shrub near the wadi, and used it to sweep away the deepest boot prints. It wasn't perfect, but the desert, relentless as ever with dust and wind, would do the rest.

He heaved the plastic bag over his shoulder and set out the final hundred yards to the truck. By the time he arrived his foot was acting up again. He heaved the bag into the bed, got behind the wheel, and tried to slot the key into the ignition. It didn't fit.

His heart fluttered in a moment of horror. Then he looked down and realized it was the key to his other car—the Fiat sitting in the garage outside Damascus. *Which means the key to the Toyota . . .*

He unzipped the small suitcase on the seat next to him, pulled out the khaki trousers he'd been wearing that morning. In the front pocket he found the key to the Toyota. He drew a long, deep breath and was unable to suppress a smile. *And what other errors have I made?*

He twisted the rearview mirror to look at himself. His hair was matted in sweat, and there was a red band around his forehead where the suit's hood had pressed in. Nothing that wouldn't fade in time. All in all, Sultan felt a surge of pride. After so much groundwork—the meeting with Petrov, the travel, dealing with the maid—he had done what he'd set out to do.

The little truck sparked obediently to life, and he steered toward the dirt trail to the east. Progress was slow, the truck bounding over ruts and channels in the hardpan earth. He navigated for eight miles using a GPS handset, then stopped near a featureless stand of scrub. Sultan got out and retrieved a small camping shovel from the bed of the truck. Ten minutes later the garbage bag containing his equipment was buried. This was the one bit of evidence he didn't want to be found—nothing to do with the residues on the outside of the suit, but rather what was inevitably within. He had considered burning everything, but he'd been told by the Russian who provided the gear that it would produce thick black smoke under an open flame. Now was not the time to draw attention.

Sultan kept driving eastward, and as he did he was struck by the boundlessness of the desert. Under a faultless sky, the land here seemed every bit as hard and detached as his homeland. Which of them concealed more atrocities he couldn't guess. Twenty minutes later he reached a semi-improved gravel road. Just before climbing the shoulder onto the raised roadbed, Sultan tossed the camping shovel through the window and into the brush.

The little truck bounded onto the road and quickly picked up speed.

THIRTY-SIX

The Hyundai fit nicely into Achmed's garage, if that's what it could be called. To Slaton the standalone building looked more like a chicken coop on steroids, a fifteen-by-twenty-foot rectangle of corrugated siding and plywood over a beaten dirt floor. When Slaton pulled the twin doors shut, one creaked like something from a bad horror movie. The other had to be dragged through the dirt. There was nothing secure about the place, but it at least put the car out of sight.

The backyard was surrounded by a head-high stone wall, and Slaton couldn't see the windows of any neighboring house—which meant he couldn't be seen in return. All around the yard were piles of discarded machinery, most of it rusting, and uneven stacks of sun-baked scrap lumber. The neighbor had a dog, which might have been a good early warning system had the creature not barked incessantly.

Ever since entering the neighborhood, Slaton had been watching for anything or anyone out of place. So far, he'd seen poverty and hard work, a few hints of criminal enterprise. But nothing at all worrisome.

Salma appeared at the back door, and her uncle was right behind her. From a distance he stared at Slaton menacingly. An understandable reaction to a guest arriving with an MP5 in hand.

Slaton leaned toward Ludmilla, and asked quietly, "Does Achmed live alone?"

"As far as I know. Why do you ask?"

"It's always a good thing to know before you walk through an unfamiliar door with a weapon."

To that Ludmilla had no reply.

Slaton set out toward the house.

A charmer Uncle Achmed was not. He was average in height with a stocky build. His unkempt black hair could have used Salma's attention and he hadn't shaved in days. He invited them inside with all the cordiality of a prison guard on overtime.

Slaton ignored another hard stare as he carried the MP5 through the back door. There would be no equivocation regarding who he was or why he was here. Having firepower nearby was mandatory from this point on.

They assembled in what passed for a living room. Brown water stains leached down one wall like a curtain. A pair of threadbare couches, one tan the other shamrock green, faced a flat screen TV. Slaton saw a paused image on the screen that he recognized from the movie *Titanic*: the two young lovers at the bow of the ship. Achmed reached for the remote, thumbed a button, and Rose disappeared before she could fly.

The low ceiling was stained by cigarettes, and the scent of stale tobacco clung to the air. The rest of the furnishings looked like rejects from a college dorm, and a sputtering box air conditioner blew a hurricane from a side window.

Slaton sat with Ludmilla on the tan couch, which looked reasonably stable.

"My niece tells me you need to get out of Syria," Achmed began. His voice was raspy, but at least he spoke English. Slaton wasn't surprised. For a smuggler of any attainment, it would be an essential corporate skill.

"I came to escort Ludmilla out. Unfortunately, things went a bit sideways at the salon. Salma and Naji may now also be at risk."

"A bit sideways?" Achmed repeated. "I heard you blew up half the street."

"An exaggeration," Slaton deadpanned. "It was no more than a quarter."

The Syrian might have grinned but it was hard to tell through the uncropped stubble.

Slaton said, "Your niece tells me you know how to move things discreetly. And maybe how to avoid the authorities."

"I know a few gaps in the border. And I have friends in Lebanon."

"What exactly do you smuggle?"

An upside-down U fixed on the Syrian's lips. "That is not a nice word. I am a businessman, pure and simple. Food, watches, phones . . . whatever is selling. I merely prevent the government leeches from taking their cut."

"Have you ever moved people?"

"I have never been that kind of trafficker!" Achmed said indignantly.

"Good to hear. But it looks like you are now."

"I am not so sure. Friends tell me what is happening. There is a blockade around the city, like those at the height of the war. Getting out of Damascus for the next few days . . . it might be impossible."

"No, what's impossible is for your niece to stay in her uncle's home. Salma and Naji have disappeared. The Mukhabarat won't know if they've been abducted or killed, or if they're helping Ludmilla. When they don't turn up in a day or so, they'll assume it's the latter. At that point, the Muk will get their act together and start looking, and they'll start with family."

Achmed seemed to search for a countering argument. There wasn't one.

Slaton said, "Look, I know we're putting you in a bad spot. If you don't want to help, that's fine. We'll leave right now."

Achmed's eyes shot to his niece, who was on the floor with Naji. She nodded, and for the first time Slaton saw more uncle than smuggler in the Syrian's rough-hewn visage.

"All right," Achmed said. "I will try to come up with something, but it will take a little time. Other than Salma, few people know where I live . . . I keep it that way for professional reasons, you understand. I think we are safe here until morning."

"Probably," Slaton allowed. He stood up from the couch, the springs creaking in relief. "While you work on getting us out of town, I could use help with something else. Ludmilla has some information we need to look at—it's on an SD card. Do you have a computer or a tablet we could use?"

"In the back room," said Achmed, pointing down a short hall. "There is a new laptop on the table."

Slaton pulled the SD card from his pocket, and said to Ludmilla, "I'd like you to hear this as well—it will help us both get a clear picture." She got up and followed him toward the narrow hall.

Slaton took the MP5 with him. As he left the room, he looked back at Achmed. He'd gone down on one knee to tickle Naji. On last glance the boy was giggling, with Achmed smiling the smile of a happy shark.

Soon—very soon—Slaton knew he would have a decision to make: whether or not to trust yet another stranger.

It was another hour before Sultan reached a properly paved road. Soon after, the small town of Burush came into view. It was a low-slung and amorphous place, warrens of earthen huts clotted amid swales in the featureless desert. There seemed no obvious reason for the town being where it was. No river or lake, no notable road intersection. It was simply the kind of settlement that arose by default, that came into being because there wasn't anything like it within a hundred miles.

Sultan pulled the truck to the side of the road. He left the engine idling, his misfortune with the key earlier having heightened his caution. He sat still for a time contemplating the town before him. The four original Rashidun Caliphs had built a vast empire, stretching from the Caucuses to the Black Sea, and around the Mediterranean to Algiers. The hills before him would have been at the bottom of that territory—indeed, near the edge of civilization itself fourteen hundred years earlier.

Will I be so fortunate? he wondered. *Could these lands someday be mine?*

"Only if I make it so," he whispered, putting an end to his musings.

From the glove box he removed three virgin burner phones. He powered up the first and saw a reasonably strong signal. He next brought his secure phone to life, and after double-checking it wasn't connected to any network, he navigated to a menu of three carefully edited voice recordings. He queued up the first file, the one with the female voice, then dialed 999 on the first burner.

As the connection ran he held his breath: calling emergency services in Sudan was rather like summoning a plumber to fix a failed water main. In his favor: a rapid and efficient response was not required.

A dispatcher came on the line, his voice reedy and distant. He was almost certainly in El-Obeid, the capital of North Kurdufan. As he had practiced many times, Sultan nested the phones together and played the recording.

He'd procured the woman's services easily—six bead necklaces from the blanket that was her shop, purchased at the end of a slow day. After that transaction, he'd told her she had a particularly mellifluous voice. *I produce a radio program in Jordan. We've been looking for a voice actress for a new series. Would you mind reciting a script into my phone for later evaluation?* The woman would not have smiled more broadly if she'd stumbled upon a bag of gold in the street. She went through six takes as he coached her to achieve just the right mix of clarity and urgency.

Now, listening to the playback, he thought she *was* really rather good. Her harried account of a tragedy traveled less than an inch to the only audience she would ever have, ending in a flurry of fearful sobbing. The dispatcher was midway through his first question when Sultan ended the call abruptly.

He turned the phone off and threw it through the window into the desert. He began driving again, ever watchful for other vehicles. The most troubled areas were behind him, but in Sudan it was always best to remain wary. Ten minutes later, on the far side of Burush, he went through the exercise twice more. The other two voices were male, obtained through similar contrivances in the slums of Khartoum. Both were convincing, panicked one-line messages that reinforced the woman's call. A few added details. Slightly different background noise. Those burners, too, went skipping into the desert afterward.

With another portion of his mission complete, Sultan doublechecked the gas gauge. Satisfied, he settled in for the balance of his journey. East to Khartoum for fuel and dinner, then northeast into the night.

And twelve hours later, the shoulder of the Red Sea.

THIRTY-SEVEN

The back room of Achmed's house was even more of a bachelor dump than the front. A warped box fan near the closed window chewed up air with a vengeance. There was a sheetless mattress on the floor, and boxes had been stacked against every wall. Clothes littered the floor like leaves beneath an elm in autumn. His first thought was that Achmed hated to do laundry. Then Slaton realized many of the shirts still had tags, and it all fell into place. A smuggler who trafficked textiles never needed to do laundry.

The laptop looked brand new, and was already up and running. Slaton pushed aside empty soda cans and half a bag of potato crisps to make room on the desk. He clicked on the mouse and the screen came to life. Thankfully there were no passwords. He made sure the micro SD card was locked to prevent corruption of the data, then plugged it into the port.

"Let's hope the card isn't password protected or encrypted," he said.

"If it doesn't work," Ludmilla replied, "I can tell you much of what was said at the meeting."

"I'm sure you can, but hearing the transcript would be better. It might help you remember more. I think there's a good chance the recording will be unprotected. You told me Petrov's man came to collect the shoe, so they probably never expected anyone to get their hands on the raw data."

A menu of what was on the stick came up on the screen. Slaton saw three audio files. He played the first and heard a man speaking in Russian.

"What is he saying?"

"I don't recognize the voice, but he is only counting."

"That's good, a system test. I'm guessing they would have preferred to transmit from the mike directly to a more secure system, but the room you were in had probably been caged by the Syrians to prevent electronic emissions—that would leave no choice but a hard recording."

The second file was similar, but slightly more muffled—perhaps a test after the recording unit had been installed in the shoe. The third file was much larger than the other two.

Slaton opened it.

The quality of the recording was good. He not only heard Petrov and Rahmani, but also Kravchuk's muted translations. Less audible was the voice of the other interpreter, Sofia Aryan. Ludmilla had already explained her fate.

Because Slaton was not fluent in either Arabic or Russian, he stopped and started the recording repeatedly to allow Ludmilla to translate. The audio began during the premeeting photo op, which according to Ludmilla was the usual grip-and-grin, followed by some empty banter while the heads of state posed for cameras.

Once the doors closed, however—clearly heard in the recording—things quickly turned more interesting. The exchange began cagily, talks of a delivery and Iran being surrounded by enemies. Then it turned more specific.

Rahmani: "How deadly is it?"
Petrov: "It makes Novichok look like weed killer."
Rahmani: "And it can be aerosolized?"
Petrov: "My technicians guarantee it. (Pause) This agent will provide you a strong new capability, but I will say what I've said before . . . chemical weapons must only be used for defensive purposes. I trust you would never employ them unlawfully. The international community is watching, as they should be."
Rahmani: "I understand. But we are increasingly set upon by the Arabs. This will help keep them at bay."
Petrov: "I should remind you, any such capability must be kept out of the hands of others—I think we both know who I am referring to."
Rahmani: "Hezbollah or the Houthis? Certainly not. They have their uses, but technology escapes them. Iran alone will have access. And only our enemies will risk being targeted."
Petrov: "Which ones?"

Rahmani: "The usual suspects."

Petrov: "And just to be clear . . . you will never initiate first use?"

Rahmani: "A weapon such as this can only be defensive. The Saudis are a paper tiger. They spend hundreds of billions of dollars on the best military technology, yet their soldiers and airmen do not have the will to use it. The rest of the Arabs across the Gulf, the Emeriti and Qataris, are worse yet. If we ever choose to attack, there are far better methods."

Petrov: "I have been told your own technicians are making great strides with this class of weapons. Soon you may no longer need our help."

Rahmani: "We did not sit still after pausing our nuclear program to appease the West. Our Revolutionary Guard employs teams of scientists who have developed many such weapons. The Syrians could never have gotten the upper hand in their war without our contribution of chemical agents. This will give us a new level of lethality."

Petrov: "You understand, in the terrible eventuality you should ever employ this agent, it cannot be brought back to Russia. We are still being blamed for the misfortune that befell Skripal in Salisbury."

Rahmani: "That ugly business with the polonium?"

Petrov: "Nothing has ever been proved. All the same, I can tell you the variant you will receive has never been tested in Russia. There is not even a record of its creation."

Rahmani: "Rest assured. This agent would only be employed as a last resort. An insurance policy, if you will."

Petrov: "Then we are in accord as ever, with a common goal of peace in your corner of the world."

Slaton listened to the entire recording twice. Ludmilla's translations were consistent. At the end of the second run, he backed away from the laptop.

She asked, "What do you think? Is it damning enough?"

He was silent for a time, lost in thought. "Oh, it's damning," he finally said. "The CIA will be all over this."

A silence came between them, until Ludmilla said, "There is something about the conversation that bothers me—I sensed it during the meeting as well."

Slaton felt it too, although he couldn't place a finger on the disconnect. He pulled both hands across his cheeks as if to wipe away the fatigue. He'd been going nonstop for nearly twenty-four hours.

"I think we should both sleep on it," he said. "We may not get much rest tomorrow."

THIRTY-EIGHT

As expected, the three calls from Sultan's burner phones instigated a haphazard response, yet one that progressed more quickly than he'd imagined.

It all began in El-Obeid where an emergency services dispatcher yawned as he listened to a distraught woman claiming to have discovered two bodies in a remote building somewhere in the hills north of Burush. This was less than a revelation. Reports of bodies being discovered in the badlands of Darfur was rather like getting word of waves on the sea, but the dispatcher kept to his task all the same. The woman talked nonstop for less than a minute, at which point the dispatcher tried to ask the usual questions. Unfortunately, before he could finish his first query, the connection was broken. He sighed, then wrote down everything he could remember, along with the number she'd called from, on a standard report form—a digital record of calls to emergency services had long been in the works, but funding had never been found.

Being a methodical man, the dispatcher took his time with the report, all while sipping his afternoon tea. Ten minutes later, he deemed it satisfactory and carried it across the room. He was placing his two-page missive in the INCOMING basket when, by chance, a second dispatcher dropped in a report at the same moment. The two papers collided, and the dispatcher's coworker, one of the few women who worked in the call center, straightened them out and said, "Bodies in the middle of nowhere. You?"

The man blinked. "The desert, north of the Al-Fashir highway?"

The woman's brow furrowed. After a thoughtful pause, she retrieved both statements from the basket. They exchanged reports and began reading. The details were essentially the same, the but the reports had clearly come from two different sources: the phone numbers were not the same, and one caller had been female, the other male.

They walked together to a wall map of Sudan that dominated one side of the room. The area in question was virtually unpopulated, and had in recent months been stable—at least by local standards. All the same, rebels had been known to call in false emergencies, hoping to draw first responders into kill zones. Aside from creating a general sense of chaos, they often were able to appropriate either weapons or medical supplies.

The two dispatchers were staring uncertainly at one another, wondering what to do, when a third coworker approached with a report of his own. They all exchanged a three-way look.

"North of Burush?" the woman asked.

With a look of surprise, the third man nodded.

More papers were exchanged, and after two minutes it was the woman who said, "Let's see what the chief thinks . . ."

The chief agreed. The three tightly spaced calls were worthy of an investigation. At his behest, the dispatchers worked together to stick an accurate pin on the wall map. When they did, it became apparent that they were dealing with a known location—an army survey two years earlier, meant to chart possible enemy redoubts, had noted the abandoned compound. That was the good news.

Less encouraging was what they could do about it. The infrastructure for emergency response in Sudan resided largely in Khartoum. As distance from the capital increased, resources degraded inversely. To no one's surprise, there wasn't an ambulance within fifty miles of the buildings in question. And even if there had been, no road came within ten miles of the place.

The regional police were not much better off. When the request for assistance came in, the officer in charge of the North Kurdufan constabulary confessed his limitations, gave his regrets, then did what he always did: he punted to the Ministry of Defense.

The end result of it all was that, three hours after the first call had come in, a single Tamal light tactical vehicle was dispatched from regimental headquarters. The team consisted of a driver, a gunner, and a combat medic. They set out shortly before sunset with a full fuel tank and no small amount of caution.

It took slightly over an hour to reach the assigned coordinates, yet the driver had no trouble finding the place. Indeed, he had been to this valley twice before in recent months during routine defensive sweeps, and he'd annotated the three buildings on his personal topographical map.

Under a partial moon and clear skies, they saw the place from a distance. The driver stopped a judicious hundred yards away. Nothing in their orders gave reason to expect resistance, yet in these hills caution was the rule. The gunner had brought a dated set of night vision goggles. The NVGs weren't anything he'd been issued—the Sudanese army's budget provided for little beyond guns and ammunition, and much of that surplus—but rather a cheap Russian item he'd purchased on the black market. The device had maddening limitations, including very short battery life and little magnification. All the same, it had warned his squad of an ambush three months earlier, attesting to the value of his investment.

The gunner studied the buildings.

"Well? Do you see anything?" the driver asked.

"Nothing moving. I see one body on the ground near the door. And maybe a pair of feet next to it."

"Are you sure they are dead?" the medic asked.

The gunner was silent for a time, then lowered his optics. "I think so. There are also animals on the ground."

"Animals?" the driver repeated.

"Two cows."

The medic, who was technically in charge, said, "Let me see."

Over the next five minutes each of the three men took in the scene. "I don't like it," said the gunner.

"Neither do I," agreed the medic, "but we've come this far." He looked at the other two as if waiting for a volunteer. He didn't get one. It was time to lead by example. "All right," he said, "cover me."

The gunner took up his station behind the bed-mounted Khawad 12.7mm heavy machine gun. The driver grabbed an antiquated H&K G3 rifle from the rack behind the passenger seat and took up a shooting position behind a fender.

In the dim light the medic walked toward the compound like a kid approaching a haunted house. He stopped ten paces short of the front door and studied things for a full minute. His flashlight beam danced over the building and surrounding grounds. Finally, he settled the tiny cone of light on the nearer body and edged closer.

From the Tamal, the others watched him get within a few steps of the bodies. Then their commander turned away suddenly and came back to the truck on a jog.

"Let's get out of here," he said.

"But . . . why?" asked the gunner.

"There were two men, both dead. And animals all around. A vulture, two rats . . . even a full-grown jackal. Something is wrong here. Death is everywhere."

The driver didn't argue. He put the Tamal in gear and drove south for a mile. At that point they stopped and the medic got on the radio. He told the command post what he'd not told his companions. The body he'd seen up close displayed a number of unusual symptoms. The eyes of the victim, who on all appearances was a *baqqara*, had been wide open and the pupils fully constricted. There was evidence of vomit and loss of bowels in the final moments of life. He'd seen many bodies in the course of his duties, but never one showing that combination of indicators. By virtue of his training, he thought he knew what it meant.

And if he was right . . . they were going to need help.

High command was skeptical at first, the officer on duty reluctant to commit scarce resources to a job that seemed best suited to an undertaker. The medic, however, had a reputation as a steady sort, and he'd clearly been shaken by what he'd seen at the compound.

A larger and better equipped unit arrived three hours later. The lieutenant in charge—the company's captain was not an "out-front" leader—took a few dozen pictures with a mobile phone. These were forwarded to headquarters and given to the staff doctor, who'd been called in on his night off. The doctor had considerable training in combat medicine, courtesy of a visiting Chinese detachment three years earlier. The Russians, the Americans, the Chinese—somebody was always trying to ingratiate themselves with the government, and military trainers were cheaper to send than surface-to-air missiles.

What the doctor saw in the photos shook him to the core. Both victims displayed pinpoint pupils, along with evidence of uncontrolled salivation, defecation, and urination. The limbs had ended in awkward positions, stiffened from uncontrolled muscle spasms. He saw the same symptoms in the cows.

The doctor went to the command post, dialed the number of the battalion commander, who was just climbing into bed. After explaining his suspicions, the doctor said, "Sir, we very much need help."

THIRTY-NINE

Sultan knew he had to take the utmost care in entering Saudi Arabia. The Saudis spent a great deal on technology, and the chance of getting through an airport or border checkpoint without being photographed was effectively nil. Other passages, however, were far more opaque.

Conveniently, his intended destination in the kingdom, the Red Sea port of Jeddah, was separated from Sudan by the most straightforward of obstacles—one hundred miles of typically placid sea. He spent that afternoon and evening on the road, bypassing Khartoum, following the Nile for a time, before a right turn took him to his launching point, a diminutive Sudanese fishing village.

If the place had a name it was not listed on any map. Somewhere north of Port Sudan, but south of Egypt, Sultan would have been helpless to find it without the miracle of GPS.

The timing of his arrival was not left to chance. If the village was sleepy by day, it was positively catatonic nearing midnight. He saw not a single illuminated light. Even at idle speed the Toyota rocked over potholes on the only road into town. The sweet scent of the desert was overpowered by a salt-laden breeze. In the dim light he saw the outlines of a dozen sandstone huts, and beyond that a makeshift stone jetty cast a shadow into the crescent-shaped bay. On the lee side of the jetty, beached above the tide line, were a half dozen dhows. The village fleet waiting for another day's light.

All, that is, except for one.

Sultan parked the Toyota next to the only other vehicle in sight, a dilapidated sedan of indeterminant make. He got out, took the key with him, and walked straight to the shoreline. He had no luggage, and aside from the key in his pocket he carried nothing other than one forged passport and a modest wad of cash. With any luck, he would need neither.

His ride was waiting just offshore—twenty feet of wood and canvas, backed by an impossibly small outboard motor. His passage across the narrow sea, along with his reception on the other side, had all been prearranged—not unlike a vacation package booked through a travel agent. His tribal network once again proving its value.

At the water's edge he removed his shoes. Sultan paused momentarily, the waves lapping over his feet onto the scalloped beach. The warm sea felt soothing on his aching ankle. Even cleansing in a way. He supposed it was understandable, given his earlier work that day. The boat lay no more than fifty feet offshore, its skipper standing in knee-deep water. Holding a painter at the bow, he looked like a trailhand waiting for a rider with a saddled horse. The man was young and strong, his sinewy frame steady in the gentle surf. Even under starlight his skin appeared dark and sun-hewn.

With his shoes in hand, Sultan waded through the shallows. As he neared the boat, he said in Arabic, "Peace be upon you."

"And to you the blessings and mercy of God," the young man replied.

"Thank you for being prepared. Will we reach the Saudi coast before daybreak?"

The young man checked his timepiece—not looking down at a watch or a phone, but rather up at the partial moon and stars. "The winds tonight are good. It can be done, God willing."

Sultan reached the boat and put a hand to the rail. He started to lift himself up, and the skipper offered a helping hand. Sultan ignored it, and after three tries managed to flop over the side on his own. He landed ingloriously on top of a fishing net.

The young man pushed the bow seaward and vaulted effortlessly over the rail.

"You know where I am to be dropped?" Sultan asked.

"Thirty-five kilometers north of Jeddah, the place we call Crescent Bay."

Sultan nodded. The name of the bay meant nothing to him, but the young man clearly knew what he was doing. He watched him crank the little outboard to life and twist the handle into gear. Once they were under way, clear of the jetty, the skipper lifted a small sail. It snapped taut under the steady southern breeze. The boat leaned away from the wind and began cutting into open sea.

Sultan didn't try to banter with the young man, instead letting him do his job. He squirmed for a comfortable spot next to the fishing net. It was a miserable place to sleep, but he had to try. He pushed away visions of the previous days, the maid and the *baqqara,* and imagined where he might be sleeping in a week or a year. Someplace far better, certainly, than the deck of a fish-fouled canoe.

In no time, the gentle rocking of the boat closed his eyes.

FORTY

Slaton stirred on the stroke of sunrise, shards of eastern light claw-ing at the edges of the sheet-draped window. There was noth-ing like being a fugitive to turn one into an early riser. He looked around and saw Kravchuk, Salma, and Naji sleeping soundly on an assortment of mattresses on the floor of the bedroom. Not wanting to wake them, he stepped into the hall with the silence of an assas-sin.

Achmed was already awake, and Slaton found him hunched over a worn breakfast table. The table was covered by a regional map, mugs anchoring three corners. The one nearest Achmed was full, judging by a curl of rising steam. When he saw Slaton, he pointed to a half-full coffee pot on the kitchen counter. Slaton thanked him and used the pot to fill the mug resting on Jerusalem.

The map was laminated, confirming that this wasn't Achmed's first rodeo. There were smudges and impressions, most centered on Damascus, and, more disconcertingly, what looked like a bullet hole somewhere north of Aleppo.

Achmed was marking a line with a grease pencil as he refer-enced a pad full of notes.

"Looks like you've been busy," Slaton said.

"I think you are right—we do not have much time. The police in Syria are slow, but they are not stupid. They will seek for Salma's relatives, and when they arrive at my door you can't be here."

"Won't it be difficult to travel?"

"Difficult, yes . . . but I made a few calls this morning. I think there is one route that will keep us clear of the authorities."

"All right," Slaton said, pulling a battered chair into place. "Convince me."

———

The coffee was strong and did its job. Slaton followed along the map as Achmed briefed his plan.

"There is a souk on the southwestern edge of Darayya," he said. "Many of the merchants come from villages and farms to the south. The desert in that direction is open, the watch thin. It is what you might call the city's back door. There are few paved roads, and many of the merchants bring their wares to market using hand carts or donkeys."

"The police don't keep a presence?" Slaton asked.

"They make rounds in the market, but more to put down petty thieves and pickpockets. The other major cities in Syria are all to the north, Beirut to the west. That means little commercial traffic passes through Darayya."

"And beyond Darayya? I thought the police had the city locked down."

"In most areas checkpoints have been doubled. But I talked to my contacts this morning, and they tell me the watch in Darayya is less than usual—I think units have been shifted to more promising sectors. We have seen this before. There were very strict blockades of Damascus during the war, but traffic in and out of Darayya was mostly unchecked."

Slaton studied the map. The souk had been circled. From Achmed's house, it could be reached by traversing the city's southern neighborhoods. This avoided the central districts that were under greater scrutiny, as well as the major arteries leading north and east. The topographical map showed the desert beyond Darayya to be flat and featureless, a few tiny villages dotting the landscape. He noted two corridors marked in black that led west toward Lebanon.

"These routes you've marked—they're not far from the Golan Heights."

"Which is why they are useful. The police leave the protection of those hills to the army. Fortunately for us, the army units near Mount Hermon always look the other way."

"Waiting for the Israeli invasion?"

"Exactly. We will pass right behind their backs."

"Have you used this corridor before?" Slaton asked.

"Yes, but rarely. There is usually no need. I have friends who run licensed transport companies. They keep a few trucks with hidden compartments, and I pay a gratuity to the inspectors at the border—no one looks too closely. Of course, I am more an importer than an exporter. The kinds of things I bring into Syria . . . no one much cares about them. Mobile phones, videos, designer clothing."

"So, you've never moved people in the other direction?"

"Never. But the principle is the same."

"You're wrong," Slaton countered. "If you lose that kind of shipment, people die."

For the first time Achmed's confidence seemed to waver. "Salma and Naji are my only family. I would do anything to keep them safe."

"Good. Because it might come to that."

The Syrian's eyes narrowed suspiciously. "I think I can get you to the border. But I must ask—what then? You say you work with the Americans, but this gives me little confidence. I see how they have treated my country."

Slaton nodded. The man had a point. America's involvement in Syria had been anything but committed. They'd provided aid and assistance to a handful of rebel groups, only to cut them off at critical junctures. They'd drawn red lines on the use of chemical weapons, then backed away. Announced troop withdrawals, then changed their minds. It wasn't the kind of strategy that built trust. In truth, however, Slaton was encouraged by Achmed's skepticism. It implied the mindset of a man who really *did* care about his niece and her son.

Slaton said, "The fact that I'm here is proof the Americans want Ludmilla. If I can get her to the border, they'll be waiting. Get me that far, and I promise to do everything in my power to convince them to take Salma and Naji as well. For what it's worth . . . I've got a little boy at home myself. He's about a year younger than Naji, and I'd like very much to see him soon."

Achmed met Slaton's gaze.

"In the end," Slaton said, "I think our objectives are the same. But to make it happen, we both need to trust a stranger."

FORTY-ONE

The skipper made good on his promise, pulling behind a spit of sand on the far side of the Red Sea just before sunrise. The narrow coastal plain along the western shores of Saudi Arabia was known as Tihamah, one of the few regions of the country where vegetation prevailed.

Sultan looked out and saw land that showed not a single human mark, the most distinguishing characteristic being a narrow ribbon of beach separating land and sea. Having already furled the sail, the skipper killed the tiny engine. The boat came still twenty yards offshore, and he flicked his finger down toward the gunnel. His intent seemed clear: *Out you go.*

Sultan looked into waters that were famously crystalline, yet there wasn't enough light to gauge the depth.

"No problem," the young man said as if reading his mind. "Only to your knees."

Sultan took off his shoes, socks, and pants and bundled them into a roll. Wearing only his underwear, he wondered if the Rashiduns before him, in their day, had suffered such indignities. He supposed they had—and probably far worse.

With one leg over the side, he paused, and asked, "Tonight?"

"I will be here," the young man promised, "one hour after sunset."

Sultan looked all around, saw nothing but low sandstone cliffs and sea. He slipped silently into the water—it came nearly to his hip. He looked back and asked, "Will you stay in the cove all day?"

"No. The Saudis patrol these waters. It would also be a waste of time. Today I will do real work."

Sultan raised his eyes inquisitively.

"I promise to not catch so many fish that there will be no room for you."

With that, the young man lifted a long pole and began pushing the dhow silently back to sea.

Sultan waded awkwardly through the warm water. On reaching land he sat in the sand to put his pants and shoes back on—the simplest of tasks, but one he'd never been able to manage while standing.

When he was done, he stood and regarded the coastline. The sun was breaking the horizon, capturing the coast in its welcoming glow. He had never set foot in Saudi Arabia, and it occurred to him that he, like any good Muslim, was obliged to make a pilgrimage to Mecca. At that moment, he was no more than fifty miles from the Kaaba, and on reaching Jeddah he would be closer yet. Would this be his best chance? No, he decided. One day, soon enough, he would complete the hajj on his own terms.

Sultan began walking, the light of a new day showing him the way. It seemed an affirmation. The spit of land where he'd been dropped bent softly inland, a crescent of sand and crushed shell. Where the crescent joined the mainland, he discerned a worn path leading north. So far, everything precisely as briefed.

He spotted the car five minutes later. It turned out to be a standard white taxi parked on an uneven dirt apron. He saw the driver behind the wheel, his face illuminated by the glow of a mobile screen. The driver glanced up, saw him coming, and put down his phone. Neither man went through the contrivance of a wave or a nod. There likely wasn't another taxi, or for that matter another passenger, within twenty miles.

Sultan climbed in back and exchanged a traditional Arabic greeting with the driver. He then said, "You know where we are going?"

"I was given an address."

With nothing more said, the car set out into a fast-rising morning.

As Sultan was nearing Jeddah, across the Red Sea three Iranians were on the verge of success. They had earlier that morning received the most specific directions yet for a delivery. On the three previous days, they'd embarked on cross-country journeys, only to return empty-handed.

Today, they were sure, would be different.

They set out before dawn, driving north out of Khartoum on a secondary road. At the prescribed location they found their marker: a blue plastic grocery bag fluttering from the branch of a thorny scrub. On face value, it was the kind of thing one encountered on any drive through the desert. Yet this particular bag was not a random bit of wind-driven jetsam. They knew because it was directly behind a distinctive roadside culvert, and because the culvert itself was precisely thirty-two kilometers beyond the Blue Nile Bridge.

The Iranians had followed their directions to the letter.

All three got out of the Land Rover and began walking. The desert here seemed familiar, little different from what existed outside Tehran. Spindly, tough-looking shrubs nipped at the cuffs of their trousers, and every footfall sent tiny stones over ferrous dirt.

They found the canister directly behind the bush, lying in the dirt near a discarded soda bottle. Roughly the size and shape of a household fire extinguisher, the cylinder was shiny and smooth, clearly constructed of high-grade steel. At the neck was a complex valve with twin activation handles that appeared to operate in series—both would have to be activated to disperse whatever was inside. Also like a fire extinguisher, the valves were secured by safety pins, and the pins themselves retained by zip ties. Three levels of precaution, all reassuring.

The Iranians stood staring for some time. Finally, they had what they'd come for. After so many false trails, it seemed a shock to succeed so suddenly and completely.

All that was left was to deliver the canister safely to Tehran.

The technician took over—after being little more than a tourist for the last week, his *raison d'être* was now realized. He performed a perfunctory test with a small portable sensor. The negative results seemed a moot point: if there was a leak or contamination, none of them would still be standing. He carefully lifted the canister and carried it to the Rover. In the rear cargo bay, he packed it in a hardened Pelican case, cradled in foam inserts designed specifically for their prize. For extra measure, he stuffed in two thick hotel towels—the witless maid, they agreed, would never miss them. To the approval of his companions, the technician took particular care in protecting the valve. After closing the case, he eased it under a mesh cargo net that would keep it from shifting.

Everyone climbed back into the Rover.

The drive to the airport was unusually quiet. One hour after collecting their prize, the Iranians pulled into a quiet corner of Khartoum International Airport. Their private jet was fueled, the crew waiting, a flight plan to Tehran already filed. They collected their baggage, including the new acquisition, and headed into the corporate terminal. The keys to the Rover were dropped with the receptionist, a pleasant young woman who bid them a happy journey and promised that their vehicle would be returned to the rental company. The rest was simplicity itself.

As was often the case in Third World states, the government of Sudan gave loose oversight to who was granted access to the country's lone corporate aviation terminal. Visiting dignitaries and royalty were routinely welcomed, so too the occasional shady arms merchant. The departure of the three guests from Tehran turned out to be a non-event. They had experienced negligible scrutiny on entering Sudan—a concession, no doubt, to the Iranian government—and leaving proved even easier. In the main building all three men showed their passports to a lonely immigration officer who waved them through with barely a glance. There was no inspection of luggage, including the custom-built Pelican case.

Ten minutes later, the sleek business jet, whose provenance was as murky as its generic paint scheme, began taxiing toward the active runway. Minutes later it was airborne, arcing northward into a cloudless sapphire sky.

While the departure of the Iranians raised few eyebrows that morning, it would be scrutinized far more intensely in the coming days. For the most part, the inquiry would be unproductive. The investigation into how authorizations for the visit had been granted would go nowhere, lost to a byzantine bureaucracy and an uncooperative regime in Khartoum. The receptionist at the terminal would be questioned, as would the staff of the Corinthia Hotel. Little would be learned, although the untimely death of the housekeeper who'd cleaned the Iranians' rooms would be tagged as highly suspicious.

Yet one track of inquiry would prove useful.

As a rule, the comings and goings from executive terminals were monitored with great discretion. High-net-worth individuals abhorred being subject to surveillance, and governments seeking foreign investment were generally happy to comply. The most discreet operations kept no cameras at all. Those that did employed state-of-the-art systems that were tightly managed. The best networks were virtually impenetrable, and could be disabled or wiped clean on orders from above.

The executive terminal at Khartoum International, as it turned out, was not up to these standards. An aging network of cameras recorded everything that happened on the private jet ramp, and the server on which those images were stored was protected by laughable cyber security measures.

The one thing investigators would never realize was that Sultan was perfectly aware of all these deficiencies.

FORTY-TWO

Achmed left the house without mentioning where he was going. To Slaton's relief, he returned fifteen minutes later driving a blue-and-white taxi.

He parked it in back near the garage, and came inside carrying a full black garbage bag. He hauled the bag to the green couch and spilled out a pile of well-worn clothes. "There are abayas and hijabs for the women—it is best not to draw attention in the souk."

"What about me?" Slaton asked.

From the pile Achmed extracted an extra-large sweatshirt with a hoodie. "You will have to manage with this—be thankful it is not summer. Only old men wear robes anymore in Damascus."

Ludmilla and Salma began sorting through a dozen robes of various colors and sizes. Slaton didn't ask where the clothes had come from, nor the taxi. He guessed it was probably owned by a neighbor, someone who could be counted on to not ask questions. As was the case in all countries run by cruel and oppressive regimes, trust began next door.

Naji ran to the pile and began throwing garments in the air. He squealed something in Arabic. Probably, *What about me?* Slaton guessed.

Achmed shooed him away. Children required no disguise. The unpleasant truth, Slaton knew, was that Naji was the best bit of camouflage they had.

"We should hurry," Achmed said. "The Mukhabarat have been seen in a nearby neighborhood."

"What about Salma's car?" Slaton asked. "If they find it here they'll know you're involved."

"After we leave a friend is going to take it away."

"Does he know to keep it out of sight?"

"His shed is bigger than mine . . . with a bit of paint, a new license plate, he will have a new car by this evening."

Not for the first time, Slaton recognized the instincts of a seasoned trader. He tried the hoodie on for size.

They were on the road ten minutes later, and Slaton was once again struck by the digression of his situation. His actions at the salon had been necessary, but also a kick to the proverbial hornet's nest. He was now riding through one of the most dangerous cities on the planet in a borrowed taxi. He had two weapons at his disposal, and his team consisted of a hairdresser, a linguist, a four-year-old child, and a man who smuggled mobile phones and pirated Hollywood movies.

Achmed, who was driving, said, "I made calls before we left the house. It is as expected. There are police around the souk, but fewer than usual."

Slaton sat next to him in the front passenger seat, and the women and child were in back—all in accordance with local customs. Salma and Naji looked perfectly convincing. She wore a drab abaya, her son the same shirt and jeans he'd been wearing for two days. The bottoms of Naji's pants left a two-inch gap above his shoes—Slaton remembered seeing Davy in the same predicament only a few weeks ago. Ludmilla was also abaya-clad, and would probably get by as long as she kept her hijab loosely over her Slavic cheeks. Even if challenged, she could respond in fluent Arabic. Yet she did have one handicap: the MP5 Slaton had duct-taped to her side. There had been no choice but to secure it beneath one of the robes, and Ludmilla had volunteered. Fortunately, the weapon was relatively compact. The stock was collapsed and he'd detached the suppressor—the two spare magazines were in his own pockets. He didn't like not having the weapon immediately available, but it seemed the best compromise.

Slaton himself was the least genuine of the group—he had the hood pulled over his sandy hair, and a pair of wrap-around sunglasses were ready on the dash in front of him. In his past life with Mossad he'd taken up far more elaborate guises, to include hair dye and agents that darkened the skin. Today, there was no time for such contrivances. As a group, they were relying heavily on Achmed's experience to keep them out of trouble.

There had been little conversation since leaving the house. Slaton glanced in back and saw tension in two partially covered faces. The same with the smuggler next to him. The only thing lightening the mood was the endearingly off-key singing of Naji who was stuck on the looping chorus of a preschooler's tune he'd heard on TV.

Achmed navigated a winding path through neighborhoods, and so far had avoided main roads. More than once he turned into what looked like a dirt driveway, only to emerge on yet another street. At one point he veered into the parking lot for the city sanitation department. Slaton saw row after row of garbage trucks, many derelict and clearly out of commission. Achmed explained that during the war the entire operation had been abandoned, garbage no longer being a priority. Now the main lot had fallen to a veritable graveyard of garbage trucks—with the smell to prove it. Achmed used it well. They traversed a half-mile-wide apron of dirt without seeing a soul.

It was invaluable local area knowledge, the kind of advantage that could never be gleaned from reconnaissance photos or maps. The more Slaton saw, the more he liked the strategy. The police might be scouring the city and locking down chokepoints, but in the residential warrens of Darayya it was Saturday as usual. Women hanging clothes on lines, men fixing cars. Kids darting from one dusty courtyard to the next.

"Can we reach the souk entirely on secondary roads?" he asked.

"We will have to join a boulevard to cross the river," Achmed said. "But it is not a busy street. After that, the souk is only minutes away. We will leave the taxi there."

"That leaves quite a gap to reach the Lebanese border."

"Twenty-five kilometers, more or less. There are a few farms, but it is mostly open desert."

"So, if we're ditching the taxi, I assume you have a plan for traveling the rest of the way?"

"I have many plans. But I have chosen the best—"

Achmed's eyes suddenly flickered with caution.

Slaton looked ahead and saw a military truck approaching in the opposite direction. It was slightly smaller than the Ural he'd stolen yesterday, moving slowly. He weighed whether to retrieve the hidden

MP5. A squad of soldiers, between eight and ten men in uniform, were seated on twin benches in the truck's open bed. They didn't look particularly alert, most either talking or keeping their heads down against the sun.

Achmed kept a steady speed, but soon it became apparent that the narrow lane wouldn't accommodate both vehicles—stone walls of various heights lined the road on either side.

"Pull over!" Slaton said, pointing to the next driveway on the right.

"No," Achmed argued. "If I do that the truck might block us in!"

"*Do it!*" Slaton ordered.

His hard tone worked. Achmed pulled the car to a stop in the recess of the next driveway. The truck came closer, not yet slowing. Sun glinted on its windshield, preventing Slaton from seeing the driver's eyes. He mentally rehearsed the moves required to retrieve the MP5.

He said, "If I engage these guys, I'll get out of the car first. I'll use the nearest wall for cover." He looked at Achmed. "If there's still room, move the car. Forward, backward . . . anywhere but here."

Achmed nodded.

Slaton devised a plan to fit the scenario. If he could access the MP5 quickly enough, he would put his first two rounds through the truck's windshield—not to kill the driver, but to convince him that continued motion was in his personal best interest. From there he would pair rounds on the nearest rack of infantry, beginning with whoever was moving most quickly.

The truck was a mere fifty feet away.

Slaton knew his blueprint was notional, subject to a hundred variables.

Thirty feet, speed still steady. He got a glimpse of the driver, saw him chatting amiably with someone in the passenger seat— probably the unit's commander. A junior officer or sergeant.

Slaton made eye contact with Ludmilla, who seemed to understand—she half turned in her seat and gripped the hem of her abaya.

Achmed waved cordially to the driver.

Salma appeared to be praying.

The truck passed uneventfully. Slaton turned, kept watching until it disappeared in a cloud of tan dust.

"Okay," he finally said. "Crisis averted. Let's go."

Achmed put the car in gear, and the collective sigh was palpable. That is, from everyone except Naji. Never once through it all had he stopped chirping his happy tune.

FORTY-THREE

Achmed explained the next steps as the souk came into sight.

"We will leave the taxi and go into the market. On the far side a friend has provided what we need to reach the border."

"And what is that?" Slaton asked.

"It will become clear when you see."

"What about the timing? The Americans need to know where and when to meet us."

"Very early tomorrow morning . . . I would say between two and four. As we discussed earlier, the hills south of Deir El Aachayer."

Slaton pulled out his phone, turned it on, and sent the message. When an acknowledgement came thirty seconds later, he turned the phone back off.

Achmed found a parking spot on a narrow side street. Slaton pulled his hood low over his forehead and donned the knock-off Ray-Bans he'd taken from a box full of them in Achmed's hall closet.

Everyone got out and assumed the briefed formation. Achmed was in the lead, Slaton at his side. The women brought up the rear with Naji between them. So arranged, they set out into the market trying to look like the family they weren't.

The report from the Sudanese army, detailing a suspicious event at a remote site in Darfur, stirred a surprisingly concise reaction from the controlling regime—if the recognition of shortcomings could be considered effective governance.

The army was convinced they might be dealing with a potential biological or chemical event. This was entirely outside the wheelhouse of a fighting force designed for chasing down rebels who traveled primarily on foot. For the government, requesting outside help was a maddeningly fluid concept. Their patrons changed from year to year, and sometimes from day to day. Russia, China, France, Egypt, and Saudi Arabia had all left recent footprints in Sudan.

The politics of the day in the Horn of Africa were driven by any number of factors: military sales, food aid, infrastructure projects, and more often than not, outright bribery. As it turned out, on that Saturday, as had been the case for much of the last year, the Americans were the ally of choice. Their NGOs were increasingly committed, and there had even been recent whisperings of arms sales. Best of all, the new administration in Washington was determined to lay bare the Chinese Belt and Road Initiative for what it was: a combination land grab and protection racket on a global scale.

Which was why, in the early hours of that same morning, the foreign minister of Sudan had dialed his counterpart in Washington, D.C., with an impassioned plea for help.

The U.S. Air Force C-130, operated by the Tennessee Air National Guard, landed on a dirt strip outside the village of Umm Badr minutes before noon—although to those sitting in the cargo bay, the term "landing" might have been charitable. The Hercules was built to land on unprepared surfaces, but the meeting between aircraft and earth on the very short, fifty-meter-wide strip of dirt was closer to a controlled crash.

The flight had taken off that morning from Incirlik Air Base in Turkey. A team from the DOD's Chemical and Biological Defense Program, or CBDP, had taken up permanent residence there, a rotating squad of nine men and women who were fully prepared for rapid mobilization: their three standard pallets of equipment included personal protection suits, decontamination gear, and various sensors for detecting, marking, and sampling both chemical and biological agents.

The Hercules reached the end of the landing strip, and once stopped, the aircraft commander simply set the parking brake, started the auxiliary power unit, and shut down the engines. There was no separate pad for parking. The aircraft's integral boarding stairs were lowered, and the first person off was the lieutenant colonel in charge of the CBDP team.

He was met by the CIA's Khartoum station chief, a man named Bates, who'd driven from the embassy in the city.

"What's the latest?" the colonel asked.

"Nothing new," Bates replied. "The Sudanese suspect there may have been an incident of some kind, and everyone's been waiting for you. Nobody wants to go near the place."

The commander frowned. "Any idea if it's chemical or biological?"

"I'm guessing chemical, but my expertise is pretty limited."

"How far back are the Sudanese?"

"One kilometer."

The rear loading ramp of the Hercules began to pivot down, and somewhere inside the cargo bay a motor rumbled to life.

"Make it two," said the colonel. "And make sure they stay upwind."

The CBDP unit, highly mobile by definition, was assembled around two standard Humvees. The Hummers were preloaded with all the necessary equipment and a high-end communications suite that could, if necessary, contact national command authorities directly. Of the nine team members, seven set out in the vehicles, while the remaining two, including the lieutenant colonel, stayed with the Hercules for logistical support and security, and to establish a forward-based command post.

The team set out under a blazing midday sun and reached the compound in less than an hour. The team leader, a captain, established an observation post as per protocol—on high ground and upwind of the incident site—while a corporal geared up in a protective suit. The captain studied the buildings much as the Sudanese had the night before. Also like the Sudanese, he was bothered by what he saw. Dead people, dead animals. No evidence of a firefight.

He walked over to the corporal, who was nearly ready to go. "Careful on this one, Josh. It could be the real deal."

The corporal didn't argue, and minutes later he was climbing into one of the Hummers, which would take him to within a hundred yards of the buildings. From that point he would be on his own.

The first readings arrived ten minutes later. The M4A1 Joint

Chemical Agent Detector was the best bit of hardware they'd received in years. It was designed to sense not only chemical warfare agents, but also toxic industrial vapors. A handheld device, the M4A1 provided real-time detection of nerve, blister, and blood agents. Best of all, at least from a command and control point of view, the unit was net-capable, able to send a snapshot of results at any moment via a secure comm link.

Which was how, within ninety minutes of the CBDP team arriving in Sudan, their findings reached various nodes of the command structure in Washington, D.C. Among them was the director's suite on Langley's fifth floor. This instigated a burst of secure phone calls, and one hastily scheduled meeting.

With a rough idea of what they'd stumbled upon, and knowing it would take time for higher headquarters to sort out a response, the CBDP team elected to not wait in place for subsequent orders. Within seconds of retrieving the corporal and putting him through decontamination, the captain repositioned his team away from ground zero.

Far, far away.

Anna Sorensen updated Coltrane on the Syria mission in the director's office.

"Slaton hopes to get Kravchuk out tonight," she said, dispensing with the code name Corsair.

"Has an extraction point been chosen?" he asked.

"The border with Lebanon, roughly due west of Damascus. I have a team from the Beirut embassy standing by in support. It's a remote area, so we should be clear on the Lebanon side. But there is one complication."

"There always is," Coltrane quipped.

"It's actually more diplomatic than operational. It involves the owner of the salon where Kravchuk took up hiding. According to Slaton, she was fearful the Syrians would go after her for aiding the enemy."

"She probably has a point."

"Slaton thought so too, so he included her and her four-year-old son in the plan. He wants us to take them into Lebanon with Kravchuk."

Coltrane blew a sigh of exasperation. "This thing is starting to blow up. By all accounts, Slaton didn't go lightly in Damascus. He laid waste to an entire street and two Mukhabarat men ended up dead. If the Syrians think this woman was complicit, and she later ends up in our custody—they're going to pitch a fit."

"No more than they will when they realize we have Kravchuk."

Coltrane weighed it all. "All right, Slaton made the call. We'll figure out how to deal with it after everyone is safe. Right now, I'm more concerned with what's going on in Sudan. Are you following it?"

"I saw the initial report," Sorensen said.

"It occurs to me that this incident might be what Kravchuk heard about at the summit."

"She used the word attack," Sorensen argued. "Terrible as it is, I don't see how a pair of dead cattle herders qualifies as a terrorist event."

"True," Coltrane said. "This looks more like an accident."

"Or a demonstration?" Sorensen ventured.

"Possibly. Whatever it is, we need to get to the bottom of it."

"Who's taking the lead on the event in Sudan?"

"The army has control of the site, and more resources are being sent downrange. By this time tomorrow, we should know exactly what we're dealing with. I think it's safe to say, this threat didn't originate in Khartoum—they were the ones who called us in. I actually have it on good account that this is scaring the hell out of the regime. I'm assigning a working group to figure out where this nerve agent came from. Once we know that, we'll have a better idea of how to react."

"Kravchuk might be able to shed some light on it."

"Maybe she can," Coltrane said. "So, let's hope Slaton comes through tonight."

FORTY-FOUR

The souk was big and busy, the obvious hub of Darayya. Like most markets across the region, it was a grocery and pharmacy and community center all in one. To Slaton's eye, there was something visceral and connective about it, as if the entire square where it existed comprised a single living thing.

He saw hundreds of tiny shops, the majority of which, he was sure, were set up each day. Notwithstanding the lack of brick and mortar, it was nothing less than the community's bedrock. Every kind of fruit and vegetable was offered, brimming in baskets and crates that came straight from the fields. Flatbread was stacked high on carts, offered either in bulk packages, or stuffed with meat from simmering skillets. The air was thick with scents: the tang of fat dripping on grills, the sweetness of fresh-baked sweetbread, the mingling accents of exotic spices. Slaton took it all in with a curious sense of familiarity. Take away the car license plates, the occasional flag, and he could have been in a market anywhere from Marrakesh to Karachi.

The main thoroughfare was defined by a high corrugated roof that ran along one side. Opposite that, vendors sat beneath the same shade tents one might see at kids' soccer games in the States or on beaches in Spain. People were everywhere. Old and young, men and women. The crowds bogged down in shoulder-to-shoulder traffic at chokepoints.

Achmed carved through it all like a knife.

"At the far end we will find our transportation," he said to Slaton under his breath. "It was provided by a man named Rafa."

Slaton didn't venture a reply. After some coaxing, Naji had agreed to ride on his shoulders. It not only conveyed an image of family, but also helped conceal Slaton's face. Those who did glance his way focused on the cute child—a perfectly natural human behavior. While one hand anchored Naji's legs, Slaton held his phone near his chest with the other. This allowed him to keep his head canted downward. Twenty years ago, it would have seemed a peculiar behavior—walking on a busy street while carrying a child, not watching where you were going. These days it was perfectly normal. And a surprisingly effective countermeasure.

Notwithstanding these visual screens, Slaton's eyes remained busy. He scanned the stalls in the periphery, the crowds ahead. He made sure the women didn't get separated. He kept an eye out for roving pickpockets, not wanting one to bump into Ludmilla and discover an MP5 under her abaya. A great many things could go wrong in a crowd so dense.

"Have you seen any police yet?" Slaton said in a low voice, cocking his head toward Achmed.

"Only one uniform, some distance away. The usual."

Let's hope it stays that way, Slaton thought.

A chicken scuttled in front of them, flapping and clucking, and a young boy was right behind giving spirited chase. Naji giggled. When Slaton stepped to one side to dodge the boy, he bumped into an old woman. She said something in Arabic, a few words of which he caught. Enough to know that it hadn't been, "Have a nice day." He easily ignored it.

Achmed turned from the main avenue into a broad alley. Fifty feet farther on was a cul de sac of sorts. He came to a stop, and before them, deep in the shadow of a building, Slaton saw an untended vegetable cart. The cart was fifteen feet long, five wide, with two wheels supporting a flat cargo deck. At the other end a gooseneck hitch rested on a brick. Beyond that he saw a worn leather harness and, tied to a post, the engine: a disinterested donkey with its mouth deep in a feed bag.

"You *are* kidding," Slaton said. He lifted Naji off his shoulders and set him on the ground.

"Look closely," Achmed replied.

Slaton did. The donkey was a donkey. The cart, too, seemed unremarkable. Its cargo bed was hip height, and there was a short wraparound rail on the sides and front. The load consisted of dozens of produce crates, most half-empty. Carrots, lettuce, oranges, dates, melons. His eyes returned to the cart, and on second glance he *did* discern something unusual in the undercarriage. A sidewall ringed the deck, perhaps eighteen inches in depth.

"A compartment?" he asked.

"Rafa is the other kind of smuggler. He makes fewer trips than I do, but they are far more lucrative."

"Drugs?"

Achmed cocked his head indifferently. "I do not judge my fellow man. He makes a good living . . . and he is very careful."

"How big is the space?"

"He tells me there is enough room for two people."

Slaton stared at the Syrian. "Ludmilla and . . . me?"

"Only until we are clear of the city. The rest of us are Syrian and won't be challenged. Once we reach the desert everyone can walk until we near the border."

Slaton smiled noncommittally, his gray eyes a blank.

"The door to the compartment is on the other side," Achmed said.

Slaton looked over his shoulder toward the market. Rafa, whoever and wherever he was, had been clever. The cart was backed into a shadow where two buildings merged. The right side was completely screened from sight.

Achmed retrieved a folded tarp from the cart and draped it strategically to give even better cover. He told the women the plan, and assigned Salma to stand watch on the market while they prepared to move.

When everyone was in place, Achmed unlatched an artfully concealed access panel on the side of the cart. Slaton studied the compartment. It was big enough for two, but only just. Ludmilla looked doubtful, and Slaton hoped she wasn't claustrophobic. He'd seen the routes Achmed had mapped out, and knew they'd be traveling over rough terrain. It wouldn't be comfortable.

Ludmilla steeled herself, and after a nod from Achmed to confirm the coast was clear, she bent down and wedged herself into the slot. Once she was inside, Slaton leaned down. Instead of climbing in, however, he whispered something in Ludmilla's ear. She looked at him wide-eyed, then nodded.

Slaton stood straight. He saw Salma give a little wave behind her back. Two young women were approaching.

"Hurry!" Achmed prompted. "Get in!"

Slaton bent down a second time, his head and shoulders disappearing. He then backed out and stood straight. He was holding the MP5, but kept it low and out of sight.

The two young girls disappeared.

With the weapon in a casual grip, Slaton addressed Achmed. "I have one minor change to your plan . . ."

Sultan had managed little sleep on his overnight voyage. That being the case, when he arrived in Jeddah with five hours to kill before his appointed meeting, he knew how to spend it.

Much like his travel, the safe house had been prearranged. It turned out to be a three-bedroom townhome, one of four in a characterless row, that had been rented online. After the driver delivered him to the assigned address early that morning, it had been simplicity itself to enter a code on a keypad at the door. On first glance he'd thought the place needlessly spacious, but a gloriously comfortable bed erased any misgivings. When the bedside alarm went off slightly after noon, he was glad to have had the foresight to set it. The buzzer jolted him out of a sound sleep.

Sultan got up stiffly and stretched, the muscles in his legs knotted from yesterday's exertions. As he washed at the bathroom basin, he heard the call to midday prayer beckoning from outside. He felt no urge to comply. Today he would do God's work, but not by putting his knees to a mat.

He was on the street minutes later, keeping diligently to the directions he'd been given. He had never before been to Jeddah, although, like any Muslim, he knew it by reputation. The second largest city in Saudi Arabia, it was best known as the gateway to Mecca and Medina, the most holy sites in the faith.

He had no trouble blending in. His features were loosely Arab, and for men the local dress code was remarkably varied. Some wore Western clothes, while others preferred traditional white *thobes*. He himself had opted for a simple *thobe*. Two months earlier, during the hajj, a casual glance would have placed him as one of the millions making their once-in-a-lifetime pilgrimage. Women, Sultan noted, were not given such freedom when it came to clothing—

without exception, every one he saw was covered from head to toe in a flowing black abaya.

Sultan checked now and again to see if he was being followed. He saw shop owners outside storefronts, taxi drivers chatting in small groups. None of them held his attention. But then, counter-surveillance was hardly his forte.

He found himself studying the city, with its new streets and postmodern construction. The sidewalks were unbroken, the curbs freshly swept. The House of Saud's largesse was evident on every corner. Sultan imagined that he might bring the same to his own homeland. The Saudis' success, of course, was not attributable to hard work or ingenuity, but rather one stroke of good fortune. In fifty years, they had built an entire country from scratch, palaces and towers and condominiums risen from the sand. A tribe that had for thousands of years been sandal-clad on top of camels had, in less than three generations, found themselves stomping Guccis on the accelerators of Mercedes.

A gilded world derived completely from black gold.

But they are weak because of it, Sultan thought as he ambled down the spotless boulevard. *And that, God willing, shall be their downfall.*

FORTY-FIVE

The café was half a mile from the safe house, a modest space embedded in a modern commercial district. Sultan arrived five minutes early, and so he stood outside under what might have passed for a tree, a spindly acacia trimmed in the shape of an umbrella. Owing to the hundred-degree heat, the outdoor patio was deserted at midday, yet he saw a decent crowd inside through the broad front windows. His phone buzzed a message: I'm inside.

Sultan walked in and found Akeem Nazir at a high counter sipping milky coffee from an insulated paper cup. He was wearing civilian clothes—Sultan knew he was not scheduled for duty today. All the same, there was no mistaking his profession. Nazir had the regulation haircut and bearing of a soldier. They embraced like the old friends they were.

"It is good to see you," said Nazir.

"And you, my friend."

"How long has it been?"

"Four months, I think," Sultan said. "Your last visit to Amman."

Nazir nodded enthusiastically. "Yes, I remember. I was home on leave."

The two had not seen one another in months, this a matter of security. Yet one last meeting was required.

Nazir gestured to a second cup on the counter. "I bought you a coffee. Sugar, no milk."

Sultan took it and smiled, not mentioning that he had recently given up coffee—one of the many deprivations he'd imposed on himself to promote a more pious image.

The two had grown up together on the outer fringes of Amman,

Jordan. Nazir was one of the few boys in school who hadn't belittled him for his crippled leg, and who hadn't teased him for his strange accent. Everyone knew that young Ahmed Sultan al-Majid was not a native Jordanian. That he came from the north was a given, although just how far north would have come as a surprise.

The two boys had bonded as boys did, playing video games and watching movies, pilfering oranges from the grove on the way to school. For Nazir it was not an exclusive friendship. He occasionally diverted to play soccer with boys who were more athletic, and regularly attended a different mosque. Nazir had never been the most street-smart child—indeed, he'd been the kind of boy who always found himself looking right when life was on his left. All the same, he was the closest thing to a best friend Sultan had ever had. And perhaps ever would.

They were thirteen when Nazir's father interrupted their friendship by taking a job in an oil field in Saudi Arabia. He moved the family away and, despite promises to stay in touch, the boys quickly lost track of one another. Three years later Nazir's father was killed, along with two other men, when a coking tank at the refinery exploded. The Saudis responded as they typically did when foreign workers fell victim to industrial accidents—they wrote modest checks to the widows, hired replacement workers, and built a new coking tank.

It was here that fate intervened. Because Nazir and his mother were Muslims from a neighboring country, one further accommodation was made: they were offered citizenship in the Saudi kingdom. Nazir's grieving mother was forced to make dire calculations. As a Muslim woman with no education and limited prospects, she saw but one chance for her only child: Nazir was about to turn seventeen, and if they took citizenship and remained in Saudi Arabia, he would be eligible for military service. There he could get training, a chance for a productive life.

These details Sultan had learned only recently. One year ago, he'd had a chance run-in with a cousin of Nazir's in Amman. It came at a time when an improbable scheme had been brewing in Sultan's head. He did a bit of research, reestablished contacts in his ancestral home. His plan progressed, at each juncture escalating into something larger, something more ambitious. Only when he learned of Nazir's assigned duties in the Saudi Air Force did the final peg fall into place. A means to an end that had long seemed no more than a dream.

Sultan leveraged the networks of his extended family, and found a tribe who were only too willing to help. He discovered that Nazir still made annual trips to Amman to visit uncles and cousins. Also, that his boyhood friend was disenchanted with military life, and that he blamed the Saudis for his father's death. It all fit perfectly. When Nazir next visited Amman, Sultan arranged a "chance meeting." Their friendship rekindled quickly, and Sultan cultivated the relationship for months before finally making his pitch.

As hoped, he'd found a willing ear.

"I think we should not talk here," said Nazir.

"I agree," replied Sultan.

"I have everything you wished to see in my car. On the way to our destination, we can drive past the air base."

Sultan nodded benevolently, a gesture he'd been working on. "Then God willing, it shall be so."

FORTY-SIX

A bird warbled somewhere in the tawny undergrowth, a warning to its equally invisible brethren. Slaton wasn't the only one watching for threats. The desert was thick with life, robust species adapting continuously to harsh conditions. Creatures that found a way to survive.

He was out on point, leading the donkey by a tether—a compulsory skill for any operator who worked the Middle East. Salma and Naji were riding on the cart, their legs dangling over the back. They were sharing an orange plucked from one of the crates. A dumbfounded Achmed was crammed beside Ludmilla in the cart's false bottom. Slaton could only imagine what that ride had to be like as the cart bounded over ruts like a bicycle over train tracks.

Achmed had been livid in the souk when Slaton refused to join Ludmilla in the compartment. That, however, was a line he would not cross. From Slaton's perspective, to be trapped inside, unable to respond to threats, was entirely unacceptable. He would gladly have allowed Achmed to walk beside him as they made their way out of the city, but when he'd started protesting loudly, with another group of women nearing, Slaton made his decision—it was neither the time nor the place for negotiation. One silencing blow to the solar plexus later, he'd folded his guide into the compartment and shut the door. Since then Achmed had remained quiet. Whether it was out of common sense or fear, Slaton couldn't say. They had cleared the souk uneventfully, seeing only one distant pair of policemen amid the outer ring of vendors. Twenty minutes after that they were absorbed by the desert.

It had been two hours now, and the last vestiges of Damascus were barely visible behind them. He guided the cart between shocks of tan scrub, keeping to lower elevations wherever possible for concealment. The terrain was rough, but positively pastoral compared to the volcanic plateaus he'd traversed the previous night in As Suwayda.

Slaton was fighting exhaustion, but happy to be clear of the city. The most treacherous part, he knew, still lay ahead—the Lebanese border would be watched closely. Mercifully, a high cloud deck had drifted in to frustrate the sun. It cut the heat to something bearable, and better yet, if the clouds remained in place they would have the benefit of a dark night.

He was sure their little troop would appear normal from a distance—a family heading home from the city. Unfortunately, the odds of passing any close inspection were virtually nil. For that reason, the MP5 was concealed between crates of oranges at the front of the cart, easily accessible.

"Naji has to use the toilet," Salma called out.

Slaton brought the donkey to a stop. His eyes swept the horizon all around.

"Okay. Let's all take a break."

Salma and Naji dismounted, and she led her son off into the scrub. Slaton went to the right side of the cart. The hidden compartment could only be opened from the outside, a latch blended into the underside of the wooden deck. Since it was designed for hauling drugs, nothing else would have been considered.

Slaton opened the door and helped Ludmilla out. Achmed came next, but Slaton knew better than to offer a hand to the pissed-off Syrian. The smuggler looked weary. His eyes creased against the light and there was dust in his beard. He tried to stand straight, working his limbs like they needed oiling. He leveled a burning gaze on Slaton, but said nothing before meandering into the desert.

Ludmilla looked unsteady. "You okay?" Slaton asked.

"Yes. But it is very uncomfortable in there." There was hollowness in her eyes, fatigue in her voice. She, too, worked her arms and legs to get circulation returning.

"I'm sure it is. Did Achmed have bad things to say about me?"

"He did."

"I don't blame him."

"How much longer until we reach the border?" she asked.

"Sometime after midnight. We're making good time."

She seemed to think about it, then asked, "Once we're with the Americans, where will they take us?"

"I don't know. Probably either the Beirut embassy or an airport."

"They will want to debrief me."

"Yes. But they'll also know you're tired. You'll have time to rest."

"More, I think, than the SVR would give me."

Slaton regarded her thoughtfully. "Are you going to miss it?" he asked.

"Russia?"

"Home."

Ludmilla bent her head thoughtfully, as if she hadn't considered it. "I have spent many years on overseas postings. My husband passed away a long time ago."

"I'm sorry to hear that," he said.

"It wasn't a happy marriage. We had already separated, and there were no children. My only relative is a sister in Murmansk. I haven't spoken to her in years. I keep a flat in Moscow, but it hasn't felt like home in a very long time."

He nodded. "I know how you feel. I once had the same problem."

"And now?"

"Now I do have a home. I highly recommend it."

"But still . . . here you are."

"Yeah . . . here I am." He gestured toward the desert. "Naji and Salma are on a call of nature. I suggest you do the same, then hydrate. There are water bottles on the back of the cart."

Ludmilla walked away with her hand on her back.

He turned his attention to Achmed, who was standing alone in the distance. Slaton decided it was time to make amends. He walked over, and said, "I'm sorry about what happened back at the souk. There was no time to argue."

The Syrian said nothing.

"I appreciate all you've done for us. If it's any consolation, you'll be rid of us soon."

"I was thinking the same thing."

Slaton half grinned. "We're not in the clear yet."

"No, we are not. And if you put me inside that cart again, I will be of little use."

"I was thinking the same thing. You and Ludmilla can walk with us. If we see trouble coming, she goes back inside. You're our best chance to talk our way out of any bind."

"If there is trouble it will come near the border—and talking with anyone we encounter there is pointless." Achmed went to the cart for a water bottle.

Slaton took out the map. He'd chosen the southernmost of the two corridors Achmed had plotted. He saw Mount Hermon in the distance, an ever-present reference. With a compass he could have taken cross bearings on a few peaks and come up with a reasonably accurate position. It was only a fleeting thought, probably the product of training received years ago far to the south of that same mountain. Today, of course, he had a far more precise method of determining their position.

He turned on his phone, opened the special applications, and within seconds was looking at grid coordinates accurate to less than a meter. He plotted them on the map, then took it to Achmed.

"At the rate we're going," Slaton said, "we should reach Lebanon an hour or two after midnight." He pointed to their destination: a notch in the border south of Deir El Aachayer.

"Yes, I would agree. And your people will be waiting?"

"Of course—they promised."

Achmed looked at him doubtfully, not recognizing the black humor so common among operators. "Let us hope it is so. Lebanon also has secret police. I have been told they are not a welcoming lot."

"I've met a few, and I can tell you they're not."

Achmed looked at him oddly, but let whatever was brewing pass.

Slaton gathered everyone near the cart and updated them on the plan. There were no objections. Minutes later, with the high clouds holding fast, the cart was again rocking westward into the deepening hills.

FORTY-SEVEN

There was no attempt at counter-surveillance as Nazir led Sultan two blocks to a parking garage. It could hardly be expected. What little Nazir knew about tradecraft he'd learned from the handful of messengers who had delivered Sultan's instructions over the last year. They explained which messaging app was the most secure; implored him to pay in cash for anything related to the mission; told him how many times a throwaway phone could be used. Nazir had not made any glaring errors, and as a result the mission was on track. Sultan even surmised, with perhaps reaching optimism, that Nazir's lack of training was a hidden advantage. At this point it hardly mattered—his position inside the Royal Saudi Air Force made him irreplaceable.

They passed an ornate mosque, and once again Sultan was reminded of prayer. He ignored it more easily than ever, and just before reaching the garage he was struck by a contrasting impulse when they came upon a small grocery store. He saw baskets of fruit lined up on the sidewalk, and just inside the door an overweight man sat on a chair drawing from a hookah. He had a fleeting urge to dare Nazir to steal an orange, much as they'd done as boys. It was, of course, nothing more than nostalgia. Neither of them would ever be so carefree again.

On entering the garage, Nazir guided him to a corner on the first level. He stopped at the trunk of a sand-colored sedan. It was an official vehicle of the Royal Saudi Air Force, a staff car with the service's crown-and-wings emblem displayed on the door. After a cautious look around, Nazir popped the trunk.

Sultan stood staring at two gadgets. The most unique was a

near twin to the one he'd installed in a remote building in Sudan. Two mismatched canisters, silver tubing, a few valves.

"It looks like the other," he said.

"There are subtle differences," replied Nazir, who had built them both. "I was forced to alter the mounting brackets, and the triggering mechanism is unique. But the essential operation is the same."

"You modeled them on the equipment you work with?"

"Yes. Many of the parts are spares from the squadron's inventory, but a few I had to machine myself. Tell me about the demonstration . . . did everything work as planned?"

"As far as I could tell, perfectly."

"Did the gauge on the main canister go to zero?"

"Yes, it discharged fully."

Nazir smiled for a moment, then fell more somber. "And the agent? Was it effective?"

"As we expected." Sensing Nazir's discomfort, Sultan thought it best to not mention the number of victims or how they'd apparently suffered. Nazir, he knew, had a sensitive side. He'd always been the boy who rescued stray dogs, brought meals to infirm neighbors. Indeed, the same compassion, he supposed, that had caused him to befriend an outcast cripple.

"And what have we here?" Sultan asked, turning to the second device in the trunk. It was a drone larger than any he'd seen before, taking up half the compartment. The body of the aircraft was relatively small, but the two-foot-square framework around it supported eight propellers.

"I purchased three others like it," Nazir said.

Sultan regarded his friend quizzically.

"I gave considerable thought to how it might be done," Nazir expanded. "An attack with one drone would have a marginal chance of success. But if others acted as decoys, or swarmed in a mass attack—the chances of success would increase."

He nodded slowly.

Nazir went on, "This model can run autonomously, fly a preprogrammed course. That denies one of the best defenses against such attacks, which is to jam the standard control frequencies around the site being guarded."

"You have done your homework."

Nazir closed the trunk. "The drones will do what we need them to do. Would you like to see the apartment as well?"

"No, I think not. It is best we don't draw attention to the place. You gave me the address, and I saw a satellite view. It seems ideally located with respect to our target." Sultan deftly avoided the true reason he didn't want to go near the apartment: he knew it would eventually be searched, and very thoroughly. He wanted no chance of leaving any trace that he'd been there. No hair, no fingerprint, no captured image. DNA was a particular concern. His genetic profile was not recorded in anyone's database, but it could be linked to another that was well known by certain intelligence agencies. In time that would work in his favor, but it was vital that he control the release of that association.

Nazir said, "I chose the apartment with the most direct line of sight. The complex is the closest available, but well outside the security perimeter."

"You did well to acquire a friend in the military police unit—having inside knowledge of the protection plan could prove vital."

"Thankfully, he enjoys cheap bourbon." Nazir began moving toward the driver's side. "I will take you to view our objective. But understand, we cannot go near—security has already been heightened for the event. An official vehicle like this might get us to the entrance, but you would have to show ID to get inside. There are also cameras throughout the building."

"You are right, it can't be risked."

"There is a pad not far away reserved for military vehicles—I can take you there with no trouble."

They got into the car, and Nazir set out over an oil-black road. Sultan mused how fitting it was—the Saudis had so much crude they were using it to pave their streets. The road bore them westward, toward the site of their impending attack. Nazir waxed nostalgic as they drove, talking about their shared childhood: the pranks, the girls, the memorable teachers.

In the beginning his reminisces struck Sultan as intended, recollections of happier times. Yet as reality descended—where they were heading, and for what purpose—he fell more reticent. His gaze cooled and he diverted to the window.

The past is the past, he thought.

And the future? That will be very different for both of us.

FORTY-EIGHT

It was a thirty-minute drive to Jeddah Economic City, although as such conveyances went it was not unpleasant. The road was good and the traffic modest, and the air conditioner in the car blew like a Siberian wind. As promised, Nazir diverted for a drive-by of King Abdullah Air Base.

"That is where I work," he said, gesturing toward a large hangar in the distance. Roughly ten large transport aircraft lay on the tarmac beyond, lined up in tight formation.

"Where are the aircraft you maintain?" Sultan asked.

"You can just see one there, beneath the shelter."

In the distance Sultan saw a sleek jet under a shed of sorts. It had a distinctive green and white paint job, and was surrounded by support equipment.

"They are BAE Hawks," Nazir said. "The Air Force uses them primarily as advanced trainers. The jets in my squadron, of course, are specially modified."

"And this is not your permanent base?"

"No, our unit is on a temporary deployment. We are normally based in Tabuk."

Sultan watched the air base until it fell out of sight, and soon the city itself began to fade in the usual urban manner. Stoic bank buildings gave way to lesser commercial edifices, and these ceded to industrial areas and warehouses. Beyond that residential areas bloomed on the outer fringes. It was here, at the end of the outer urban orbit, that their objective appeared like a mirage. Rounding a bend, a vast tract of desert sprawled before them, mile after endless mile of featureless terrain. Which only made their target stand out all the more: in the distance, rising like a giant marker from the heavens, was the tribute that would forever be central to Jeddah Economic City.

Sultan had viewed countless pictures of the structure, but now, presented in all its scale and glory, and in a nearly finished state, he had to admit it was breathtaking. Over eight years in the making, Jeddah Tower rose from the table-flat desert with all the drama of a mountain rising from the sea, which was befitting for its singular purpose—to give the Saudi Kingdom claim to the tallest building in the world.

It had originally been named Mile-High Tower, but that ambition had been truncated by failings of geology—as it turned out, the layers of porous limestone so perfectly adept at sourcing crude oil were less suitable when it came to supporting five-thousand-foot skyscrapers. Even so, at 3,281 feet, Jeddah Tower would be at its dedication the tallest building on earth, more than double the height of the Empire State Building, and comfortably above the behemoths on the north shores of the Saudi Peninsula—yesterday's monuments to excess in Kuwait and Dubai. In a matter of days, a new champion would be crowned.

The tower's triangular footprint was evident from a distance, keeping the effects of wind to a minimum—needed to preclude nausea for the upper floor residents. As envisioned by the architects, the massive tower would one day be ringed by canals and a harbor connecting to the sea, and a new city would evolve around it. Shopping, conference centers, the world's finest restaurants. Like the tower itself, the biggest and the best. Sultan had seen the brochures, a dream in high-gloss print.

Nazir pulled the car into a parking area thick with military vehicles. There were sedans like their own, but also more tactically oriented models. Presently, all were empty, their occupants pulling duty nearby.

Nazir said, "The military and National Guard are working feverishly on their precautions. The king himself will preside at the event, and every important prince will be there, along with the rulers of many of the Gulf States."

"I am not surprised; the crown prince would never miss such a chance to gloat." The guest list had never been secret. Kings, emirs, sheiks—every leading Arab from across the region would be present for the tower's dedication.

They got out of the car and stood by the hood, marveling at the massive structure. Nazir pointed two-thirds of the way up. "You can see the observation deck."

Sultan studied intently. This was the first, and certainly only, time he would see it with his own eyes. The platform jutted out from one side of the tower, a great concrete tongue sticking out at the world. It was expansive enough to hold three tennis courts. He couldn't appreciate the view from where he stood, yet Sultan had seen photographs taken from the rail. From twenty-two hundred feet above the desert floor, it offered a panoramic vista of the entire Red Sea. A view fit for a king. *Or in two days,* he thought, *three kings, twenty-two princes, six emirs, and ten heads of state.* A rare concentration of Arab leadership.

Sultan forced himself to turn away from the spectacle. Roughly one mile in the opposite direction, he saw the apartment complex. "Which unit?" he asked.

Nazir followed his gaze. "Second building from the right, center unit, top floor."

"A direct line of sight."

"Yes . . . it is perfectly situated."

"Which will make it even more convincing." He reached beneath his robe and retrieved three Ziploc bags containing what was left of the material the maid in Khartoum had collected. He gave it to Nazir.

"Do you have any questions about how to distribute it?" Sultan asked.

"No. I remember everything."

"Good."

They talked for another ten minutes, discussing the details of how the agent would be dispersed, the angle from which the attack would commence. At the end, Nazir confided his plan for escaping Saudi Arabia in the aftermath.

On this last point, the Fifth Rashidun averted his gaze despairingly. Quite out of character, he said a prayer for his friend, petitioning that Allah, the most gracious and merciful, would watch over Nazir to the end.

FORTY-NINE

Night fell quickly, the high clouds holding fast to blot out the last traces of daylight. From a distance, the five weary shadows behind a donkey drew an image more befitting a scene from The Nativity than a CIA-run extraction op. Or so Slaton hoped.

Leading the tiny caravan westward, he wished he still had his night optic—it had ended up in the charred rubble of the Ural outside Chez Salma. He didn't beat himself up over it. The last five days had been busy, thousands of minor decisions made. It was only natural that he'd made a few mistakes.

Conveniently, his phone came with a "tactical flashlight" application that emitted red light—the best wavelength for retaining night vision, and less evident from a distance than white light. He'd paused every half hour to plot the phone-derived GPS position on the map, always including Achmed to cross-check his work. They'd performed the most recent update minutes earlier, and decided a slight adjustment to the north was required. Once the course was set, Slaton picked out a point on the horizon—a red light on a hilltop radio tower that was certainly in Lebanon—and used it as a reference. It was accurate enough, and allowed him to avoid constant use of the phone. These days in the field, the conservation of battery power was second only to ammunition.

"Where will I live?" a voice asked.

Slaton cast a glance back and saw Ludmilla. Since being freed from the hidden compartment she'd been walking with Salma and Naji.

"You mean once you get to the States?"

"Yes."

"I don't know. The CIA has a relocation program for people who need to disappear."

"Petrov's SVR has a program to find those people."

"So I've heard," Slaton said.

"Have you ever known anyone who's gone into hiding like that?"

A hesitation. "Yes."

"Was it successful?"

"So far. As to where you end up, it's pretty much up to the agency. Small towns are probably best. But if you have a request . . . they might listen. Wherever you go, you'll have an advantage because your English is good."

She was silent for a time, then said, "I wonder if I have done the right thing."

"In defecting?"

She nodded.

"Given what happened to the other interpreter, I don't think you had much choice."

"I suppose not, but still it seems so . . . unfaithful."

"I don't think you're being unfaithful. I think Petrov and his oligarch friends are turning their backs on Russia."

Ludmilla seemed to think about it for a long time, then said, "You have a child."

Slaton looked at her inquiringly. It hadn't been posed as a question.

"I see how you look at Naji," she said. "You have a father's eyes."

"I have a son, a little younger than him. And a wife."

"You must miss them terribly."

"I do."

"Can I ask, then . . . why do you do this kind of work?"

Slaton kept his eyes ahead, scanning the distant terrain. "I've been asking myself that question for a long time."

Sultan left Jeddah chasing a splendid sunset, a paint-by-numbers canvas of red and orange that beckoned like paradise. He watched it until the last strands of color were swallowed by the night.

He had reconnected with his driver near a mosque on the north side of the city, the man waiting just as he'd been that morning. His silence, too, was unchanged. The entire course ran in reverse: an

hours-long car ride, a walk through low dunes, the young fisherman waiting with the dhow.

They set sail for Africa under a cloak of darkness, a fresh offshore breeze adding a push. Sultan was perfectly happy to see the
Saudi kingdom recede into the shadowed marine haze. He tried,
but failed, to shake his final image of Nazir. He'd embraced his old
friend on parting, but only now did he recognize the gesture for
what it was: not a show of affection, but one of remorse. He had put
his friend in an impossible situation.

With the land of Mecca receding astern, Sultan forced it all away.
It was time to embrace his new beginning. He sat down on a bench
at the bow, his feet kicking for space amid piles of mackerel—the
young man had indeed not wasted the day. Sultan wondered idly
if he would ever set foot on the peninsula again. It wasn't out of
the question—not given the anarchy he was about to set off—but
returning here was not his goal. He was determined to seize his
legacy, the one written in the blood of his father. Do that, and God
could sort out what was rightly included.

The Saudis, the Emiratis, the Russians—yes, even the Russians—
were helpless to stop him now. Everything was in place, moving
forward by a clock that could not be stopped. When the vital hour
came, Sultan would be in place. It was time to go home now, and
there fulfill his birthright.

Finally, home.

Two black Chevy Suburbans rumbled over hardpan earth, their
suspension groaning with every rut. Both vehicles displayed diplomatic license plates, although there was nothing to suggest which
particular mission they might be tied to. Collectively, the Suburbans carried four men and two women. All were employees of the
CIA's Beirut station, and all were armed. The team had of course
been given strict rules of engagement—they were only to engage
threats as a matter of self-defense. It was the kind of order, everyone knew, that was far easier to give than to decipher in high-stress
situations.

The run from the Beirut embassy had so far been uneventful,
two hours of road-trip boredom through rolling hills. Their mission tonight was highly unusual, although straightforward on its

face. They were to rendezvous with between two and four individuals at the Syrian border, and deliver them as quickly as possible to a waiting jet at Hariri International Airport on the south side of Beirut.

All good on paper.

The first complication turned out to be the terrain. The exact spot of the expected rendezvous was far off the beaten path. Actually, far off *any* path. Chevrolet Suburbans, as a rule, were designed for modest off-road travel. The two in question, unfortunately, were less capable than most owing to an extra two thousand pounds of armor plating, bullet-proof windows, and self-sealing run-flat tires.

The terrain seemed to get worse as they went. The drivers did their best, but half a mile from the meeting point, with everyone tumbling around like dice in a cup, the team leader ordered a cessation of the hostilities. After a brief discussion, the consensus view was that one of the SUVs was going to get hung up soon—a differential on a rock or a wheel in a rut. Because they were getting close, it wasn't an insurmountable complication. Four members of the team dismounted, collected their gear from the trunk, and set out on foot.

They reached the rendezvous point fifteen minutes later, and the first thing they did was double-check the grid coordinates. Satisfied, two members lifted night optic devices and began scouting for patrols. They primarily looked across the border into Syria, but took an occasional sweep behind. When it came to Lebanon, one never knew.

With no one in sight, including their prospective charges, everyone settled in and tried to get comfortable. It had the makings of a long night.

FIFTY

By one o'clock that morning Slaton knew they were getting close. There was a temptation to move quickly, to dash the last two miles before they could be seen. He knew it would be a mistake. This was the highest threat area, and there would certainly be border patrols. Some units would be active, searching and deterring. Yet according to Achmed, who was the local area expert, Syrian patrols here often remained static, concealing themselves to watch common crossing points.

The cloud deck overhead was breaking, moonlight filtering through the gaps. Slaton brought the procession to a stop. He looked back and saw Naji atop the cart, his legs dangling over the side, feet bicycling in the air. A vision of Davy on their boat came to mind: sitting on *Sirius'* beam and kicking at waves. With practiced discipline, he forced the image away.

Achmed came to his side and pointed ahead. "There are two hills, low but very distinct—almost twins."

Slaton picked them out in the dim light. "Okay, I see them. Maybe two miles."

"Even less. They are directly on the border. Split them, and the meeting point is just beyond."

Slaton didn't need to check the topo map—he'd already memorized the terrain at the finish line. He did a slow 360, taking in the horizon in every direction. It was apparently contagious—in the periphery he saw the others doing the same. Nerves were on edge. Everyone knew they were close.

Naji, who was standing on the cart, said something to Uncle Achmed.

"We look for cars, Naji," Achmed replied in English.

"I see a car," Naji replied.

Achmed smiled the smile of a patronizing elder.

Slaton did nothing of the kind. He followed Naji's young gaze and saw it fixed on a point to the south. Slaton's shooter's eyes battled the gloom, and soon he saw it as well—faint glints in an otherwise vacant night.

"Move, move!" he commanded, gesturing toward a dry riverbed a hundred feet distant.

Everyone complied.

The donkey, unfortunately, did not.

Slaton tugged on the lead, but the creature wouldn't move. He pulled harder—it was probably the wrong move, but there was no time for patience. A whack on the rump finally did the trick. The cart began rocking toward lower ground.

Slaton took one glance over his shoulder and realized it was too late. The glimmer resolved into headlights—two sets actually, that were headed straight for them. He could tell they were moving fast by the way the lights flickered over the jarring terrain.

Once everyone was in the ravine, Slaton began shouting orders. "This is probably a border unit. When they get here, don't try to hide or run. Whatever they tell you to do, comply."

"Should I get into the compartment?" Ludmilla asked.

"It won't do any good. Just stay in the back of the group and try to keep your face covered. I'll be nearby."

Before anyone could ask where he was going, or why, Slaton sprinted toward the cart. He retrieved the MP5, then ran west, keeping low. Twenty seconds later he threw himself behind the biggest rock in sight and readied his weapon.

The situation was going south fast. For the first time since entering Syria, Slaton remembered what Sorensen had put on offer. With perhaps a minute to spare, he pulled out his phone and typed a message for Langley, detailing the situation. After seeing the SENT confirmation, he added a second message: Might need that emergency backup you offered. Launch immediately if possible.

He was scanning the nearby desert when a reply came: Copy all. Wilco on backup.

Slaton heard the vehicles coming before he got a visual. Something relatively small, engines revving high. This close to Damascus, it could only be a government patrol—Syrian army regulars or Desert Guard. Anywhere else, and he might have considered other suspects: bandits, rebels, a tribal militia. That gave a small degree of predictability, but it was hardly comforting.

He planned as best he could. As with his engagement last night, the suppressed MP5 provided both advantages and disadvantages. It forced him to work close—in this case, a mere forty yards from the clear area next to the wadi where he guessed they would stop. Yet it also offered a measure of stealth, which was good—unlike last night, he wouldn't be shooting at tires. There was a slim chance Achmed could talk his way out of the predicament. He was an experienced smuggler, and Slaton guessed that at that moment he was practicing his story. There was also the chance of a bribe—he had told Slaton he was prepared for it.

The more likely outcome: the police would take everyone into custody and search the cart. And when they got a good look at Ludmilla, any hope of fast talk or bribes would go out the window. Everyone in southern Syria was looking for her, and the commander of the unit that corralled her had his next promotion guaranteed.

If that was how it all went down, Slaton's hands would be tied. He guessed he could get off three rounds, maybe four, before the unit realized they were under attack. Unless they were a particularly disciplined unit, everyone's eyes would be on the four travelers and the cart. That meant the key was to start in back: one by one, take out the rearmost individuals.

The headlights came back into view, flickering closer. When the vehicles were a hundred yards distant, he began to feel them—with his body flat on the earth, vibrations in the hardpan desert. Slaton remained still.

The trucks came in hard and fast, skidding to a stop in a cloud of dust and fury—as predicted, centered in the clearing. Also as expected, their headlights were trained on the wadi, cutting the matte-black night like twin sets of knives. The vehicles turned out to be identical, and Slaton recognized a pair of UAZ-469s: Russian-built military utility trucks, four-wheel drive, built for rugged terrain. Their canvas tops had been lowered for night work, which put all the occupants in plain sight. It was a good configuration for Desert Guard soldiers who needed to be able to see in every direction.

And a better one for a sniper.

Slaton was set at a ninety-degree angle to the contingent, roughly forty yards distant. He counted seven men—four in the lead vehicle, three in the second. Every set of eyes was on the wadi. He also saw that one man in the lead vehicle, passenger seat, was wearing night optics—the reason they'd been spotted from such a distance.

The man wearing the optics flipped them up and shouted something in Arabic.

Achmed replied.

Slaton understood none of it. He settled his reticle on the lone man in the back seat of the rear UAZ, thinking, *Someday I need to learn the damned language.*

The driver of the rear vehicle produced a spotlight and trained it on the cart. Achmed and the others stood frozen in the beam like prisoners caught in a jailbreak. Two men from each vehicle got out, moved forward, and pointed their weapons at the captives. One of these was the man Slaton had been targeting. He shifted his aim to the spotlight holder.

More shouting, increasingly insistent.

Achmed began to reply, but was immediately cut off.

So much for talking his way out of it.

The guard detail edged forward, menace in every step. Their weapons were fixed on the group, and for a moment Slaton feared they would open fire. Achmed was shouting, pleading. The leading soldiers shouted back. The situation was degrading, on the edge of a massacre. Then the commander took charge. He fired a pistol into the sky, three rounds reverberating to shut everyone up. The commander dismounted and began moving forward.

Achmed slowly put his hands on his head. The women did the same. Only Naji was an outlier—he stood at his mother's side, his body racked by sobs and his face buried in her robe. Slaton was glad for that—it meant he wouldn't see what was about to happen.

His decision tree had reached an end. No more branches. He took the time to amend his targeting priority, reflecting the tactical situation. He began to pressure the trigger, his initial five shots planned.

The first flew toward the spotlight carrier, who at that moment was the only person in the rearmost UAZ. The man slumped immediately from a headshot. The spotlight fell to the dirt, and that sudden change of illumination immobilized everyone. Everyone except the assassin. Slaton shifted quickly to the four men in front—they had to be next, because they had weapons ready. He first took down the most distant, two rounds, and as he was tumbling toward the wadi Slaton struck the man to his right with another two.

Then the night exploded.

His suppressor, along with the subsonic ammo, had kept the report to a minimum. Even so, the MP5 was hardly silent, and some flash was inevitable. How quickly his adversaries discovered his position depended on two things: their angle of view, and how well trained they were. Unfortunately, at least one knew what he was doing.

The nearest of the soldiers out front sensed Slaton's position and began returning fire. It wasn't anything direct, but high-rate semi-automatic suppression. It had the desired effect.

Slaton took cover behind the rock while bullets ripped through the scrub around him, bits of stone and vegetation flying. He then engaged that soldier, sending two rounds center of mass. The man went down spinning, hit but possibly not out of the fight. By that time two others had joined in, high-rate return fire that was beginning to focus.

Slaton again put his head down, waiting for the lull when they hit the end of their magazines. He heard Achmed shouting. An engine roaring to life.

The return fire paused.

Slaton lifted the MP and began seeking out targets. Smoke and haze had taken hold, obscuring the visibility. He distinguished two shadows moving, but he held his fire—he couldn't confirm they were enemy. Then he recognized the commander—he was running back to the lead truck. The driver was still at the wheel, ducking low. Slaton tracked the second figure and got a better look—the last man standing was helping his wounded partner up. Slaton hit their combined center of mass with four rounds—from the angle he was shooting, the two were virtually one target. He couldn't tell where his rounds hit, but hit they did. Both went down convincingly.

Five down, two to go.

The commander and driver were the only targets left, both in the lead UAZ. Not surprisingly, they were reacting to the fast-changing odds—the truck shot forward, its wheels chewing dirt and gravel. Slaton fired twice at the driver, but the truck was sliding sideways and bouncing wildly. He doubted he scored any hits.

With a break in the return fire, he instinctively performed a tactical reload. He settled his sight again on the fast retreating truck. He fired four evenly spaced rounds at each of the two seats. Someone—almost certainly the commander—tumbled from the passenger side and went pinwheeling into the desert. The truck kept going. It lurched suddenly downward, into the wadi. Either the driver had lost control, or he was smart enough to break the line of sight to the sniper who was decimating his unit.

Slaton leapt up and began running.

FIFTY-ONE

Slaton never got a follow-up shot on the truck. He caught one glimpse of the retreating UAZ, but the limited range of his MP5 precluded a realistic shot. The sound of the truck's engine faded quickly in the night. The scene around him was surreal, swirling smoke caught in the headlight beams of the remaining UAZ.

He ran toward the wadi and saw everyone crouched behind the cart. "It's all clear!" he called out.

Achmed was the first to appear, head and shoulders edging out. The others soon followed in a cluster, arms locked around one another like freshly released hostages. Which, in essence, they were.

"Is everybody okay?" Slaton asked.

Nods all around.

He double-checked the casualties, looking for signs of life. Four were clearly dead. One man, the driver who'd been holding the spotlight, was breathing but unconscious, blood oozing from a neck wound. Spent brass was everywhere, along with two empty magazines. The smell of spent gunpowder was thick. Slaton pulled the Sig from his thigh pocket and addressed Achmed. "Do you know how to use this?"

A nod.

He handed over the weapon and pointed to the survivor. "Watch him."

Slaton set out to the spot where the wounded commander had fallen out of the truck. Halfway there he heard a moan and leveled the MP5.

As he closed in he heard breathing, wet and rheumatic. He followed the sound and found the man lying in a heap near a clump of sage. The headlights of the remaining UAZ sprayed enough light to give him a decent look. The commander was face down in the dirt and writhing. Reassuringly, Slaton saw both his hands—empty, as was the hip holster on his belt.

Taking no chances, he kept the MP5 on the man until he was a few steps away. "I need light," he called out.

Achmed took charge, and seconds later the dropped spotlight was trained on them. Slaton saw a wound high on the man's back. Blood was turning the dirt beneath him dark. The commander was conscious, but in a lot of pain. He made no threatening moves, but then, Slaton doubted he was having threatening thoughts. He slowly half rolled the man and saw a face wrenched in agony. The man was looking straight into the barrel of the MP. Less than two feet away, it must have looked like a train tunnel. His expression fell to that of a man facing his executioner.

Slaton weighed the merits of an interrogation, but decided against it. He doubted he would get anything truthful, and time was becoming critical. He leaned down and the man recoiled. Slaton searched him with his free hand, but found no weapons. Satisfied, he rolled the man until he was facing away, then pulled the back of his uniform coat up over his head. He screamed in pain, the contortion putting pressure on shattered bone and torn nerves. Slaton got a better look at the wound and decided it might be survivable. There was clearly internal damage, but the bleeding was minimal. The only other injuries he saw were scrapes and contusions—what you got from falling out of a moving truck. The maneuver with the jacket had secondary benefits. It covered the commander's eyes like a hood, and trussed him, given his injury, to the point of immobility.

Satisfied the area was secure, Slaton went back to the cart and called a meeting.

Those who resided near the airport—and there were notably few— were rarely awakened in the middle of the night. The neighboring townships were small to begin with, and the airfield had been set back a sensible distance into the desert. There was a small university two miles from one end of the runway, a camel and livestock research facility near the other. The only permanent residents within three miles of the place were a handful of farmers—and as a rule, desert ranchers were not the sort to complain.

Cradled centrally on the craggy western plateau of Saudi Arabia, Al Jouf Airport serves as the province's principal commercial field. There are but a handful of flights each day connecting to hubs around the region, a sparseness that reflects well the surrounding community. Yet as is the case with all airfields in Saudi Arabia, Al Jouf carries the designation of a dual-use facility—military operations are also conducted.

There had never been any continuous presence. The First Gulf War had been the highwater mark when the United States Air Force took the place by storm, forward deploying fighter squadrons for round-the-clock operations. Things had settled considerably since. There were a few exercises each year, mostly involving the Saudi Air Force, which ran during civilized hours. The occasional survey or air diversion stirred the dust now and again, these too keeping to daylight.

Yet there was one outlier.

Every few months, on no particular schedule, a handful of unmarked trucks would appear at Al Jouf. They arrived without fail in the middle of the night, and set up shop on a remote taxiway on the airfield's north side. The contingent pitched a small city of tents, unloaded equipment and spotlights, all of which was centered around a modest portable hangar. There were never more than a dozen men and women involved, all of whom wore an eclectic mix of civilian clothing and store-bought camouflage.

The questions of who they were and what they were doing were largely left unasked. When anyone did make a query, no answers came. The air traffic controllers claimed to know nothing, and the airport administrator professed to be equally in the dark. In truth, this might have been the case, a contract of mutual indifference. The commercial side of the airfield, which included the air traffic control tower, closed each day between midnight and six in the morning. And it was then, during this recurring window of darkness, that the little compound came alive.

On that night, just after one in the morning, the silence around the airfield ended abruptly, although shattered would have been too harsh a word. A dark gray shape accelerated down the runway, the slightest hum emanating from its single turboprop engine. The low acoustic signature was by design. With long straight wings, not unlike those of a glider, the aircraft was built less for speed than endurance. An aerial loiterer. After an unusually short takeoff roll, the craft levitated into the sky like a second-rate magic trick. What little sound there was soon faded into the blackness. Though the operators could not know it, not a single farmer awoke. Nor did any of the students in the nearby university dorms. The camels and cattle at the research center never stirred inside their pens.

Yet for all that stealth and remoteness, the departure of the MQ-9 Reaper drone got a great deal of attention in a command center half a world away.

FIFTY-TWO

Slaton had killed the truck's headlights, along with the spotlight, as a matter of security. He used the red-light app on his phone to illuminate the topo map, and invited everyone closer. They huddled together like campers around a fire. He tapped his finger on their present position, and addressed Achmed.

"We have to assume the guy who escaped will call for backup. How long will that take?"

"It is difficult to say. The spacing between units varies, but most are the same size. I would say twenty minutes minimum, perhaps as long as an hour. Expect one or two units like the one that found us." He looked obviously at the dead soldiers in the distance. "By daybreak, I promise you, there will be an army searching for us."

"Okay, so we need to move fast." He again referenced the map. "I'm going to take the truck, make for this road." He pointed to a highway, roughly two miles north, that ran parallel to the wadi. "If anyone shows up, the first thing they'll see is me making a run for the border. I'll draw anyone who takes the bait north, away from you. Achmed, I want you to lead the others." He drew a line with his finger. "Stay in the wadi until here. At that point it's only a few hundred yards to the gap between the hills and the border. Make a straight shot for the rendezvous point. You remember where it is?"

"Yes, I remember."

"All right," Slaton said, "let's move."

"But you will be alone in the truck," Achmed said. "If they follow you and get close, won't they wonder where the rest of us are?"

Slaton folded the map and gave it to Achmed. "Leave that to me."

———

There was only time for brief goodbyes. Ludmilla, whose escape from the Four Seasons had started everything, looked at Slaton gratefully. "Thank you for everything you've done."

"We're not across the finish line yet. I've still got the memory card. If it looks like I'm going to get captured, I'll ditch it in the desert. If that happens, you'll be the sole source for what was said at the meeting."

"I heard the recording. I can remember almost everything, word for word."

Salma came forward and gave Slaton a kiss on the cheek. Naji was in tears. He could have no grasp of what had just happened. Slaton hoped his mother had shielded him from the worst of the firefight. Kept his face buried in her abaya until the killing was done. Even then, he would have heard the noise and the chaos. Sensed his mother's fear. Slaton took solace in the fact that the alternative would have been far worse. Had he not acted, everyone would have been captured. Ludmilla could have expected a one-way trip to Moscow. The others would have been taken into custody by the Syrian Mukhabarat, interrogation and execution a virtual certainty, at least for the adults. Naji's life might be spared, but only at the crushing expense of losing his mother.

Achmed beckoned the others, and they set out along the wadi on a fast walk. He was forced to carry the still-sobbing Naji. They quickly fell to silhouettes in the darkness, and then nothing at all. The tiny group of refugees disappeared into the night.

Slaton got straight to work.

He checked the survivors one last time. The man who'd been holding the spotlight had died, but the commander was hanging on. Slaton removed his hoodie and wedged it beneath the man's shirt over the primary wound. The man said nothing.

Slaton hauled two of the other bodies to the UAZ and put them in seats, one in front, passenger-side, the other in back. He could have put a third in back, but decided it wasn't necessary. When reinforcements appeared, as they certainly would, and if they had night optics, also likely, they would see a vehicle with multiple oc-cupants making a run for the border. That would be enough.

He strapped the bodies in using seat belts, but they slumped like the dead weight they were. He searched the truck, and beneath the back seat found a set of jumper cables and a first aid kit. He used the jumper cables to strap the man in back upright. The first aid kit contained two rolls of stretch bandages and a spool of surgical tape. He used these to bind the second body in place.

It would have to do.

He unhitched the donkey, slapped it on the rump again, and watched the beast amble away. One more element to add to the confusion. Or so he hoped.

He cranked the UAZ, flicked on the headlights. In the beams a flicker of motion caught his eye. His hand was on the MP5 before he realized what it was: the night breeze had picked up a plastic grocery bag. He breathed a sigh of relief and watched it roll across the desert, a modern-day tumbleweed.

Slaton set a course northward. He passed the still-trussed commander on the way out. The man had wormed his head out of his upturned jacket and was leaning on one elbow. It looked awkward, but Slaton understood—he was contorting himself to minimize the pressure on his injury. He watched Slaton drive by, seeming more lucid now. Slaton didn't wave, didn't slow down, but he tossed the remainder of the first aid kit toward the man as he passed.

The UAZ's headlights strobed the desert in front of him. The terrain was rough but manageable. It would be slow going until he reached the highway. With any luck he might come across a semi-improved road, something that wasn't on the map.

Slaton saw a tactical radio mounted in the dash, and it brought back to mind the events of two nights ago. The radio was on, but the volume had been turned down. He spun the knob and heard a conversation in rapid-fire Arabic. He was sure it was the driver who had gotten away coordinating with backup units.

Slaton cursed under his breath.

Someday I really need to learn this damned language.

FIFTY-THREE

After ten minutes, Slaton came upon a dirt trail. It wasn't anything improved, no raised bed or crushed gravel, but simply a well-worn path through the brush. The truck he was driving, he imagined, had probably helped create it, a thousand patrols over the same channel of earth.

He followed the trail north using his phone for navigation. He wanted to give Achmed and the others at least thirty minutes. Slaton did his best to be obtrusive. He kept his headlights on, high beams engaged. He turned on the spotlight and jammed the handle into an empty tube near the spare tire. It spun in circles like a drunken lighthouse.

Even more conspicuously, the UAZ's engine would be nice and hot. To anyone using infrared optics, it would stand out like a lone star in a black sky. The only thing Slaton didn't do was lean on the horn—but he might if anyone got close enough to hear. At one point he weighed the idea of getting on the radio and broadcasting his coordinates in English. It would get everyone's attention, but he deemed it too obvious. A red flag that would soften his diversion.

Careening toward the main road, Slaton decided he was doing everything he could to highlight himself. One way or another, he was going to be seen.

Things went well for another five minutes. Slaton found the main road and turned left, putting the border with Lebanon only a few miles ahead.

It had always been a coin toss from which direction reinforcements would come. He'd expected they would appear in the north, ideally once Lebanon was within reach. In that scenario, he could put the accelerator to the floor and make a run for the border. The UAZ wasn't fast, but he reckoned that any unit chasing him would be driving the same make and model. If he could reach the border first, he would drag any pursuers along the edge. Once they got uncomfortably close, a quick turn would put him safely into Lebanon. That would buy all the time the others needed.

As it turned out, with less than a mile of the main road behind him, things began to go wrong.

He saw two sets of headlights ahead and to his right. Not *on* the road, but making a beeline for it from the desert. Slaton pushed the UAZ harder. The angle of the headlights didn't change; they were fixed solidly at his two o'clock position. He didn't need a radar to know what that meant—they were on a collision course. The unit had a visual on him, and they were taking an intercept angle to cut him off.

He put the accelerator to the floor, but not much happened. Ninety kilometers per hour became ninety-eight. It was all the vehicle would do. The angle was almost steady, the enemy perhaps falling back slightly toward three o'clock.

As they closed in he could make out the shadowed vehicles attached to the paired headlights. The geometry was inescapable—they would merge in less than two minutes. Slaton thought he might be able to get out ahead, but only slightly. He fully expected a barrage of fire as he passed. The odds of not taking a hit, from what were probably minimally trained conscripts shooting from a vehicle speeding over rough terrain, were heavily in his favor.

But odds had a way of biting you.

Surviving that, there were further problems. He was already at maximum speed, so he might get some separation while his pursuers fell in behind and accelerated. But the road would give them a more stable platform. The idea of taking potshots all the way to the border was hardly appealing. He might get away with it. Duck low and hope for the best. Send an occasional round in return. Yet there was also the chance of further reinforcements. The radio had gone silent, and he guessed the Syrians had either changed frequencies, or more likely were using mobile phones to coordinate. That would be the smart move—they knew he had one of their vehicles, and therefore one of their radios. These might not be elite troops, but they weren't stupid.

It all went through Slaton's mind in a matter of seconds, a tactical decision process. One final factor had to be considered. If anything went wrong, if the adverse odds added up, he would be stopped. Fighting his way out of that jam wouldn't be an option—this time they would have numbers and he wouldn't have the element of surprise. Given what happened earlier, he'd be lucky if they didn't shoot him on sight. Either way, they would realize he was alone, the bodies of their comrades strapped in as decoys. From that point, regardless of Slaton's fate, the hunt for the others would commence. Which meant he might not accomplish his primary objective. The same would be true if he dashed across the border into Lebanon.

In either case, Ludmilla and the rest might not reach safety.

There was no choice.

Slaton slammed on the brakes.

Through a skid, he steered for the right shoulder. Once he'd slowed enough, he threw the wheel hard left, hairpinning into a reversal. The little truck bounded across the tarmac onto the opposite shoulder, fishtailing through dirt, spewing gravel and dust. Straightening out in the opposite direction, he accelerated again for maximum speed.

Slaton glanced over his shoulder. Two sets of headlights were straightening out behind him. Locking on like targeting beams. They were half a mile back, but he had no doubt they were talking to other units, reporting the new vector.

Slaton got out his phone, opened the special applications using the retina scan feature—no small feat of multitasking under the circumstances. He didn't try to send a message. *Texting while driving is probably illegal in Syria,* he mused. Instead, he thumbed down on an app he'd not yet used. Sorensen had explained what it was— an emergency voice line that would cut straight to the CIA/SAC operations center.

The software programmer who'd built it, apparently, had a black sense of humor. The icon was labeled 911.

With his right foot pegging the accelerator to the floorboard, Slaton waited for the phone to do its magic as he shot back once again into the heart of Syria.

At 7:15 in the evening, Langley's hallways were quiet. The rank and file had gone home, and those who remained fell into one of two general categories: the beginnings of the graveyard shift, and a few overtime heroes. Anna Sorensen, of course, was in neither category. She had an ongoing op in Syria that was reaching resolution.

The Special Activities Center had recently been blessed with its own proprietary command center, a reflection of the increasing scope and secrecy of its missions. The one going on at that moment, west of Damascus, was a case in point. Minutes ago, Sorensen had been sitting in the cafeteria, jabbing a plastic fork into a half-eaten chicken Caesar salad, when a message buzzed to her phone: Slaton had called for help.

She burst into the ops center, passing beneath a door topped by her agency's motto: *Tertia Optio*. It was Latin for The Third Option, an apt moniker for an agency whose missions fell in the gray area between diplomatic and military responses.

"Where is he?" she asked breathlessly.

There were six people manning "the boards," referring to the three primary wide-screen displays. A comm tech behind the center console answered. "Five miles from the Lebanese border. He just did a one-eighty—he's heading back toward Damascus now."

"*Toward* Damascus?"

"We don't have eyes on," the technician said, referring to a lack of real-time satellite coverage. "His previous message said—"

"I *know* what it said. He was going to take a stolen vehicle to act as a decoy while the others made for the border on foot. Is there any word from our unit in Lebanon?"

"The station team is in place. I have an open line with them, and so far they report no contact. They asked again how many to expect."

"Tell them three is most likely, but to take whoever shows up. Kravchuk is the one we have to get out."

The technician began typing.

Sorensen sided up to a young woman at another console, the keeper of the bigger picture.

"Where's my Reaper?" Sorensen asked.

"Thirty-five nautical out."

"All right. Set up a link with the crew flying it—I want to follow this."

FIFTY-FOUR

There comes a time in most ops when every bit of planning, every well-thought contingency plan, goes soaring out the window. It came for Slaton shortly after he turned back east. He wasn't surprised when he saw a second unit bearing down. He was *very* surprised to see how big it was.

There were five sets of headlights—multiple intensities and configurations. Different vehicles for a different type of unit. He guessed they were military. Syrian regulars, perhaps, who'd been diverted from a nearby assignment. Most likely, checkpoint duty on the outskirts of Damascus, searching for a Russian defector.

Now I'm up against the army, he thought. Worse than the numbers was the geometry—the new force was bearing down from the road ahead. Caught in a pincer, Slaton checked his phone. The only choice was to go off-road. Unfortunately, the path he'd taken earlier was nowhere near. He remembered catching a glimpse of an unimproved trail minutes earlier.

But where was it?

In dim light he scanned the left side of the road, willing the offshoot to appear. The headlights were getting bigger, brighter. In less than a minute they would merge. He saw nothing for twenty seconds. The headlights coming at him were blinding. He gave it ten seconds more. Slaton was about to give up, simply turn into open desert, when a break in the scrub appeared. It was a pure ninety-degree turn. Best of all, it led away from the wadi where he'd started. Away from Achmed, Ludmilla, and Salma. Away from Naji.

Slaton whipped the wheel left, and the UAZ skidded onto the side road. The passenger in his right seat shifted, the body slumping halfway out the door. There was no point in keeping up appearances, so he unbuckled the corpse's seat belt and gave it a shove. The body tumbled out onto the dirt siding. If his pursuers saw it, they might slow to take a look. A few seconds bought.

The road was in fair condition, and Slaton kept up his speed. The UAZ battered ahead, throwing him on and off the seat like a carnival ride. On one pothole he went completely airborne, two hands on the wheel his only connection to the truck. He saw a flash of motion to his right. The landing was violent, and he heard a terrible crack in the chassis. The truck kept going. Slaton looked down and realized what had gone flying—his MP5 was gone. He'd wedged it between the seats as best he could, but clearly not well enough.

It didn't matter. The force he was up against now was overwhelming. His eyes strained to see the path ahead, stones and ruts caught instantaneously in the flickering beams of the headlights. He had no idea where the trail was taking him. Wherever it was, he knew more backups might be there to greet him.

Through the bumps, Slaton realized the phone in his pocket was vibrating. *How long had it been going off?* He pulled it out and saw a call.

With one hand fighting the wheel, he hit the green button and shouted, "A little help would be much appreciated right now!"

"We're working on it." Sorensen's voice, steady and clear. "Are you okay?"

"Just great. But I do have an army breathing down my neck."

"We don't have eyes on you yet."

"I'm northbound on a minor road, roughly five miles northwest from where I split with the others."

"Hang on . . . we're pinging the phone." A long pause. "Okay, we've got you."

"Look, I'm a little short on ideas right now. What about that contraption from the ACME Corporation you mentioned?"

"Yeah, it's on the way."

"I haven't been trained on how to use it."

"It's intuitive. Just grab hold and hang on."

Slaton paused. "If that's your complete operational briefing, Deputy Director, it does not instill confidence."

"I'm not here to instill confidence. I'm here to get your ass out of harm's way. Now listen closely . . ."

The pilot looked calmly at his displays. His Reaper was cruising at twelve thousand feet, cutting effortlessly through the black sky.

Two CIA employees were directing the mission from a trailer at an airbase outside Riyadh, Saudi Arabia. Having the controllers in theater was a CIA quirk, more to do with legalities than any operational advantage. Yet there were minor technical benefits to the arrangement. The Air Force ran drone operations from Creech Air Force Base, north of Las Vegas, twelve thousand miles and, more critically, 1.2 seconds removed from its aircraft. As it turned out, that lack of signal delay could tonight prove critical.

The Reaper was flying with its lowest possible electronic signature. At that moment, the only emanation was a single link to a satellite. No radar, no navigation lights, no laser designator. The primary sensor was a thermographic camera mounted in the aircraft's chin, video from which streamed upward via a secure satellite link. The Reaper carried no weapons. Indeed, all external hardpoints had been removed in order to keep its weight and radar return to a minimum. The only external store, at that moment stowed in a conformal pod, had never been operationally deployed. That was about to change, and once it did the radar cross section of the aircraft would be hopelessly ruined.

"Any air defense activity?" the pilot asked, addressing the sensor operator in the chair beside him. Both were sitting at consoles bristling with flight information, sensor data, and the controls for their respective duties.

"Nothing yet. This model was upgraded with a new radar absorbent coating. They say it's pretty effective."

"Let's hope."

As insurance, the pilot had flown a wide arc around Damascus, although it might not have been necessary. Drones had long been a fixture in the skies adjacent to Syria. On any given day they scouted and probed and wandered the borders, and occasionally strayed across. Everyone was doing it—the Americans, the Saudis, the Russians, the Iranians. For the most part they were only here to look, although the one exception was Israel—for Syrian air defenses, anything approaching from the Golan was viewed as nothing short of an invasion. Aside from that, little fuss was made. The regime only cared about the regime, which meant protecting Damascus. More to the point, anyone who wanted to go pyrotechnic on the royal palace would use something with far greater punch than a Reaper. A barrage of cruise missiles, a gorilla package of fighters with smart bombs. Altogether, it meant the Reaper crew had some leeway for tonight's mission. One misguided drone, even if it were to be spotted, wasn't likely to draw a response.

"Ten miles on a bearing of three-two-zero," the sensor operator said, referencing location data on their moving target being streamed from Langley.

The pilot banked ten degrees right.

"Still nothing on the camera. If we . . . wait, hang on."

The pilot saw it as well in the video feed: beneath the drifting coordinate symbol, a lone hot blob fronting a cloud of dust. As they closed in the software began to filter and define, and soon the white blob resolved to become a vehicle. One man driving.

Their objective in sight, the sensor operator zoomed out and saw a group of five vehicles giving chase. Half a mile farther back was a second, smaller group.

"This guy really could use some help," the sensor man said.

As if on cue, the pilot pulled back the throttle and eased the nose down. The vertical speed on his flight display registered a gentle descent of five hundred feet per minute. "Prepare to deploy."

The Reaper closed in.

FIFTY-FIVE

Sorensen transmitted the basics of the extraction procedure. "You'll need to keep up your speed as best you can."

Slaton was jolted airborne in his seat again, nearly getting tossed into the back with his other deceased passenger. *Easy for you to say,* he thought. He had a death grip on his phone—lose that and he would truly be alone. His eyes were locked on the onrushing trail a hundred feet ahead, the limits of the feeble headlights. "I can't see the road very well. Does it continue straight ahead?"

"As far as I can tell, yes. What's your speed?"

Slaton checked. "Sixty-five . . . that's kilometers per hour."

A pause. "Okay, that's thirty-five knots. The drone operator would like a little more."

Slaton cursed under his breath. He chanced a look back and saw his pursuers. Not gaining, but holding steady. He realized his back seat companion had disappeared, no doubt bucked out into the desert.

He pushed the accelerator down slightly, trying to keep some semblance of control. He put the phone back to his ear. "How far out is my ride?"

"Stand by . . ."

"One hundred and ten knots," the pilot called out. "In line with target now. Throttling back."

"Wind three-four-zero at twelve," the sensor operator announced. "That gives us a ten-knot headwind component."

"Landing gear down. Ninety knots. Flaps extended."

"Groundspeed seventy-eight. Range to target . . . five hundred feet."

The pilot reached for the special icon on his touchscreen weapon select panel. "Ready . . . and . . . trap deployed."

"You think they saw us?" the sensor operator wondered aloud. Moments ago, they'd passed directly over the trucks pursuing Slaton, yet they could no longer see them—the Reaper's only operating eye, its IR camera, was locked on the UAZ ahead.

"Doubtful," said the pilot. "Even if they did, there's not much they can do about it."

"They could take potshots. We're a big target."

"If it was daytime, maybe, but I don't think they're stargazing right now. Anyway, nothing to be done."

"High on glidepath."

"Correcting. Give Langley the one-minute call."

The sensor operator typed out the message, sent it. As soon as he looked up, something in the distance drew his attention. He slewed the camera and adjusted the magnification.

"Ah, boss . . . we have a problem."

The pilot shifted his eyes from the truck that was filling his screen and saw what was ahead. *"Holy crap!"*

"David, we have an issue!"

Slaton flicked his eyes momentarily to the phone. As if doing so might transmit his disbelief. He had a lot of *issues* right now. The urgency in Sorensen's voice didn't bode well. "What is it?"

"The road you're on . . . it ends in two miles."

"I'll never keep up this speed over open desert."

"Actually, that isn't an option. The road doesn't turn into desert. It dead ends into a ravine—a pretty deep one."

He glanced over his shoulder. The headlights were still there, jolting over the road. Thanks to his kamikaze-inspired driving style, the convoy had fallen back slightly. But they weren't going away. "A U-turn is not an option!"

"The Reaper is right behind you."

Slaton glanced behind again, this time searching higher . . . and he *did* see something. It was only a glimmer at first, then a slim shadow materialized. His head swiveled like a spastic metronome, alternating between the road ahead and the sky behind.

"Okay, I see it!" he said, shouting to be heard over the UAZ's straining engine.

"You're only going to have one chance, David! The drone can't go any slower. If you miss the handle on this pass, there won't be time to come around again."

Slaton didn't respond. He kept glancing back as the drone closed in. The Reaper was fifty feet behind him now, no more than twenty feet over his head. It was gaining definition, a shadowed apparition materializing out of the night. It seemed huge, like a massive bird of prey swooping down for a kill. He discerned the landing gear and fuselage, the long thin wings. And finally, the "trap" as Sorensen had referred to it. He knew the term was short for trapeze, which seemed eminently appropriate—two heavy ropes connected by three composite bars. A circus act beneath an airplane.

He could hear the drone's engine now, saw the aircraft bobbling as the pilot tried to hold a steady path. Slaton put the phone to speaker and dropped it in his front shirt pocket. Contorting in the seat, he put his right foot on the gas pedal, his left hand on the steering wheel. He half stood to get as high as possible, his knees bending for balance—he felt like he was at sea in a storm.

The drone was closing in at the relative speed of a steady run—eight miles an hour, maybe ten. Slaton focused on the lowest bar of the trapeze, a two-foot-wide objective swaying under the aircraft. He decided to grip it with one hand, then launch himself upward to get a second handhold.

Twenty feet now. The Reaper dipped suddenly. The pilot corrected, but too much, and the bar lifted out of his grasp.

"Lower!" he shouted, not even knowing if the phone could pick up his voice. The din of the truck's engine was drowned out by that of the drone's.

Slaton took what he hoped was his last glance ahead, then wished he hadn't. The dirt road in the truck's headlights went momentarily to scrub—then nothing at all. Only a black abyss that blended into the night.

The bar dropped abruptly, smacking the truck's tailgate. For a moment he thought the drone was going to crash into the truck—part of the landing gear actually touched the spare tire. Slaton reached out and got his fingers to the bar, only to have it swing out of reach. He sensed the cliff coming, some internal clock counting down. The bar oscillated back to a point just above him, but it was beyond his reach and moving away. His only way home was just out of grasp.

Slaton screamed in frustration. The UAZ shuddered.

His internal clock hit zeros.

Time was up.

He took his foot off the gas, stepped momentarily on the seat, and launched himself upward. One hand skipped off the bar, but the other snagged the rope on one side. He didn't so much pull himself skyward as the UAZ fell away beneath him. Slaton was dangling by one hand, and he felt the Reaper lurch. His weight had changed the dynamics for the pilot. Increased weight, increased drag.

The Reaper's engine rose to a screaming pitch. The churning propeller was behind Slaton, a "pusher" mounted on the aircraft's tail. One more bit of sensory overload. The bar was swinging wildly, and he timed the oscillation to get a grip with his second hand. He failed on his first try. On the second he got the bottom bar.

Hanging by two arms was better than one, but still a finite existence. Within minutes his hands would tire, give way. Having two solid points of contact, he looked up and studied the trapeze. Nylon loops above him were available as either handholds or footholds. There was also a harness of sorts with straps and what looked like a quick-release buckle.

With the oscillations dampening, he started to climb. It was all arms and shoulders to begin with. The noise was deafening, the wind extreme. He guessed the pilot was flying at the Reaper's minimum maneuvering speed, but for Slaton it was like climbing a rope ladder in a Category 2 hurricane.

His hands began to tremble, but the strain was relieved when he got his left foot on the lower bar. From that point it was a matter of maneuvering until he had four points of contact. He did his best with the harness, which distributed the weight further.

Huffing like he'd scaled a mountain, Slaton shouted toward his shirt pocket, *"Okay, now what?"*

He heard no response. At first, he thought it was due to the noise. Then he checked his pocket. The phone was gone, lost during his leap to reach the trap.

Slaton was again on his own.

He did his best to get comfortable, but soon realized it was a relative term. Looking into the night, he tried to determine which way they were flying. The ground was barely visible, but he guessed the pilot was flying at five, maybe seven thousand feet. Slaton hoped he didn't go any higher. At ten thousand oxygen deprivation became an issue—something his rescuers would certainly know.

He wished he'd queried Sorensen for more details about the system. For all his skepticism, the maneuver had actually worked. He'd been extracted from nearly impossible circumstances. Yet one great question loomed as he took in the scene around him— highlighted by the fact that he was at that moment hanging five feet lower than the Reaper's landing gear.

"What the hell do I do now?" Slaton said into the night sky above Syria.

FIFTY-SIX

"What the hell do we do now?" Sorensen asked.

The operations center had gone quiet, transfixed by the as-tonishing scene. The mission had crested in a minute of heart-gripping terror. Because the Reaper's camera was tracking the UAZ, it had followed the vehicle unfailingly as it went airborne and plummeted into a sixty-foot-deep ravine. Slaton was clearly no longer in the driver's seat, but the question of whether he too had plunged over the cliff loomed heavy. The tension had only been cut when the sensor operator slewed the camera back toward the trapeze. They all saw the operative known as Corsair clinging one-handed to the bottom bar. Everyone in the ops center had watched breathlessly as he clawed his way upward. The collective sigh was audible when he stabilized beneath the drone and strapped into the harness.

"We've been updating our options, ma'am," said the comm of-ficer. "The navy has a littoral combat ship standing by thirty miles off the coast of Israel, the *Jackson*. Unfortunately, the seas are high—eight to ten feet. We've never tested a recovery under condi-tions like that. It would also take nearly an hour to get there."

"Too long. What about the other possibility?"

"That's more promising. Our station chief in Tel Aviv has been working out the details since the mission was green-lighted. All the authorizations are in place—airspace, search and rescue."

"How far away is the zone?"

"From the Reaper's present position . . . forty-six nautical miles. At current speed, roughly thirty minutes."

"Okay," Sorensen said, hoping Slaton could hang on for that long. "Then that's where we're going."

Slaton rearranged his feet, trying for a better stance. His hands were beginning to cramp, and he intermittently wrapped his forearms around the upper bar to relieve the pressure. The harness helped, but the straps were too narrow, cutting into his back and shoulders. He was mentally logging ideas for improvements in the design.

Hopefully I'll live long enough to put my suggestions in the box, he thought.

The engine noise had lessened—no longer thunderous, but a steady drone. This suggested the aircraft was no longer climbing and had reached its cruise altitude. Even so, the rush of wind was unrelenting. In effect, he was riding outside an airplane like a barnstormer at an airshow.

He estimated, referencing the stars and the geography he could make out on the clear night, that the drone was taking him southwest. He saw the coastline in the distance on his right. Damascus and Beirut were obvious, one over each shoulder. At this point Slaton was along for the ride, but there was a vague sense of comfort when he realized his destination: he was headed into Israel. From the agency's point of view, it made sense. Friendly country, capable military, good intelligence organizations. Still, the question of what would happen when he got there weighed heavily. When Sorensen had first briefed him on the extraction method, he'd been less than impressed. She'd shown him a video of a soldier making the transition from a fast-moving Hummer onto the trapeze.

For Slaton, that had been enough. The whole concept seemed so speculative, so risk-laden, he'd not bothered to watch the rest of the video. Now he wished he'd stayed for the end of the show. He couldn't imagine how the drone was going to land with him hanging from the trapeze. He'd done his best to survey the aircraft's belly, yet in the darkness he could see no sign of a compartment or higher handholds, no cradle that would put him above the level of the landing gear. A parachute would have been worth its weight in gold. Try as he might, he couldn't imagine what the plan was for dismounting this carnival ride.

The engine suddenly throttled back. The Reaper's nose tipped down. Whatever the plan was, he was about to find out.

The first thing Slaton noticed was a void of light on the ground ahead. It was the shape of an oval, a great black hole many miles wide. He was intimately familiar with the area—as a teen he'd spent years on a kibbutz not far from here. He knew he'd been delivered over the Golan, and was now soaring over northern Israel. The approaching emptiness was surrounded by a necklace of yellow light. He saw Tiberias on the edge to his right, beyond that Nazareth.

Slaton put it all together and knew precisely what he was looking at. He was descending toward the Sea of Galilee.

With that realization, the endgame resolved. The Reaper was low now, perhaps a thousand feet above the ground and still descending. The noise lessened considerably passing over the northern shore of the lake—a lower RPM on the engine, the onrushing hurricane one category lower.

Then Slaton saw something that crystallized what was about to happen.

Dead ahead, in the center of the lake, he saw a pair of lights. They looked like spotlights, separated by perhaps fifty yards. The powerful beams were playing the sky like a Hollywood premiere. One flickered momentarily across the Reaper. It wasn't blinding, but Slaton saw it coming and closed his eyes to preserve his night vision. The light fell away, and when he looked again both began flashing on and off, long and short intervals. It might have been Morse Code, but he didn't try to decipher it. They could only be telling him one thing.

Slaton readjusted his four-point stance, then twisted free of the harness. The drone seemed to be slowing. The spotlights went steady and focused on a spot on the lake between the two sources—which could only be boats. The drone was getting very low, very slow.

He saw water now in the beams of the lights. It looked black and cold, and a slight chop gave texture to the surface. With a quarter mile to go he looked down and adjusted his feet, making sure there was no way he could hang up on the trapeze. He decided the best move would be to simply let go, fall away with the wind.

The pilot had the drone skimming just above the surface, perhaps twenty feet separating Slaton's feet from the water. In a fleeting thought, he remembered as a schoolboy having to memorize the depth of the Sea of Galilee. Now the number escaped him, but at the time he recalled thinking it was deeper than he'd imagined. He could never have foreseen how critical that bit of learning would one day prove.

He felt like he was water skiing from the ladder, gliding just above the lake. The target of crosshatched light was coming at him like a train in the dark. Which was pretty much how it would feel if he didn't get his water entry right.

Legs together, arms across the chest. Spine straight, chin tucked.

He loosened his grip, then let go, freefalling into the night.

He struck the water at sixty miles an hour. It felt like hitting a brick wall. Slaton did his best to maintain his entry position, but the impact was crushing. The shock translated through his body, and his limbs flailed outward, no longer under his control. For an instant he felt pain in a half dozen places, ligaments finding new limits, joints pressed bone-to-bone. Yet there was one positive to the severe impact: it arrested his descent quickly. The deceleration was rapid, and he quickly sensed that forward motion had stopped. There was lingering pain in his ribs and one shoulder, but everything seemed to be working. He'd tried to time his last breath, but the impact had knocked the wind out of him. Even so, old training kicked in.

Slaton remained motionless, letting his body go limp in the lake's weightless void. The water was frigid, but he tuned that out as well.

He was ten, perhaps fifteen feet below the surface. As he knew would be the case, he was completely disoriented. With a partial lungful of air to work with, he couldn't afford to swim in the wrong direction. Fortunately, whoever was on the surface knew what he was facing. He saw the lights playing frantically across the surface, his bubbles rising toward them.

Slaton stroked upward.

He surfaced seconds later. Before he could get his bearings, or even blink the water from his eyes, a strong hand seized the back of his shirt.

FIFTY-SEVEN

The boat was small and low to the water. Slaton saw another like it nearby, roughly a twin.

The hand was pulling him tight to the gunnel. Slaton reached one arm over the top, but his effort ended there. After hanging beneath an airplane for half an hour, and swallowing a good portion of the Sea of Galilee, all strength suddenly left him.

It didn't matter.

A second hand took hold of his arm, and he was hauled unceremoniously into the boat. He flopped to the deck like a boated tuna, spent and exhausted. For the second time in less than a minute, Slaton let his body go still. He relaxed with his eyes closed. When he opened them again, he saw a face that told him two things.

He was safe.

And he was indeed in Israel.

Anton Bloch, the man who had so many years ago recruited him into Mossad, into the life that still haunted him, was smiling down like a benevolent God. Which, as a former spy chief, he most certainly was not.

Slaton saw two other men in the boat, both young and fit. Bloch himself had retired, but the new director permitted him to keep a hand in the game. And there was no more fitting hand to play than this—Slaton, in so many ways, was Bloch's crowning legacy.

Slaton worked himself onto a wooden bench along the port side. He coughed up more water, spit it over the side. Someone put a blanket over his shoulders. The man in back cranked a small outboard to life and began steering toward shore. The other boat fell in behind. Slaton looked skyward, searching for the Reaper. He saw nothing.

"I see you haven't forgotten how to make an entrance," Bloch said in his brusque baritone.

Slaton worked his right arm—the worst of the hits from his entry. "And I see you aren't playing golf."

"Are you all right?"

"Aren't I always?"

"We have a doctor standing by on shore."

"A good thing. The Americans could use some refinements to their extraction methods. I would characterize the endgame as suboptimal."

Bloch smiled, a difficult process in which minor fissures appeared in his stony visage. "According to the Christians, the Sea of Galilee is where Jesus walked on water. You, it seems, are not so blessed."

Slaton relented, allowing a smile of his own. His only reply was to look out over the calm lake.

"Welcome home, David."

During the same minutes that Slaton was being hauled out of the Sea of Galilee, three travelers walked wearily from Syria into Lebanon. Though they could not know it, they were a mere fifty yards past the border when three men and a woman materialized out of the gloom.

"Welcome to Lebanon," the lead man said in Arabic.

The reception committee were dressed in casual clothes, and even in the darkness their features belied their Western heritage. Through a series of handshakes and greetings—simplified by the fact that everyone spoke at least rudimentary Arabic—Ludmilla, Salma, and Naji were introduced to four officers of the CIA's Beirut station.

"Is this your entire party?" the lead American asked.

Ludmilla said, "There were two others. We separated from the man who was guiding us out, but I think you've been in touch with him. The other is going back to Damascus."

The American nodded. "We have two cars waiting. We should go now."

No one argued, and Lebanon's three newest arrivals set out again northward. Three of the Americans led the way, while the woman fell in behind. Ludmilla, exhausted from the travails of recent days, had trouble keeping up. The Americans seemed to be in a hurry. But then, in her experience, they usually were.

"Where are we going?" she asked the woman officer behind her.

"To the airport. There's a jet waiting."

"Where will it take us?"

"I don't know."

Ludmilla suspected the woman was being truthful. She paused, half turned, and looked back into the dark hills. She couldn't say where the border was—there was no fence or wall or berm like in some areas. She only knew it was not far behind her. In the pre-dawn darkness, she wondered if Achmed was still watching them. Suspecting he was, she raised a hand into the night and waved goodbye.

"We really should hurry, ma'am," the woman said.

Ludmilla turned and began walking again, her stride suddenly energized, curiously light and free. More than it had been in a very long time.

FIFTY-EIGHT

The masters of intelligence agencies, at least those worthy of their positions, do not forfeit sleep by choice. Like the parents of a teenager prone to bust curfew, they do so out of worry. The waiting is the worst, those idle minutes in which dire scenarios permeate every thought. The ding of an incoming secure message can straighten a spine as well as any unexpected knock on a front door. Satellite feeds are watched for good news like a driveway for headlights. The main difference for spymasters is a sobering one: the chances of an actual catastrophe coming to pass are exponentially higher.

Sorensen monitored Slaton's mission throughout the evening from the Langley operations center. When she finally got word from Anton Bloch that Corsair had been pulled from the Sea of Galilee, cold and wet and bruised, but fundamentally intact, it was ten o'clock D.C. time.

As it turned out, her night was only beginning.

What should have been relief at the completion of a successful mission was drowned out by the quagmire of a secondary crisis. Within moments of word coming from Lebanon that Ludmilla Kravchuk and two Syrian nationals were safe and sound on an agency plane near Beirut, an update arrived regarding another operation.

Sorensen's division had ceded control of that investigation to the DOD, which was far better equipped to analyze chemical attacks than the CIA. The incident in Sudan, which had taken the lives of two individuals, along with a herd of livestock and various carrion feeders, had initially been categorized as an "unknown chemical event." The preliminary report now before Sorensen narrowed things down. The culprit turned out to be a potent nerve agent, the specific signature of which was not in the army's extensive library of such substances. A chemical analysis of swabbed samples, however, proved the agent to be remarkably similar to Novichok-class weapons long attributed to Russia.

Within minutes of reading the report, Sorensen was on the phone with Dr. David Gyger, the DOD's preeminent expert on chemical weapons. She had met Gyger once, and remembered a man in his sixties who held a PhD from Princeton and an MD from Harvard. More off-putting for Sorensen, both then and now, was that his voice reminded her of her late father's.

"How sure are we that this is a Russian product?" she inquired.

"The chemistry is certainly of Russian origin—we've identified a unique chemical structure common to all variants of Novichok. But the answer to your question isn't so simple. While the design of the agent is provably Russian, it's not out of the question that it could have been licensed and produced elsewhere."

"You're saying they could be selling their recipe?"

"I find it unlikely, but the possibility can't be ruled out. There is also the manner of dispersal to consider." Gyger described, in perhaps more detail than necessary, the dispersal hardware that had been recovered from the site. "We are clearly looking at a binary employment system, two precursor sources combined and aerosolized. In the past, the Russians have tended to be more direct, using liquid agents applied to skin through clandestine methods. The latter method is far more controllable, more specific when it comes to targeting."

Sorensen thought about it, and a question rose to mind. "I'd like your opinion, Doctor. Given that this attack took place in the middle of nowhere, and the victims, by all accounts, were no more than random passersby—why would someone go to all this trouble?"

"I wondered the same thing," Gyger admitted. "I can think of only two reasons. The first would be that we are looking at a demonstration, an implied threat if you will."

"But that only works if you know who's responsible. If ISIS or some Al-Qaeda branch had claimed responsibility, it would be a model terror weapon. But nobody is taking credit."

"Precisely. Which leaves option two. This is some kind of test—someone is making sure both the agent and the delivery system are effective."

"Okay, but who?"

"I can tell you it's not the Russians. They would do that kind of thing in-house, in their own Siberian backyard. If I were to guess, I'd say we're looking at a state actor—someone from the region who wants to be sure their new weapon works before they actually use it."

"That's not very comforting."

"Not at all."

"One more thing," Sorensen said. "The hardware that was recovered—the canisters and metal tubing. Does it give you any idea how this weapon might be employed?"

A hesitation. "I've gone over the photographs thoroughly. The actual hardware is fairly straightforward. It reminded me of certain small-scale firefighting systems, which include any number of commercial applications. A closet with high-voltage electrical relays, inaccessible compartments on a ship, the engine bay of a city bus."

"Good to know, but that hardly narrows things down."

"I wish I could be more specific, but the possibilities are almost endless. There *were* some peculiarities in the mounting hardware—the shape and anchor points implied a very specific purpose. But without some idea of where to look . . . I'm afraid I'd only be guessing."

Sorensen hung up to find another call waiting—a connection she herself had initiated ten minutes earlier. Somewhere above the Mediterranean, a company jet was whisking eastward. Among the eight people on board was a Russian defector who claimed to have knowledge of a pending terrorist attack.

Sorensen found herself talking to the leader of the extraction team, a man whose name was actually Smith. "What do you have so far?" she asked, eschewing any conversational openers.

"We interviewed Kravchuk for roughly twenty minutes. At that point she was pretty much asleep in her chair. We decided to let her rest."

"Okay, but what did you get?"

"She gave a pretty detailed recount of the meeting between Petrov and Rahmani." After providing the highlights, Smith said, "I made a digital file of the interview and sent it to you via secure link. Your comm guy there should see it any moment."

"Okay, I'll check."

"Kravchuk also said the guy who brought them out had an SD card with an actual recording of the meeting. She said the two of them listened to it together before leaving Damascus."

"Okay, we should have access to that soon."

"Kravchuk and the others," Smith said speculatively, "they've been asking about him—the guy who led them out."

"He's fine, made it out of Syria no problem," she said, knowing Slaton might have viewed it differently.

"Good to hear, I'll pass it on. Once Kravchuk wakes up, I'll have another go at her. For what it's worth, I think she's legit."

"I think so too. When will you arrive stateside?"

"According to the pilots, midday your time."

"All right. Keep me posted."

Sorensen cut the connection, then immediately looked at the comm officer. She wanted to compare Kravchuk's interview with what was on the SD card Slaton was carrying. It was going to be a long night, but one thing was clear. Her two ongoing operations— one in Syria and the other in Sudan—were fast becoming one.

FIFTY-NINE

It seemed entirely fitting, Sultan thought, that he was viewing the desert around him in the light of a new day. His journey from Sudan had gone well—he'd caught the dawn flight out of Port Sudan to arrive in Baghdad, spent and weary, on a clear midmorning. A car had been waiting at the airport to deliver him on the final leg of what had once seemed an improbable journey.

"Finally, I have come home," he murmured. He'd meant the words for himself, but the man next to him in the back seat responded.

"It must seem a very long time," he said.

His seatmate was clad, rather asynchronously, in a worn Western business suit with a red-and-white keffiyeh framing his face. Such was the incongruity of present-day Iraq, a land trying to find its way in the world after so much war and sectarian violence. The endless national rehabilitations, the world-class corruption. The man sitting beside Sultan had lived through it all. His bushy black hair and mustache attested to his lineage every bit as much as his name: Ibrahim Ayman Al-Tikriti.

"It will be a large gathering," Ibrahim said. "A handful will remember you. Friends, family, your father's old business partners. Everyone remembers the old days fondly."

"Everyone but me," Sultan said.

"I should tell you to exercise caution—there will be a number of important clerics in attendance."

"I suppose it is necessary."

"Never underestimate the value of religion. The title you wish to claim is without parallel in the modern era."

"The title I wish to claim is a matter of heritage and history—no one can deny my right."

Ibrahim tipped his head to one side. "The Shiites control Baghdad and the south, but their grip is weak. If they lose Iran's backing, they will be helpless. The Kurds are troublesome as ever, but they keep to their territory. They can be dealt with later. You will give true Iraqis the two things they desperately need; a war to preoccupy and weaken our enemies, and a legitimate leader who can reunite our nation."

"You make no mention of the Americans. They still have a presence in Iraq, military bases."

"It has fallen to only a token force. The Americans stay behind their walls. They will be distracted by this new war, and we should encourage them for a time, let them use our air bases freely. We can stand back and watch Saudis and Iranians annihilate one another. As they do, we will quietly get stronger, consolidate power. When the dust settles, a new Middle East will emerge, and the rightful ruler will be waiting to lead it—the Fifth Rashidun."

Sultan diverted his gaze and looked searchingly out the window. The landscape seemed familiar, but he supposed it was not much different from Jordan. Thatched hardscape, distant brown hills. Plots of green rimming the wandering Tigris River. He wished the bond he felt was a direct memory, but that had never been plausible. He'd left this place when he was eighteen months old, bundled into a car with his mother and two guards—or so he'd been told. A fast ride to the airfield, an unrecorded departure. All because his father had deemed it so. And just like that, after a one-hour flight, his history, his very existence had been wiped away.

He, of course, remembered nothing of those days. Indeed, his mother hadn't told him the story, had not confided his lineage, until his fourteenth birthday. Yet others here had never forgotten. Elders had tracked him from a distance, made sure he became educated. They kept the prospect of his return alive. They all knew the reason for his being expelled from the family. Knew that his mother had been exiled with him, in disgrace, apparently, for having issued a defective heir.

Ironically, in the end, that banishment had saved them both. And the clubfoot that had caused him to be shunned as an infant would only support his rise inside the hierarchy of faith. Blind clerics had once been all the rage. A cripple, surely, must be imbued with the wisdom of the Prophet, peace be upon him.

He looked down at his foot. It hurt more than usual, but that was to be expected after so much travel. The defect could have been surgically repaired after birth, at least in part. But his father had simply shunned him as imperfect. How ironic that, after so many years, he, the shamed and crippled child, was the one left standing tall.

The city of Tikrit began to encompass them. Sultan looked more closely, saw rows of grand buildings pockmarked from the wars. All seemed in various stages of recovery. What the city had suffered was incalculable, indeed the inverse of the largesse that had once been showered upon it. Twenty years ago, the roads had been the best in Iraq, the utilities the most reliable. Every member of the tribe who'd wanted work had found it. Those who didn't were guaranteed food and medical care. Here in Tikrit, the pulsing heart of the nation, *everyone* was in the tribe.

The new government had appropriated the most ostentatious palaces, and of these there were many. The grandest, of course, had been built for his father, while others had risen for uncles and sisters and important patrons. Sultan had researched many of them on the internet, a parade of images documenting their besieged histories. The most famous had been either obliterated in battle or desecrated during occupations, the Islamic State reveling in the latter. Yet a few of the minor houses had come through unscathed.

The edifice that began filling the front windscreen did not look familiar. It was modest in scale, but in reasonably good shape. Even from a distance he saw intricate carvings in the sandstone, soft curves and expansive balconies.

"It is one of the few palaces to survive untouched," Ibrahim said, following his gaze. "It was built for one of your cousins, but he fled to Greece just before its completion. The local council has taken control, although there is a rumor the governor wants to turn it into a tourist attraction."

"That will not come to pass, God willing."

Ibrahim looked at him and smiled approvingly.

The driver followed the semicircular driveway to a high portico. A uniformed guard was waiting, and he opened the back door. Ibrahim led the way. A soaring archway fed into a courtyard brimming with greenery, much of which, Sultan suspected, was not native to Tikrit. After passing through a massive pair of ornately carved doors, which seemed better suited to a mosque than a home, Sultan found himself standing on a floor of black-and-white tile in a checkerboard pattern. All along the edges, like so many pieces on a chessboard, two dozen men stood arranged in neat rows.

On some unseen command, everyone bowed their head and said in near unison, *"As-Salaam Alaikum."*

The Fifth Rashidun responded in kind. He could not deny that he was moved. He'd left these old sands thirty-four years ago, before his second birthday. Yet somehow it felt intimately familiar. The faces around him were his people, the roof over his head their sanctuary. On the far wall he saw two flags. One was a variant of the black standard carried by the first four Rashidun Caliphs. The other was the flag of Iraq, although not the contemporary version. This red, white, and black tricolor displayed the three stars and handwritten message that had been removed in 2004: the *takbir*, "God is great," that had been scripted in the regal hand of his father.

Saddam Hussein Abd al-Majid al-Tikriti.

SIXTY

Slaton had officially broken with Mossad more than five years earlier. It was rather like an ugly divorce: he'd long ago lost track of what his ex was up to and where they were living. So it came as no surprise when, sometime before daybreak, he and Bloch had been dropped in front of a building he'd never seen before.

It could only be described as a bunker. Set deep in the bedrock of a minor hill, the building was long, rectangular and deeply nondescript. Given the approximate duration of the drive, and the direction from the Sea of Galilee—his navigational instincts were not to be denied—Slaton guessed the place to be somewhere in the hills of the upper Jezreel Valley.

In the predawn Bloch had ushered him inside past layers of security and, without any suggestion of a debriefing, deposited him in a functionally appointed sleep room. One cot, one blanket, one pillow. In that moment, Slaton had been profoundly grateful.

He woke, according to a clock on the wall, at two that afternoon. Rolling out of the cot, his first sensation was that his mouth was sandpaper-dry. An ice pack gone to water, stretch-bandaged to one shoulder, reminded him of his brief encounter with the agency doctor—an officious woman who'd given him a once-over when he arrived at the bunker. He unwound the stretch bandage and tossed aside the now room-temperature plastic pouch. He rolled his shoulder as a test, and deemed it sore but serviceable.

Slaton had stripped down to his boxers to sleep, and he discovered that the filthy clothes he'd been wearing through three days of desert travel and firefights—not to mention being dropped from an aircraft like a human bomb—had been replaced by something similar. And of course, in his size.

Retirement had not dulled Bloch's eye for detail.

There was a tiny shower in the adjacent bathroom. The water was warm and wonderful. The muscles in his neck were crossbow-tight, a predictable consequence of tension, fatigue, and hitting a lake at highway speeds. He rolled his head under the stream until things loosened up. After dressing, he stepped into a hallway that seemed brilliantly lit and turned in the direction of the most noise. Through the first door on his right were a half dozen men and women chatting in a small cafeteria. Bloch was at a corner table, sitting alone and looking contemplatively at a large plate in front of him. On it was a thick steak, and what looked like potatoes Lyonnaise.

The sound level crashed when Slaton stepped into the room. Everyone looked at him as they might a stray Rottweiler who'd wandered into a backyard. News of his adventures, apparently, had preceded him. He nodded cordially on his way to the coffee pot. There he filled a Styrofoam cup to the brim, then took a seat across from Bloch.

"Steak for lunch?" he asked.

Bloch finally looked up. "I really shouldn't."

"What . . . eat it?"

"Moira has convinced me to become a vegetarian."

"You don't look convinced."

Bloch picked up a fork and serrated knife, but still did not attack. He sighed. "When I am at home it seems easier. But at times like this . . . I have doubts."

"You used to have doubts about much more consequential things."

Bloch said nothing.

"Would I be helping if I offered to eat it for you? I haven't had a real meal in days."

Bloch looked at him severely, then began sawing off a hunk of the steak. The look on his face when he savored the first bite was nothing short of ecstasy.

Slaton let his old boss relish the moment, before asking, "So what is this place?"

Bloch lifted his eyes to the ceiling. "Some years ago, the army built a network of remote command bunkers—a bit of insurance against strikes to more obvious command and control nodes. They are occupied on a random cycle, but on any given day most go unused."

"So, for Mossad—this is like your version of an Airbnb rental?"

"It seems an efficient use of resources."

"Have you heard anything from Lebanon?"

"Your Russian defector, a hairdresser, and a young boy have all been safely retrieved."

"That's good to hear. What about the SD card I gave you—did you upload it to Langley?"

"Precisely as you asked," Bloch said.

"Did you look at it yourself?"

"Of course."

Slaton never expected anything less. Mossad was due something in return for their assistance. "What did you make of it?" he asked.

Bloch shoveled in a second piece of meat, taken close to the bone. He directed his knife at Slaton as a maestro would wield a baton. "It is the worst news I've heard in years. Iran has acquired a new weapon of mass destruction. I instructed Director Nurin to run an analysis of how and where such an agent might be used, and what possible countermeasures are necessary. We of course will prioritize vulnerabilities in Israel, but other targets must be considered."

"You *instructed* Nurin?" Slaton mused. Raymond Nurin was Bloch's successor, the presiding director of Mossad.

"Strongly advised, if you prefer. In this instance, we are in complete accord. Anything you can add would be appreciated—you spent a good deal of time with this interpreter."

"I think we both might benefit from a conversation with Langley."

"Your new controller, Miss Sorensen?"

"She's far more agreeable than my old controller."

Bloch feigned pain. "You strike me to the quick, David."

"Yeah, right. I'm guessing you can set up a secure call from this place?"

"If not here, then where? This outpost was built for secure communications." Bloch then acquired a more circumspect gaze. "Can I surmise, then, that your mission for Miss Sorensen is not yet complete?"

"Are missions ever?"

"I suppose not."

The sweet smell of heated butter and garlic wafted in from the kitchen. "Did you bring your own chef?" Slaton asked.

"Our budget is never so generous. One of the men on my protection detail is an excellent cook."

"Which is why he's on your protection detail."

"Why waste talent? He tells me all his ingredients are from sustainable sources. The cattle are grass fed and free range, whatever the hell that means. Mind you, all of this is classified at the highest level . . . Moira can never hear of it."

"Your secret is safe," Slaton said. "And while you're working out that communications link . . ." he pointed to Bloch's plate, "do you think I could get one of those?"

SIXTY-ONE

"Sergeant!"

Nazir froze, which wasn't hard to do. He was wedged headlong inside the engine bay of a jet, a two-seat BAE Hawk trainer. As a powerplant specialist, he was responsible for keeping the unit's Adour turbofans perfectly maintained. He counted his wrenches carefully—he'd brought three into the cavity, and it was sacrosanct to not leave any behind—before backing out onto the work stand.

He looked down and saw Captain Mahrez striding across the glossy concrete of the air-conditioned hangar. "Yes sir?"

"Number three is due an oil service on the accessory housing next week. I want you to do it today—we can afford no mistakes for tomorrow's event."

"I will take care of it as soon as I am finished here," Nazir promised.

"What are you working on?"

"A minor leak in a hydraulic line. I tightened a B-nut and performed the pressure check."

Mahrez began to turn away.

"Sir?" His supervisor paused. "I was hoping for some time off this afternoon. I have worked extra shifts the last three days, and it is my mother's birthday—"

"We are all working overtime this week!" Mahrez interrupted.

"Yes, sir. But I would only need a few hours. I can return after evening prayers."

Fortunately for Nazir, Captain Mahrez imagined himself a man of reason and compassion. Nazir knew he was the son of a distant member of the royal family. It had been enough to earn him a commission, but nowhere near what it took to gain a slot for flight school. That being the case, Mahrez did what most third-tier royals did—he went through the motions of a job he cared little about, with the end date of his obligatory four-year hitch circled in red on his calendar. At that point, having "served," he could expect a comfortable position at some state-run company. He would spend the rest of his life idling through soft promotions at a place like Saudi Aramco, overseeing expatriate workers who broke their backs in the field. The likes of welders who repaired refinery coking tanks under dangerous conditions.

"All right," Mahrez said. "If you can finish the accessory housing, take your leave. But be sure number five is ready for the scheduled practice."

The captain walked away.

With a sigh of relief, Nazir eased back into the engine bay of number 4 and finished what he was working on. Ten minutes later he buttoned up the access door, picked up a rag, and began wiping grime from his hands. He tried to recall what he'd blurted about his mother. Had he said he was going to see her? *No,* he thought reassuringly. *I only said it was her birthday.* And it very nearly was—early next week.

He heaved a sigh of relief.

In truth, his mother no longer lived in Jeddah—she had recently returned to Jordan. He was glad for that. She had never acclimated to life in Saudi Arabia, and he'd easily convinced her to return to the Hashemite Kingdom. He wished she'd gone farther away, but that could be dealt with later.

He looked to the far end of the hangar and saw the next jet in his work queue. A fan blade inspection wouldn't take long at all. He set out with his toolbox across the spotless floor. As he did, Nazir felt a surge of satisfaction as he composed the message he would send tonight.

Package is installed. Delivery will be right on time.

"It must be put to a stop!" the white-bearded sheik shouted.

Sultan listened dutifully.

They had moved to a smaller room, twelve of the most important clerics in Iraq seated on pillows before him. Sultan was also seated. He had been briefed by Ibrahim prior to entering the room on certain religious protocols, and to the best of his abilities he'd abided by them. The men in this room were powerful, collectively if not individually, and the sway they imparted upon their flocks was essential to achieve success.

For over an hour the holy men had had their say. One by one, they outlined their grievances. Those from Baghdad were united—the Shia clerics in the city conspired with the government at every turn, trying to freeze out Sunni influence. Intersect marriages were forbidden, schools forced to use only Shia-approved textbooks. Sunnis were never given consideration for influential government jobs.

"If they have their way," a squat man with nicotine-yellowed teeth complained, "there will be nothing left for us but to sweep the streets and pick up garbage!"

Sultan nodded with feigned interest. At essence, these were the same Sunni-Shia arguments that had been raging since the death of the Prophet Muhammad fourteen hundred years ago.

He found himself studying the room. What had seemed a gilded place on first glance showed signs of age on closer inspection. A corner of the ceiling displayed water damage and rotted wood, and many of the floor tiles had hairline cracks. The air was stagnant and carried the unmistakable hint of mildew. He wondered who had lived here through so many years of conflict. As a child, he remembered being told that voices in a home never die. They echoed between the walls, decreasing in volume but never going silent. The sounds of anger and ecstasy, of joy and grief. If that were true, this place, surely, had stories to tell.

A minor argument broke out on the left side of the holy formation, two bearded men raising fingers at one another. Sultan sighed.

As vital as these men were, the soon-to-be Fifth Rashidun understood that they needed him more than he needed any one of them. Only the last remaining son of Saddam Hussein could pull everyone together—a theological coalition to join their respective theaters of battle.

"Enough!" he shouted.

The squabble went silent. Sultan looked across the group, meeting each set of eyes for a moment. With order established, he decided it was time. Time to begin the speech he'd been waiting a lifetime to deliver.

"I have heard your troubles, listened to your hopes. Now it is time to share with you my own vision for Islam . . ."

SIXTY-TWO

The bunker on the rim of the Jezreel Valley was unmistakably an army affair. The chairs were gray metal, the walls olive-drab. There were steel toilet seats that would last a hundred years, and closets stocked with prepackaged meals that might outlast them. The only decorative touch in the building, if it could be referred to as such, was an official photograph of the chief of the general staff of the Israeli Defense Force. Israel's equivalent of a three-star general, decked in full regalia, brooded high on a wall near the vault-like entrance.

The communications center, too, had the IDF's utilitarian hallmarks. Most of the connections were old-school, hardened landlines that networked to regional military outposts, and two dedicated lines linking to Northern Command headquarters in Safed. More advanced technology, however, was not completely ignored—one secure satellite link had been installed. Taken together, Slaton recognized time-honored military doctrine: the more lines of communications you had, the greater chance that at least one would work when you needed it.

Bloch coopted a workstation and used the satellite device to connect to the Special Activities Center at Langley. Knowing Mossad as he did, Slaton was sure that every word spoken would be logged in the databases of the agency's own Glilot Junction headquarters complex.

"Good afternoon, David," Sorensen said, her face streaming across the grainy feed.

"Not where you are," he replied. "What is it . . . ten a.m.?"

"It was a long night. I have to say, you look surprisingly relaxed given what you went through."

"I had some time to rest. You should know that a certain former Mossad director is listening in."

"I expected as much. Hello, Anton."

"Good morning, Miss Sorensen. Our paths cross again. And once more, with David in the crosshairs."

"Thank you for coming to his rescue."

"As you and I both know, David is far more dependent on us than he imagines."

Slaton didn't bother to respond.

Sorensen said, "We've gone over the SD drive. It essentially backs up what Kravchuk told us. President Petrov promised to deliver a new and very lethal nerve agent to Iran."

Bloch said, "As I told David earlier, such a development would be viewed gravely by Israel. Do you have any information about how or when this transfer might take place?"

"Actually, we are quite confident it already has."

Slaton's attention ratcheted up—this was news to him.

Sorensen went on, "Two days ago there was an event in Sudan, a very remote area in eastern Darfur. The emergency services hotline received a series of three calls. All reported fatalities at a tiny desert outpost in North Kurdufan."

"How many fatalities?" Slaton asked.

"As it turned out, two."

Slaton's gaze narrowed. He had an ominous sense of where Sorensen was going.

"This area is extremely remote, and it took some time to get the right investigative team in place."

"And what did they find?" Bloch asked.

"This."

Sorensen's face disappeared from the screen and a still photo took its place. Slaton saw a compound consisting of three dilapidated buildings. Only one of them looked habitable, and in its entryway lay two bodies. Outside were a pair of decomposing bovine carcasses.

Sorensen said, "The victims were eventually identified as a cattle herder and his teenage son. They had no ties to any nefarious organizations, either inside Sudan or elsewhere. Interviews suggest that in the last week rumors have been circulating in nearby villages that the valleys to the east were favorable for grazing."

"They were lured to this place," Slaton surmised.

"Apparently. The route to the so-called promised land would have taken them right past it. By chance, the first team the government sent in to investigate was led by a medic. He got a close look at the bodies, and recognized enough warning signs to pull away and call for backup. It probably saved his life. There were a few more missteps, but by the next morning the Sudanese understood they were looking at something out of their league. They quietly informed us of the situation, and we sent a team in. The DOD keeps a Chemical and Biological Defense Program response team on standby at Incirlik Air Base in Turkey."

Sorensen began stepping through more photos. Both bodies from different angles, the area around the compound. In the background technicians in hazmat suits could be seen. "Have you confirmed the use of a nerve agent?" Slaton asked.

"Yes, the tests were definitive. We also found a staging site a short distance away." More photos. From some ancient training, certainly administered by the IDF, Slaton recognized an open-field decontamination area. Two full suits lay accordioned on the ground, the booties still in place. A spray bottle of what had to be decontamination fluid was discarded next to one of them. Somewhere in the back of his mind warning lights began to flicker. Faint and ill-defined—but definitely there.

"Any idea who was wearing these suits?" he asked.

"That's the million-dollar question. We were able to recover DNA evidence from both—hair and some sputum. Unfortunately, there were no matches in any of our databases."

"What about region or ethnicity?" Slaton asked. He knew this was a growing track of analysis, the intelligence agency equivalent of commercially available DNA heritage profiles.

"We just got the results. Both samples matched positively as Persian. One registered as being Azeri, a common ethnicity among the ruling class and Revolutionary Guard."

"So, let me get this straight," Slaton conjectured. "You're suggesting the Iranians are testing nerve agents on humans in Sudan?"

"I know it's far-fetched, but that's how the evidence is stacking up. We're still pursuing a couple of other leads."

Bloch said, "The Iranians have long pursued nerve agents. They suffered greatly during the Iran-Iraq war when Saddam Hussein used his extensive arsenal against them. Tens of thousands of Iranian conscripts died terrible deaths on the front lines. But the chemical program has never been a top priority for the mullahs. They view nuclear weapons as more imperative, a response to what they view as a threat from Israel. This would suggest a major change in strategy."

Slaton said, "I take it you've analyzed the agent?"

"It's definitely Russian, an offshoot of the Novichok line. We watch their program closely, and have an extensive database of samples we've been able to acquire and analyze—don't ask how."

Another photo appeared on the main monitor. Slaton saw what had to be the delivery system, two shiny cylinders connected by an intricate web of tubes and brackets.

"This is the hardware used to deploy the agent. It employs a binary process, each canister having a precursor compound. Independently, either chemical is harmless. Put them together, aerosolize, and you've got a deadly product. We're still running estimates, but the projected lethality is on par with anything we've ever tested."

Slaton studied the device on the screen. "The engineering looks very . . . specialized."

"What do you mean?" Bloch asked.

"I'm not sure," he hedged. "Certain parts look more complicated than they need to be. The mounting hardware has unused attach points on the sides, and the overall arrangement seems odd."

"Some of our technicians noticed the same thing," Sorensen replied. "Unfortunately, trying to guess the intended use is a pure guessing game. We're moving the whole assembly stateside for further study, but that will take time. For what it's worth, we've identified the cylinders as Russian."

"How?" Bloch asked.

"Our engineers identified characteristics in the metallurgy that signify Russian manufacture. The piping and mounting hardware are Chinese—the kind of thing you can get at pretty much any hardware store on earth."

Slaton heard a loud chime in the audio background. After a pause, Sorensen said, "I need to ring off—something just arrived and I need to have a look."

"Brief us in when you can?" Slaton asked.

A pause. "David, you did really well . . . you got Kravchuk out.
I was assuming you'd be on the next flight home."

"Then you don't know me as well as you think."

"Okay. We'll talk soon."

The connection broke, and for a time Slaton stared at the monitor. He was wondering the same thing Sorensen had been wondering. *Why not just go home?*

He remembered long ago, in a Mossad safe house, being spurred
by a piece of junk mail into discussing the prospect of retirement
with another operative. Like Slaton, the other man had never considered it, but his reasoning was novel: he said he never expected to
live that long. *It takes twenty years to get a retirement, right?* the man
had said. *What are the chances?* His words had proved prescient:
he'd died six months later in a tunnel explosion in Gaza. For Slaton, that theory had hardened for years afterward. The notion of
drinking double Scotches in a hardwood-paneled room, reminiscing with friends about the good old days—it simply had never been
part of his future. Then he'd left Mossad, started a family.

He felt Bloch's eyes on him.

"I find myself wondering why you want to see this through,"
Bloch said. "I think it might be because you see a threat to Israel."

"I see a threat to us all."

The former director nodded, although Slaton doubted he was
convinced.

"Don't worry about my motivations," Slaton said.

"As you wish. And while we wait for Miss Sorensen to call us
back?"

Slaton considered it. "I'd like to listen to that SD card again.
Can you pull up the file on a computer?"

"But of course."

SIXTY-THREE

Having listened patiently to grievances from the assembly of clerics, Sultan spent thirty minutes airing his own.

For too long, he admonished, the caliphate of Mesopotamia had been divided, torn apart by infighting—exemplified by what he had just heard. The Western powers had invaded, bringing with them their high-tech armies and apostasy. They sold weapons to the oil-rich Saudis, gave hope to the Kurds, flew missions from Turkish air bases, conspired with the Jews. Not only was Iraq defeated and subjugated, but it was surrounded. Muslims near and far were desperate for change, a leader who could bring the faith together as one.

And now that leader had arrived.

He delivered his message confidently and with all reverence for the Prophet, peace be upon him. Sultan set out his vision, beginning with an end to the turf wars between the various factions. This, he told the sheiks, had long been Islam's problem. The faith had fractured into too many sects, too many tribes, to fully exercise its power. The pope ran a flock of nearly a billion and a half, a top-down hierarchy of faith in which one man set the course. The Vatican had its share of politics and backstabbing, to be sure, but when the white smoke announced a successor, Catholics across the world fell in line. Only when Muslims found that kind of unity could they leverage their true power.

Sultan promised to bring a revolution to the heartland of Iraq, one that would spread like wind-driven fire. "For the first time in fourteen hundred years," he said in summation, "a rightly guided caliph will rule."

He watched the clerics closely, twelve bearded faces that comprised a rogue's gallery of Sunni Islam. What began as scattered affirmation rose into a chorus. Soon all were standing with arms raised, praising Allah.

Sultan set what he thought might be a regal expression.

After an appropriate interval, he launched into his parting soliloquy. He timed his ending perfectly, the call to afternoon prayer sounding from speakers outside. He watched them race one another to the door, each wanting to be the first to the mosque across the street. Schoolboys in a contest of piousness.

He was alone in the great conference hall for less than a minute when Ibrahim appeared. He filled the doorway at the far end of the room and began clapping theatrically, each meeting of his hands echoing across the empty hall.

"A command performance!" he said as he walked across the chipped tiles.

"I am glad you approve. Was it convincing?"

"Absolutely! I can't remember when I last saw them align behind anyone."

"Perhaps fourteen hundred years ago?"

Ibrahim chuckled and stopped a few steps away. For the first time Sultan noticed the scars on his hands. Ibrahim had been imprisoned after the war, ostensibly because he was a high-ranking member of the Ba'ath Party. His family ties would have been enough—he was a half nephew of Saddam. Yet Ibrahim had done well, escaping from prison ten years earlier. Now, like Sultan himself, he had found his way back to the family. Ready to regain control of a country that had lost its way.

"Never forget," Ibrahim said, "the first Rashidun Caliphs were no different from you. They were men of flesh and blood who saw opportunity and seized it."

"Perhaps."

"It is time to meet the party elders. Are you prepared?"

Sultan sighed. "The sheiks were exhausting . . . but yes, let's get it over with."

"Expect a more productive session. There is no need to show deference to this lot. They scheme not for paradise, but for profit and territory. And none will have it without your blessing."

"As it should be."

"As it once was," Ibrahim corrected. "My advice is to be generous with al-Jaafari and al-Ahmed. They will be your generals, which makes them more important than the rest."

"They control the bullets?"

Ibrahim smiled.

"There, you see? I am learning."

"You have your father's instincts. Give me ten minutes." Ibrahim disappeared to assemble the new meeting.

Sultan winced and looked down. His weak foot had gone numb. He stood and began pacing the room, which usually helped. He took in the stained carvings on the ceiling, the dank rugs on the walls. This place had once been grand, and it would be again. He wondered if the first four caliphs had taken hold so easily. Having the clerics in line, he now needed only the backing of the Ba'ath Party . . . who, of course, had instigated the entire scheme.

And why wouldn't they?

For decades the party had controlled every facet of Iraqi society. Under the rule of his father, no one could assume a position of importance—university professor, doctor, teacher, hospital administrator, government councilman—without first taking membership in the Ba'ath Party. Then came the war, and the traitorous government installed by the Americans. Baghdad fell to be dominated by Shiites who turned the nation on its head. They banned Ba'ath Party members from any position of importance—just as the Americans had done to the Nazis in the aftermath of World War II. Virtually overnight, Iraq had lost a generation of its best technicians and leaders. Lost its national identity.

But now the party was resurrecting itself, and by virtue of his lineage, Sultan was its chosen leader. The Sunni councils and governors had come quietly on board, as had critical leaders in the military. Everyone would do their part. The transition would play out quickly once the war to the south began to rage. The ayatollahs would be monumentally distracted, fighting for their survival. Tehran would pull assets from southern Iraq to defend the homeland. The Saudis, like usual, would rely on the Americans, who would balk at the thought of yet another war.

Yet the Ba'athist's web of preparations went far beyond Iraq. Beyond the walls of one minor palace in Tikrit. In the Empty Quarter of Yemen, a group of Houthi commanders, fed up with being bombed by Saudi fighters, were quietly being rearmed for a new offensive. Another multiplicand to the chaos. Sunni militias in Syria, long on the back foot, would renew their fight against the government. Hamas recruiters in the West Bank had been getting a surge of volunteers, the urgings of local clerics having the predicted effect.

His father's old networks, once widespread and reliable, had never really died. They had only gone dormant, waiting for the needed spark.

Waiting for the arrival of the Fifth Rashidun.

SIXTY-FOUR

There were times Nazir wished he had better training. Or for that matter, any training at all.

The drive from the air base to Jeddah Economic City seemed uneventful, yet he increasingly found himself watching the rearview mirror. A white Mercedes held his attention for a time, seeming to come and go, until he realized he'd been watching two identical cars. One of the drivers was male, the other female—a new reality in the kingdom.

He reached the apartment complex and parked his Air Force sedan across the street. He selected a spot between two work vans in the nearly empty parking lot of an under-construction strip mall. Military staff cars were relatively common throughout the kingdom, yet Nazir knew the price of apartments in Skyview Towers were well beyond the means of a staff sergeant. Along the same lines, he'd changed into civilian clothes after leaving the hangar.

He went to the trunk and paused for a look around. Other than a pair of foreign workers—Sri Lankans, he guessed—who were installing a window in one of the new shops, there was no one in sight. He opened the lid and lifted out a cardboard box. It was extremely light, the drone inside weighing little more than the box itself.

He crossed the street and took the stairwell to the third floor. He'd been told by Sultan's messenger that the only active security cameras were in the rental office two buildings down. The elevator lobbies were wired for surveillance, but the cameras had not yet been installed. This, however, could change at any time, and by keeping to the stairs there was virtually no chance of his image being captured.

He encountered no other tenants on the way up, but that was

hardly surprising. His block of apartments was the newest, and on last count only three of the twelve units had been rented. The other blocks, too, remained mostly empty. As with the rest of Jeddah Economic City, the House of Saud's urban planners were taking a "build it and they will come" approach.

Once inside the apartment, he threw the bolt and set the box on the kitchen island counter that served as his work bench. The place looked unchanged from his last visit. It was minimally furnished; there was a fusty brown couch, a scratched dinette ensemble, and one sheetless mattress on the floor in the bedroom. There were no dishes in the cupboards, no clothes in the closets. Given the tools scattered across the counter, along with the drones and their associated controllers, the place looked more like a workshop than a home.

He opened the box, removed the drone, and set it on the counter next to three others. Nazir already knew what his next chore would be. He reached into the pocket of his cargo pants and extracted the three Ziploc bags Sultan had given him. He began in the bedroom, opening the bag with the most material and scattering a bit at the head of the mattress. The bathroom was next. He scattered contents from all three bags around the sink, and left two toothbrushes, which bore the name of the Corinthia Hotel in Khartoum, on the counter next to a tube of toothpaste. Two disposable razors he set down next to a travel-sized can of shaving cream—he'd already flushed half the contents of the can down the toilet.

He went to the shower and turned the handle to let the water flow for a moment—the first time he had ever done so. Then he shook out what remained in the bags over the wet screen on the bathtub drain. Nazir pocketed the empty bags; he would dispose of these later.

At the kitchen counter he tinkered with the drones, removing a propeller from one, opening the battery compartment of another. Each had its respective controller, and he made sure fresh batteries were installed in all four. He scattered a few tools around the counter, then stood back and measured the effect. It was good. Just the right blend of haste and industriousness. He turned toward the window of the main room.

A broad balcony was fronted by a sliding glass door. Nazir stepped out to the balcony, lit a cigarette, and reminded himself to take the butt with him. His part in the plot could never be hidden, but the bulk of the blame had to go elsewhere.

The panorama before him was the reverse of the one Sultan had seen yesterday. This was clearly the apartment's selling point, the money shot for brochures. The balcony promised to one day offer a commanding view of the budding city, which so far was largely notional. Today there was but one focal point: roughly a mile distant, the triangular monstrosity that was Jeddah Tower. The entire concept could not have been more symbolic: a nation coalescing around a future king.

But plans, Nazir thought, *have a way of changing.*

He lifted a set of binoculars from the only piece of furniture on the balcony, a ten-riyal plastic table. He looked out across the flat desert to the north, then dragged the optics in a line toward the tower. Nazir settled his gaze on the observation deck two thousand feet above the ground.

Symbolism, he thought again. *It can indeed be a powerful thing.*

SIXTY-FIVE

Slaton had taken a seat at a small conference table. With a pair of scissors and glue stick in hand, he was cutting and pasting—much as Davy might be doing at that very moment in preschool. When Bloch came into the room, he looked at his most accomplished assassin like he'd gone off the deep end.

"May I ask what you're doing?"

"I'm making a case." Slaton set aside the scissors and glue.

Bloch took a seat next to him.

"First of all," Slaton said, "we have to remember that this recording was made surreptitiously, and certainly on Petrov's orders. So the question becomes, why would he do that?"

"Absolution," Bloch ventured. "If the nerve agent is ever misused, he has to be able to cover his motives for giving it to Iran."

Slaton shook his head. "Listen to this line again." The laptop Bloch had provided was on the table. Slaton queued up the section he wanted and hit play.

Petrov: "Just to be clear . . . you will never initiate first use?"

Slaton cut the audio. He waited.

Bloch thought about it. "He's leading Rahmani. Drawing him to say certain things."

"Exactly. When I first heard the raw recording, I thought it sounded odd. The exchange between the two men, the flow of the conversation—it seemed stunted, deliberately phrased. There were pauses where there shouldn't have been."

"Go on," Bloch said.

"Voiceprints are getting very accurate. It's becoming increasingly difficult to manufacture a false recording. But Petrov would have very convincing evidence if—"

"He's going to splice it," Bloch finished.

"That's what I'm thinking. Look at this . . ." Slaton shuffled three pages. He had printed out a transcript, then clipped and rearranged certain sentences. He turned the first page to face Bloch.

Petrov: "This agent will provide you a strong new capability, but I will say what I've said before . . . chemical weapons must only be used for defensive purposes. I trust you would never employ them unlawfully. The international community is watching, as they should be."

Rahmani: "I understand. But we are increasingly set upon by the Arabs."

Slaton exchanged a glance with Bloch, then turned to a second page.

Petrov: "I have been told your own technicians are making great strides with this class of weapons. Soon you may no longer need our help."

Rahmani: "We did not sit still after pausing our nuclear program to appease the West. Our Revolutionary Guard employs teams of scientists who have developed many such weapons. The Syrians could never have gotten the upper hand in their war without our contribution of chemical agents. This will give us a new level of lethality."

Bloch said, "Petrov is placing the blame on Iran for providing chemical weapons to the Syrian regime."

"Russia has long been the main suspect, but this puts the blame squarely on Iran. Perhaps not the primary objective in what's going on, but a nice opportunistic touch." Slaton shifted to the last page.

Petrov: "I should remind you, any such capability must be kept out of the hands of others—I think we both know who I am referring to."

Rahmani: "Hezbollah or the Houthis? Certainly not. They have their uses, but technology escapes them. Iran alone will have access."

Petrov: "And just to be clear . . . you will never initiate first use?"

Rahmani: "Rest assured. This agent would only be employed as a last resort. An insurance policy, if you will."

Petrov: "Then we are in accord as ever, with a common goal of peace in your corner of the world."

Slaton set the papers aside. "With the right audio technicians, and some good editing software, you can create an entirely new conversation. One that provides an entirely new narrative."

"There is no mention of the delivery of samples. Petrov could maintain that this new agent was a Russian design, but that Iran produced it, tested it . . . and perhaps used it."

Slaton locked eyes with his old boss. "I don't like where this is taking us."

Bloch pushed his chair back, ran a hand across his meaty chin. After a moment of contemplation, he said in a perfectly flat tone, "There is something I should tell you, David."

Slaton straightened in his seat. In his experience, the more neutral the former director's voice, the more damning his impending words.

"As I told you earlier, when I heard what was on this recording I suggested to Director Nurin that we quickly evaluate where this agent might be used. I talked to him a few minutes ago and he had the preliminary answers."

"That was quick."

"You are surprised at our sense of urgency? Israel's most hated adversary has acquired a new weapon of mass destruction, and by all appearances tested it on innocents. That is a rash move on their part. Rashness implies haste. If the Iranians are in a hurry, then so are we."

"All right. So, where might it be used?"

"We first studied our own vulnerabilities, of course. The Knesset will assemble this week in Jerusalem, but security there is generally good. The prime minister is hosting a dinner for the Egyptian foreign minister tomorrow evening."

"Where?"

"9 Smolenskin," Bloch replied, referring to the Israeli prime minister's official residence.

"Has security been tightened?"

"Of course. There is also a regional security conference in Tel Aviv, taking place at a hotel on the coast."

Slaton looked squarely at his old boss. He knew they were thinking the same thing.

"I agree," Bloch relented. "None are symbolic enough to be likely targets."

"What else then?"

Bloch's hesitation was like a held breath. "We analyzed external events, and there is one that stands out light years beyond the others."

"I've been a little too busy to keep up with current events— enlighten me."

"At noon tomorrow there will be a dedication ceremony for Jeddah Tower."

"The big skyscraper?" Slaton asked. He'd heard about the project, but little more—keeping up with who had the tallest building on earth wasn't a priority on the ranch in Idaho.

"The biggest ever. It has been under construction for years, and the House of Saud is eager to gloat over its newest bauble. The ceremony has been months in the making, and it will be very well attended. The king and crown prince, most of the royal family. Over a dozen emirs and heads of state from across the region."

"Is this an indoor or outdoor event?"

"Where better to appreciate the grandiosity? The tower has an observation balcony—it is half the size of a football pitch, suspended two thousand feet in the air."

Slaton considered it. It would make an attractive target. Yet the outcome of such a strike seemed unconscionable. "Targeting so many leaders with an aerosolized nerve agent? That would be a flat-out act of war."

"Yes . . . but only if it could be verified who undertook the attack."

"*We* know. Or at least we have some damning evidence. And the Iranians know that Kravchuk defected. She was at the meeting between the two presidents."

"Everything you say is true. But would it deter Rahmani from risking such a strike?"

The two stared at one another. Slaton *still* felt something amiss.

The words in the transcript, the messy killing of two poor cattle herders, the calls to emergency services in Sudan.

It was just coming into focus, coalescing in his mind, when a technician on the far side of the room said, "I have Miss Sorensen back on line from Langley . . ."

SIXTY-SIX

The source was one of many Sultan had been provided—part of the wandering network cultivated and maintained by the faithful since the diaspora of the Ba'ath Party. His call was answered on the second ring, then immediately ended. He waited five minutes for the response, which came from a different number, undoubtedly a throwaway phone.

"I am glad you called," said the distant voice. The accent was regional, familiar—not far from Sultan's own Jordanian inflection. He had never met the man, but he might have if he'd tried—only days earlier they'd been in very close proximity.

"I must know the status of the Russian woman," Sultan said.

"We believe she crossed into Lebanon last night. A Desert Guard unit nearly had her, but someone intervened."

"*Intervened?* Who?"

"We cannot be sure, but we suspect a CIA operation."

"CIA?" Sultan repeated. "What leads you to that conclusion?"

"A number of units ended up pursuing a man in a stolen vehicle. The method of his escape was extraordinary. The kind of thing only the Americans would attempt."

Sultan didn't press any further, his thoughts advancing to what it meant. "You have contacts in Lebanon, do you not?"

"I suspect we both do. I have already referenced my most re-liable man. He was able to learn that a small jet of questionable ownership took off very early this morning out of Beirut. An eye-witness report leads me to believe the interpreter was on board."

"Are the Russians aware of this?" Sultan asked.

"I was going to call them soon—but I hoped to talk to you first."

Ibrahim, who was standing nearby and monitoring the call on an earbud, nodded to Sultan.

"Very well," Sultan said. "I am sure you did all you could. Tell the Russians what has happened—it is more a problem for them than for us."

"I agree," said the source.

"Are your travel arrangements made?"

"That was next on my list. One way or another, I will be in place tomorrow."

The two went over the timetable, then the source ended the call abruptly.

As Sultan lowered the phone, Ibrahim pulled his earbud free. He said, "The Americans were very efficient."

"As they can be. But it hardly matters. The interpreter couldn't possibly know the details of the attack. And even if the target is identified, we have the insurance of our diversion."

Ibrahim agreed. The two men settled at a table, a tray of tea and honey between them, and began a deep discussion about how to organize the rising caliphate.

Six hundred miles west, outside the police headquarters building of the Damascus Governorate, Inspector Omar Hadad tossed the disposable phone into a dumpster. He went back inside and took the elevator to his colonel's office.

"What is it, Hadad?" the colonel asked, looking up distractedly from a file he was reading.

"I have a new lead on our Russian interpreter. A highly confidential source claims to know where she's gone."

The colonel removed his reading glasses. "Very well . . . so why aren't you out chasing it?"

"I would like to, but it requires that I travel abroad—for that I need your approval."

"Where must you go?"

"Jeddah."

The supervisory brow furrowed. "That is delicate ground. It would require strings to be pulled. Our relations with the Saudis are strained to say the least."

"True, but we do still *have* relations. I fear if we don't catch up soon, this woman will disappear forever. Her case, of course, is of little direct interest to our affairs. Yet if we could steer the Russians toward her . . . I think it might reflect very well on our president."

The colonel pretended to be thoughtful before saying what Hadad knew he would say. "Make the arrangements then. And happy hunting."

SIXTY-SEVEN

Sorensen was plainly energized. "We have a pretty clear picture what happened in Darfur. Our priority has shifted to figuring out who introduced this weapon to Sudan. If an attack really is in the planning stages, we need a trail to follow. Yesterday I assigned a team to start a crash investigation—all agency assets available, no restrictions about whose nose gets out of joint. It's messy, but tends to get results. I also got the backing of NSA for their sheer data-crunching ability."

"Let me guess," Slaton said. "Start with transportation hubs?" He and Bloch were back at the same work station for the video conference.

"It seemed like the obvious place to start. The Sudanese have been mostly cooperative, especially after we told them what happened to those herders in Darfur. In truth, we didn't need their cooperation. Sudan has long been a haven for terrorists, so we committed some years ago to keeping an eye on things there. It's not hard. The country only has a couple of commercial airports worth watching, and the road network is about the same—two northbound border crossings. We accessed the monitoring networks years ago."

"Accessed," Bloch commented.

"Okay, call it a breach. We've gone over the security camera footage from the two airports with immigration: Khartoum International and Port Sudan."

"And?" Slaton asked.

"NSA is getting outstanding results with their new facial recognition software—it's pure black magic. The bad news is, we can't match any individual unless they're in our database to begin with.

We went back a week before this event and got roughly three dozen hits. We examined every profile exhaustively, and were able to track most of them up to where they are at this minute. Money launderers, nickel-and-dime arms merchants, soldiers of fortune. No matter how we twisted it, none seemed like realistic suspects for the trafficking and employment of Russian nerve agents."

Slaton said, "Transporting something like that is extremely risky. I think whoever did it would have avoided commercial airports entirely."

"That was our next line of pursuit. Unfortunately, there's no way to monitor thousands of miles of desert frontier, especially when the neighboring countries are every bit as dysfunctional. The Sudanese make an effort to monitor maritime shipping, primarily in Port Sudan. That was going to be our focus . . . until we stumbled on this."

The screen filled with a video. Three men could be seen walking through a lounge of some kind. All were dark-haired, olive-skinned, and sported brooding five o'clock shadows. The one in the middle was carrying a hardened Pelican case, the other two dragging standard roller-bags. Moments before they disappeared through a heavy glass door, all three faces appeared in good focus. The eighteen-second clip looped back to the beginning.

After the clip ran three times, Sorensen froze on the best frame.

She said, "The footage you're seeing is from the corporate terminal at Khartoum International. Needless to say, not many wealthy businessmen vacation in Sudan. Anybody who shows up here is in town for business, most of which is on the shady side."

"You hacked this camera network as well?" Slaton suggested.

"Actually, the Chinese did."

After a lengthy pause, Slaton finished with, "And . . . you hacked the Chinese."

"The details are beyond my technical grasp, but in essence, yes. We acquired footage for all of last month. As you can see by the time and date stamp, this took place at ten o'clock yesterday morning."

The video flickered, and a new picture appeared, this time an exterior view. The three men walked across the tarmac to a waiting jet. Slaton studied the Pelican case closely. It wasn't a rifle case, but something thicker. Hardened and lockable, no doubt with custom foam inserts. Judging by the center man's irregular stride, it was also heavy. All three men strode up the boarding stairs and disappeared. Within three minutes, the airplane was taxiing.

Sorensen said, "NSA was able to match one face as a known. The guy in the middle, the one carrying the case, is Mohammed Mahdran. He's a major in VAJA, and known to have been given high-level assignments in the past."

"Sounds pretty conclusive," Slaton said distractedly.

"We went back two weeks," Sorensen said, "but didn't see any corresponding arrival. We think they went into Sudan by some other means."

"Where did the jet go?" Slaton asked, suspecting the head of the Special Activities Center had already figured it out.

"We found two solid radar tapes—one from Israel, the other from one of our missile boats that was transiting the Suez. The jet flew straight to Tehran."

Slaton exchanged a look with Bloch. The thoughts that had been brewing earlier returned. "Show me both clips again," he said.

A few beats later, the videos ran in sequence. Slaton studied every corner of the screen. He noted how the men moved, checked the periphery. For a moment, as they passed a desk inside the corporate terminal, he saw a receptionist in the background. On the ramp outside he discerned a fuel truck in the distance, perhaps a driver at the wheel. He noted a wave from the pilot to the approaching passengers, and an empty baggage cart near the jet's cargo bay. He mentioned all of it to Sorensen. She promised to follow up, and said her own analysts were going over the video as well.

"So, you don't know how this team got into Sudan," Slaton said. "But they're clearly leaving with a suspicious package."

"Essentially, yes."

"And whatever it was, they took it straight to Iran," Bloch added.

"There's one last thing," Sorensen said. "We think we've identified the car they were using. It's a Land Rover, rented last Thursday from an agency in central Khartoum. The name on the contract is a legend, and not a bad one—it has certain hallmarks that point to VAJA."

"Was the car tracked by the rental company?" Slaton queried.

"No luck. The Rover was GPS capable, but that feature uses ground-based signals to send location data. Sudan doesn't have the digital infrastructure to support it outside a very narrow geographic area. Basically, rental car companies there don't bother."

"What about the mileage?" Slaton asked.

"A good question—that's always recorded. The usage was high, averaging over two hundred miles a day."

"Enough to go to Northern Kordofan and back," Bloch surmised.

"More than once. We think we have a bead on where they were staying, a hotel called the Corinthia. It was booked in the same false name as the rental car. We're checking cameras there, but nothing has come in yet. I'm doubtful it will add to what we already know."

Bloch summarized, "So we have three Iranian nationals carrying a suspicious package onto a jet. Individuals whose DNA could conceivably be matched to samples found at the site of a nerve agent attack. And all this took place soon after a meeting in which the Russian president promised to deliver a new nerve agent to Iran."

He looked at Slaton expectantly.

Slaton said nothing.

"You don't look convinced," Bloch prompted.

"What doesn't fit?" Sorensen seconded.

Slaton shook his head. "Everything fits perfectly . . . which is what I don't like. Iran knows Kravchuk is missing, and she was *at* the meeting between Rahmani and Petrov. Since my work in Syria last night wasn't exactly stealthy, they'll assume the CIA has her in custody. If Iran uses this nerve agent, the evidence linking it back to them is overwhelming. But I can think of one other scenario . . ."

Slaton waited.

Sorensen said, "A false flag op? You think someone is setting Iran up?"

"It makes sense."

"Russia?" Bloch suggested.

Slaton hesitated a beat. "I'm not sure. If we hadn't gotten Ludmilla and that recording, they might have used it to manufacture an excuse. But what if the Russians are working with some third party? Somebody who set up what happened in Darfur. The decon suits you found with the DNA inside—that bugs me. It was too easy. Why would anyone leave evidence like that behind?"

"All good points," Sorensen said, "but we're only speculating.

I have to go with what we know, and what we know forces me to think preemptively."

Bloch said, "David and I were discussing precisely that when you called. We have to assume these three men delivered some amount of this nerve agent to Tehran. If that is the case, it could be employed at any time." For Sorensen's sake, Bloch went over Mossad's analysis of likely targets in the days ahead. Not unexpectedly, the same one had drawn her attention.

"Jeddah Tower is the most obvious," she said. "And it happens tomorrow."

They went over it all once more, yet the calculus was inescapable: if the nerve agent was used there, with ties to Iran, it would result in a war that would shred the Middle East. Or in Bloch's words, ". . . it would do for the Middle East what nuclear power did for Chernobyl."

Sorensen and Bloch agreed to leverage their respective agencies for answers.

When the call terminated, Slaton was staring at Bloch.

"I've seen that look before," the former spymaster said.

"While the two of you go about your business . . . I should get in position."

Bloch's dour expression never faltered, as he said, "I'll have the Office make the arrangements."

SIXTY-EIGHT

Nazir arrived at the apartment just after daybreak the next morning. He looked out the wide window at the tower in the distance, saw it glimmering under the low eastern sun. Rising from such desolate terrain, it looked like the backdrop of a science fiction movie—a great spire of civilization on some bleak and distant planet.

He turned back inside, went to the kitchen counter and regarded the four drones. He had purchased them individually, two in separate stores and two online. It seemed a necessary precaution: who would buy four identical models given how expensive they were?

In the last hour Nazir had altered one to make it unique. He checked the hardware one last time, in particular the attach points and valve connections. Everything fit perfectly. The parts had mostly come from work. He'd removed an assembly yesterday from the number 4 jet, and logged the installation of new dispersal hardware. It was a standard repair, every step by the book and signed off by his supervisor. Nothing less was permitted from the elite maintainers in his squadron. Nazir had noted the parts he'd removed from number 4 as damaged. This typically meant they would be discarded, although no one was going to check whether they actually ended up in the dumpster behind the hangar—at least, not until it was too late.

Looking at the modified drone, he considered testing the servos with the remote. Nazir decided that wasn't necessary. If they didn't work, he wasn't going to fix them. *I only work on real airplanes,* he mused. His eyes settled on the dispersal fitting, and he noted the color of the stained nozzle: green. It was only a coincidence, but satisfying all the same. It could just as easily have been red or white. As it turned out, green was the signature hue of a nation—and the ever-proud flag of the Kingdom of Saudi Arabia.

The convenience of working with the best intelligence agencies was never appreciated until lost. This was Slaton's dominant thought as he gazed out the oval window of an Airbus-A321 taxiing to the terminal of King Abdulaziz International Airport in Jeddah.

For the last seven years Slaton had largely been on his own when it came to maintaining identities and procuring forged passports—not only for himself, but for his wife and son as well. He had bought countless burner phones, established credit card accounts, all while trying desperately to not leave a trail. At times, it bordered on a full-time job.

Yesterday, however, he'd had a welcome return to Clandestine Incorporated. On the way to the airport in Tel Aviv, a young woman had provided him a flawless package: driver's license, passport, visa to enter Saudi Arabia, credit cards, and the ultimate fringe benefit, a generous wad of cash. He was sure it was all backstopped in databases, and in the worn wallet there were even photos of two children who could have passed for his own, a strikingly attractive faux wife, and an active library card that probably carried one obscure spy novel as slightly overdue.

Slaton was, if the documents and backstory could be believed, a Swedish journalist arriving to cover today's grand opening of Jeddah Tower. Sweden had been chosen for his strength in that language, journalism because it would afford him the greatest possible access. Press credentials, for a conservative and little-known Stockholm daily, had thoughtfully been included, along with a high-end digital camera.

He'd flown last night from Tel Aviv to Dubai, and spent a leisurely night in the kind of airport hotel a feature writer might procure—a decent place, but nothing over-the-top. The layover had been necessary due to the rushed timetable, but also served as a buffer after his initial flight from Tel Aviv.

Everything had worked flawlessly in Dubai, Mossad's forgers holding to their unassailable standards. Now it was time to test the documents again. The aircraft drew to a stop at the gate, and the long jetway dinosaured into place.

Slaton stood and meshed in with the crowd of new arrivals.

———

Across the community of nations, the sharing of intelligence is undertaken with utmost reticence. The reasons for this reluctance are many and good. Sources can be put at risk, vital information leaked. Lines of communication can be compromised and strategic objectives sacrificed. Yet there is one exception to the greater rule: information was always shared in the face of imminent danger.

Which was why, in the early hours of that morning, the CIA had taken action. After a briefing from Sorensen, Director Coltrane decided time was critical and elected to bypass the usual channels. Instead of running a presumed threat to the Saudi royal family sideways through the U.S. State Department, the CIA delivered the bad news directly to the Saudi Arabian National Guard, or SANG, the service responsible for protecting the House of Saud. The CIA suggested, with all necessary tact, that security for the Jeddah Tower opening ceremony be tightened, with particular attention given to an attack using chemical weapons.

The Saudis listened, but were clearly skeptical. The tower's isolation, in the SANG's view, was strongly in their favor. Aside from one cluster of mobile construction offices, there was not another building within a mile of the skyscraper. Plans for an eventual subway line beneath the tower, which would connect to the city, were on the drawing board but had gone no further.

For the sake of due diligence, the tower was searched from top to bottom. Over a hundred men took part, including architects, construction crews, and engineers, all of whom had unique perspectives on dead spaces, access points, and air handling systems. Nothing was found. Every vehicle in the parking garage was searched, and barriers and checkpoints were doubled on the only access road. Those guests planning to arrive by helicopter were quietly told to make new arrangements, and as a matter of convenience another two dozen armored limos were booked. These too were searched.

In the end, the commander of the National Guard was satisfied, and he declared without reservation to the crown prince, "Every precaution has been taken. The ceremony can proceed as scheduled."

SIXTY-NINE

With the advent of the digital age, raw intelligence for spy agencies relies increasingly on crunching vast amounts of data. Inputs arrive from countless sources. CCTV cameras, mobile phones, computers. Household appliances and industrial software. Photoreconnaissance from satellites and drones. Sometimes the data is accessed willingly and with legal authorization, other times less so. The NSA alone processes so much information that mathematical standards had to regularly be revised to characterize the sheer amount of data collected. The latest nomenclature, gegobyte, involved thirty zeros after the one, a quantification of information incomprehensible to anyone outside the scientific community.

The dilemma for programmers and analysts had long been sorting through the digital haystack to find the occasional needle. Yet for all that committed processing power, and the endless plethora of sensors, there was another less common source of intelligence that was often overlooked: the eyes and ears of experienced field officers.

On that morning, as supercomputers in Utah chewed through quintillions of pixelated images and voiceprint comparisons, David Slaton was standing in a fifty-deep line at the immigration counters of King Abdulaziz Airport in Jeddah. He was stretching his neck, which was still stiff from his swan dive into the Sea of Galilee, when a face in the crowd caught his eye.

Although it wasn't quite the face. Slaton was drawn to something familiar in the way the man stood. His posture and bearing, the way his clothes hung on his slight frame like old curtains. Mild alarm was his first instinct, thinking he'd spotted a tail.

He immediately conjured up the mental map he'd drawn on

entering the arrivals corridor. As was his practice, Slaton had already identified every way out of the broad hall. The proper exits were at the far end of the room, rows of wide-open double doors through which arriving passengers exited after clearing one of the twenty-odd immigration booths. These doors were posted with armed guards who seemed alert. Slaton guessed the doors could be locked down quickly, perhaps even remotely. It was an option for egress, but one that came with severe limitations. A second avenue of escape would be to go back from where he'd come, into the terminal. This was generally the least promising option in airports. The best way out, in his view, involved the seven doors on either side. Through these he had watched immigration officers come and go. The doors were labeled NO ADMITTANCE in both Arabic and English, and controlled by a card-swipe lock. He saw two weaknesses in the system. First was that the locks had no keypad for a code. Pilfer an employee ID, and with one swipe, abracadabra. The second shortcoming involved the pneumatic arm attached to each door. These regulated a smooth closure, but also held the door open for a period of time—between four and six seconds, depending on the door. That was more than enough time from where he stood, and all he would need was a distraction. Getting through would be simple, and better yet, the immigration officers he would encounter on the other side were conveniently not armed.

With all these assessments made, Slaton ventured a second, deeper look at the man to his right. He was wearing Western clothing, a cheap gray coat over standard business casual. Worn leather shoes and wire-rimmed glasses. It was when the man reached up and pushed his glasses higher on his nose that Slaton made the connection. He was looking at the man he'd seen outside Chez Salma, the one who'd risen out of the lead sedan to survey the street.

If the man was practicing tradecraft, Slaton didn't see it. For a time he seemed preoccupied with his passport, and later took out his phone and began texting. As his queue advanced, he fell directly under the lens of a ceiling-mounted security camera yet made no attempt to avert his face. Slaton had avoided that line for precisely that reason—its proximity to cameras.

Given what he knew, Slaton supposed the man was either Syrian Mukhabarat or a midlevel policeman. Had he somehow tracked him here? It seemed doubtful, especially with Slaton standing thirty feet away. It struck him that Syria and Saudi Arabia didn't have the warmest of relations. Was the man here for some reason tied to this afternoon's ceremony? Had the Syrian president been invited? All questions that needed answers.

Slaton was dealt a minor setback when his own line came to a stop: a large family at the booth ahead was having an issue. While a supervisor was called in, the Syrian in the adjacent line edged forward. Slaton had been in the lead, but it now looked like he would be second going through the exit doors. Changing lines was not an option. Too much attention drawn.

The confusion at the top of Slaton's line ended, and things began to move. But it was too late. The Syrian cleared customs while Slaton was on deck. He watched the slight man disappear through the nearest paired exit doors.

Slaton was waved forward. His documents cleared uneventfully, and once again he gave silent thanks to Mossad's forgers—in his opinion, the best in the world. He hurried to the double doors and set out into the terminal. He bypassed the baggage carousels and went straight to the curb. His eyes swept left and right, searching for the gray coat and wire-rimmed glasses. He finally saw them, moving near the front of the taxi queue. Slaton walked as quickly as he dared, making a beeline toward the lead cab and pulling out his phone. He passed within ten feet as the man slid into a cab, all the time thumbing away as if texting. Seconds later the cab was gone, and Slaton diverted behind a skycap booth and paused to check his work.

He'd recorded the scene as a video, getting more frames per second than he could possibly get by clicking away. Frame by frame, he flicked through the video and found the two images he wanted. One was a head-on capture of the man's face as he bent to get in the cab. The other was a perfectly clear picture of the taxi's license plate.

SEVENTY

"His name is Omar Hadad," Sorensen said. "He's a detective inspector with the Damascus police, criminal investigations division. He flew in directly from Damascus this morning and landed ten minutes after your flight."

"It didn't take you long to figure all that out," Slaton said. He was sitting in the driver's seat of a car he'd just rented, still in the parking garage.

"We aim to please. The images you sent were good, and I put the highest priority on it. You say you saw him in Damascus?"

"Yeah, outside the building where Ludmilla was holed up. Two standard-issue government sedans came looking for her, and this guy got out of one to take in the scene. I got a brief look at him."

"And now he turns up in Jeddah. Do you think he followed you?"

"Can't rule it out, but I don't think so. He would have had to know where I was going, which means the Syrians have already busted the identity Mossad gave me. I don't think that's the case, and even if they did they'd never react so fast. I also didn't get that feel when I spotted him. If that was his idea of surveillance, he was terrible at it. I think he's just what he appears to be—a Damascus cop who gets important assignments."

"Like hunting Ludmilla Kravchuk down?"

"And going to Saudi Arabia for . . . whatever."

"Whoever he is," Sorensen said, "I think we should keep an eye on him."

"'We' meaning me? It's a big country. How am I supposed to find him?"

"You don't have to—we already know where he is."

Slaton grinned. "At this moment?"

"Twenty seconds ago . . . that's the best I can do."

"The cab?" Slaton guessed.

"The company tracks its cars with a software we're familiar with. The taxi he took stopped in front of a car rental agency along the Jeddah Corniche." Sorensen provided an address in the city's shoreline resort district. "And, wait for it . . . the cab went off duty one minute later."

Slaton loaded the address into his map application and started the car. "Why does someone take a cab to a car rental agency? Why not just rent one at the airport?"

Sorensen backstopped what Slaton himself was thinking. "Because he doesn't want to leave tracks. I'm betting he used an alternate name to rent the car."

"Okay. While you and your supercomputers check on it, I'll head in that direction."

A hesitation on the Langley end. "Time is getting short if Jeddah Tower really is the target. Do you think this is worthwhile?"

"I have no idea. Honestly, I wish he was Iranian. I wish he'd flown in from Tehran carrying a big Pelican case."

"That would make more sense," Sorensen agreed.

"Yeah," Slaton said, wheeling his car toward the garage exit. "As if any of this makes sense."

Captain Mahrez walked across the tarmac where the squadron's six jets were lined up. Not seeing who he wanted, he addressed the senior enlisted man in sight. "Where is Sergeant Nazir?"

A master sergeant who was making a logbook entry stopped what he was doing. "I haven't seen him since earlier this morning, sir."

"Is he not supposed to be on duty?"

The master sergeant pulled a roster from the thigh pocket of his work overalls. He scanned it quickly, and said, "Yes, he is."

Mahrez looked up and down the flight line. He saw fifteen men of various ranks and specialties prepping the aircraft. "Do you have another powerplant specialist on duty?"

Another check of the roster. "Yes, sir. Tech Sergeant Said is available if needed."

The captain looked relieved, then raised a finger to make his point. "Very well. But when Nazir shows up, tell him I am putting him on report!"

Nazir was at that moment in a gas station restroom on the western outskirts of Jeddah. He'd returned to base one last time, not wanting his absence to be noticed too soon. After eating a late breakfast in the enlisted dining hall, he'd slipped out quietly. Half a mile outside the front gate his transformation began.

He first abandoned the staff car and retrieved his recently purchased motorcycle. Now, behind the bathroom's locked outer door, Nazir took off his fatigues and donned civilian clothes from his backpack. He dropped his fatigues in the trash bin, using wadded paper towels from the dispenser to make sure it was concealed. And just like that, his career in the Saudi Air Force, such as it was, reached its inglorious end.

He went back outside, and at the pump topped off the gas tank on the motorcycle. He next filled a pair of plastic ten-liter gas cans. He loaded these onto the bike, one in each of the paired saddlebags. The bike was a two-year-old Honda CB300F, a standard road bike that got nearly eighty miles to the gallon. With a full tank and two extra cans, he was sure he could reach the Iraqi border. That five-hundred-mile journey would begin later today, and he expected to arrive on schedule, shortly after nightfall. He was to seek out a particular marker along the remote four-hundred-mile-long barrier wall. There he would be met by a driver and spirited into Iraq. By the time he reached Sultan's palace in Tikrit, sometime around midday tomorrow, his revenge for his father's death would be complete. The Saudis would find themselves hurtling into a terrible new war. And Nazir would begin life anew.

With everything ready, he straddled the bike. Nazir donned his helmet, spun the engine to life, and set out one last time for the apartment.

SEVENTY-ONE

Nazir arrived twenty minutes later.

As usual he parked across the street from the apartment block. He was crossing the street when his eye was caught by a sight that made his heart skip a beat. Half a mile away, meandering across open desert, he saw a roving security patrol. The vehicle seemed in no hurry, and he forced himself to ignore it. Sultan had told him the National Guard would be active this morning.

Nazir's nerves were beginning to fray. By not showing up for work this morning, he'd crossed the point of no return. He and Sultan had been planning this day for months, and while he thought they'd covered every detail, now, as the strike played out in real time, doubts began to creep in.

Captain Mahrez would have noticed his absence by now. Hoping to muddy the waters, Nazir had called from the gas station and explained to the squadron's admin clerk that he was ill with a stomach virus. Calling in sick was not a red flag, but the standard procedure was to do so before a shift started—especially on a day when a performance was scheduled.

He took the stairwell to the apartment. Once inside, Nazir shut the door, threw the bolt, and leaned into the wall. He swept his eyes over the place and decided nothing had changed. He went to the counter, retrieved the first drone—the one with the canisters—and carried it to the balcony. Five minutes later everything was in place.

He took out the burner phone he'd recently purchased and powered it up for the second time in what would prove to be a very short service life. The first had been earlier that morning, just long enough to install the latest secure messaging app.

He tapped on the only contact and sent a message: EVERYTHING IS IN PLACE.

The reply took nearly a minute: UNDERSTOOD. NO SPECIFIC THREATS NOTED. MEETING TONIGHT AS SCHEDULED.

Nazir waited. Nothing else came. The clock on the phone read 11:13.

He placed the handset on the counter and stood looking out the window. *Forty-seven minutes,* he thought. If nothing changed, all he had to do was keep his eyes on the tower and send one final report. He planned to do so from a distance, taking the bike a few miles north toward the main road. The slightest of head starts for his escape.

Barring any last-minute changes, he would then be home free.

Slaton drove as fast as the traffic permitted. The route to the rental agency took him west toward the coast, bypassing the Ash Shati district. He turned parallel to the sea on King Abdul Aziz Road, the primary coastal boulevard, until the directions on his map reached an end. He parked along a curb between two larger vehicles, leaving ample room in front—if he had to leave quickly, he didn't want a multi-step maneuver to get back under way.

In the distance ahead he saw an amusement park, quiet for the moment in the midmorning heat. Beyond that the Red Sea sprawled out toward Africa. The car rental agency was directly across the street. It turned out to be an Avis outpost, the usual counter with a half dozen agent stations, only half of which were occupied. While making the drive, Slaton reasoned that the day of the week and time of day might work in his favor. He'd been right. It was Monday morning, the start of a business week, and the place looked busy.

He was close enough that he didn't need binoculars. Through the agency's wide front window, he saw a line of customers corralled inside crowd control stanchions. There were ten people waiting, but Omar Hadad was not among them—he had already reached the counter and was talking to the leftmost of the three agents on duty.

Avis' setup could not have been more standardized. The rental counters were at the base of a three-story office building, and to the left was a three-level parking garage. There was a door connecting the two, and even a sign with a large arrow and English lettering that Slaton could read from across the street: THIS WAY TO CARS.

He surveyed the parking garage and saw the exit behind his left shoulder. To keep track of its fleet, Avis would permit only one way out. Regardless of which way Hadad turned when he reached the street, Slaton could easily fall in behind. He tried to get a feel for the flow of traffic on his left, then adjusted his mirrors accordingly.

Slaton left the car running and waited.

SEVENTY-TWO

The observation deck of Jeddah Tower was prepared, a gathering fit for a king. All the regalia fitting such a grand occasion had been put on display. A red carpet led from the entrance to a low stage, and this was backed by silk drapery in regal colors. At long tables on either side, ice sculptures presided over golden flatware and cutlery, with trays of the finest delicacies lying in wait. Above it all, on a newly installed flagpole, the green standard of Saudi Arabia snapped smartly in the breeze.

The few guests who'd arrived early were being kept inside, milling noisily in the reception hall on the 157th floor. The deck was populated by an army of caterers, sound technicians, waitstaff, and security teams. The man in charge of the latter was Lieutenant General Muhammed al-Bandar. As commander of the Saudi National Guard, he looked worriedly down at the ground almost half a mile below.

He saw cars backed up on the road at the lone security checkpoint. The general hoped it didn't get any worse. The last-minute change to deny helicopter travel had thrown the plans of dozens of dignitaries into disarray—the sort of men who were not accustomed to waiting.

Al-Bandar's executive officer, Major Samir, appeared at his side. "We've finished one last search of the building, sir. Nothing was found."

"Good," the general said, the distance in his voice implying his thoughts were elsewhere. "Has the king arrived?"

"Yes, he is on the way up now—elevator fifty-six. The crown prince is with him."

"And the rest of the guests?"

"Eighty-six invitees are in the building." Samir looked down at the road checkpoint. "Will we adjust the schedule if some are delayed?"

"No," the general said, having already made that decision. "It would create too many complications." He checked his watch. Thirty-six minutes. "We can trust the royals to mingle for a time. Plan on opening the door ten minutes before noon."

Samir acknowledged the order.

"Has there been anything else from the Americans?"

"No," Samir said, shaking his head. "Since throwing their little grenade in our operation, they have gone silent."

"The Americans are a lot of things . . . but they are typically not reactionary. There is something behind their warning."

"But a chemical weapon? Did they not explain the source of their suspicions?"

"No, not really." The general regarded his long-time aide, who he thought quite competent. "Tell me, my friend . . . what are we missing?"

Samir's gaze drifted to the balcony, then out over the sea. After a long pause, he said, "I can think of nothing. Everything is going to plan."

The car turned out to be a white Ford sedan, and Hadad was in a hurry—Slaton knew because he was violating virtually every cate-chism of automotive tradecraft. He kept a judicious distance behind Hadad, and thankfully traffic was heavy enough to provide con-cealment.

When Hadad had turned onto the city's main westbound ar-tery, it seemed obvious he was headed for Jeddah Tower. This gave Slaton pause. Might Hadad himself have come to deliver an at-tack? Might the generic white Ford in front of him be transporting a binary chemical weapon? He tried to make the notion fly, but it didn't feel right. He was weighing other possibilities when his gaze snagged on something in the distance: resolving out of the haze, a great spire reaching for the sky. The building truly was massive, although like so many structures on the Saudi Peninsula, more an endeavor of ego than engineering. If hubris were an architectural style, he thought, Jeddah Tower would be a masterpiece.

His phone vibrated. He saw a call from Sorensen.

Slaton picked up and said, "Our friend seems to be in a hurry."

"And I know why," she responded. "I just discovered that he was originally booked the first flight out of Damascus today, but the airplane had a mechanical issue. He bought a last-minute business class ticket on a different carrier."

"Sounds expensive."

"Especially for a Syrian policeman—he used his own credit card. Sounds like he has somewhere important to be."

"The way it's looking right now, it's the tower. Maybe he has an invitation to the ceremony." Slaton was sure the destination was no surprise to Sorensen—at the very least, she would be tracking his own phone. The building was gaining definition in his windscreen.

Quite abruptly, the Ford ahead shifted into the right lane and shot onto an exit. Slaton maneuvered quickly, doing his best to copy the move without being conspicuous.

"Check that," he said. "It looks like our cop is headed elsewhere. I'll get back to you . . ."

Captain Mahrez said a silent prayer as he watched the jets leave the parking apron. Six for six today, no maintenance turnbacks. The squadron's seventh aircraft, a maintenance spare, hadn't been needed. He watched with no small degree of pride as the formation taxied toward the active runway in tight pairs. 1 and 2, 3 and 4, 5 and 6.

His handheld VHF radio had been quiet. It was tuned to the squadron's discreet maintenance frequency. If anything went wrong between the ramp and the runway, that was how he'd hear about it.

His brick remained silent.

SEVENTY-THREE

Slaton followed Hadad for roughly a mile, then watched the Ford pull into a nearly empty parking lot. Across the street was an apartment complex—the buildings looked new and mostly unoccupied. He slipped his own car behind a dormant bulldozer a quarter mile from the apartments. He would have preferred to be closer, but there was little traffic and virtually no cover on the final stretch of road.

Across the street from the apartments a strip mall was under construction, a half dozen minor stores with block walls and a roof, but waiting for drywall and windows. Outside were a handful of contractor trucks, electricians and air conditioning. In the direction of the tower Slaton saw a few clusters of vehicles. The largest was what looked like a staging area for security, roughly ten armored personnel carriers and light utility vehicles parked door-to-door. He recognized this for what it was—reinforcements for the larger contingent around the base of the tower. He saw another group of what looked like catering delivery trucks, and not far from that, in the center of a wide dirt lot, two work vans were parked with their rear doors open. Between them three men were busy setting up a fireworks display—wooden racks with mortars being placed in rows. This too made sense. According to Sorensen, today's festivities would run into the evening, including a private dinner for the regent and certain select guests. For such an over-the-top event, a fireworks display seemed a fitting climax, and photos of the great tower backlit by pyrotechnics seemed predestined.

He turned his attention back to Hadad. Slaton watched him circle to the back of his rental car, open the trunk and lean inside. He retrieved something small and stuffed it into the pocket of his coat. Slaton was a long way off, so he couldn't be sure, but he thought it might have been a matte-black handgun.

His attention ratcheted up. Both he and Hadad had taken commercial flights this morning, no weapons permitted. Now the Syrian was armed and he was not. Still behind the car, Hadad closed the trunk and pulled out a mobile phone. He placed a call that lasted less than a minute, after which he set out toward the apartment complex on a purposeful walk. He approached one of the central buildings, drew the object from his pocket—definitely a gun—and walked directly into the main entrance.

Hadad disappeared inside.

"What the hell?" Slaton muttered.

General al-Bandar was in the reception area, watching the king welcome the emir of Kuwait, when his phone vibrated a unique double buzz. This was the setting reserved for one particular caller—the command center's emergency hotline.

He answered breathlessly. *"What is it?"*

"We have a report of a threat, sir, but it is very vague."

"Where?"

"The caller didn't have time to say. He claimed to be a visiting Syrian policeman. He said he was going to check out a suspicious man he'd seen on the perimeter."

Al-Bandar rushed outside to the observation deck. He went to the rail and looked out over the desert. Under a cloudless sky, he could see fifty miles in every direction that wasn't blocked by the building at his back. "Where did the call originate?"

"We are trying to find out. This policeman said he would attempt to handle the matter on his own—he said there is no immediate threat to the ceremony."

Were the general a balloon he might have burst. First the Americans tell him to expect a nerve agent attack. Now foreigners were engaging suspicious characters. "A Syrian policeman is going to save us all!" he spat incredulously.

Not surprisingly, there was no reply.

Hadad found the correct door easily: apartment 304.

He took a moment to study the entrance. Like any Syrian policeman, Hadad was intimately familiar with doors. He'd kicked in his share, and knew how to find the weak points. Deadbolts, chains, hinges. Some could pose problems. Businesses sometimes installed solid-core wood doors. Criminal organizations preferred steel-encased items. For anything like that a good breaching device was always preferred. What he saw here, thankfully, was nothing of the sort. It was a new-build apartment complex, and the developer had clearly chosen low cost over security. The cheapest of the cheap.

He saw a simple striker plate seated into a one-by-four jamb, no sign of a second plate above or below. Not being a large man, Hadad took the time to set his stance solidly. His main concern was to breach on the first try—the only way to keep the element of surprise. He reasserted his grip on the Glock—placed in the rental car by Sultan's network—and held it close with a bent elbow, barrel up and away.

He reared back, brought his left knee high, and with careful aim lashed out.

The kick might have been perfect . . . had the door not opened in that instant.

Hadad's heel had barely made contact when the door was pulled inward. He lurched forward, the momentum of his kick taking him into the apartment in an uncoordinated lunge. His gun hand reached for the door jamb to keep from falling flat on his face. He managed to get his front foot on the ground, but his legs were spread wide in a virtual split, his balance completely gone.

It was in that awkward position that he came face-to-face with the man he'd come to kill.

Nazir saw the gun clearly.

As a jet engine mechanic, he was not skilled in the dark arts. All the same, like military men and women around the world, he *was* versed in the basics of self-protection. And he knew a threat when he saw one.

His heart kicked, adrenaline flooded in, and he threw himself at the stranger. Nazir's first instinct was to go for the gun, and he got one hand on the man's arm. For good measure he followed with a knee to the stomach. He heard a grunt, and as they fell into the wall he got a second hand on the weapon. That was when things began to go wrong. His left hand unfortunately was clamped directly over the muzzle, and his adversary was the first to recognize it. A shot rang out, and Nazir's hand exploded in a mass of blood and tissue. He screamed in pain.

The two men briefly stood straight, like a pair of grappling dancers, then tumbled toward the kitchen in a maelstrom of thrashing arms and kicking legs. They ended up side by side, bent awkwardly over the waist-high main counter. The intruder butted Nazir in the face, dazing him. He did the same right back. He still had his functioning hand on the gun, and was able to force the barrel away. Then his adversary, who was not a large man, began pummeling his face with an elbow. Every blow brought stars, and Nazir tried to hold on.

He saw a wrench on the counter, and realizing something had to change, he let go of the gun and went for the wrench. He no sooner had his fingertips on the shaft when a second shot sounded.

The third and fourth Nazir never heard. His last conscious thought was that he wished he'd not taken one last look from the balcony. Ever the reflective type, he had wanted to take in the scene for a few final minutes.

And it had cost him his life.

SEVENTY-FOUR

Hadad sank onto his haunches, his lungs heaving like twin bellows. There was blood everywhere, some of it certainly his own. Nazir lay motionless on the floor, a pool of red spreading beneath him.

Hadad pulled himself to his feet using the counter for support. His nose was in agony, the cartilage surely crushed. He tried to touch it and winced, and his hand came away even bloodier. Staggering to the sink, he turned on the tap and seized a dishrag. He gingerly dabbed away blood, first from his hands, then his face. His vision was fuzzy, and he pulled the cloth gently over his eyes. Things seemed to get clearer.

Beginning to recover, he remembered what had to come next. Hadad set his gun on the counter, pulled out his phone, and placed a call.

Sultan himself answered. "Is it done?"

"Yes," Hadad croaked, failing to keep the pain out of his voice.

A long pause. "You've done well then. It will not be forgotten. Make sure everything is staged as we discussed, then make your second call."

Hadad said that he would. As he did so, however, he found himself looking out the window. The big tower seemed very close. "Are you sure I am far enough away?" he asked.

"Yes, I told you . . . the wind is very predictable near the sea. It will drive the agent away."

Hadad wasn't so sure, but before he could argue the point Sultan ended the call.

He pocketed his phone and looked around the room. The drones and equipment were already scattered about. There wasn't really much to do. He looked down at Nazir's body, and thought, *The hard part is done.*

Hadad collected his thoughts and began rehearsing his next phone call. The number would be the same he'd called earlier, the National Guard emergency line. He would give his location and claim to have the situation in hand. One more element to the confusion. A false sense of security instilled.

Hadad's eye caught on the open front door. For all the chaos, there wasn't the slightest scratch on it. He went over and began to swing it closed. Halfway through the arc, a large boot flew in and kicked it straight back in his face. It crushed his nose a second time.

When the second double buzz arrived, General al-Bandar was ready. He had the phone halfway to his ear before the first cycle ended.

"Tell me what you've found!"

"We were able to triangulate the call from the Syrian policeman," said the voice from the command center. He followed with a rough estimate of the direction and distance from the tower.

The general was already on the balcony, and in the given direction he saw blocks of apartments and a small shopping mall under construction. "Put together a response!" he ordered. "Immediately!"

Hadad was wavering on his feet, a cold-cocked boxer deciding which way to fall.

Slaton held the Syrian upright, spun him against the entryway wall. When awareness flickered back into his eyes, Slaton leaned in and barred an arm across his neck. He kicked the door shut with a heel while his eyes swept the condo. He saw a dead man on the floor with multiple bullet wounds. There was a gun on the kitchen counter—probably, but not definitively, the one he'd seen Hadad carrying. Slaton saw and heard no one else, but a hallway to the right led to other rooms. These had to be cleared.

Hadad was a mess, his face battered and bloody. Slaton searched him thoroughly for other weapons, found none. The most useful discovery came from the jacket's inside pocket. A worn leather credential holder. Slaton flipped it open. There was no badge, but instead a card embossed with the seal of the Syrian Ministry of the Interior, Damascus Police. Next to that was a photo ID, and an identity card with the man's name in both Arabic and English. Inspector Omar Hadad, criminal investigations division. Sorensen's metadata analysis had been dead-on.

Slaton wrenched his captive away from the wall and marched him toward the hallway junction. Passing the counter, he picked up the gun—a Glock 17 Gen 4. He released his captive long enough to perform a press check, saw a round in the chamber, then reasserted his grip on Hadad's collar. He kept the detective out front as they approached the hallway—not as a human shield, but because he knew Hadad would react if he was out on point and there *was* a threat in back. Nothing happened.

Hadad regained his faculties, began standing straighter. Slaton addressed this by driving a knee to the man's stomach. The Syrian doubled over and fell to the floor. Slaton made a quick search of what turned out to be one bedroom, two closets, and one bathroom. All were clear.

He went back to Hadad, bent down, and readdressed the moaning policeman.

"Do you know who I am?" Slaton asked in English, the most likely language they would share.

Hadad shook his head. "No."

"Then I have you at a disadvantage." Slaton nodded toward the Glock in his hand. "Or maybe I should say, *another* disadvantage."

Hadad's eyes blinked as he tried to follow.

Slaton said, "Three days ago I saw you outside a hair salon in Damascus, a place called Chez Salma. You arrived up in one of two cars that had come to arrest Ludmilla Kravchuk. You were in the back seat, and at one point you opened the door, got out, and took a look around. That was right before all hell broke loose."

Hadad's eyes narrowed. "You . . . that was *you*?"

"Small world, huh? I'm the guy who lit off that truck full of Hezbollah rockets."

Hadad looked at him despairingly.

"It seems strange that our paths should cross again so soon . . . and here of all places. I'm guessing neither of us has come for the hajj. In fact, I'm pretty sure I'm here for the same reason you are— the dedication of this big new tower. Something like that could be a tempting target for Saudi Arabia's enemies."

The Syrian said in heavily accented English, "I received information about a terror plot. I came to intervene." He gestured all around the room.

Slaton stood and took in the room more carefully. He saw two large drones on the main counter, some tools and hardware. On the balcony outside were two more drones, one on the floor, another on a cheap plastic table. The one on the table was clearly different—it had been modified with two small canisters and a network of metal tubing. The hardware looked very similar to the images Sorensen had shown him from the incident in Darfur. The idea of being a few steps away from a fully primed weapon of mass destruction should have been unnerving to both of them. Yet as Slaton looked at Hadad, he thought the inspector seemed far more worried about the Glock.

Something didn't add up.

Slaton pulled Hadad to his feet and herded him across the room. With all the finesse of a sledgehammer, he dumped the Syrian in the corner near the balcony sliding door.

Slaton asked, "When did you receive this information about an attack?"

Hadad hesitated a bit too long. "Last night."

"But instead of calling the Saudis to warn them, you decided to fly here and save the day yourself?"

Silence.

Slaton went out to the balcony and studied the drone rigged with hardware. Then he looked at the one next to it, and the two inside. Why four? he wondered. Two would offer a backup. But four . . .

He reached out and, using the barrel of the Glock, tapped the two canisters in turn. Both sounded empty. He picked up the modified drone and thought it seemed surprisingly light. Slaton looked at the distant tower and checked his watch. The ceremony was to begin in ten minutes.

He knew he was missing something, and time was running out.

Slaton pulled out his phone and took three pictures of the drone from different angles, then uploaded them to Sorensen. He followed up with a call.

"You're in the apartment complex?" she asked immediately.

"Number 304."

"We just got word that the Saudis are responding to a reported threat in that building."

"Where did the report come from?" he asked.

"I don't know."

Slaton looked at Hadad.

"We got the pictures you sent. What else is in there?" Sorensen asked.

"Altogether, four drones, one dead guy, and a certain Syrian detective."

"Then you've done it! I'm looking at the pics you sent and I see the canisters. They look almost identical to the ones from Darfur."

Slaton kept staring at the drone.

"David . . . what is it?" Sorensen asked, sensing his doubt from thousands of miles away.

"This is too obvious. Think about it. Whoever is running this show knew we would find the equipment in Darfur. I think they *wanted* us to find it, along with the links to Iran."

"You still think this is a false flag op?"

"Has to be. The Jeddah Tower event is an obvious target, so they might have anticipated an intervention."

"So what we're looking at is a diversion? A bit of last-minute insurance to throw everyone off the real threat?"

"I think so."

"Where does that put us? The ceremony starts in eight minutes."

After a long hesitation, Slaton said, "If the threat in this apartment isn't genuine, then the real one is still out there . . . and it's probably imminent."

"The Saudis will be there shortly. They can call up a chemical weapons unit from the army to inspect the canisters."

"Not in seven and a half minutes they can't."

"What other option do we have?"

"I can only think of one." Leaving the call connected, Slaton set the phone on the table. He picked up the entire drone assembly, carried it inside, and set it on the floor at Hadad's feet. The Syrian still seemed less concerned about the drone than the Glock in Slaton's hand.

Slaton edged to one side and pointed the gun downward. He took careful aim at the larger of the two canisters and his finger went to the trigger. He paused momentarily to gauge Hadad's reaction.

There was none.

Slaton said a silent prayer. Then he pulled the trigger.

SEVENTY-FIVE

The sound of the shot mixed with a metallic *clank,* and a jagged hole appeared dead center in the first canister. Slaton stood still, waiting. Watching. Ready to run. There was no hissing stream of mist venting from the breach, no ooze of green liquid. Nothing at all. His next shot drilled the smaller canister. Same breathless moment. Same result. Empty. Hadad had flinched at the shots, but he ignored the canisters. He looked at Slaton like he was a madman.

It had been a gamble, but not as big as might be imagined. Even if there had been precursors inside, either one would likely be harmless by itself. Slaton picked up the phone again. "The canisters are empty. This is definitely a tactical misdirection."

"Okaaay . . . good to know," said a cautious Sorensen. He knew she'd heard the shots over the open line. "So now what?" she asked.

"We're back to square one. Do you have a schedule of how this event is going to play out?"

"If not, I'll get one ASAP."

"While you do that—" Slaton's thought was interrupted by the sound of engines revving in the street out front. The Saudi National Guard was indeed responding.

If he remained here, in a room full of terrorist hardware and bloody suspects, one of whom was dead, he would have some serious explaining to do. He would be disarmed, detained, and hauled off for interrogation. At some point he would convince the Saudis to contact Sorensen, who would vouch for him. At that point, Slaton would be released. All of which would take hours, if not days. In the meantime, the real attack would proceed and he would be out of the fight.

Slaton moved out onto the balcony and scanned the horizon 180 degrees. One thing seized his attention. Half a mile away, the fire-works display being assembled. Could *that* be the method of an aerosolized attack? In the hands of the right bombmaker, he sus-pected it could. Large-scale fireworks were essentially mortars—only smaller in caliber, with recreational fusing and designer warheads. It was a possibility that had to be ruled out.

He heard shouting out front. Slaton glanced at Hadad. He was curled in a fetal ball, rocking in the corner. Slaton doubted that would change as adrenaline wore off and pain kicked in.

He leaned over the rail of the third-floor balcony. The second-floor unit below had a duplicate balcony. On the ground level was a stone deck surrounding a community swimming pool, the water sparkling in the midday sun. From where he stood, the twenty-five-foot drop onto travertine was an invitation to broken bones. He might leap out far enough to reach the pool, but he wasn't sure how deep it was—a detail every bit as important to special operators as it was to kids jumping into backwoods swimming holes.

Slaton adapted to the situation.

He gripped the balcony rail firmly, vaulted over the side. Re-versing his grip, he then lowered himself as far as he could by walk-ing his hands down a pair of rails. With his legs dangling beneath the base of the balcony, he began to oscillate back and forth. While he maneuvered, he heard a crash as the door of 304 was breached.

On the next inward swing he let go, aiming for the second-floor balcony. He landed awkwardly, striking the rail with one leg. He twisted as he hit the tile, and his phone shot out of his pocket. He reached out with a hand, but too late—he watched the handset flip over the edge. Moments later he heard the crack of plastic and glass shattering on stone.

"*Dammit!*"

He got up gingerly, his right hip stinging with pain. *That's going to leave a mark*, he thought as he went to the rail. He saw the shat-tered phone, pieces strewn across the deck. He could only ignore it.

The pool was fifteen feet down, ten feet outward. With a running start, he could make a horizontal leap, the depth of the water no longer an issue. It would make for a spectacular escape. It would also create noise, a visual spectacle. And if he didn't get his last step right, he could end up crashing onto the stone deck. There was a time for Hollywood and a time for practicality.

This was the latter.

Slaton lowered himself down the second-floor balcony as he had the one above. The final drop was a manageable ten feet, and he rolled onto his good hip in near silence. As he got back to his feet he heard shouting from above—Hadad being taken into custody.

He ran on an angle to the east, hoping to not be spotted by the Saudi team securing the apartment above. The fireworks staging area was half a mile from where he stood, entirely across open ground. There was no way to reach it without being seen. Slaton weighed the idea of going back for his car, but decided there wasn't time. He set out on a sprint across the sunbaked desert.

As he ran the shouting from above faded, and for the first time Slaton noticed a new sound. Somewhere in the distance, the unmistakable resonance of jet engines tearing through the sky.

"And . . . delta . . . now."

The words came over the radio in Lieutenant Colonel Jamil Issa's unmistakable cadence, the flight leader's words spaced at a precise interval so that on his final command all six aircraft moved in perfect synchronization.

The Saudi Hawks aerial demonstration team maneuvered as one, the five trailing aircraft flying with reference to a stable lead. The pilots made ever so slight adjustments of pitch, roll, and power to reconfigure the flight into a precise delta formation.

The flight leader looked over his shoulder and was happy with what he saw. His men were in good form and, with five minutes to go until the flyby, the rituals of their "warm-ups" were nearly done. The flight was twenty miles from show center, and Issa was feeling relaxed. Some performances required considerable planning, including the extensive study of ground references necessary to guide him through maneuvers. Today no aerobatics were involved. It was only a "pass-in-review" in delta formation, a simple flyby, although he was quite aware that his audience would include the king and crown prince. His reference point for show center, Jeddah Tower, could not have been more obvious—on any day as clear as this one, it could be seen for a hundred miles. All the leader had to do was get his timing right. He checked the aircraft clock, saw that his inbound run would begin in three minutes. He was to arrive at the ceremony at precisely 12:05.

Colonel Issa checked with his narrator, who was at the ceremony with a handheld radio. Everything was running on schedule. Issa banked into the last turn of their distant holding pattern. The only chore left was the final system test.

As he rolled into level flight, Issa keyed his microphone. *"Smoke check, three . . . two . . . one . . . now."*

In perfect synchronization, all six pilots depressed a switch to activate their respective aircraft's smoke generator. In the engine bay of each jet, dye-infused oil was released from a five-gallon reservoir and metered onto the exhaust pipe of an Adour turbofan engine. The high-grade steel exhaust shroud maintained a temperature of between five and seven hundred degrees Celsius, and the oil vaporized on contact.

For all the engineering, the result to viewers on the ground was typically a pleasing one. Six sleek jets trailed six plumes of smoke. In the case of the Saudi Hawks, two red, two white, and two green. This initial activation was only a test of the system, undertaken beyond the visual range of spectators at show central. After five seconds Issa ended the exercise.

"Smoke off . . . three . . . two . . . one . . . now."

Six thumbs again acted in unison. In the tail sections of each jet, valves shut off the oil feed and awaited their next command. All, that is, except for one.

In the tail of the number 4 jet, flying slot, a distinctly different mechanism activated. Modified switches in the engine bay engaged a shunting device, disabling the primary smoke generator in favor of two smaller canisters that had been installed by a certain engine mechanic—a Jordanian national who now lay dead in a nearby apartment.

The next time the pilot of number 4 switched on his smoke, in less than five minutes, what would stream from the tailpipe of his jet was an odorless and colorless compound manufactured in a distant Siberian laboratory. And the effect it would have on those on the ground would be anything but pleasing.

SEVENTY-SIX

It wasn't the fastest half mile Slaton had ever run, but probably the most grueling given the rough terrain and his mounting list of minor injuries.

He watched the staging area closely as he ran. Barring anyone hidden in the trucks, there were only two men working the site. Both wore off-white coveralls and appeared to have identity cards hanging around their necks on lanyards—evidence that they'd been screened at some level by the Saudis. Both men were six inches shorter than Slaton, both slight in build. Forced to guess, he would have pegged them as being Indonesian, maybe Sri Lankan or Thai. Their work vans were large and displayed identical logos, a company called Innovative Pyrotechnics. None of that dissuaded Slaton from the possibility that they could be terrorists preparing to launch an assault.

What *did* make him doubt it, however, was the men's behavior. Both seemed wholly engrossed in their tasks, one packing mortars into a rack of launch tubes, the other connecting wires to a relay on a control stand—a table set up behind one of the vans. In the few minutes it took Slaton to reach them, neither man cast a single outward glance. They never noticed the tall man sprinting toward them, nor did they seem interested in the multiple security details in the distance. Neither looked at all on guard. If these two were in fact a terrorist element, they were among the coolest operators Slaton had ever seen.

Nearing the first van, he drew the Glock and trained it on the nearest man—the one connecting wires to a relay box and laptop computer. When he finally look up, his reaction further reinforced Slaton's thinking. There was surprise, perhaps a touch of fear, but no suggestion whatsoever of a response. The electrician didn't even shout to alert his partner.

Having the first man's attention, Slaton put his finger to his lips in the universal silencing motion. The man nodded tentatively. Closing to within a few steps, Slaton flicked the Glock's barrel twice, motioning in the direction of the man's partner. The electrician began moving slowly. The man working the tubes was so engrossed in his task he didn't look up until Slaton had the other man five steps away. His reaction was identical.

Once the men were standing next to one another, he said in English, "Don't move. Do you understand?"

Two nods.

Slaton edged closer to the racks of mortar tubes. They all looked similar, with minor variations in the size of the tubes, the projectiles, and the color of their caps. He saw no metal cylinders, no unique launcher loaded with some kind of higher-grade mortar. Slaton was no expert when it came to pyrotechnics, but nothing seemed suspicious. Every bit of factual evidence screamed the same thing: he was looking at two guys setting up tonight's firework display. And nothing more.

He'd hit another dead end.

He needed to call Sorensen, but he'd screwed up and destroyed his phone. Slaton reckoned both men in front of him had phones. But what number to call? The 911 app he'd accessed the night before wouldn't be loaded. He hadn't memorized a backup number. Slaton was working through it all, trying to figure a way to reestablish comm with Langley, when something far to the west caught his eye.

Something red, white, and green . . .

A short segment of six smoke trails dissipating high in the desert sky.

Sorensen recognized the threat at virtually the same time Slaton did, although it wasn't the sound of jet engines that cued the connection. She was sorting through the loss of communications with Slaton when a call came in from her resident chemical weapons expert, Dr. Gyger. She told the comm officer to have him call back, but when Gyger persisted she picked up.

"I've been studying the hardware arrangement that was uncovered in Sudan," he said. "I think I may finally have an answer for you."

"You know where it came from?" Sorensen asked.

"Not yet, but I think we've identified what it is. Both the canisters and wiring are part of a smoke generation system."

"Smoke generation? You mean like what the army uses in the field to hide the movement of formations?"

"Same general idea, but on a much smaller scale. This is an aviation version, very high-grade equipment—it's what the Blue Angels use at an airshow to create their smoke trails."

Sorensen literally dropped the handset.

She hurried to a nearby workstation and began looking for a printout she'd seen only minutes ago: the schedule of today's events at Jeddah Tower.

On the tower's observation platform, General al-Bandar finally got a bit of good news. The leader of the raid on the nearby apartment called to say that the situation was under control. There had been, by all appearances, a plot brewing involving a number of drones. One man was presently in custody, while another had been killed.

To say the general breathed a sigh of relief was a massive understatement. He'd been seconds away from shutting down the entire event, which would have meant pulling the king and crown prince away from a podium and hustling them to safety—this in response to a conspicuously vague threat. It was an insufferable choice, but one that, if he were to err, could easily end his career.

He put his phone back in his pocket with relief, sure that he'd dodged a bullet. He watched the crown prince, who was midway through his remarks.

"Is everything all right, sir?"

Al-Bandar looked to his left and saw an Air Force major, the narrator of the Saudi Hawk team. He was coordinating the fly-by scheduled to arrive immediately after the crown prince finished his remarks. The general realized his apprehension must have been obvious.

"Yes," he said. "A minor incident, but everything is under control."

The major nodded, and al-Bandar saw him glance at the prince's

He looked at the two vans. Saw the Indonesians staring at him. And then . . . the obvious.

There was no time for subtlety. Slaton strode toward his two captives. They were still standing next to one another, and he raised the Glock to a point between them. He fired one round that went screaming past at shoulder height. Of the two, the one on the right, the electrician, reacted more favorably.

"No, please! What do you want?" the man said, his voice cracking.

Slaton swept the gun toward the nearest rack of mortars. "Is this setup operational?"

The man looked at him dumbly, as if the question hadn't registered. It was probably the stress.

"Are these things ready to go?" Slaton demanded.

"Not all of them, but most are primed and ready."

"Show me how it works—quickly!"

The little man scurried toward the table. His partner didn't move.

On the table Slaton saw banks of wiring that connected to various circuit boards. Each of the boards was tied in to a laptop computer. Slaton was no expert, but he knew professional fireworks displays were orchestrated by computers, often accompanied by music.

He glanced at the onrushing formation of aircraft. They were getting close, maybe five miles and moving fast.

He knew that most fireworks didn't go particularly high in the air. Two hundred feet? Five hundred? It was a question he'd never considered. Certainly not the last time he'd seen a display—this summer when he and Davy and Christine had attended a Fourth of July celebration in a small town in Montana. Whatever the answer, Slaton knew he had one thing in his favor: flight demonstration teams flew exceptionally low.

"Here is the sequence," the electrician said, pointing to the laptop screen.

Slaton saw a list of probably forty names, all in creative English, for the various groupings: Dandelion, Starfire, Waveburst . . . Any single one, he reckoned, was a salvo of two or three or four tubes launched together for the best effect. There was a timing interval next to each one. In essence, he was looking at tonight's show in the controller's format.

"Which ones are ready to go?" he asked.

"The ones in large font," said the electrician.

Roughly half the titles were listed in caps and highlighted. "You could launch those now?" he asked.

"Yes, they are wired and ready. It only takes a master code to arm the system."

"You have it?"

"Yes."

"Do it!" Slaton ordered.

The electrician went to work. A red box came up centrally on the screen, and he entered an eight-digit code like a missile officer about to launch a salvo of ICBMs.

Slaton could hear the jets now, their engines ripping through the air. They were barely a mile away, on a course that would take them almost directly overhead.

"It is ready," said the slight man, casting a guarded glance at the approaching formation. "Select any one that is prepped and hit enter."

In the moment it took Slaton to reach for the computer mouse, one name at the bottom of the list seized his attention.

Grand Finale.

Colonel Issa made a slight correction to the right. His wingmen held true.

His last reference point was nearly upon them, and he prepared to make the call-out for smoke. He was far too engrossed in the timing to notice two work vans passing beneath the nose of his aircraft.

"Smoke on, three . . . two . . . one . . ."

SEVENTY-EIGHT

Lieutenant Colonel Issa was a combat veteran. In his eighteen-year career, he'd flown extensively in the war in Yemen, and also taken part in a half dozen lesser skirmishes. That being the case, he was intimately familiar with being shot at. He'd seen anti-aircraft artillery. The odd shoulder-fired SAM. Plenty of unguided small arms fire. None of that prepared him for what engulfed his formation.

The explosions were all around, the sky filling with airbursts of varied brilliance and color. Issa heard a flurry of tiny impacts on his jet—he would later reflect that it sounded like flying through heavy rain. He had no idea what had just happened, but his reaction was instantaneous.

The final command to engage smoke was replaced by *"Break out! Hawk Flight, breakout!"*

The six BAE Hawks, which moments earlier had been glued to one another in tight formation, were already beginning to wobble. Every pilot's attention had been locked to the aircraft next to him, but in the periphery they'd all seen what Issa had—explosions all around.

When jets fly in close formation, there is a standing procedure for separating in an emergency. It is covered in every briefing, and designed as a controlled maneuver. The jets on the left and right turn aggressively in their respective directions and climb steeply. The next two in line mirror the move, but to a lesser degree. The intent is to get separation, to keep wingtip from striking wingtip, until all aircraft are a safe distance apart.

Owing to the adrenaline of the moment, what actually happened was something closer to a bomb going off—six individual pilots reacting with nothing less than survival instinct. The four aircraft veering left and right did so with varying degrees of emphasis, shooting outward at odd angles and high into the sky.

Issa, the flight lead, began a sudden climb. The timing of his impending command to switch on the smoke generators had been so near, the reaction to the explosions so abrupt, that two of the team members actually did turn on their smoke. Numbers 2 and 5 soared up behind corkscrewing trails that rose high into the desert sky. One was green, the other white.

By no more than pure chance, number 4 did not activate his switch. He, in fact, had been put in the direst position of all. Flying the slot, below and behind the flight leader, the pilot knew he was surrounded by teammates engaged in various aggressive maneuvers. Turning to either side was not an option. His duty in the breakup was essentially to keep the status quo. In another situation, a gentle descent would have been permissible, but as it was, flying at high speed and extremely low altitude, he had no such option.

The number 4 pilot watched his lead climb away, then checked over his shoulder and saw the others careening skyward at odd angles. He was so distracted by these maneuvers, not to mention the explosions that caused it all, that he nearly made the classic aviator's error—for the briefest of moments, he forgot to fly his own jet. When he turned back and focused ahead, his entire forward windscreen was filled by the largest building on earth.

In a panic he yanked back on his stick, aiming toward the nearest sliver of blue sky. It would later be determined that the pilot of number 4 put nine and a half Gs on his jet in the last-ditch move, necessitating the grounding of his aircraft for a precautionary inspection. Camera footage would eventually document that the tail of number 4 passed less than thirty feet from the observation deck. No less than the king himself would claim to have felt heat from the jet's exhaust moments after it passed.

All of this was taken in by a group of stunned guests, chief among them the crown prince. As six hyperventilating pilots scattered high into the sky, he looked on lividly. The prince had not seen the fireworks that precipitated the disaster. Instead, he finished his speech expecting a breathtaking flyby, only to find his Saudi Hawks scattering like doves from an onrushing falcon. Then confusion went to fear as the number 4 jet nearly struck the observation deck. The prince immediately began drumming up invectives for Lieutenant

Colonel Issa, although his ire would reverse before they could be delivered.

The director of the CIA's Special Activities Division called the Saudi National Guard command center, who called General al-Bandar, who called his major, who called the rapid reaction team. Within minutes, the team was bearing down on the site from which the premature fireworks had been launched.

The general moved quickly to buttonhole the crown prince, and at a whisper explained how close they all might have come to an agonizing death. Before the prince could respond, al-Bandar ushered him and the king into the safety of the lobby.

Half a mile from Jeddah Tower, one expatriate Israeli and two perplexed Indonesians stood watching the spectacle. To Slaton's eye, the six distant specks in the sky seemed to be reassembling. He warily eyed the two fast-dissipating trails of smoke. He had no way of knowing if either, or perhaps even both, carried elements of a deadly nerve agent. The smoke was drifting away from where he stood, but toward the big tower. The surreal scene was made even more bizarre by the introduction of music. When the grand finale barrage had launched—sixty-one mortars in the space of ten seconds—an audio accompaniment had begun blaring from great speakers near the tower. The classical piece was now flooding across the desert at rock-concert volume, the ground actually vibrating.

Not unexpectedly, Slaton saw a group of six armored vehicles bearing down. At least twenty men, he guessed, and no doubt heavily armed. Probably also on edge. He ejected the magazine from his Glock and dropped it in the dirt, ejected the round from the chamber and locked the slide open. He set the gun on the table and stepped away.

The Indonesians stood staring at him.

There was nothing more Slaton could do. He would make his case to the commanding officer as best he could. Try to talk his way up the chain and get through to Sorensen. To anyone who would listen, he would explain the precautions that needed to be taken: the demo team needed to land at a remote airfield, and the pilots would be well served to get out of their cockpits and run like hell upwind.

The heavy vehicles ground to a stop, and men in full combat gear began pouring out. They shouted in Arabic, which neither he, nor he suspected the Indonesians, understood. It didn't matter. The tone was sufficient. Slaton put his hands behind his head. The Indonesians, still watching him, mirrored the move.

Slaton grinned, and said, "It's okay, you guys aren't in any trouble. Just cooperate."

The first men reached Slaton, forced him to his knees, and began searching him for weapons. As they did, the music rose to a crescendo. A soaring rendition of Wagner's "Ride of the Valkyries" thundered across the desert into a featureless sky.

SEVENTY-NINE

The second rendezvous at the farmhouse in Uruguay took place five days later. Slaton was the first to arrive. He had been sprung from detention in Saudi Arabia after less than twenty-four hours, but a circuitous route to South America had taken another three days. He'd spent last night in the house alone, Sorensen having again given the caretakers a holiday. The front door remained unlocked.

Sorensen arrived at midmorning, although precisely when Slaton couldn't say—there wasn't a clock anywhere in the house. They sat on a burnt-tile terrace out back in the shade of a towering eucalyptus, a fresh pot of coffee between them.

"The crown prince of Saudi Arabia asked me to express his appreciation," she said.

Slaton sipped from his mug before saying, "Thanks for getting me out so quickly. He wanted to meet with me while I was in custody, but I explained that it might not be a good idea."

"Afraid someone might commemorate the event with a photograph? That could prove awkward for both of you."

"That's the least of it. Anton would be furious."

She smiled. "Don't worry, I covered for you. I told the Saudis you were a very important asset. I said we wanted to get you back as quietly as possible." Sorensen had stopped for sweet rolls at a nearby bakery, and she plucked one from a box.

Slaton said, "I haven't been watching much news, but as far as I can tell this whole thing is being swept under the rug pretty effectively."

"And why wouldn't it be? The nerve agent was never dispersed. Other than one very screwed up dedication ceremony for Jeddah

Tower, and a murder in a nearby apartment, there wasn't anything particularly newsworthy. The Saudis realize they've had a severe security lapse. The man you found dead in the apartment—he was the one who installed the hardware on the airplane."

"Who was he?"

"A mechanic in the Saudi Hawk squadron."

"Really? An inside job?"

"Essentially. But he wasn't a Saudi national." Sorensen explained Nazir's background.

"His father died in an oil field accident?"

"Yes. And once we began looking at Nazir, it led to something else." She licked sugar glaze off her fingers, and said, "Let me grab my iPad." Sorensen went inside.

Slaton looked out into the still morning, the rows of olive trees stately and enduring. This house, this place, seemed innately simple. More and more, he appreciated simplicity.

If there was any recompense for being Anna Sorensen's secret assassin, it was that he didn't have to fill out after-action reports. By design, there could never be any record of his actions downrange. Slaton knew that The Farm, the agency's school for clandestine training, would never invite him as a guest speaker or analyze his op for teachable moments. Better yet, the CIA's army of lawyers would never scrutinize his tactical decisions for possible violations of conduct. It was a freedom, he supposed, no other state-sponsored operator in the world enjoyed.

Sorensen returned with her tablet and pulled her chair nearer his. She set the iPad screen-down in her lap, and said, "We've learned a lot in the last few days. Your instinct was right—this was a false flag attack. The primary intent was to start a war between Saudi Arabia and Iran."

He nodded thoughtfully. "And who was behind it? Petrov?"

"We think he was involved, but only tangentially. By supplying the nerve agent, Petrov enabled the true culprits. As the recording you recovered suggested, he wanted very much to cover his tracks."

"Now that you have the recording, couldn't you hammer him with it?"

"We could try. And in return, he would say it's all a fabrication. Director Coltrane has decided to let Petrov stew. We have the recording, he knows it. It's leverage, but in the big scheme of things, not much more."

"So, who was he working with?"

With the tablet still in her lap, Sorensen began a lengthy briefing—one that Slaton had the impression she'd been rehearsing on her inbound flight. She explained that a resurgent Iraqi Ba'ath Party was spreading its tentacles throughout the Middle East. They were renewing ties with militias and governments. With a detective in Syria named Hadad. She told him about a boyhood friend of Sergeant Nazir's, a man whose name Slaton had never heard. The title to which he aspired, however, was one of legend.

"A Fifth Rashidun?" he asked incredulously.

"Right now, there are only rumblings. But if this attack had succeeded, if a full-blown war had broken out between the Gulf Arabs and Iran? This man would have been ideally placed to take advantage."

"Okay. But what makes this guy so special?"

Sorensen lifted the tablet and showed him a photograph. It appeared to have been taken from a security camera, probably at an airport. The image had all the hallmarks of having been digitally enhanced, and as such was remarkably clear. Dark olive skin, black hair, push-broom mustache. Perhaps a slight crookedness in the gait as the man passed through a corridor.

Slaton looked at Sorensen, saw she was holding something back. "What?" he asked.

Sorensen told him the rest. Told him about the lineage of Ahmed Sultan al-Majid al-Tikriti.

An hour later Slaton was walking through the grove alone. This had been Sorensen's suggestion—she'd wanted to give him space, and of course he knew why. He took in the smells and sights, and once again could not deny the familiarity. Distant remembrances of the Jezreel Valley came flooding in. Was that why Sorensen had chosen this place?

If his surroundings were serene, his thoughts were less so. Climbing the first hill away from the cottage, he found himself thinking of home. After so many years, Slaton had found a family, and all the love and warmth that came with it. Yet he'd long had a sense that something was missing. Something lacking since the day he'd turned his back on Mossad.

For a time he'd tried to ignore the emptiness. Later he'd tried to overpower it with hard, physical work. As a mason, he'd repaired ancient aqueducts in Malta, built retaining walls in Virginia backyards. Carved churches from coral in the South Seas. Still the hollowness was not made whole, and only now did he realize why. What did he have during his time with Mossad that he didn't have now? The answer, quite obviously, was a mission. Slaton was a soldier. Nothing more. And certainly nothing less.

He knew the world needed men like him. That much had been proved this week. Evil, like beauty, was in the eye of the beholder, yet from Slaton's point of view the events of recent days had set a new paradigm. He felt anger at what had befallen Ludmilla, not to mention her Syrian counterpart, Sofia Aryan. Salma, Naji, and even Achmed had had their lives turned upside down. All put at risk by men lusting for power.

He paused in the grove and spun a slow circle. He saw nothing but old-growth trees in any direction. Then he looked up through the canopy of foliage and saw clear blue sky. Slaton suddenly felt freer than he had in years. Felt more certain of the right course.

The question that had been in the back of his mind for a week returned to the forefront. Why had he accepted this mission? All at once, he knew. He had gotten involved because it was the right thing to do. Because, for all America's faults, he believed in its ideals. He was a convert, a believer. And if he could use his skills to make the world safer for Davy and Christine, and so many like them . . . so be it. Having settled that, Slaton knew what he had to do.

He set out back toward the cottage.

EIGHTY

For two weeks the Ba'ath Party loyalists waited. They sat glued to their television screens in Tikrit waiting for breaking news of a terrorist plot in Saudi Arabia. Curiously, none came. Their envisioned attack on the Saudi monarchy and Gulf Arabs, so near the shrines of Islam, had not gone to plan. They knew the plot had been uncovered, yet from the Saudi foreign ministry: crickets.

Sultan had taken up residence in a new palace, a reconditioned mansion on the western outskirts of Tikrit. Standing at the edge of the broad patio, he looked over the perimeter wall into a clear night. A half-moon shone down embracingly, washing the terrace and surrounding landscape in its warmth.

"The drones were a mistake," a familiar voice said.

Sultan turned to see Ibrahim approaching. He was carrying a tray with a bucket of ice, decanter of Scotch, and two tumblers. He set the tray on a high-boy wicker table near the patio's edge.

"Perhaps," Sultan replied. "But at the time it seemed a necessary contingency."

It had been a matter of some discussion in the weeks before the attack. They knew they were walking a fine line. By leaving so many traces that linked Iran to the nerve agent, they ran the risk of the target being identified prematurely. It was Sultan who'd suggested they devise an alternate delivery method, something obvious to take the heat off Nazir's insider sabotage of the Saudi Hawks.

"I tried to contact Petrov again," said Sultan.

"And?"

"He doesn't return my calls."

Ibrahim dropped ice cubes into the tumblers, made two generous pours. He held one out to Sultan, and said, "Petrov would not be where he is without being a cautious man. He'll come around."

"Will he?" Sultan took the drink, put it to his lips and tipped back. His eyes closed for an appreciative moment. "I've been told many of our contacts are drying up. Egypt, Syria, Oman."

"They will be back."

"Is there anything about Hadad?" Sultan asked.

A hesitation. "He has not been heard from. Apparently he remains in Saudi custody."

"That's not good. He knows a great deal. I fear the crown prince will take out his bone saw again."

"None of that matters!" insisted Ibrahim. "You are the Fifth Rashidun. In time these difficulties will pass, and another opportunity will arise. We must have faith." He held out his tumbler for a toast, smiling for the first time in days. "To faith, my friend."

Sultan grinned humorlessly, and said, "Of course . . . to faith."

Sultan reached out to complete the tribute, yet as the two glasses neared one another, his arm jerked violently. The two glasses crashed together, both breaking. At first, Ibrahim didn't know what had happened. He only knew there was Scotch on his face, ice cubes and shards of glass raining around his feet. Sultan seemed to fly backward toward a lounge chair. He ended up splayed across it, a massive splotch of red centered on his white shirt.

As a teenager, Ibrahim had served in Saddam's army during the Iran-Iraq War. It was a long time ago, but lessons forged in battle were never forgotten. He threw himself to the ground and began screaming for help.

To their credit, the Ba'athist security men surrounding the compound reacted swiftly. Moments after Sultan collapsed onto the lounge chair, with a beer-can-sized hole in his chest, an alert went out over the tactical frequency. The twenty-six men sprang into action.

The first trace of what they were up against came from an astute man on watch. From his perch high in a minaret, he scanned the horizon with his magnified night optics, and quickly caught sight of a black-clad figure rappelling down the side of a distant mobile phone tower.

As he called in the threat on his radio, his eyes never wavered. The speed and agility with which the attacker was descending implied a high level of proficiency. The moment his feet hit the ground, he began sprinting toward the far side of the tower. Less than thirty seconds after the arrival of his bullet, he was on a motorcycle, the rear tire spewing stones into the air.

The response crystallized quickly. Two separate units bundled into vehicles. The first group made a beeline for the nearest major road, the direction in which the motorcycle had been heading, intending to give chase. The second unit headed for the tower.

The vehicles dispatched to the tower were the first to arrive. Nine men with heavy weapons poured out and began sweeping the area. Once the all clear was given, the commander tapped a young enlisted man on the shoulder and began scaling the ladder. He'd chosen the young corporal for good reason: he was the only man in the unit who'd had any sniper training.

They found the shooter's hide easily on a maintenance platform, slightly below the apex of the three-hundred-foot tower. As hide sites went, it was somewhat predictable—high ground with an unobstructed view of the palace and surrounding grounds. More surprising was what the sniper left behind. The gun was still in place—according to the corporal, a McMillan TAC-50, Hornady .50 A-MAX ammunition. Four rounds remained in the five-round box magazine.

There were also three sandbags on the wire-mesh floor, carefully arranged as a shooting platform. Two empty burlap grain sacks had to be explained by the corporal. "A sniper lying in the prone position with a weapon gives a very distinctive profile. The bags served to interrupt the shape, and also mask the infrared signature of the shooter's body."

The commander looked at it all helplessly.

"Whoever he was," the corporal affirmed, "he knew what he was doing."

The commander looked out at the distant palace. "It looks awfully far away."

"Fifteen hundred yards. Maybe a little more."

"Almost a mile. Is that some kind of record?"

"Not even close," said the corporal "But for the man who took the shot—it was precisely what it needed to be."

The second unit sped down the highway in hot pursuit of the motorcycle. They'd assumed, correctly as it turned out, that the attacker would make for highway. To their surprise, they found the bike almost immediately. It was lying in the middle of the road less than three miles from the mobile tower. Judging by scars on the metal frame and skid marks on the asphalt—clear in the illumination of their headlights—the bike had gone to ground at high speed and slid to a stop. Sensing victory, the commander ordered his men to search the area. They didn't find their man. Undeterred, an extended search was undertaken. To everyone's bewilderment, not a single footprint or trace of blood could be found. The rider had simply disappeared.

Though he had no way of knowing it, the commander might have glimpsed the sniper in the first moments after their arrival. Had they looked high into the sky, slightly to the south and very near the half-moon, they might have glimpsed a man hanging beneath a drone who was donning a steerable parachute.

ACKNOWLEDGMENTS

Assassin's Strike is the seventh book in the David Slaton series. When I wrote the first book, *The Perfect Assassin,* it never occurred to me that Slaton might find himself so busy. That journey would never have been possible without a team of professionals behind me— men and women who are every bit as competent as Slaton himself.

Thanks to my agent, Susan Gleason, whose support never wavers. Thanks to Tom Doherty, a legend in the business and all-around nice guy. My editor, Bob Gleason, is a constant source of inspiration—some of my fondest memories as a writer have been, and will always remain, our extended "what if" conversations.

I am deeply indebted to the team at Tor. Linda Quinton, Elayne Becker, Robert Davis, Eileen Lawrence—you are all essential. So too, Deborah Friedman, for seeing what I so often can't.

Finally, I would like to thank my family. You were there for book one, and I know you'll be there for the next. No writer could ask for more.